THE
TOOTHACHE
TREE

THE TOOTHACHE TREE

A NOVEL BY

Jack Galloway

ST. MARTIN'S PRESS

NEW YORK

Design by Claudia Carlson

Library of Congress Cataloging-in-Publication Data

Galloway, Jack.
    The toothache tree.
    I. Title.
PS3557.A41554T6 1989   813'.54   88–29876
ISBN 0–312–02659–5

First Edition

10 9 8 7 6 5 4 3 2 1

To Nancy,
whose love never let up.

▼ ▼ ▼ ▼ ▼ ▼ ▼ ▼ ▼ ▼ ▼ ▼ ▼

1

No one could really like Jimmy Jamison, but that should come as no surprise. No one did.

He was more than a loner—a distant, standoffish man who seemed to exude disdain. Though possessed of no particular talent, skills or training, he nonetheless wore a postured air of detachment and superiority like a cloak.

Thus endowed with no redeeming faculty, the man was at least capable of driving an automobile, even a fine one—a pedestrian skill that had enabled him to become chauffeur to the Hamilton Caine family, of Houston. The position tended to confer upon him a sense of dignity far beyond what he deserved, no doubt contributing to his continual look-down-the-nose hauteur.

Technically, Jimmy Jamison did not work for the Caine family at all. His paycheck came from Texas Consolidated Utilities Corporation, not coincidentally headed by Hamilton Caine, where Jamison was listed on the employee roster as a member of the Transportation Department. Said department also included four full-time pilots and a dozen or so support personnel. Among the equipment inventory were an eighteen-passenger Gulfstream jet, an eight-passenger Beechcraft prop jet, a vanilla-plain Cessna 172, and a fleet of 177 company cars, at last count. With such an assortment of personnel and machinery, it was not difficult to hide a family chauffeur from the watchful but often clouded eyes of the Internal Revenue Service and/or company shareholders.

The only corporate-related duties Jamison ever performed were occasionally delivering Hamilton Caine to the office in the morning, or transporting him to or from the company hangar at Houston Intercontinental Airport. Whatever other chauffeuring Caine required during the day was provided by some other corporate employee stationed at the firm's forty-story downtown office tower.

True to the code of the servant class, the man had long ceased to be known as Jimmy Jamison. "Jimmy" sounded too undignified, and family servants of that ilk never seem to have last names. Thus it was simply "James"; and it was "Martha" for the housekeeper; "Wilma" for the maid. It was "Claudette" for the cook (how chic to have a French-name cook) and "Gilly" for the gardener. The latter's name was actually Guillermo, but that was too complicated to pronounce and much too Mexican-sounding to suit the Caines. Besides, "Gilly" sounded quaint.

One of the traits that made James so easy to dislike was his steadfast laziness. It was the man's determination that his sole purpose in life was to chauffeur the family limousine, and occasionally to see to its maintenance and to that of all the other family vehicles—the sporty little Mercedes convertible which Mrs. Caine drove when she preferred to drive herself, the sleek Jaguar coupe which Mr. Caine preferred to use likewise, and the big, powerful Jeep Wagoneer station wagon which had been purchased for its four-wheel-drive capabilities, though it would be difficult for anyone to comprehend why. Caine certainly never went hunting or fishing; and the likelihood of snow in Houston is on the order of once every ten years. Maybe.

As stated, Jamison—James—only drove the vehicles. He would never have so much as lifted a finger to maintain a single one of them.

The majority of simple citizenry has never experienced what it is like even to have a full-time family maid—much less a cook, a housekeeper, a gardener, and a chauffeur. If one were to reflect upon such things, one might recall the era when American motion pictures were produced primarily to be pleasant experiences. A family chauffeur, if there ever was one, was usually pictured behind the steering wheel, opening doors for the master or mistress, or else puttering around the garage at the family mansion. There, he would most likely be clad in black rubber boots and matching apron, sponging or chamoising the big, black family limousine, or maybe spit-polishing a Stutz or a Cord down to the last gnat speck.

Not so with Jamison. Not on your Duesenberg. The thought of soiling one of his spindly fingered hands completely repelled him. He took the cars out for that—washing, vacuuming, anything akin to work. It was more costly that way, but the Caines didn't worry too much about that. The company paid for all that sort of thing anyway, writing it off, in turn, from the corporate income taxes; so what's to worry?

The important consideration from the Caine standpoint was that being tall and thin, James wore the chauffeur's uniform nicely. Also, despite his haughty demeanor, he did manage to affect an adequate air of servility when responding to orders from the master or mistress. He kept his mouth shut; and he was virtually always available when called upon. He resided in a small apartment over the gargantuan garage (at least that much true to the movie tradition) and he hardly ever went out for long or did much of anything. He spent most evenings alone in his apartment, either watching television or reading—activities not altogether reprehensible until you examined what it was that he read.

Pornography. That's right, the sanctimonious, supercilious schnook indulged himself in smut. Dirty books. *Really* dirty books. Filthy little pamphlets and magazines sprinkled with salacious pictures in full-color, close-up detail.

When off duty, his smartly pressed uniform neatly closeted and his officially obsequious demeanor quietly laid away, the Caine family chauffeur liked to wallow in literary filth, using the pages of his smut collection as inspiration for sick fantasies and solo perversions. To his credit, though, he always kept his perversities to himself, never venturing forth onto the streets of Houston to find someone with whom to share his depravity, or to foist off his flights of fantasy upon anyone else. Jimmy Jamison was a loner.

In addition to his literature, James had one other abiding passion, at which he modestly excelled. The man loved to play video games. That was perhaps another sort of vice, but at least it could be indulged in public without fear of censure.

James had just the right haunt for both of his cravings. Southwest Video-News was one of those ubiquitous 24-hour "newsstands" that dot most American cities, peddling an assortment of magazines and newspapers, for respectability, but also stocking a large assortment of hard-core porno. Those were kept in a back room that was partitioned from the honest-to-goodness magazine shoppers by saloon-style swinging doors with signs on them that read: NO ONE UNDER 18 YEARS OF AGE ADMITTED. Often as not, there was a back room beyond the back room where, for a nominal price, customers could stand on a filthy floor in supposedly private little cubicles and peer at raw-sex porno films—hetero-sex, homo-sex, beasty-sex, take your choice. It was all good, dirty fun, if that suited your point of view.

To be sure, that sort of emporium had existed for many years, but its like took on new financial sustenance with the advent of video games. To the regular clientele of cheap-thrill voyeurs was added the newest addict—the video game freak. As Jimmy Jamison was both, the familiar neighborhood dirty-book parlor became a virtual Valhalla.

Southwest Video-News was just as good, or as bad, as they came; and James visited the place almost daily. Shun-work that he was, he could always manage to steal away for an hour or so; but then, family chauffeurs who don't car-wash do end up with a lot of nothing-to-do time. Given his peculiar interests, the school term was made to order.

It was his regular duty, on weekdays, to deliver the Caine's only child, fifteen-year-old Hamilton Robert Caine, Jr., to a highly exclusive and even more highly expensive private institution of secondary learning known as Wingate School, and to pick him up at the school grounds when classes were dismissed in the afternoon. Such a routine activity provided James with twice-daily opportunities to snitch a little video-game time, unless there was some sort of conflict with Mr. or Mrs. Caine's need to be chauffeured.

There hardly ever was, especially in the afternoons, so it became a matter of daily ritual for the tallish, uniformed chauffeur of the society-Caines to exit the family enclave about an hour and a half before the Wingate School's final bell, at 3:30 in the afternoon, and pop into Southwest Video-News for a fast half-hour or so of doing battle with "Galactic Crusaders," or nimble-wristing his way through a few games of "Journey into the Unknown." A quick trip after that into the NO-ONE-UN-DER-18 room provided nobody's-friend James with more printed grist for his depravity mill. Then he could be rapidly on to Wingate School in plenty of time to pick up The Brat, as he privately referred to the Caine family's son and heir.

The chauffeur was at least discreet in his clandestine activities. Southwest Video-News was located several miles from both the Caine's River Oaks mansion and the forested Memorial-Area location of Wingate School, but just a short jaunt out of the way between the two. James always parked the long, black limo in the paved alley behind the place—nicely hidden from public view by a tall, waxed-leaf ligustrum hedge on the alley's rear borderline, and an oversized dumpster can belonging to a furniture store adjacent to his favorite retreat. Thus concealed, the parking spot was a perfect location for an ambush.

▼ ▼ ▼

September, in some parts of the United States, is a time for renewal that borders on the spiritual. However enjoyable the lazy days of summer picnics and frolics at the beach might have been, the September advent of crisp autumn air, falling leaves and campus bonfires always brings a welcome change. That's the way it seems to be in movies and many textbooks, at any rate.

It is a romantic image that has undoubtedly been accomplished through the years by persons residing in the northern tier of states—or maybe in England. No author of such autumnal propaganda could ever have been to Houston, Texas.

September in Houston is still among the doggiest of the dog days of summer. Unless the lush, green, San Augustine-grass lawns of spring have had tedious, costly watering throughout the summer, and at least two doses of fertilizer, they'll have been burned brown by the blazing suns of July and August.

The month is in the peak of the hurricane season, with all the terror and threat of destruction that weather phenomenon portends.

Temperatures usually remain in the low- to mid-nineties, often with relative humidity numbers to match. It's relentlessly hot, sticky, and oppressive to anyone who has to wear clothes— not too bad for a sun-worshipping nudist with a good shade tree and no job, but guaranteed to wilt the collar or droop the hairdo of anyone else going from a (usually) air-conditioned residence to a (normally) air-conditioned car to an (absolutely) air-conditioned place of business.

Despite the discomfort the weather provided inside his mandatory uniform jacket, white shirt and black tie, the month of September was especially welcome to Jimmy Jamison. Now in his third year of employ with the Caine family—or, rather, with Texas Consolidated Utilities—James was especially delighted to settle back into his favored school-session routine: daily trips to the dirty-book/video store in conjunction with delivering The Brat to or from school.

The summer just ended had been too hectic to suit James. The Caine boy, still too young to drive a car legally on his own, had to be carted around everywhere he needed to go—a function usually performed by loving but long-suffering parents when they are so unfortunate as not to have a chauffeur: to the dentist, to tennis two or three times a week, and even back and forth an interminable number of times that summer to a week-long tennis tournament. There were also occasional trips to take the boy to and from summer parties in the evenings. Perhaps because of the Caine youth's rather striking good looks, as he blossomed into his mid-teens, he was becoming increasingly active amid an affluent, adolescent social circle.

"A pain in the ass," was James's opinion. It is true that a teenage scion like young Hamilton Caine, Jr., can be a tremendous burden on someone with the antisocial propensities and dedicated sloth of Our Man James.

Now, though, summer was over—at least by the calendar. The Brat, now in his freshman year of high school, was properly deposited back at Wingate School, and all was once again right with the Caine family chauffeur's picayune, sordid little world.

It had been that way for a little over two weeks. To be precise, it was September 17th, at 2:15 in the afternoon, when James wheeled the long, black Cadillac out of the garage and headed slowly out the brick-paved driveway.

There are a number of affluent residential areas in and around Houston; and then there is River Oaks. In any of several neighborhoods—some of them incorporated towns of their own—a business or industrial kingpin and his family can hang their hats and lounge about their swimming pool, tennis court, the back-yard spa or the indoor Jacuzzi, depending upon the weather, and hold their heads high with pride. But to those who seriously aspire to the city's aristocracy, there is only River Oaks.

The Hamilton Caine home on Azalea Vale was certainly not the largest in the area, but neither was it modest. It sat on a beautifully manicured four acres of land—a rambling, multi-leveled structure totally devoid of any particular architectural style. But then, there are those who would call that a style of its own. "Eclectic," one might say if pressed for a compliment.

With tall columns, cut-glass windows and three roof gables, the house had a white brick facade and wood trim that varied in color from year to year, depending on the moods of the mistress and her decorators. That year, it was earth tones, with the exterior tonal theme echoed inside the front entry and from room to room throughout the downstairs area. The next year it might be mauve and green, but for then, it was earth tones.

There was difficulty, from time to time, establishing just how many bedrooms and baths the mansion contained; their numbers seemed to remain in almost as periodic a state of flux as the colors of the exterior paint. There might be six bedrooms and eight baths during one period, seven and nine during another—

or maybe only four palatial sleeping accommodations, each embellished with a fountain-dotted, private pleasure pool suitable for a good-sized Roman orgy. Style is change.

An inordinate number of bedrooms was not really necessary, after all, as the Caines had only the one child. Thus it was delightful pursuit for the mistress of the house to redo, and redo, and redo again. It amounted almost to a fixation; and she might as well have retained a full-time architect, decorator, and builder on the payroll along with the regular household staff.

All of this construction and reconstruction might have made family life difficult, but the Caines could always tough it out during those periods in the villa at Acapulco, the condominium at Aspen, or in the occasionally rented cottage at Majorca. In a severe pinch, there was also a far-from-modest, two-bedroom suite maintained year-round by the corporation in the luxurious Hotel Melton, at the western edge of downtown Houston, overlooking vast and beautiful Memorial Park. Its major reason-for-being was to provide quarters for visiting business clientele and, occasionally, foreign dignitaries and minor-league royalty, who were lavishly fêted by the Caines.

At the time, though, there was no construction in progress on the River Oaks mansion, where the current color scheme was considered by the mistress to be a fitting complement to the tall, stately trees that dominated the grounds. Majestic oaks, graceful longleaf pines, a smattering of sycamores and a sweetgum or two shaded over the vast lawn, an integral part of the arboreal splendor that pervaded River Oaks. In the midst of a Houston summer, the overall effect was that of a series of soothing oases dotting the concrete desert of the streets—islands of impregnable verdancy laced together by macadam rivers of simmering heat.

On that particular afternoon, James made his way in utmost air-conditioned luxury from the back-yard garage of the Caine enclave and into the late-summer heat beyond. There was no summer-burned grass here, to be sure. Gilly The Gardener had labored long and hard to ensure that such a fate would not befall the Caine family expanse. There was always something in bloom within the carefully sculptured garden plots—from the azaleas of early March to the camellias of January. It was a beautiful, soul-satisfying place for a man like James to work. Whether or not he had a soul, he most assuredly had it made.

Employees and habitués of Southwest Video-News had long since become accustomed to Jamison's tall, slender presence in the well-tailored chauffeur's suit, so they rarely if ever paid him any mind. Most of the patrons were just as secretive about their being there as he was—schoolboys who shouldn't have been there in the first place, and grown men who always looked embarrassed at their own presence—so there were never any greetings exchanged, and hardly ever any eye contact. The customers, in fact, paid remarkably close attention to what they were doing, assiduously to avoid noticing anyone who might be noticing them. The cashiers attempted always to appear blasé about everything. (How else could they take money and give change for dirty books?)

In the video parlor, the tall, uniformed man scored spectacularly well at "Journey Into The Unknown." After running up a near-record total of points and earning three free games, for which he would collect tokens for use at some future date, James slithered his way through the swinging doors into the back room. He leafed quickly through a Saran-encrusted copy of *Hell In Leather*—something for the sado-masochistic crowd, no doubt—eschewing that in favor of the latest edition of a periodical of prurient pleasure entitled *Lots of Love*.

He paid for the magazine, which was properly placed in an inconspicuous brown paper bag, and departed his usual route out the front door, down the sidewalk to the right, and through the small alleyway where the limousine was parked in its usual location—headed out, in order to make a dignified exit.

The first thing he saw when he rounded the back corner of the furniture store was the muzzle of a .45 automatic, just inches from his face.

"I hate to sound old hat, friend," said a voice behind the pistol, "but just be quiet and do what I say, and no one will get hurt."

Spoken in a hundred or more detective stories and twice that many TV movies, the pronouncement sounded well-rehearsed;

and it also sounded sincere—at least, James hoped the part about not being hurt was sincere. He was more than happy to oblige.

"Wh . . . what do you want?" he stammered.

"First," said the man with the gun, "put this tight across your mouth."

He handed James a strip of two-inch adhesive tape, and the chauffeur quickly obliged.

"Now walk quickly to the other side of the car," the man said; and James once again did as he was told, positioning himself behind the rear bumper of the shiny black limo and into a corner formed by the dumpster and the ligustrum hedge. "Now take off your clothes."

Jimmy Jamison stared at the gunman in disbelief.

"Hurry up," the man said; and James decided that such would be a good idea. He hurried. While shucking his uniform, James tried his best to make a carefully recorded mental image of his assailant.

As he recalled, the man was about medium height and build—maybe five feet, nine or ten inches tall, and perhaps a trifle huskier than most—with a flat stomach and what appeared to be muscular arms. He could have been anything between thirty-five and forty-five years of age. He had black, slightly curly hair, and a rather heavy mustache to match. It was the type of mustache that not every man can wear, indicating that the area between his nose and upper lip was longer than most— or at least that it grew more whiskers.

The man made no apparent effort to disguise his appearance. Nor did he seem to make any especially menacing gestures with the gun; he was simply rather matter-of-fact about it all. He was, however, wearing gloves—not exactly the most comfortable thing to do on a hot September afternoon—indicating that he was taking the precaution of leaving no fingerprints. He was also taking no prisoners.

"Now turn around," the assailant said after James had stripped down to tee shirt and baggy boxer shorts. "And if you make any unnecessary moves, I'll blow your head off. Put your hands behind you."

The chauffeur mumbled some kind of muffled plea from beneath the tape, almost a whimper, then quickly thrust his hands behind his back and stood statue-still.

Quickly, the gunman wrapped a quarter-inch rope tightly around James's wrists, looping it over and over again until secure.

"Now lie down."

James nodded assent and crouched gingerly to the pavement, glancing skyward as he did so in hope that the merciful gods would send a police helicopter by at just that unpleasant moment. But none came.

The gunman trussed the lanky man in his underwear rather quickly into something resembling the fetal position, making his victim feel like one of those wriggling calves he had seen on television, roped and tied by a professional cowboy. Then the man with the mustache produced a somewhat heavier rope from a hiding place somewhere beneath the dumpster, and he tied that one to the chauffeur's wrist bonds. The other end of the rope went around the leg of the trash container, then around the captive's ankles and back again. The job was finished with a quick, expertly knotted double half-hitch.

With the tie-up completed, the man fished into James's pants pockets for the keys to the limo, opened a front door and stripped off his own clothing, placing it with no particular care onto the front floorboard. Getting into the chauffeur's jacket was not easy. The man was not a beanpole like James, but he managed to get most of it buttoned. The pants, though, were impossible, so he put his own jeans back on.

Once costumed, the man ran quickly around the dumpster and retrieved three large furniture boxes from an adjacent trash pile, arranging them so they would preclude visibility of the prostrate figure from either direction in the alley, or from the street. He then picked up a small valise from behind the dumpster and tossed it onto the front seat of the limousine.

"Remember," he said, placing his gloved left index finger gently across his lips, "mum's the word."

As he was about to leave, the gunman spotted the brown paper sack from the newsstand on the ground, stooped to pick it up, and plucked out the salacious magazine. Its title, *Lots of Love,* was fittingly attested by a copulating couple on the cover.

"Marvelous," he remarked, with a wry half-smile and a glow of dedicated devilishness in his eyes, and he tossed the magazine at the helpless James. Blowing the victim a kiss, he added, "Lots of love to you too, sweet-face . . . and lots of luck!"

With that, the man jumped into the Cadillac and drove away.

▼ ▼ ▼ ▼ ▼ ▼ ▼ ▼ ▼ ▼ ▼ ▼ ▼

2

The existence of Wingate School was announced only by a small, tasteful sign that marked its entrance off Memorial Drive. Beyond that, the campus was all but hidden within the piney woods of that western section of Houston.

The so-called Memorial Area that surrounded the school was certainly one of the most desirable residential locations in the city, second only to River Oaks in prestige; and it was probably even more appealing to those who preferred natural beauty to manicured estate living. It was also considerably more democratic, with homes ranging in size from modest, three-bedroom bungalows to mansions every bit as imposing and ostentatious as those in River Oaks. As the area was quite large, the less affluent could co-exist in easy harmony with those of greater pretention, a situation aided by the natural screening of its woodsy setting.

The forest was composed of a natural stand of mostly loblolly pines and a sprinkling of assorted hardwoods, which included several varieties of oak, hickories and gum trees, plus assorted other flora. It marked the southwestern edge of the great Southern pine forest that stretched eastward into the legendary Big Thicket area of East Texas, across the Gulf Coast states and all the way to the Atlantic Ocean.

Amid this beautiful forest on a secluded, huge campus, was Wingate School.

You would never find Wingate mentioned in the newspapers

on Saturday morning among high school football scores. There was no varsity football program. There were intramural athletics, to be sure, which were looked upon by the schoolmasters as a singularly important adjunct to the proper development of the minds and bodies of their teenage charges. At Wingate, unlike public schools, students actually received instruction and serious coaching in their athletic endeavors—rather than the piddling, perfunctory pretensions of physical education programs in the tax-supported schools. In the proper seasons, the school taught soccer, tennis, volleyball, tumbling and elementary gymnastics. Although none of it was mandatory, the people at Wingate stressed that healthy bodies were important to the development of healthy minds, and that athletics not only stimulated their growth and development, but also provided a necessary physical release from the stress of mental development and the emotional furies of adolescence.

But it was development of the mind that was, demonstrably, the goal of Wingate School.

The school had been founded in the 1940's, with a first-rate administration and a faculty staffed with highly skilled, professional educators—the best, in fact, that the student body's heavy tuition fees could buy. Due to an outbreak of puberty among children of the junior high school level shortly after the second World War, which continued unabated ever after, Wingate added the traditional seventh and eighth grades of study to its original four-year high school curricula in the late 1950's. That addition provided the economically gifted students with a solid continuity of guided teaching and learning opportunities, from their earliest significant biological stirrings to their matriculation into college. In fact, from an educational standpoint, most college students should have had it so good.

Language was taught there, as a living thing. And literature. And history—as an exciting, true adventure story. And music. And the physical sciences—with a tendency on the part of the science faculty to relate their seemingly arcane intellectual pursuits to the world around them. The school's sprawling campus-in-the-forest helped in that respect. With just a short jaunt into the trees, students could witness the living realities of a variety of small-scale ecosystems co-existing with the modern world in the real-life raw. But science wasn't all that was pleasantly taught in the outdoors. On nice days, of which there were many during the Houston-area school year, it was nothing to find a half-dozen or so Wingate classes being conducted on the school grounds—adjacent to, or even deep within, the surrounding woods.

Being a private school, there were no politics with which to contend. Textbooks were selected for their clarity and capability of imparting knowledge—not by some ponderous committee intent upon placating every pressure group in the entire state and, if they could get away with it, imparting a little politically or religiously tilted propaganda while they were at it. There were no racial quotas at Wingate. No forced bussing. Nor any other artificial impediments to the achievement of the purpose for which there were schools in the first place. They simply taught at Wingate. And darned well.

Thus, while it was true that only the wealthy could afford to send their children to Wingate School, by no stretch of convoluted prejudice could it be dismissed as merely a snob school for rich kids.

▼ ▼ ▼

The new fall semester had barely begun when the man who had hog-tied Jimmy Jamison threaded the stolen Cadillac limousine down the winding, tree-arbored drive to a parking place in front of Wingate School. Tuesday, September 17th; 3:25 in the afternoon.

Having noted that Wingate was not justly accused of being nothing but a snob school for rich kids did not mean to imply that there were not snob kids in attendance. There certainly were—in abundance; but a blanket indictment of general snobbery would be just as unfair, and as untrue, as to say that because of the school's academic excellence, all of its students were mental giants. Generalizations always ring wrong.

The jury was still out on Hamilton Caine, Jr. On both counts. Known to his closest friends as "Ham," the youth was certainly not long on humility; and he clearly was not dumb. Just as clearly, he could be loud.

"That's the stupidest thing I ever heard!" he all but yelled at Kevin Andrews, as the two stood at their lockers following the final school bell of the day.

"It's true," Kevin replied. "I know it is."

"Where does it come from?"

"I don't know. It just does."

"What does?" asked Randall Edwards, who had just arrived at his nearby locker.

"Oh this idiot," Ham Caine explained, "is trying to tell me that boys bleed just like girls do the first time they have sex."

"That's right," Kevin defended. "There's some kind of little sack inside—just like girls have—that gets busted and bleeds out."

"Out where?" Hamilton continued to press.

"Right out the end of your dick."

"Where did you get that idea?" the Edwards kid asked.

"Everybody knows that. And besides, Curtis Richards told me. And he ought to know."

The Richards youth was well-known for his sexual prowess. Now a junior at Wingate School, he was reputed to have been logging conquests since the seventh grade.

"Curt Richards is full of shit," Caine replied.

"Oh yeah?" countered Kevin. "Then why don't you just ask him yourself?"

By coincidence, the young Lothario in question was among a group of upperclassmen walking down the hallway at just that instant.

"I will," said Caine, refusing to be awed. "Hey Curt."

"Yeah?"

"This asshole says you told him that boys bleed the first time they have sex, just like girls do."

"That's right," the famous young lover replied. "I know that for absolute sure."

"Man, that's nothing but total bullshit!" Ham Caine declared.

"How in the hell should you know?" retorted Curtis Richards. "The only thing you ever screwed was your fist."

"Yeah, and maybe a Coke bottle," added Kevin Andrews.

Everyone laughed—except Ham Caine.

"That's not true," he barked in self-defense. Staring Richards straight in the eye, he added, "I just don't go around bragging about it like you do."

"Oh really? How many times have you done it? And who are the unlucky girls?" Richards asked in reply.

"That's none of your damned business. It's uncool to tell other guys what girls you've made out with," Caine declared.

Joining in the fun, Randall Edwards asked Caine, "Did any of them know it at the time?"

Laughter all around. Except for Caine.

"They knew it all right," he replied, half-smiling. "You've never heard such moaning and groaning."

"You never heard such bullshit, either," Edwards added.

They had him on the run, now.

"Where'd you manage to do all this making out?" asked Curt Richards. "In the back seat of your daddy's limousine? Did your chauffeur take you out to park?"

That was a low blow. The older boy had his own car—a brutish-looking, powerful, Mustang convertible. None of the other three kids, all freshmen, was old enough to have a driver's license—although all but Caine were enrolled in driver's training classes and did some driving on their own.

As the proudly promiscuous Richards youth sauntered away, Randall Edwards abruptly changed the subject. "You should have been with us last weekend, Ham, we had a blast. My dad bought one of those skeet-thrower things—you know, a trap?—and we spent almost all Saturday afternoon busting clay pigeons. My shoulder is still bruised from that damned twenty-gauge. It doesn't kick an awful lot, but after you shoot-up three or four boxes of shells, you sure know you've done it."

"I wish I could have gone with you," Caine replied. With a touch of petulance he added, "I wish I'd just gone, and not told anybody anything. Nobody around the house would have known the difference."

Vividly, he recalled the scene when he asked permission to go . . .

▼ ▼ ▼

"Mother," he called, carelessly tossing his school books onto the velvet softness of a down-cushioned sofa in the parlor.

"I'm busy now, Hamilton," Mrs. Caine replied. She was sitting in a chair across a marble-topped coffee table from the sofa where her son had dropped his books. A man dressed immaculately in white flannel slacks, topped with a double-breasted, brass-buttoned, blue blazer, pink shirt, and a red kerchief tied jauntily inside the open collar, sat in an adjacent, matching chair.

"I'm sorry, Mother, but I need to ask you something now."

"Hamilton," his mother replied, as though his urgencies meant nothing. "This is Mr. Gilchrest. He is our new decorator; and he's going to be working on some preliminary designs for the parlor and dining room while your father and I are away."

Mr. Gilchrest rose and offered his hand to the boy. Like all the others before him, he radiated masculinity like an iceberg radiates heat.

"Why, I'm so pleased to meet you, Hamilton."

The boy accepted the decorator's handshake—resisting, but just barely, the temptation to crush the limp offering with all the strength he could muster.

"Please leave us to our business now, Hamilton," Mrs. Caine requested. "We have a great deal to accomplish and not much time. By the way, we are having a small going-away dinner party tonight, here at the house, and I expect you to be dressed and presentable by seven o'clock."

"But Mother, I need to ask you now. Randy Edwards has invited me to go with him and his family to their ranch at Wimberley this weekend. Can I go?"

"Just look at him," his mother said. "Have you ever seen such a sight? Especially those shoes. Why in the world he has to wear those silly, ill-fitting—what do you call them, deck shoes?—I'll just never know. He even tries to wear them without socks; but that is where I absolutely draw the line."

"He's such a handsome young man," the decorator said, much to the boy's embarrassment. "And he favors his mother *so* much. Small wonder he is so good-looking. And I couldn't agree with you more about the deck shoes, although they are quite the rage among teenagers these days. I think he'd look fabulous in penny loafers. Or maybe tassel-tops."

He was right about the resemblance between mother and son. But it was only superficial.

Both were exceedingly blonde. Her hair was immaculately coifed in an upswept, semi-bouffant manner that appeared at once to be elegantly formal and studiedly casual. The boy's hair was straight, a trifle long, and inclined to be unruly. Both had the same, finely chiseled facial features; and if the truth were known, she had to fight a constant battle, using electrolysis treatments and every sort of emollient imaginable, to deter the same trace of a mustache that now graced the upper lip of her only child.

The major detail difference in the two was in the eyes. Hers were almost harshly green—cold and impassive, like those of the most unapproachable alley cat. The boy's were bright blue; but they had the capacity to fluctuate in intensity from what amounted almost to a soft glow, to blazing fury. And the heat was now beginning to show.

"Mother, please. I don't want to be rude, but I've got to tell Randy something tonight."

"Now Hamilton," she replied, "I have told you that I am busy. I do not have time to discuss the matter with you at the present. You know that your father and I are getting ready to go on a cruise, and I don't enjoy the idea of you running off to someone's ranch while I'm gone. We'll discuss it later."

"No, Mother! I need to discuss it now! Why won't you let me go to Randy's folks' ranch with them? I never get to do anything like that. Randy says he has a great time with his dad up there all the time. My dad is never even around. All that is ever around here is guys like him," the boy said, pointing to Mr. Gilchrest with obvious derision.

"Hamilton!" his mother said sternly. "That is quite enough! The conversation is concluded."

"No it isn't. I want to go to Wimberley with Randy and his folks. And I don't see why I can't. And I have to let them know right away. I'll go call Dad." Caustically, he added, "If that's all right with you."

"It is not all right with me. And your father is out of town. He won't be back until barely time for the dinner party this evening." She was trying desperately to keep her temper in check—but losing the battle.

"He's always out of town! He's never here!" The boy was almost barking now. "I might as well not even have a father! Where is he? I'll go call him, wherever he is. I know he won't care if I go. He could never care less what I do."

"He is away on business," Mrs. Caine replied. Her jaw had become firmly set, and her eyes had turned to steel. "And I'm here *trying* to conduct business of my own. And *you* are being impertinent and interfering. Now I will tolerate no more of this! You are excused. Please go to your room."

With exquisitely bad timing, the elegant Mr. Gilchrest rose in an ill-advised attempt to placate the youngster. Placing his hands on young Caine's shoulders, he said to the boy, "Hamilton, I know you don't mean to be rude. Now you and I are going . . ."

Ham cut him off in mid-sentence. *"Get your slimy, faggot hands off of me!"* he yelled; and he stormed out of the room.

▼ ▼ ▼

The stormy mood remained as young Caine sat quietly at his upstairs bedroom window, watching and waiting, with a can of Coca-Cola and a large bag of potato chips for company. From his vantage point, he had a good view of the driveway and garage area in back of the house.

The chips were nearly gone, and he was on his second Coke when he saw James, the chauffeur, descend the stairs from his quarters and head for the family limousine. Ham Caine was out of his room and downstairs as quick as a grin.

The youth waved his arms frantically as the limo began to roll, signaling the chauffeur to stop. James looked questioningly at young Master Caine as the boy threw open the back door and plopped down onto the rear seat.

"Are you going to the airport to pick up my dad?" the boy asked.

"Yes, I am," the chauffeur replied.

"Then I'm going with you."

"Whatever you say, sir," James agreed, with a touch of sarcasm that did not go unnoticed. He knew full well that the senior Mr. Caine would look strongly askance at the youth's presence at the airport, and he hoped silently that The Brat was about to get into a world of trouble.

Ham Caine didn't think so, though. Even if he did, he would have thought, "What the hell?" His mother wouldn't give even the slightest consideration to his request to spend the weekend at the Edwards ranch. He reasoned that he could at least have his father's attention—a rare commodity as far as the boy was concerned—for the time it would take to drive from the airport back to the River Oaks mansion.

The closer the limousine got to Houston Intercontinental, the more excited the fifteen-year-old became. He was really looking forward to having a good half-hour's heart-to-heart conversation with his father. Why, he wondered to himself, hadn't he ever thought of that before?

The youth stood waiting in the wide expanse of the sliding doors of Texas Consolidated Utilities' private hangar when the large, impressive Gulfstream taxied to a halt. Bubbling with excitement, he ran to greet his highly successful father as the corporate kingpin stepped off the plane.

Hamilton Caine, Sr., had to stoop slightly to pass through the open doorway of the corporate jet. He was about six-feet-one and trim, an obvious reflection of the hours spent weekly at a workout spa in the muscle-toning ritual necessary to feed his savage ego. His sandy hair was graying heavily at the temples, a color combination which was nicely complemented by the custom-tailored suit that he wore—light gray with brown, red, and blue pinstripes. In his right hand, he carried the ubiquitous talisman of the corporate executive—a heavily stuffed, brown leather briefcase.

He greeted his eager son by bellowing, "What in the hell are you doing here?"

"I just came out to meet you . . . so we could talk on the way home."

"Whatever possessed you to do that?"

"I just thought it would be a good time, since you wouldn't have anything else to do but sit in the car and ride home."

"Well you thought wrong!" The senior Mr. Caine strode over to the chauffeur, who stood elegantly erect holding open the back door of the limousine. "Whatever got into you to let this boy tag along to the airport, don't ever let it happen again. Is that clear?" There was an unquestionable touch of menace in his voice.

"Yes sir," the errant servant replied in his most obsequious tone. He resented the personal rebuke, but he perversely enjoyed the pain the scene was producing for The Brat.

"Now listen young man," the father continued, totally oblivious to the crestfallen countenance of his only child, "Arthur and I have a great deal to discuss on the ride back into town, and we don't have time to put up with any of your foolishness. Do I make myself clear?"

The "Arthur" to whom Caine referred was the squat little man in the mouse-colored suit who had disembarked from the airplane behind him. He was the company's vice president for corporate finance.

"But Dad, I only . . ."

"You only nothing," the father interrupted. "You only wait until we get home; I'll deal with you there."

For a moment, Ham Caine considered walking away and finding his way back to the River Oaks mansion the best way he could. Or perhaps, not at all. Instead, he crawled disconsolately into the front seat beside the smirking chauffeur, whom he silently hated, and said not a single word more during the entire ride home. That suited the president and chairman of the board of Texas Consolidated Utilities Corporation just fine.

The same stormy mood prevailed throughout the dinner party that evening, at least as far as the shiny-blonde high school kid and his society-conscious parents were concerned; and there were no tears of parting in the white-bricked mansion on Azalea Vale when Hamilton (Sr.) and Melanie Caine departed on their journey the next day.

▼ ▼ ▼

Now, with the jibes of Curt Richards and the others still stinging in his ears—especially the comment about the chauffeur—it became even more apparent to Ham Caine that his high school freshman year at Wingate School was going to be a drag.

Next year . . . he could hardly wait. Next year he would be sixteen, and he could have a car of his own; he considered that to be a foregone conclusion—a Z-car, perhaps; or maybe a Corvette. To him, that meant freedom—liberation from the tyranny of depending upon someone else for locomotion. For wheels. But with his own car, he wanted to believe, the opportunities would be endless . . . girls, parking, sex for real . . . who knows?

He knew at least two guys his age who were already driving their own cars, and to heck with the legalities. One of them already had two tickets; but if your folks are wealthy, so what?

Such would not do, though, for the Hamilton Caine family. In the first place, it meant something they'd rather not have to worry about—a family responsibility best put off as long as possible. In the second place, it must be considered that Hamilton Caine, Sr., headed the city's—in fact, the state's—largest public utility company, subject to regulation at more than a dozen governmental levels. It just would not do to flaunt the law in order to let his son drive an automobile a year before he could legally do so.

Thus with no personal wheels, and the added embarrassment of being chauffeured to and from the campus, young Caine dreaded his freshman year in high school. He shouldn't have;

because in spite of all the parties and other activities of the just-ended summer, he had plenty of reasons to be happy to be back in school—if he would only stop to think about it.

Wingate School had often provided the most rewarding experiences of his formative years. He had enjoyed Camp Rio Alto, in the Texas hill country, for a couple of the four summers he had spent there; but as he got a little older, the camp activities began to cloy, becoming too stultifyingly juvenile to suite his growing maturity. It was adult companionship and guidance that he craved, not kiddie games. And at home, of course, the boy's father was always otherwise occupied.

The marriage of Hamilton Caine, Sr., to the former Melanie Banks, Houston social butterfly supreme, had become more one of corporate appurtenance, not familial delight. It suited his ego and his business purposes to remain married to the city's most visible socialite, but home life was not what pleased him most. Or at all. A trip now and then, okay. A few lavish parties every year, certainly—all good for the image. A picture on the society pages glimpsed dining with his lovely spouse at one of the city's best restaurants, fine. But something like, "Let's take the kid with a tent and disappear into the mountains for a few days," was not what Hamilton Caine was all about.

And more's the pity for the kid. He needed exactly that sort of thing. He needed an occasional roughhouse before bedtime, or to be picked up and tossed on his butt across the back lawn. Needed to have his hair tousled. He needed someone to make gentle fun when his voice was changing, and to kid him until he blushed about that ever-more-prominent growth of peach fuzz on his upper lip. He needed football and baseball games in the Astrodome. Popcorn and hot dogs.

He never got any of that. Instead, he got stereos. He got his own color television set. And a VCR. He got toy cars and airplanes, ridey-horses and talking clowns—rooty-toot-toots and rummy-tum-tums enough to stock a toy store. He got summer camp and fine schools; but he never got a father.

But at school, there were friends and intelligent, caring faculty once again—companionship to be depended upon every day of the school week. So it was good for Ham Caine to be back—even if he did figure that the freshman year would be, as he called it, "a bummer."

Not the least part of that consideration was the fact that he had to consort, even the tiniest bit, with that chauffeur, James.

"Man," he confided to Randall Edwards just the week before, "that guy's a world-class nerd. He's dorky to the absolute max."

But there he was, as far as the boy knew—that "dork," that "nerd"—waiting as usual in the shining black limo that afternoon when young Caine left his teasing, arguing friends and classmates in the hallway. Mercifully, at least, the guy no longer got out to open the car door for the kid. He had been asked, "please, puh—leeeease," not to.

For the man actually behind the wheel, the next few minutes would provide his sternest test. He had scouted the situation daily since the school term began. He knew where the limo was always parked, which side the kid got in on, the speed at which they drove away, the right turn onto Memorial Drive—all of that. But he had no way of knowing, nor of determining, what went on inside the car. Was there any interchange between the driver and the boy? Was there a greeting? Did anything get acknowledged? Requested? He would simply have to wing it. Everything else, he had practiced.

"Hullo."

That's all there was. Just, "Hullo," as the Caine family's only progeny plopped with a load of school books onto the limo's back seat—way back there—and closed the door. Not too hard to reply to that one. The man simply nodded his head, as he figured a good-mannered servant probably should, then methodically started the car and drove out the driveway—hoping that the boy in the back seat would not notice the undersized fit of the chauffeur cap perched precariously on his curly topped head. No one else said hello, no one waved good-bye. It could not have been easier.

Two hundred or so tenuous yards down Memorial Drive was the entrance to a fledgling real estate development that had not yet gotten off the ground. Site preparation had begun, but work had been halted for the time being. A quick turn off the thoroughfare and the limo was effectively swallowed-up in the trees.

The boy didn't notice the turn, nor the unaccustomed stop—absorbed, no doubt, in whatever were the contents of that school notebook he carried.

He did notice quite abruptly, after the car had stopped, when the driver suddenly leaped into the back seat and pinned the youth beneath him. Aided by the surprise tactic, and no little bit more by the fact that he outweighed the kid by some sixty or seventy pounds, the stranger quickly established mastery of the situation. In short order, the boy's mouth was taped—speechless but heavily grunting—and his hands and feet were bound behind him.

"Now pay attention to me, Buddy Boy. You and I are going for a little ride."

Hamilton Caine, Jr., game kid, responded with an attempted knee-shot to the man's groin; but his bindings prevented a complete swing-through, and he connected with the left thigh, instead.

"That smarted, twirp," the man complained. "Try something like that again and you'll take our little ride with a large bump on your head. Do I make myself clear?"

Hatred, revulsion, revenge—blazing from the young blue eyes straight into the mature brown ones—were the boy's only response. They seemed to say, "Do so, and you'll be sorry."

That was good, the man thought. The kid may not be so much of a twirp after all. He was quite obviously, though, not about to walk on his own power from the limo to the green van parked alongside, as had been the plan.

"Okay, Buddy Boy, upsie-daisie," the man said.

He dragged young Caine out the limo's back door, tossed him across his left shoulder like a sack of potatoes, and carried him to the waiting van—with the boy continually wriggling, squirming, tossing and attempting to lunge away. But to no avail; soon he, too, was hog-tied and trussed, just as the chauffeur had been. The man then pulled a long canvas bag—the type used by cotton pickers—over the head of the still-squirming youngster and tied it below his feet.

"Enjoy yourself," the abductor said. And from the dark recesses of his mobile prison cell, the boy heard the back door of the van slam shut.

▼ ▼ ▼ ▼ ▼ ▼ ▼ ▼ ▼ ▼ ▼ ▼ ▼

3

The kidnapped youth would have been hard-put to estimate how long they drove. Jouncing around in the back of the van, encased in his canvas sheath, young Caine felt as though it took many hours—maybe half a day—before the journey came to an end. It was three hours and twenty-five minutes, to be precise; but with his hands (and wrist watch) bound behind him, the boy had no way of determining that—only that it seemed interminable.

He tried to identify sounds along the way—perhaps to provide clues later on, if he survived—to his kidnapper's destination. He remembered seeing an old movie on television, in which an abducted man counted stops at street lights, identified the clickety-clack of crossing railroad tracks and the clump-calumpf of sound waves reverberating from the moving car off the trusses of a bridge trestle; and he later led police, purely from sound recall, to the lair of the villains.

No such luck for Ham Caine. He heard only the whine of the van's tires on the pavement and the now-and-then roar of an 18-wheeler truck rolling by; and he felt only the occasional, but uncountable, slow-down and stops for traffic lights, or maybe stop signs. Nothing to lead the FBI to from that.

What he was painfully aware of, though, was a persistent cramping in his right calf muscle—that, and nerve-ragging fear. The cramp he attended to by trying desperately, within his bonds, to shift to a more stretched-out position, and by concentrating with all his might on relaxing the leg. This met with only moderate success.

The fear, he could not overcome. His first, immediate fright was that he would suffocate inside the canvas cocoon, but that proved not to be so; the material was loose-woven enough to allow him to breathe. The sustaining fear was far worse. Too much had been in the news, those days, about young boys being done in by degenerate old men—no one could avoid the stories. Would he be killed? Would he be molested? Maimed, maybe? He had heard of one fiend whose favorite diversion—following God-knows-what and prior to silencing his victims forever—was to cut off their testicles with a big knife and eat them. Raw. Right in front of the victims' astonished eyes. At least, that's the way he heard it. Twice during the ride, involuntary screams tried unsuccessfully to escape through his tape-sealed lips.

Roughly the last half-hour of the journey was quite bumpy, and taken at a noticeably slower pace, indicating to the boy in the cotton sack that the getaway van had left the pavement. When the vehicle at last came to its final stop, it was several very long, worry-filled minutes before the back door was opened and the kidnapper returned for his prisoner. Prior to that, with the boy's heart pounding in his ears, he thought he could also hear the sounds of rustling around outside; but there was no sound among them that he could identify—just bumping, scraping, that sort of thing. Once, he heard a voice, or voices. It might have been the man with the mustache, or it might have been someone else.

When the door finally did open, it was upsie-daisie once again, as the man silently hoisted the bundled boy onto his shoulder and carried him a short distance. When he was set down and the canvas bag removed, young Caine found himself inside what was apparently a small camping trailer.

He lay in a tiny alcove just inside the doorway. There was a couch adjacent, with some kind of fold-down table hung on a wall next to it. The opposite wall had a rack containing some folding chairs. Past the entrance was a small kitchen area opposite a built-in dining table with bench seats. The seat upholstery matched the curtains on the adjacent window, as well as windows behind the couch and over the kitchen sink—a coarse-textured, plaid material in brown, burnt-orange, and off-white. He couldn't quite make out what was at the opposite end of the trailer. That was a sleeping area, most likely; and there were two closed doors—probably a closet and a bathroom.

The abductor stood over him, pensively studying his now thoroughly terrified captive. Slowly, he bent down and, with surprising gentleness, removed the adhesive tape from the boy's mouth and cheeks. Next, he unfolded a large hunting knife and cut away the ropes that had bound the youth for so painfully long. Still no conversation.

Slowly, tentatively, young Caine uncoiled his legs and rubbed his nearly raw wrists. Somehow—he didn't know how he was able to do it—he managed to speak, albeit in a half-stammer, half-sob. "Are you . . . you . . . are you going to . . . kill me?"

"No," the man replied, still staring intently at the boy, but with the wry half-smile he had bestowed on the chauffeur beginning to wrinkle one corner of his mouth. "I'm not going to kill you."

"Wh-what then? You going to violate my young body?" He couldn't believe he'd said that.

"Your young body is safe, my friend. You're just not my type."

"Then what? Wh-what are you af-ter?"

"Shut up and let me think," the man said. "It's been a trying day."

After a pause, he said, "Come on," took the boy by the arm and led him to a pair of stacked bunk beds in the back corner of the trailer. "Get in the bottom one."

"I need to . . . to use the rest room."

"Okay, go ahead; it's right there." The kidnapper pointed to a small doorway opposite the bunk beds.

Once inside, door closed and bladder pressure relieved, the boy quickly studied the possibility of escaping through the minuscule window, but that was hopeless. The next thing he knew, he was crying—crying harder and ever harder, until he was ultimately caught-up in a paroxysm of complete emotional release. The lad had held up bravely for as long as he could—longer than most would have, maybe—but he finally could hold out no longer. After all, he was only fifteen.

Great, uncontrollable waves of sobbing coursed through him—immense, *grand mal* convulsions that shook his body in rolling contortions like a string of small boats lashed together in a storm-tossed sea. Fear, worry, all the imagined horrors had overcome his tender young bravery; and he was helpless in their thrall. Tears literally sprayed from his eyes and cascaded down his cheeks. Twice, he shrieked aloud. Finally, he collapsed, limply, into a heap on the tiny bathroom floor.

The kidnapper thrust open the bathroom door just as a wave of nausea struck the pathetically huddled figure, and he helped guide the boy's reeling head to the rim of the commode. The boy vomited. He vomited again. And when there was nothing left in his writhing stomach, he dry-heaved. At last, under the firm, strangely reassuring pressure of the man's grasp around his arm, he was able to bring his tortured body back under control with one last, enormous sigh.

"Here," the man said, "drink this." He handed the boy a glass of water, which was quickly downed. "I don't suppose you're very hungry for supper after all that, are you?"

Again with surprising gentleness, belying his apparent demeanor and purpose, the man carefully scooped the drained youth off the bathroom floor, carried him across the tiny room to the beds, and deposited his limp body into the lower bunk.

"Lie down, kid, and get some rest. There was a tranquilizer in that water, so you should feel a lot better tomorrow."

With that, he snapped one manacle of a set of handcuffs to the boy's right wrist and the other to a steel pole that stretched vertically by a corner of the bed from the floor to the ceiling. Ham Caine reasoned that the pole had been anchored there specifically for that purpose; it was obviously not part of the trailer's standard decor.

How many other kids have been handcuffed to that pole? the boy wondered to himself. *Bastard! What did he do to them? What's he going to do to me? Will he do it while I'm asleep?*

While I'm drugged? Son of a BITCH! I pray to God I get the chance to kill him. And I will if I just get the chance . . .

On and on his mind raced, fueled by undiminished terror and sparked by the growing rage within him. Ultimately, the drug began to take hold of his tortured brain, and the exhausted, terrified teenager drifted into sleep.

As the boy's breathing became gentle and even, the man stood over him watching, with a quizzical, half-smiling, half-puzzled expression on his face. Perhaps he was trying fully to comprehend just what it was that he had accomplished; or he might have been troubling-out a decision as to exactly what to do next. At length, he turned to walk away, stopped, turned back, and studied the boy a short time more. Finally satisfied with whatever had been on his mind, he kneeled down to the bunk bed and removed the captive's shoes.

"Pleasant dreams, kid," he said. Then he rose, turned, and walked out the trailer door.

▼ ▼ ▼

It is easy enough to wish pleasant dreams. But how can anyone manage to have them when living under the fear of imminent death, molestation, or watching someone cut off and eat his testicles? Under such a threat, sleep can be only short-lived at best—even to someone drugged.

For Hamilton Caine, Jr., it was a devastatingly long night, fraught with terror . . . in and out of sleep, half-sleep, and no sleep. The drug held sway for no more than a few hours. After that, he lay in the bunk in a sleep-wake void, part dreaming and part imagining, half conscious and half out-of-it. The air around him was still—heavy with the late-summer, not-yet-fall, meteorological middle-age that had settled in like a thick coating of soggy oatmeal inside the tiny trailer.

He was aware of the handcuff on his right wrist, and of his inability, because of it, to roll over to his left, no matter how much his body ached to do so. He was also aware that, sometime during the night, a light blanket had been laid across his lower body—not needed at all. He kicked it off; and it was then that he noticed his shoes had been removed. That was nice; so he one-handedly removed both socks, also. And he thought about pajamas, and clean sheets, and about air-conditioned bedrooms, as he started to feel beads of perspiration popping out all over him.

Funny, he thought, *I can actually feel the sweat pop out. Never noticed that before.*

From somewhere in his semi-conscious, he could hear an occasional raucous, rasping sound—first loud, then trailing off, like a rip saw tearing into a fresh-hewn log. He had never heard a rip saw tearing into a fresh-hewn log, but that was the way he imagined it would sound. It was the kidnapper, the man with the mustache, the bastard, sonofabitch . . . snoring.

Grasping for something to relate to—anything to occupy his mind—the best he could come up with were memories of Camp Rio Alto. In the summer. In the Central Texas heat. And the times when, in the middle of a sultry night, he had shucked the underwear he had worn to bed (that's all any of the boys wore) and had lain there naked for the rest of the night. Several others, he learned, had done the same thing. Many of the counselors slept naked all the time, and made no bones about it; but he had long since come to the conclusion that about half of them were fags.

Does sleeping naked make you a fag? Or are you a fag first and sleep naked later?

Interesting thoughts. Serious thoughts. Silly. Shallow. Sleep. Nonsleep. He wished he were there, right then, lying naked in his bunk at Camp Rio Alto.

WHO-HOOT-HA-HOO!

The sudden outcry sent him bolt upright in his bed—until his manacle tether jerked him backward. If he had been a lot older, it might have meant immediate cardiac arrest; but not to a boy of fifteen. It only scared the daylights out of him.

WHO-HOOT-HA-HOO!

There it was again, sledge-hammering its way into the adobe fortress of his fitful attempts at sleep.

Horrible noise, a voice told him from somewhere within, as he struggled to force himself awake. *What was it?*

WHO-HOOT-HA-HOO!

By now, the frightened youth could certainly have considered that the end of the world was coming. But what was a kid shocked out of his sleep to think? How could a fifteen-year-old city boy, scion of corporate and societal bigwigs, know that the loud, startling noise was the call of a great horned owl?

He did, though. Sometime between the second and third heart-stilling hollers, as he struggled to shake out the cobwebs of his tortured mind, he had managed to identify it. After all, you don't spend four summers at Camp Rio Alto for nothing.

He was being held somewhere deep in the woods; no doubt about that now.

Many of the other night sounds heard between half-sleep and half-awake were even scarier, though not as momentarily startling as that of the giant night bird. There was one that was a kind of rattle, like a cross between the baby's toy and the Halloween noise-maker. That sound came in alternate, staccato bursts from all over the place. First it was over there; then over here; then back to there; then way off there; and so forth—a cacophony that mercifully ended as the long night wore on, only to be replaced by deafening silence.

Twice during the night, he heard the distant howling of what must have been a pack of coyotes. Wolves, maybe. He had heard them, too, at summer camp; and they always sent chills up his spine.

There was another distant noise also—too distant, and he was too deep into sleep for it to register in anything but his subconscious; but it was there.

And often came the buzz saw. And terrible silence.

Then finally, once more, sleep. Merciful, wonderful, strength-rejuvenating sleep. And dreams. Running. Falling. Slow motion. Can't move. Can't run. Won't work. Nothing functions. Ghosts and goblins. Nightmares. And off, once again, into deep . . . deeper . . . heavy . . . no-dream sleep. Sle-e-e-e-p.

BUH-LAM!

What the hell? Where am I? A shot? Explosion?

Silence. And then again . . .

BUH-LAM!

The sonofabitch is shooting at me! But he missed. How can he miss in this tiny trailer? But there's no pain. No blood. He missed me!

BUH-LAM! BUH-LAM!

Echoes from all around. Deafening. Pulse-pounding.

There'll be no way to survive the night!

But it was no longer night. When the boy managed to force his eyelids apart, he could see through a bedside window the dim light of early dawn outside. Inside, the trailer was still almost totally dark. All the more foreboding. All the more terrifying. And what about those shots?

"Wake up, Junior!" The door of the trailer had burst open and the visage of a person of some sort stood silhouetted in the dimly backlit doorway. "Time for breakfast."

It was the kidnapper. The bastard. Sonofabitch.

The boy had difficulty seeing in the trailer's gloom, and he had to squint. The man was wearing camouflage all over. Shirt. Pants. Hat. And even some kind of makeup on his face—all camouflage. He looked like some kind of demented Indian with a decorator touch: war paint in earth tones.

"Wake up, kid." A ceiling light flicked on at the man's outstretched fingertips. His left hand held three dead squirrels. "Sleep well?"

How callous can anyone get? There stood that sonofabitch man who puts a fifteen-year-old child through nineteen different kinds of hell and then asks, "Sleep well?" It didn't deserve an answer.

Suddenly, finally, it all made sense. He'd been hunting. The loud explosions really were gunshots; only the maniac was shooting at squirrels, not at boys.

"But there were four shots." The boy couldn't resist the jibe.

"One of them took two," the man replied. "Sorry."

"I need to use the rest room," the boy noted with a degree of urgency.

"Promise you won't do what you did on your last trip to the rest room?"

The boy nodded his head, tight-lipped.

That wry half-smile found its way back onto the kidnapper's

face as he fished in his left pants pocket, retrieved a two-key ring, and unlocked the prisoner's handcuffs.

After the flush of the peculiar trailer toilet, there was silence. The bathroom door didn't open, and no sound came forth. The boy must have been milking the scene for dramatic effect. If so, he did it well.

The man with the camouflaged face did not rise to the bait, however; he waited it out. After a long, empty interval, the door finally opened and the boy emerged—a theatrical gesture completely wasted, because the kidnapper, now stripped to his underwear briefs, was at the trailer sink washing the grease paint off his face.

Yet the boy persisted at taking the scene. Waiting where he stood in the bathroom doorway until the man turned around with towel to face, he intoned, "You're holding me for ransom, aren't you?"

The man looked him straight in the eyes and nodded affirmation. His face now paint-free and dried, he walked to a small built-in chest of drawers, extracted a pair of cut-off blue jeans, shucked them over his black-bristled legs, buttoned the waist and zipped the fly. No belt.

"How much?" the boy asked.

No reply.

"How much are you asking for me?"

"Demanding, not asking," the man with the mustache replied. "One hundred thousand dollars."

"One hundred thousand? That's an insult! Why not a quarter of a million? Why not a million dollars?"

"You gotta be realistic, kid; that's too much to expect."

"It is *not* too much. I won't stand for a stupid one hundred thousand dollars."

The man couldn't believe it all. "Okay, make it a hundred and fifty."

"Two hundred."

"You got a deal. Two hundred thousand dollars it is." The man had a strong sensation that he was attending a Mad Tea Party. Alice and the White Rabbit should be along any minute. Only last night, that boy was vomiting his guts out in terror; and

now, bright and early the next morning, he was bargaining to
raise the ante on his own ransom. Was everyone crazy?

The youth smiled. "All *right!*" He'd won the moment; but his
plans for winning the day might fare differently. Cockily, he
asked, "What's for breakfast?"

"You're looking at it," the man replied, pointing to the three
squirrels on the table.

"Squirrels?"

"If you haven't tried 'em, don't knock 'em."

"But squirrels are nothing but rodents, just like rats!"

"And turtles are just reptiles, too," the man rejoined, "like
snakes. But I know a restaurant in New Orleans that makes turtle soup you'd kill for."

The boy began to chuckle. Then the chuckle erupted into a
laugh.

"What's so funny?" his abductor wanted to know.

Chuckle again. "Your timing sucks!"

"What's wrong with my timing? Everything has gone exactly
according to my plans."

Then another chuckle. "It still sucks."

"I don't know what you're talking about."

"You don't know what 'sucks' means?"

"Yes, but I don't know what you mean 'sucks'."

"Then I'll tell you," again chuckling. "My parents left four
days ago on a cruise from Acapulco to Tahiti . . . on a sailboat!" More chuckling. "Who's gonna pay your ransom?"

The man regarded the news with half-stunned silence, followed by the only comment he found suitable for the situation.

"Shit! Shee-it!"

"What do you do now, Mister Hot-Shot Kidnapper?"

"Well, Buddy Boy, it looks like you are going to be my house
guest a little longer than I'd planned."

Now it was "Buddy Boy's" turn to be stunned. Almost involuntarily, he responded with expletive in kind. "Double shit!" he
exclaimed.

Young Caine had really believed that he would best the man
with that revelation. Surely, he thought, with his parents away
and virtually incommunicado, ransom demands would be out

of the question, and they could both quit the charade and go home. That thought had buoyed his spirits and had given him courage to face up to his captor.

There was also the possibility that the man would just give it all up and kill the boy in order to leave no traces, no witness to the bungled kidnapping. The captive knew that it was a chance he'd just have to take; after all, it was the truth, and the man would find it out sooner or later anyhow. Besides, he'd said he wasn't going to kill him. He could also have lied.

So the boy took the gambit, made his ploy; and it fizzled. He no longer had any viable idea what to do. After all, he wondered, what were the alternatives? Escape? Prospects not too good. Kill the man? Delightful thought; but how could he do it? Too risky to attempt anyway—at least for now. Play along with him and hope for a break? That was most likely the best strategy for the moment; but it meant that he might have to stay there for an eternity, and the bastard might yet decide to kill him. He resolved one thing for sure, though: he would never again, no matter what the circumstances, lose control of himself as he had done the evening before.

"I don't want any damn squirrel," he announced, sulkingly.

"Nobody's forcing you to eat."

"Good." The boy went back to the beds and slumped into the lower bunk again, face down.

The man with the mustache that hid the long upper lip looked down momentarily at the floor, glanced again toward the boy, then turned his gaze out a window—amazed at the previous exchange.

Gutsy kid, he thought to himself. *I hope he doesn't grow up to be a crook like his father. He might end up owning the whole damned world.*

"I don't know what you did in the bathroom to psyche yourself up like that," he said aloud, "but you sure came out swinging."

I took a piss! the boy thought silently. And he continued to sulk.

▼ ▼ ▼

Attention was then turned to the necessary chore of cleaning the breakfast squirrels. The man produced his fold-up knife again and deftly incised a ring around the neck of one of the small bushy-tails. The next slice opened the fur and skin down the animal's belly, all the way to the anus, with the man taking care not to puncture the membrane that contained the intestines. A similar longitudinal slice exposed the backbone; and the breakfast beasty was ready to be peeled.

With a firm finger-and-thumb grip on the circumscribed neck skin, and the other hand holding the squirrel's head, the hunter tore the hide away from the flesh with apparent ease— stripping each side, in turn, and pausing only a few times to slice away an unrelenting strip of cartilage or bone. The result, when the operation was completed, was a frail, white-and-reddish carcass—ridiculous looking in its total nakedness with the bushy, bulging head still attached.

The first such denuding took place in complete silence, with no audience. From the lower bunk, a pair of intent blue eyes beneath a tousled blonde mop watched with fascination at the second. By the time the neck was ringed on the third, the curious youngster was standing beside the meal skinner, studying every movement of the operation.

"Do you think I could do that?"

"Sure," the man replied, "with a little practice."

"Looks easy to me," said the youngster.

The man handed him the final animal, and the boy learned otherwise.

"Squirrels don't particularly like to part with their skins," the man said. "Now you'll have to keep a tight grip on the skin and pull with all your strength."

The boy tried again, with little success, then gritted his teeth and bore down harder—determined. With an occasional adult assist, he finally managed to get the creature peeled all the way to the genitals (it was a male) and stopped in bewilderment as to how to go about managing things from there.

"Well-endowed little bugger, isn't he?" the man asked, having noted the hesitation. "Squirrels remind me of little male toy poodles. Have you ever noticed? About two-thirds of the entire dog is peter."

The boy smiled, shyly. Yes, he had noticed that, but he

didn't comment. Then he watched as the man took over again and started to slice away the reproductive organs. Young Caine couldn't help thinking of the story of the testicle-eating ghoul he had worried about during the night, so he decided to excise that fear—along with the squirrel's oversized anatomical accomplishments.

"Here, let me," he said, as he reached for the knife and continued the delicate removal of the doodads.

The man immediately realized that surrendering the knife was a mistake. The captive boy could quickly plunge it into his gut and the game would be over. But it had been such a natural thing to do, that he handed over the deadly instrument without the slightest hesitation.

Cautiously, then, he watched the boy-surgeon's operation—planning a quick dodge, feint and lunge if a threat should appear. But the boy was much too innocent for that; and without further instructions, he raggedly finished the skin-pulling and semi-triumphantly held up the poor dead beasty to gloat. "How's that?"

"Not bad for a punk. Now you can gut him."

"Gut him?"

"Gut him. Come on, I'll show you how." The man picked up the squirrel carcass and the knife, and walked to the small kitchen sink. The boy followed.

"Now's when you can get your hands good and filthy," the man said. "The important thing is not to get the meat filthy along with them."

He then proceeded to detail to the youth the fine points of removing the animal's entrails, taking care not to puncture the bladder or the lower intestine, and thus risk tainting the meat with rather unappetizing bodily by-products. When the job was completed, a pile of offal lay in one corner of the sink, and his hands were covered with blood.

"Turn on the water, please," he requested, and he held the squirrel and his own gory hands under the faucet. The boy turned the tap and heard the whir of a small electric pump that brought at-home convenience to that trailer in the who-knows-where. As the man washed, the boy took two steps backward.

"What's to keep me from running out that door while you're standing there with blood all over your hands?"

"A lock. And Brutus," the man replied, without even looking up.

"Brutus? Who's that?"

The man put two still-wet fingers to his lips and emitted a loud, shrill whistle. "C'mere Brutus," he called. Then he nodded in the direction of the door. In short order, a very large, yellowish canine appeared outside the door and barked. Deep. Authoritative.

"Guard him, Brutus," the man commanded. The dog responded by glaring intently through the screen door at Hamilton Robert Caine, 2nd edition, and wrinkled-up the right corner of his mouth with a snarl.

The boy edged closer to the door and peered through the screen, thus precipitating an even louder snarl. With a gulp, he said, "You too, Brutus?"

By God, the man thought to himself. *The kid's got a wit.*

"Now let me tell you a story," he said to the boy.

"Once upon a time there were three clergymen who went on a fishing trip together in a small rowboat, somewhere out in Galveston Bay. One was a Baptist preacher, and one was a Catholic priest. They'd fished together a lot. The third one was a Jewish rabbi, and this was his first time to go fishing with the other two.

"Well, they fished a while into the morning and presently ran out of bait. 'Not to worry,' the Baptist said, 'I'll go get some.' So he stepped out of the boat and walked across the water to a bait stand, bought some more bait, and walked back across the water to the boat.

"The Catholic priest wasn't too impressed by any of this, but the Jewish rabbi damned near dropped his teeth. The last one he'd heard about walking on water was a couple of thousand years ago—and that was subject to dispute.

"Well, fishing was good; so good, in fact, that they ran out of bait again. The Catholic padre put down his pole and said, 'Okay, my turn.' Then he, also, stepped out of the boat and walked across the water to the bait stand. This time, the rabbi damned near fell out of the boat. He couldn't believe it. But the priest came back the same way, and they kept on fishing.

"When they ran out of bait the third time, both the preacher and the priest looked straight at the rabbi. And that poor guy— he was about to come unglued. But I guess he figured that if the other two men of God could pull it off, so could he—he'd just have to have faith. So he stood up, stepped out of the boat, and sank out of sight.

"After a while, the Baptist looked over at the Catholic and said, 'You know, we'd better show him where those rocks are, or he's gonna drown'."

The youngster looked blankly at the man. "That's a dumb story," he said.

"It's a parable, son," the man replied, "a parable. Do you know where you are?" The boy shook his head. "You're in the Big Thicket, sweetheart—the toughest, meanest, deadliest piece of tangled-up real estate in the whole U.S. of A. Out there, all around us, is swamp . . . quicksand . . . man-eating alligators as long as this trailer . . . mountain lions . . . wolves . . . bobcats . . . every kind of poisonous snake on the North American continent . . . treacherous plants . . . and sixteen other kinds of ways to get yourself killed.

"If Mother Nature doesn't get you, the cannibal Indians probably will. And if they don't, you won't stand a chance with the white men. Those redneck East Texas yahoos out there would just as soon skin you alive—just like we did those squirrels—as look at you. They don't tolerate strangers one little bit, not at all. Little blonde city boys will make 'em mad as hell just being there. And you can't go anywhere in these woods without them knowing you're there.

"The moral to the story, Buddy Boy, is that before you get any serious ideas about trying to escape . . . in case you think you can get away from me, and in case you think you can get away from Brutus . . . just remember where you are. *I* know where the rocks are; *you* would never make it."

The parable was not lost on the kid. It proved that his situation was even more helpless than he had feared. He had, indeed, heard something of the legends of the Big Thicket; and there was just enough ring of truth in what the man told him to send an unpleasant shiver up his spine.

So he couldn't run; but he didn't feel at all comfortable about staying until his captor played out his little game, either. Even if the man didn't *intend* to harm him—and who could be sure?—there remained a question of what might happen if things went wrong. What, for instance, if the man got stoned and lost control of himself?

"What are you going to do with me when you shoot up?" the boy asked.

"When I what?"

"You know, when you do drugs."

"I don't do drugs. Do you?"

"No. But come on," the boy persisted, "I thought all criminals did drugs."

"Well, I don't do drugs. And I'm not a criminal," the man said adamantly.

"What do you call kidnapping?"

He had him there. "Well, I don't make a habit of that, either."

"You mean this is your first time? Is this your first big crime?"

The only reply was a frown. "Come on, now," the man said, changing the subject. "Let's clean the rest of these critters and have some breakfast before it gets too hot in here to cook."

"Might as well," the boy agreed. "If you're gonna die, you might as well not do it on an empty stomach."

"You're not going to die, you twirp," the man chided, intending to sound good-humored.

"I'd sure like to believe that."

"Trust me."

"Ha!"

▼　▼　▼

Breakfast preparation was routine, but nonetheless fascinating to young Caine, who had never participated in cooking chores of any kind. Consequently, he knew nothing about it.

The camp chef first put on a pot of rice. While that was cooking, he split the squirrels in half down the back, salted and peppered them, rolled and sprinkled them with flour, then popped them, two halves at a time, into a skillet of hot grease.

"Colonel Sanders, eat your heart out," he proclaimed, as the breakfast offerings sizzled and sputtered their way into the grease.

"Is this going to be like that turtle soup you'd kill for?" the boy reminded.

"I already did," the cook replied. "I killed the squirrels, didn't I?"

The menu, alas, did not live up to the billing; the boy found it to be tasty, but tough. Still, the gravy and rice were delicious to a hearty appetite, there was plenty of cold milk, and the teenager was able satisfyingly to fill a stomach that had been achingly empty since the wretched retching of the night before.

With the meal nearly finished, he asked, "What's your name?"

"Now you don't really expect me to tell you that, do you?"

"Well, I've got to call you something." Pondering the subject briefly, the youth announced, "I'll just call you Bill."

"Why Bill?"

"I used to have a Teddy bear named Bill."

"A Teddy bear? You're naming me after a Teddy bear?"

The boy looked at the man's hairy body, covered only by the cut-off jeans. "Maybe I named him after you."

The man made no reply. He stared reflectively at his captive—sizing him up and evaluating their situation. It occurred to him that, if he had had a son, he might be just about this kid's age, give or take a year.

It's the age when a father can really begin to enjoy a son, to have fun with him. It's the age when youth cautiously reaches out for adulthood, dallies with it, tests and tastes of it before deciding it doesn't taste good yet and should best be put off for a while longer. But babyhood has irretrievably melted away and can no longer be recalled or tolerated, while vestiges of manhood are stirring beneath the surface, trying to pop out, but pushing only pimples to the outside, instead.

The onslaught of puberty had been kind to Ham Caine in that respect. He was blessed with an occasional zit now and

then, but nothing on the order of the craters-on-the-moon erup-
tions that plague many teenagers. He would never have acne.

Yes, a son, the man continued to muse—if his long-ago
failed marriage had managed to make one—might be just about
this boy's age, in the blush of ripening adolescence; but he
doubtless would never have resembled this example. This boy
was as fair as the man was dark. The man's hair was black and
curly; the boy's was blonde and straight. The eyes of the man
were brown, deep, and rather soft, almost like those of a wistful,
spaniel pup; but they hinted at an occasional inner glow—a
twinkle. The youth's were bright blue—inquiring, penetrating.
Indeed, everything about the pair reflected a similar black-white
contrast. The man, heavy-shouldered and almost stocky; the
boy, lean. He'd likely be tall. The boy had everything going for
him; the man was trying in desperation—and kidnapping for
ransom is about as desperate a move as anyone can make—to
reforge something out of a life that had taken too many kick-
ings, and a career that seemed to have withered away.

The contrast continued down to the clothing—the man's rag-
ged-legged cut-offs, which he had swapped for his all-camou-
flage outfit, and the boy's designer everything. The youth wore
jeans, also, but they were of the soft-brushed variety with a designer's signature on the hip pocket. His shirt, horizontally
striped in pastel-hued yellow, white and tan, boasted the proper
designer's emblem over the left breast—so obligatory to a young
gentleman of his station. His shoes (he had put them back on,
perhaps in the earlier anticipation that he might get the opportunity to make a run for it) were not the deck shoes that so upset
his mother. They were athletic in nature, but of the highly expensive, white leather variety that no one could ever refer to as
"tennies." His mother didn't like them, either.

Yes, the man's son, if he had had one, might be this boy's
age; but he would never have looked like this one.

A boy could have been great fun, though, the kidnapper
thought, as he let himself slip deeper into musing. Silently he
recalled, from Rogers and Hammerstein's *Carousel: I'll teach
him to rassle and dive through a wave when we go in the morn-*

ing for our swim. And the theme of the song: *My boy Bill, I will see that he's named after me . . . I will.*

Bill. The name and the song reverberated in his thoughts. They were the embodiment of every man's dream-wish of possessing his very own son . . . his spittin' image . . . his opportunity to mould a new person into what he perceived himself to be; his joy; his delight; his immortality, perhaps. *Bill.*

Abruptly, he was transported back to the table in the little trailer, looking directly into the earnest, searching blue eyes of somebody else's son, whom he had stolen.

"Okay," he said. "Bill will be fine."

▼ ▼ ▼ ▼ ▼ ▼ ▼ ▼ ▼ ▼ ▼ ▼ ▼ ▼

4

The breakfast mess had been mostly cleaned up, which amounted to throwing away the paper plates and cups, and putting the frying pan into the sink to soak. The squirrel entrails had been fed to the dog—an act that young Caine promptly pronounced to be, "Gross. Totally. Gross to the max!" Brutus didn't seem to think so.

"Okay, Junior, time for your nap," said the man, now named Bill.

The boy's expression loudly asked, "Are you serious?" It was barely 10:30 in the morning.

"Come on now," Bill ordered, "back into your cubicle. I've got to go make a very important phone call; and the way you eat, I'd better buy some more supplies, too."

"But nobody will be home, I tell you."

"The FBI will be, and they've got to get the message that you're alive and well, and that I'm wanting money."

"Demanding," the boy corrected.

"Okay, demanding. Now crawl into that bunk, Junior."

"Don't call me Junior," the boy snapped. After considering his situation, he added, "Please," and crawled grudgingly into the bottom bunk.

Bill snapped the loose half of the chrome bracelets around the boy's wrist again, checking to make certain the other half was secure around the steel pole. "Now you just sit tight, Buddy Boy, and everything will be all right."

Now you just sit tight, Buddy Boy, and everything will be all right.

The words reverberated inside the boy's head. He had a strong feeling that he had heard them before. Perhaps, he thought, they might even have been in the same voice. It was startling, and it puzzled him. Where could such a recollection, or such a feeling of recollection, have come from? He couldn't shake it; but with nothing to do but lie in his bunk prison, he might as well ruminate on it, roll it around in his head for a while. Nothing would come clear, though. Soon *déjà vu* gave way to Camp Rio Alto; and shortly afterward, the still-exhausted boy was asleep.

The man, meanwhile, donned a shirt, belt, and a pair of sneakers, without socks, climbed into his van and left—admonishing the dog as he departed, "Watch the house, Brutus."

A few hundred yards down the twisting, almost-hidden, woodland road, he stopped, got out of the vehicle, and replaced the license plates. He had removed them to avoid identification by his captive. It was about a thirty-minute drive from there into the little town of Woodville; but he went the other direction, instead, to Beaumont—which took over an hour. That was a planned, tactical maneuver, just in case his telephone call should be monitored or traced.

From a pay booth, he telephoned the Houston Police Department's emergency number, to make certain he would get the dispatcher. When the call was answered, he launched into a terse spiel that he had been rehearsing all the way from his secluded campsite.

In his best phony imitation of a stage hoodlum, he announced, "Okay, you'd better make sure your recorder is on, 'cause I ain't sayin' it but once. We've got the Hamilton Caine kid. He's okay. When the old man gets back into town, tell him we want two hundred thousand dollars in cash for the boy. I hope you got that."

He hung up, feeling certain that the brevity of his announcement had precluded the possibility of a trace—particularly since his call had come from another city. He had used the "we" because, as he saw it, it couldn't hurt for them to think there was a gang involved.

His next stop was a grocery store, where he bought a few random items that included a full gallon of milk. As he picked up a package of wieners, and then decided to make it two packages, he speculated to himself, *I'll be willing to bet there's not a kid alive, even a rich kid, who doesn't like hot dogs.*

Other obvious cookout items included marshmallows, canned pork and beans, and lots of crunchy chips.

Silently, he wondered, *Do rich kids eat junk food? . . . Does a trash fire smoke?*

The kidnapper made another stop, at a hardware store, then headed back to the hideaway—halting one last time to remove the license tags again.

By the time he arrived, it was almost two in the afternoon . . . and hot! When he walked into the trailer, it could have passed for a sauna; and the boy lay pitifully helpless, still handcuffed to the bedpole. He had one-handedly removed his shirt, as best he could; but he was unable to get it past the handcuffs and the steel bar, where it lay wadded and soaked with sweat. The mattress around him was also sweatsoaked. He was awake. And furious.

"I'll get you out in a minute, kid," Bill said, stopping at the small propane-powered refrigerator to put away the perishable food he had just purchased. While there, he took out a Coke and a tray of ice, placed four cubes into a paper cup, and handed them to the boy. "Here," he said, "you might like this."

As he turned and started to walk out the door, the still-unopened Coke can caught him swift and hard in the back. He turned to find the boy on his knees, almost in the middle of the trailer floor—which was as far as he could stretch from his manacled position.

"Bastard!" the boy yelled.

"I thought it was 'Bill,'" the man replied, not really blaming the kid for the outburst. He tossed the drink can back to the youth and said, "Here. Now drink that and cool off! I'll be back in a minute."

As he re-entered the trailer, the kidnapper pulled off his shirt and tossed it onto the dining table. Reaching into his pocket for the keys, he walked over to the bunks and unlocked the half of the handcuffs that was attached to the pole, leaving the other half still affixed to the boy's wrist. He then grasped the youngster firmly by the elbow, pulled the wet shirt over the cuffs, and dropped it onto the bunk.

"Come on," he said. "If you haven't finished your drink, bring it." The drink remained behind, unfinished.

Outside the trailer, the dog ran hurriedly over to sniff the boy's legs, causing him to jump in alarm.

"Don't worry about him," Bill said, "he just wants to get acquainted. You do what you're supposed to, and he won't bother you."

Leading the boy by the handcuffs, the man reached to the ground to pick up a stout chain that had been padlocked around a large-trunked tree; then he snapped the handcuffs onto the chain.

"Take your pants off," he told the boy.

It's finally come, the boy thought. *I knew he'd get around to it sooner or later*. Then aloud, "Stick it in your ear!"

"Look, kid," the man said. "I'm holding all the cards. Now do what I said and take off your pants, Jun . . ." He had almost said, "Junior," but caught himself. "Buddy!"

With the hatred of the day before burning once more in his bright blue eyes, the hapless fifteen-year-old opened his belt, unzipped and dropped his designer jeans. They refused to pass over his shoes, so he had to sit down on the ground to remove the shoes, then stand again to shuck his trousers. When the task was completed, he slammed them to the ground.

"Now stand still," the man said, and he walked back into the trailer.

The youth stood just as he was ordered—fully uncovered except for the very stylish, for his generation, pair of skimpy, bikini underwear. They were red, giving his total appearance a four-toned effect. He had one of those complexions peculiar to very few blondes—that of being capable of taking on a rich, glowing tan from the sun rather than the burn-peel-and-freckle routine common to many fair-haired people. Though decidedly blonde from the beginning, his hair had bleached to golden in the hours he had spent at tennis during the just-ended summer vacation; and his skin had toned beautifully tan along with it, like some healthy-looking Swede seen advertising health foods, Scandinavian cruises or such—all of him, that is, except his mid-section. That part, from just below the navel to mid-thigh, had remained covered on the courts by his tennis shorts. It was as white as a baby's behind, then bisected in the middle by the red briefest-of-briefs.

He stood erect and defiant, with a decently flat and hardened stomach, for fifteen. While burnishing in the light bronze tone of his skin, the summer at tennis had also managed to burn off what had remained of early-teen puppy fat, and he was overall lean and well sorted-out. His arms had taken on that muscle tone that brings a top-central vein to near the surface of the skin just above the inside of each elbow, providing a sinuous, semi-muscular look; and his legs were beginning to fill with blonde bristles. With such a body, he could stand unashamed at any poolside or in any locker room—an altogether handsome youth. And with the intense hatred now blazing from those blue eyes, beneath that golden outcropping, Adolf Hitler would have loved him.

But as he had been told, he held none of the cards; Bill had all the trumps.

Presently, the man emerged from the trailer with a spray can of insect repellent. "Hold still," he ordered; and he began to spray the boy's vulnerable body from ankle to shoulders, inside and outside the arms and legs, and all across the red skivvies. The spray was cold, stinging, acrid. He then ordered the boy to take off his socks, which he did, and he sprayed his feet, too.

Before finishing the spray job, Bill ordered, "Now close your eyes and your mouth, take a deep breath and hold it." And he sprayed the pungently scented potion onto the boy's face, neck and hair. "Okay, you can open them. That ought to keep off the mosquitoes and some of the chiggers . . . maybe."

The boy watched as the man performed the same ritual on himself.

During his afternoon of imprisonment in that steam bath of a trailer, young Caine's imagination had run wild again, and he had been once more possessed with all the fears of the previous day. Being led outside and forced to strip to his underwear had bolstered those fears. He had momentarily experienced a feeling of relief, until he saw the man glance at his near nakedness and produce that folding knife once again. He saw the blade unfolded, and watched with dread as the man stooped low, directly in front of him. The boy closed his eyes and tensed his body.

Now almost at the youth's feet, the man he had named Bill reached out and picked up the recently shed designer jeans; and with a quick thrust, he plunged the knife into the right pants leg, then scored it around in a full circle, reminiscent of the skinning incisions on the necks of the squirrels. Opening his eyes, the boy watched as the man with the knife did likewise to the left leg, then tossed the now designer cut-offs at his captive's feet. Next, the kidnapper pulled over a folding lawn chair that had been resting against the tree, unfolded it, and set it beside his captive.

"You should be cooler now," he said; and he turned to walk away.

"Hey," the boy called. "I need to use the rest room."

"Is it a stand-up or a sit-down job?"

"Stand-up."

"Then what's wrong with right where you're standing?"

"You mean right here, in front of God and everybody?"

"It works the same there as it does anywhere else," the man noted. "You can go behind that tree if you'd like."

The youngster turned to do so, but halted. Jaws set with determination, he lowered his red briefs and relieved himself right where he stood—in front of God and everybody. The man glanced over his shoulder at him, half-smiled, and walked away.

The task accomplished, young Caine picked up his newly refashioned jeans, put them on, and plopped into the chair—completely nonplussed.

For almost twenty-four hours, he had been on an emotional excursion as undulant and multidirectional as a switch-back mountain road. On three occasions—twice just now and once the evening before, when he was drugged and put into the bed—he had girded himself for the vilest of inflictions, only to be treated to acts of kindness, instead. It was terribly uncomfortable for him to be left handcuffed and burning up in the bunk all those hours; but what else, he wondered, might that guy realistically have done?

It was debilitating and degrading—humiliating—to be sitting there chained to a tree; but what else would he, himself, do under the circumstances? The youth realized that he, himself, would not be kidnapping a kid and dragging him off to some godforsaken woods for ransom; but that was not the point, as he saw it. They were there; and the deed was done. And wasn't the man, he wondered—wasn't "Bill"—acting as decently as anyone could under such conditions?

Wasn't he patient, understanding, and instructive when they were cleaning the squirrels? Even kind? And indeed, the boy realized, it was considerate of him to spray on the bug repellent; he didn't have to do that. And, no doubt about it, sitting shirtless and shoeless in the shade with his pants legs removed was ten thousand times more comfortable than lying in that steam bath inside. Even though he was chained, there was more freedom there than there was lashed to the bunk.

Maybe the guy isn't such a dork after all, he thought. *But why fret about who's a dork when you're worried about getting killed?*

And what was that man who couldn't be figured-out doing now? He was sitting down by the creek *sharpening his knife!*

Oh dear God, he's gonna get my gonads yet!

It was not until then, noticing Bill by the creek, that the transplanted youth began to take cognizance of his surroundings. The small camping trailer was parked in quite the most beautiful setting that he had ever seen. It made some of the woodland memories of Camp Rio Alto seem bare as the Sahara by comparison.

They were on the bank of a small, flowing creek, canopied-over with great trees whose leaves and branches, reaching from both sides of the creek, almost completely blotted out the sky. The banks at creek level were sandy; and on the opposite side, past just a few feet of sand, there was an abrupt, high bank, perhaps ten feet tall, up to the forest-floor level on top. Their trailer camp was almost at water level, but on an intermediate sort of shelf between the banks of the creek and the flat level of the forest above. Unlike the immediate creekside, the ground under the campsite was similar to the forest floor, strewn with pine needles and who-knows-how-many years of hardwood leaf droppings.

The tree to which he was chained was some two to two-and-a-half feet in diameter, but infant in comparison to a similar-looking one that was half-falling down the opposite bank. Maybe that was its mother, the boy thought. The bark on both trees was mostly light gray, but stained-looking here and there with smudges of green that gave it a mottled appearance overall. The trees were quite tall, with far-reaching branches and medium-sized leaves forming an overhead arbor that looked as though it might at one time have been one completely solid something that had been reticulated apart like a giant jigsaw puzzle. Then, he noticed that both the trailer and the van were painted forest green—no helicopter searching party would ever spot them under that leaf awning.

The guy had it planned, for sure.

What the boy had been studying though—the canopy above the campsite—was only two trees. There were still hundreds—thousands—of others, of every conceivable size, shape, bark texture, and color of leaf. *How many different shades of green can there be?* he wondered.

A lizard ran up his chain-holding tree. It was six to seven inches long and brown, for the moment. The same type of lizard lived in residential areas throughout Houston, especially in the vicinity of Wingate School, and he knew them well. They were not true chameleons; but they did perform a color change to match their surroundings—from medium brown to bright green, almost chartreuse: perfect convertible camouflage.

A daddy long-legs ran across his foot. It was a big one, maybe six inches in total spread. They are completely harmless, not true spiders at all, but immediately frightening to the uniniti-

ated. Thanks to campus wanderings at Wingate, young Caine
was not uninitiated—at least as regards daddies long-legs.

The only aspect to mar the aesthetic beauty of the setting was
the creek itself. It was not very wide, and it appeared to be only
a foot or so deep in most places. It was lightly brownish in
color, similar to weak tea—not really pretty or appealing at all.
But the boy thought that whatever the color, it would be nice to
be sitting right in the middle of it on that steaming September
afternoon.

He felt a nudge on his right side . . . and then a second
nudge, bringing a halt to thoughts of cooling in the creek. It
was the dog, Brutus, holding a Frisbee in his mouth and bumping the boy on the leg, begging him to play. The boy on the
chain glanced over toward the man with the knife, who was
paying attention to neither of them, intent upon his sharpening
chores. Hamilton, Jr., noticed for the first time that, in addition
to the knife, the man was now armed with a pistol, ensconced
in a leather holster on his right hip. So much, he thought, for
any idea of making a run for it. He had no hankering to get
himself shot.

Again he was nudged, this time accompanied by an ever-so-
slight canine whine. He reached down and patted the huge dog
on top of the head; and that was all the encouragement it
needed. The next thing he knew, the big oaf of a mongrel mutt
had raised up and plopped his forepaws right in the boy's lap,
with the Frisbee still in his mouth.

The boy pushed him off. The dog came back. He pushed
again. Back again. On the third time, he took the curved-edge
plastic saucer out of the canine's toothy grasp and gave it a left-
handed toss off to the side. Mission accomplished, the dog delightedly took off and was back in a blink, dropping the Frisbee
into the boy's lap.

Caine gave it another toss; but left-handed, he was not all
that good at it. Dogs forgive, though, and the play-toy was
promptly returned for another try. *Why not give it a shot with
the right hand?* So he did, with miserable results. The handcuffs clattered and grabbed at the heavy chain, which grabbed
back, and the toss fizzled.

Then the boy got an idea. He choked up on the chain with his left hand, holding it a couple of feet back from his manacled wrist, thus giving his tossing arm the weight and restriction only of that short length of chain, rather than the entire fifteen feet of it. After a few tosses, the youngster became halfway adept. And Brutus loved it, grinning from one flopped-over ear to the other as he ran after and retrieved the toy—from across the creek bank in the sand, from atop the opposite bank in the woods, from the water—panting, romping, and barking with delight.

Aware of the uproar, Bill glanced over at the boy and dog, smiled that wrinkle-cornered smile of his, and went back to whatever it was that occupied him. His back was to the field of play.

After he'd gotten the hang of it pretty well, by holding the slacked chain with his left hand, the boy carefully calculated a trajectory, took precise aim, and let fly one mighty heave with what he knew was the only opportunity he would have for the shot he so much wanted to make. The swooping arc was precise and true; and the Frisbee clunked hard against the back of Bill's head.

"Hey, watch out!" he yelled, thinking he'd been caught with a stray shot. But when he saw the triumphant expression on the boy's face, he knew it had been intentional.

"Little shit!" he mumbled in protest; then he let fly a zinger with the Frisbee, aimed right at the boy's face.

It would have missed by three feet to one side, but the target made a leaping catch, executed a mid-air swing, and as his feet hit the ground, let fly back at the kidnapper—all the while chained to a tree!

"Show-off," the man grumbled as he tossed the Frisbee back. It was a poor toss, sailing over the head and far beyond, irretrievably out of reach of the boy on the tether. It wasn't out of Brutus's reach, though; and the dog quickly retrieved the missile to the master, because he was the one who had thrown it.

Bill held the Frisbee in his hand, and was about to give it another toss when he was brought up short with an unexpected and unwanted realization. He felt as though he could see deeply into the boy; and the feeling was uncomfortable, disconcerting. It was a sense of empathy, of compassion, that he had been hoping would not come; but it was now impossible to avoid. As he studied the game youth chained to the tree, there was something in the way the kid held his body . . . something to the peculiar, inquiring slant of his head . . . something, perhaps, to be read in the boy's eyes that now stared straight into his—a sense of pride, and of dignity under adversity; but it was also a yearning, a silent plea telegraphed by body language alone. And it transported the man back to the boy.

Wordless, without preface, he crossed the yardage that separated them, reached into his pants pocket, plucked out the keys, opened the handcuffs and let them drop. The boy was free.

Yet he remained bound to the man—a mutual understanding recorded in their eyes alone. It was a privilege not to be abused, a trust not to be violated; and both had agreed, though not a word passed between them.

Unless you could call "Hoop!" a word. And "OO-HAH!"

And away the boy ran, leaping and turning; then he stopped and held out both hands in the gingerbread man's catch-me-if-you-can gesture. Bill tossed the Frisbee, low and fast. The boy scooped it up and returned the throw, arching high and long. The man missed; and it sailed past him. Brutus to the rescue. The dog fetched the gadget, ran right past the man and dropped it at the feet of the thrower.

Buddy Boy, the freed captive, paused, looked over and smiled at the man who had captured him, the man who had freed him—as openhearted, honest-candid a smile as anyone has ever had the pleasure to receive. Bill smiled back, returning in kind. The wry, held-back wrinkle in the corner of the mouth was gone. This one was all across the face . . . and all the way from the too-soft heart.

▼ ▼ ▼ ▼ ▼ ▼ ▼ ▼ ▼ ▼ ▼ ▼

5

Keep a healthy, normally active, teenage boy tied down for a twenty-four hour period and he will become as jumpy as a sackful of fleas. There is a combination chemical and physical activity constantly seething within those ebullient creatures that continues to roil even though the body itself is firmly fettered. When freed, it is like an atomic chain reaction, expanding exponentially in every direction at once—the union of a whirlwind and a pogo stick.

Being rich, pampered, and tutored in the finest schools did nothing to make young Hamilton Caine an exception. He bounded around the secluded creekside campsite—into, around, and on top of everything in sight—rejoicing in his freedom and incessantly curious about his surroundings. He leaped back and forth across the narrow creek, ascended to the top of the other-side bank to toss the Frisbee to the man or for the dog. He shinnied up a small tree, sat down on a stout branch, hooked the branch into the backs of his knees and reclined backwards to hang upside down, arms akimbo. The dog, believing this all to be for his benefit, delightedly chased along, barking and jumping after, with the two of them occasionally colliding and tumbling noisily to the ground, rolling and tussling on the sand-and-leaf terrain.

The man watched smilingly through all the frenetic activity. For many years he had considered the prospect; and now, there it was. He had a sure-enough, full-blown kid on his hands. And this one was quite an example! Bill was afraid to think too much about it, but the boy was fun to watch. *In another time*, he thought, *under different circumstances . . .* But such thoughts had to be erased. There was a project of an entirely different sort at hand.

Bill, too, had been infected with restlessness, which was amplified by the boy's rowdy display of blowing off steam. He felt the urge to explore, and to show off this beautifully dense, varied and fascinating locale that he had chosen as his hideaway—this deep-woods country that he loved so much. There had been wildlife spoor, days earlier, that he wanted to locate again if it was still around. He wanted to show the kid.

"When you get through going ape," he told him, "put on your shoes and let's take a little walk; there's something I want to show you."

Now game for anything, the boy went back to the spot where he had been freed from his tether, to retrieve his shoes and socks.

"Leave off the socks," the man said. "You'll get your ankles scratched up a little, but it'll help keep the chiggers off."

"What are chiggers?" the boy wanted to know.

"Red bugs, they call 'em; tiny little beasties that like to climb aboard delicate young bodies and burrow into the skin; parasites. You won't like them."

"How about tough old bodies?" the boy wondered. "Do they like them too?"

"They don't discriminate."

"What do they look like? What do they do?"

"You never see them. Don't even know they're there until you've got a swollen little red spot on your skin. Then they itch. They like to congregate in the lower parts of your body, especially where the clothing is tight—like under the elastic of your skivvies, the waist and leg openings. In your crotch, too, and in your armpits—anywhere there's hair. And they especially like socks. Socks just seem to collect them."

The boy remembered that other boys at summer camp, particularly older ones, used to scratch their crotches a lot and mumble something about "chiggers," but he never saw any actual evidence of such; it was just something to say when you felt the urge to scratch your crotch.

He obediently donned his white leather sneakers, and the man motioned him back into the trailer.

"Better put on your shirt," Bill advised. It has been said that in Africa, everything bites. It could be added that in Texas, everything has thorns.

"Brutus, watch the house," the man commanded, much to the dog's disappointment. He wanted to go along; but Bill was afraid he might mess things up.

"What's that for?" the boy asked, pointing to the holstered pistol.

"In these woods," the man replied as they walked from the trailer, "you just don't go around without a gun. Never know when you might have to defend yourself against a dinosaur . . . or something. Now let's go; I want to look for something. And stick close to me."

That last sentence struck the boy as sounding a trifle ominous.

The wide spot along the creek bank, that was the trailer campsite, was the exception to the nearby terrain, not the rule. A scant forty yards away, as they proceeded downstream, the woods closed in and the going became difficult. Soon the bank ceased to exist at creek level, and they were forced to climb up on top, through dense entanglements, in order to forge another thirty or forty yards farther downstream. Leading the way, Bill was caught-up in pain several times as thorn-laden vines reached out to snag a leg—first one, then the other. The boy, following behind, didn't fare much better; and soon both hikers became blood-spotted, from the bottom of their cut-offs to their shoe tops.

"These damned things will tear you to pieces if you're not careful," Bill told the boy. "If one grabs you, stop still, don't let it tear, or you'll be even worse off. Now here, hold onto this and push it behind you as you pass." He gingerly handed a cat-claw-encrusted branch to the boy.

"What is this stuff?" the young hiker questioned.

"Blackberry vines."

"The kind you eat?"

"In late spring, yes. The rest of the year, they eat you."

After negotiating that particular entanglement, the explorers were able to make the next few dozen yards with relative ease, working their way back to the creekside again.

"Where are we going, anyway?" the boy inquired.

"Right . . . down . . . here." The man dropped from the five-foot-high ledge they had encountered, back down to the creek bank, which was once more present in a sandy stretch varying from three to five feet in width. Not half as exuberantly as he had dashed about a half-hour before, the boy dropped down alongside, then looked inquiringly at the man, as if to say, "What next?"

Bill was now inching his way along the creek bank, intently studying the ground all around. Quiet was not actually necessary for the purpose, but it seemed fitting. After another twenty-five yards of silent terrestrial investigation, he spotted them, on the other side of the creek. "Come on," he said quietly; then he waded unhesitatingly across. The creek was about two feet deep at that point.

The boy followed; but he was unprepared for the shock of the creek water. There they were, tip-toeing through a steaming-hot jungle with sweat rolling down their bodies, and the tepid-looking, tea-brown creek was as cold as ice. "Wow!" was the best he could say, accompanied by a perceptible gasp.

"Chilly, isn't it?" Understatement seemed appropriate. "Now come over here carefully. Watch your step, and don't mess anything up."

The "anything" to which Bill referred was a set of four large paw tracks, neatly impressed in the damp sand near the water's edge.

"Take a look at these," the man said, lightly touching his right index finger to the rim of one of the prints.

"What is it?" The boy knew, of course, that it was an animal track, but he didn't know what kind. Whatever it was, it was big.

"Cougar. That-there's the mark of a mountain lion, Buddy Boy."

The kid felt the hair stand up on the back of his neck.

"I figure they must be four, four-and-a-half inches across," Bill continued, "and that's a mighty big 'puddy tat.'"

The man made a fist with his right hand and rested it carefully atop one of the tracks, for comparison. The track was larger. The boy did likewise, with his smaller fist easily surrounded by the pug.

"How do you know it's a cougar?"

"I don't, exactly—just that it's a mighty big cat. Look closely now. See, there aren't any claw prints. Dog tracks will show indentations at the ends of the pads from their claws; cats don't. It's the same with bears, by the way. Black bears don't leave claw prints, so I'm told; grizzlies do. But bear tracks aren't round like these; these are a cat's. They're much too big for a bobcat, so a cougar is all that's left. It's been years since we had a tiger in these parts."

The boy didn't find that revelation at all comforting; but he took on a new appreciation for the handgun on the man's hip. "I hope you know how to use that thing," he said, pointing.

"Me too," Bill replied, adding no additional comfort whatsoever. "I just wanted to find out if he was still around."

Young Caine sat down on the narrow, sandy bank of the creek—absorbing, wallowing in the mystery and danger of the moment. Why is it that grown men take such delight in scaring kids? The answer is probably because kids—boy kids, especially—delight so in being scared. Bill's young "Buddy Boy" was, indeed, properly scared—and genuinely enjoying it.

The setting could not have been more perfect for a good scare; and no cleverly contrived side-show haunted house could ever have been more authentically frightening. There on the creek, there was hardly enough maneuvering room to dodge a spit ball, much less an oversized carnivore intent on tender, young Homo sapiens for lunch.

The stream's location at that point was at the base of a virtual tunnel—narrow at water's edge, high-banked on both sides, and completely covered-over on top with an arboreal awning that would turn the brightest day into the scant visibility of late dusk. That big cat could have been lying furtively on the bank above them right then, studying their every move and crouching to spring on man or boy at any moment.

"They're not generally known as man-eaters," the man explained, "but you never can tell. They eat deer, mostly, unless they get too old and feeble to catch them. That's when they will sometimes take to eating the easiest thing of all to catch—people, particularly small kids."

Twisting the tale-telling knife a little more, he added, "This one's awfully big, so he might be old, too. I understand that once a big cat tastes human flesh, he takes a liking to it, and he loses his natural fear of man. That's when they become real people-eaters."

Although it seemed impossible, the boy's eyes grew wider.

"I read up on them once, just out of curiosity," Bill continued. "Some obscure old reference book I came across had a beautiful description of cougars and their eating habits.

"There are lots of different names for the critter, by the way, other than cougar. It's been called 'mountain lion'—especially out in the west—and 'panther', and 'painter', and several other things; but that book referred to it as the 'puma'. 'The puma,' it said, 'will eat anything it is capable of catching. And it is capable of catching anything it wants to.'"

The ice-cold creek flowing through the venturi-like tunnel had the same chilling effect on the immediate atmosphere as freon gas flowing through the coils of a refrigerator. It was superhumidified there, and unbelievably cool in comparison to the steaming-hot, jungle-like forest above them. Combined with the blood-chilling impact of the boy's situation—still captive, defenseless, the possible prey of a huge carnivore capable of catching and eating anything it wants, and positioned in the perfect location for an attack—the refrigerated atmosphere sent a shiver like nothing he had ever before experienced up the spine of the not-woods-wise city boy. His arms broke out in goose-flesh, and he felt a sudden, urgent need to urinate. He rose, walked a few cautious steps downstream, zipped open the cut-off jeans and anointed the creek bank with spoor of his own.

"That ought to keep any self-respecting jungle pussy cat away," the man said. "There's nothing that will broadcast man-scent more effectively than a good puddle of fresh pee on the ground."

In spite of the fact that the man made light of the situation, it was senses-tingling excitement for the boy—a moment worthy of replaying in the memory, and cherishing, for many years to come.

"Let's start back," Bill said, before the moment could linger long enough to pall. "I expect it's getting close to time for supper."

"Supper?" the boy asked. "What happened to lunch?"

"Yeah, what did happen to lunch?" the man repeated. At very close physical proximity now, he was able to see deeply into those now-intense blue eyes. Gone was the hatred that had blazed through them earlier that afternoon; gone, also, was the fear and suspicion that had permeated and made them impenetrable, inscrutable. Now looking directly into his own, the eyes had taken on a mellower, almost translucent coloration. They were aglow, reflecting their youthful vitality; but they were radiating, also, a newfound trust and anticipation. The older eyes registered, recorded, and reflected back—a mutual conciliation, a coming together that spoke eloquently without words.

In the new-found warmth that glowed between them, within the refrigerated creek-tunnel, the urge was impossible to resist. The kidnapper reached out his right hand and half-roughly tousled that shock of uncombed, golden hair beside him. Boy and man smiled, and they started back to camp.

▼ ▼ ▼

Their shoes and lower legs had already been initiated by the ice-chill of the creek, so the man called Bill led the return trip right through the water, eschewing the already-experienced pleasures of the blackberry thicket on top. The boy, pensive and somewhat subdued by the deliciously fearsome experience of the lion tracks, walked quietly beside him; youthful chatter seemed inappropriate. After a short distance, he managed to become accustomed to the chill of the water.

The creek bank widened, then narrowed once more as the pair sloshed out of the water and back into it again. The stream turned here, then doubled-back there; and the boy noticed that in some spots the color of the water was darker, cloudier, more like coffee with cream than its usual tea-brown. He reasoned that those might be pools, and he wondered how deep they were.

They were walking still in silence when the man suddenly let go with a broad swing at the boy with his left arm, whopping him across the chest and knocking him backwards. Though stunned, young Caine was able to recover and avoid landing on his backside. In the same, fluid movement, Bill reached into his holster, drew the pistol and leveled it at arm's length at a low-hanging tree limb directly in front of them. At the shot, an object in the tree, which the boy still had not seen, fell in a wriggling heap onto the sand. For good measure, the man shot quickly at it again, and the snake reacted with a jolted squirm. Once more, this time with careful aim, Bill squeezed off a shot that caught the snake in the top of the head and reduced its helter-skelter squirm to a slow oscillation.

"Wow!" the boy yelled. "That's some shooting. What kind is it?"

"Cotton mouth," the shooter replied. "Water moccasin. Rottenest damned reptile we've got."

"Poisonous, huh?"

"Very. The disgusting thing about these sonsobitches is that they can be anywhere. They can be on the ground, in the trees or in the water. They swim on top or dive down and swim below—I've seen them. They can get you almost any-damned-where. If they ever learn to fly, we've had it."

The serpent on the ground continued to writhe—unlikely ever again to crawl, climb, swim, or learn to fly.

"It's still alive," the boy said.

"No, that's just muscular contractions. He's dead all right," the man said as he reached down to pick up the reptile by the tail. "See, his head is almost totally blown off."

He held it at arm's length. Almost five feet long, the snake was a mottled, dark gray, with circumferential bands of black or darker gray—undistinguished, otherwise, by any kind of pattern or coloration.

"He's a big one, isn't he?"

"Big enough," Bill replied as he lay the odious creature back on the sand. He plucked a twig from a nearby bush, broke it in two, and with the two as levers, carefully pried open the snake's mouth, displaying a bright interior in sharp contrast to the lead-gray and black body.

"See how white that is? That's why they're called 'cotton mouths.' What you don't ever want to see is one of those mouths wide open, with its fangs stuck out, staring you eye-to-eye somewhere. Here, hold this," he told the boy, indicating the two twigs that held the mouth agape. "But be very careful, there's still venom in those fangs; and they can kill you."

He plucked another twig and reached it into the reptile's mouth. Touching it against the roof of the mouth, half-way back, he pushed the twig forward to extricate the fangs, which are normally retracted until the viper strikes at prey.

"Aren't those cute?" He pushed the fangs to full extension—perhaps an inch or so in length.

"See that little pit there?" he said, touching the twig to a pocket just below the snake's eyes. "Inside that is a heat-sensing device—rattlesnakes have them, too—making the bastards the first real heat-seeking missiles. That little pocket is why they're called 'pit vipers.'"

"They're the pits, all right," the boy observed, awed but ever witty.

"Come on, let's go," the man said, standing.

"What about him?"

"The critters will take care of him," Bill replied, as he once again picked up the wiggle-body and hurled it across the creek, where it landed on a clump of yaupon brush. "Still hungry?"

"Starved."

▼ ▼ ▼

Starved was also the feeling that afternoon in room B-22 of the Federal Building, in downtown Houston—starved for clues. And pressed for time. Yet despite all that, there prevailed an air of studied, professional confidence. The room was where Henry Wilson, Special Agent in charge at the Houston office of the

Federal Bureau of Investigation, had set up a command post to handle the red-hot case of what was rapidly becoming known as the River Oaks kidnapping.

Without ever having been asked, the balding, slightly stocky Wilson had stepped into the case the first thing that morning. Although kidnapping is a federal crime, the FBI can become involved only if there is evidence or indication that the captive has been taken across state lines. There was no such indication yet, but the Bureau tends to operate under the assumption that after twenty-four hours, it is considered *possible* that state lines might have been crossed. Even before that, they will intercede in an "advisory" capacity; and on a case with the probable import of this one, doing so was virtually automatic.

Those responsible for missing juveniles at the Houston Police Department could not have been less upset; and there was certainly no jurisdictional dispute. The locals felt that the FBI was expert in that sort of thing, so they were welcome to it. At that point, then, the role of the HPD became a supplementary one—supplying whatever extra manpower was necessary and handling the news media.

Although he had not yet completely assembled his forces, Wilson's battle plan for breaking the case was beginning to take shape, and he was secretly relishing the task.

"That's right," he told the two technicians who were connecting the telephones, "I want the red one to ring the instant the phone rings in the Caine mansion. How long will it take you to complete the tap?"

"It will be done as soon as we get the line cleared," the crew boss responded. "And that will be no more than five, ten minutes at the most."

"Good," Wilson replied. "The black one is already hooked up to HPD, right?"

"Right. As soon as a call comes in to the dispatcher at police headquarters, all he has to do is flip a switch and it will ring on this phone."

"And the instant that phone rings," the other technician added, holding up a small tape recorder, "this machine will start taping. If it's our man, we'll have him. Then if he's in the city, a trace will take only a matter of seconds."

"And that will work on either phone, right?" Wilson asked?

"Correct. Just as soon as we get this hot-line tap hooked in at the residence. We should be hearing from our guys out there any time now."

"It would be nice if we could be hearing from the bereaved parents some time now," Wilson noted. Half cynically and half in jest he added, "It just isn't a proper kidnapping until Mom and Dad know their precious child is missing."

"Liddell," he called to another agent in an adjoining room, "is there any word at all yet on Mr. and Mrs. Caine?"

"We haven't been able to find them yet, chief." Agent Liddell Peters was Wilson's right-hand man. "We're still trying to pin it down with the Coast Guard in Galveston; but as best we can find out, they think the sailboat the parents are on might be one called the *Heavens to Betsy*, that left port way back last June; and it's been berthed in Acapulco since then. The Mexican police in Acapulco appear to be cooperating, but you know how it is trying to get information out of them. So far, we can't get confirmation on whether the boat is still in port or it's sailed."

"So how do we get confirmation?" Wilson asked.

"Either they give it to us, or we find out for ourselves. I talked with one of our people in the American Consulate there in Acapulco about ten minutes ago, and he's working on it directly."

"Well keep them all hot on it, the Mexicans too," Wilson ordered. "I'm afraid our child-snatchers might start getting antsy if they don't make some kind of contact soon with the boy's parents; and that could spell trouble."

The red telephone rang loudly, and one of the technicians answered.

"Okay," he told Wilson. "The Caine hot line is set up."

"Good work," the boss replied. Almost abstractly, to the telephone, he added, "Now call, you bastard."

Considering himself to be relieved of guard duty, the dog, Brutus, ran to greet the pair of explorers when they reached the campsite. He had a peculiar and highly effective method of demanding attention, which he proceeded to demonstrate on young Caine. Darting in from behind, the big, yellowish dog wedged his head between the boy's legs and raised up, lifting him completely off the ground and sending him sprawling. As the boy lay on the ground, the dog leaned over and licked him on the face . . . so much for any attempt at maintaining a fear of the big dog by the kid.

The man, meanwhile, had gone directly to the green van, opened the door and stepped inside. As soon as he was able to escape the dog's affection, the boy followed, watching as Bill fished into a pocket for a set of keys and unlocked a large chest. Reaching into the chest, he fumbled briefly with the contents, then leaned back with a handful of bullets and began to reload the pistol.

"What's in there?" the boy inquired, indicating the chest.

"Big boy's toy box."

"You mean guns and stuff?"

"Yeah, guns and stuff."

"Will you teach me how to shoot?"

Bill paused to reflect. "No, I don't think so."

"Why not?"

"Have you forgotten? I just kidnapped you. You think I'm going to put a loaded gun in your hands?"

The answer was too logical and obviously too final for continued argument, so the boy pushed it no more. Later, maybe.

Slamming the van door shut, Bill asked, "Do you know how to make a fire?"

"Sure," the boy lied. Then he thought better of it and added, with a shrug, "Sorta."

"It's show-and-tell time," the man said. "Let's make a fire pit; but first, we have to clean off a spot." He reached under the trailer and pulled out a hoe and a shovel, then handed the hoe to the boy.

"Push back a circle about six feet in diameter," he said, "about right here." He indicated a spot on the ground between the trailer and the creek. "We don't want any loose sparks to set our playhouse on fire."

The boy obeyed, raising a mound of leaves and forest-floor debris around the perimeter of the circle. Bill then took the shovel and dug a shallow hole in the middle of the cleaned-off spot.

"Now look up on top there," Bill said, indicating an area above their campsite ledge. "You see that stand of pine trees?" The boy nodded. "Go up there and get me a double handful of pine needles from underneath those trees. You're going to learn how to make a fire with just one match."

When young Master Caine dutifully returned with a double armload of pine needles—easily twice as much as needed—the man carefully sprinkled and mounded half of them into the hole he had dug. While the boy was away, Bill had gathered an assortment of hardwood twigs from the immediate surroundings (never any problem finding kindling in that forest). He showed the boy how, and explained the importance of stacking the smallest twigs, first, in a tepee-like pile atop the pine needles. Another tepee was established atop that one with larger twigs and broken-off branches—all obtained from wood that was lying on the ground, as Bill explained, because it had to be dead and dried-out to burn properly.

The next step was to gather an assortment of larger firewood, from an inch to three or four inches in diameter, with Bill breaking all but the thickest of them into usable-sized chunks by pulling them toward him with both hands, against pressure from his knee. The boy emulated, and soon they had a respectable pile of firewood on the ground. As they worked, Bill explained to his young guest the importance of using hardwood if they intended to cook on the fire, which they did, because pine fires produce a turpentine flavor and smoke laden with tar. The boy, throughout, was an eager listener and participant.

"Okay, buddy," Bill said at last, "see if you can make a campfire out of it . . . but one match is all you get." He handed a box of kitchen matches to the kid.

The boy struck and carefully cradled a match in his hands, lighting the pile of pine needles in several different locations, as Bill suggested. Soon, the needles were ablaze and billowing smoke, and flames began to ignite the kindling.

"Bingo," the man said. "Buddy has built himself a fire."

"I like that," the boy said, grinning.

"You like the fire?"

"No, the name. I like you calling me Buddy."

With a slightly pursed lip that brought a wrinkle to his chin, Bill studied the idea briefly. Then he replied, "I think it has a pretty good ring to it myself. Maybe with a little coaching, it just might fit real well."

The boy smiled, reached out his hand with arm upraised, and the two shook hands in the manner preferred by the younger set—elbows down, and hands clasped high.

"Take off those wet shoes," Bill said, removing his own and placing them near the fire. "Maybe they'll dry out while we're cooking supper." Buddy followed suit.

The man went back to the van to retrieve an axe for the heavier firewood; and he had just slammed the door shut when the boy exclaimed, "Bill, look at that!"

He was pointing to the ground right behind the trailer. Bill looked; and he discovered a small field mouse—maybe four inches long excluding the tail. As luck would have it, the huge-eared rodent ran right at Bill, changing course when just a few feet away and providing the man with an excellent opportunity to show off.

With no attempt at a fast draw, the man methodically removed the pistol from its holster, cocked the hammer and swung it into the path of the scurrying varmint, rolling it beautifully, thoroughly dead. In one shot.

"Gosh, you're good," the boy observed. "Please teach me how. I promise I won't try to shoot you."

"I'm sure you won't," Bill replied, reholstering the weapon, "'cause I'm not going to give you the chance. What time is it now?" As a woods-camping habit, he had removed his wrist watch some time ago.

"Five twenty-five."

"Let me know when it gets close to six, and we'll try to catch a newscast."

The boy had a digital, capable-of-doing-everything watch; and he set it to buzz an alarm.

Meanwhile, there were camping chores to be done. With the medium-sized firewood now ablaze, it was time to add the heavier material. It was also time to locate some long sticks for roasting wieners. Bill led the boy to a clump of yaupon—a ubiquitous, unloved underbrush, cousin to holly, which is attempting to cover the entire world from a base of operations somewhere in East Texas.

"I don't know of any other earthly reason for the existence of this junk," Bill said, "but if you can find a decently straight stalk of it, it makes a good weenie-roasting stick."

Two "decently straight" stalks were quickly located and amputated at the base with the man's ever-useful folding knife. As Buddy watched, Bill whittled off every branch, twig and appurtenance from the main stem, ending-up with a tapered stick about four feet long.

"Now it needs a point," Bill noted, "and we don't need the bark to flavor our hot dogs." With the knife blade, he stripped away the bark from the narrow end, some four inches back, and proceeded to whittle a sharp, tapered point.

"Far as I know, this stuff isn't poisonous," he said. "A lot of what you might find in these woods is, but I know this won't hurt you."

The boy watched the trimming and whittling with genuine interest, making no comment. Bill was becoming adept at reading those blue eyes, though, and he carefully considered their latest entreaty before he said, "Here, now you make the next one." He handed the once-dreaded knife to the boy.

Without so much as a smile of acknowledgement, Buddy went to work on the stick. The knife was sharp enough, as he knew it would be, but some of the branches were reluctant to part company with the mother stem, thus requiring more effort than he had expected. Halfway through the task, the beeper on his watch went off; and he said, "It's four minutes to six."

"Good," the man replied. He went into the trailer, brought

out a battery-operated radio, and tuned-in a Houston radio station. The boy continued to whittle.

At six o'clock, there were the usual overproduced ruffles and flourishes touting the world-class capabilities of the radio station's news team, an acknowledgement of the sponsor, and the newscaster led off:

Authorities are still trying to piece together clues in the disappearance and apparent kidnapping yesterday of the son of prominent Houston industrialist Hamilton Caine . . . and the parents have not yet been located.

Late last night, the Caine's chauffeur was found bound and gagged in a Southwest Houston alley. The man who assaulted him had taken his clothing and the Caine family limousine.

James Jamison, the chauffeur, told police that the assault took place around three o'clock in the afternoon, and that he had been en route to the exclusive Wingate High School, in Memorial Woods, where he was to pick up the Caine's only child—fifteen-year-old Hamilton Caine, Junior.

The boy was seen leaving school and getting into a black Cadillac limousine at the school grounds when classes let out at three-thirty. He has not been seen nor heard from since. The limousine was found today, abandoned, barely one mile from the Wingate School.

Meanwhile, authorities have been unable to locate Hamilton Caine, Senior, and Mrs. Caine, who are said to have departed Acapulco, Mexico, last Friday . . . on a sailboat bound for the island of Tahiti, in the South Pacific. Attempts to reach them by radio have thus far been unsuccessful.

Caine is president and chairman of the board of Houston-based Texas Consolidated Utilities—the largest public utility company in the state of Texas. Mrs. Caine is a prominent Houston socialite.

According to HPD Detective Sergeant Wesley Price, Houston police received a telephone call late this morning from a man claiming to have the Caine youth in custody, and demanding ransom. The FBI has entered the case.

On the weather front . . . observers are keeping a close watch on a tropical depression that sprang up sometime during the night in the Gulf of Mexico. The National Weather Service says conditions are favorable for that system to develop into the season's fifth tropical storm. If it does, it will be named Elizabeth.

And at City Hall today . . .

Bill clicked the switch and the radio went silent. "What do you think, kid? You're famous."

The boy thought enough of the gravity of the situation to remain silent. Whittling on the roasting stick was a good outlet, so he attacked the task with renewed vigor.

"I'm surprised they haven't reached your folks yet," Bill noted. "Surely they've got a ship-to-shore radio on that boat. My guess is that they've probably gotten hold of them by now, but the radio station hasn't found out about it yet.

"Let's see," he continued. "Today's Wednesday. I figure it should take a maximum of two days to get a helicopter or an amphibious Navy plane out to pick up your folks—probably from Hawaii—and get them back to Houston. That would put them back in town on Friday, most likely, but not before banking hours are over; so it might be difficult for your old man to round up two hundred thousand in cash until Monday, at least. That's going to give you and me plenty of time to get good and sick of roasted weenies."

Seizing the opportunity, Buddy said, "I would eat a squirrel again if you'd let me shoot it." Bill only glared at him in silence.

▼ ▼ ▼

Roasting wieners on a long stick, over an open fire, is a good time for reflection and relaxed conversation. A can of pork and beans, lightly laced with ketchup and pancake syrup, was simmering on the stove-top in the trailer. Bill was sipping pensively from a can of beer, while the boy who had just been nicknamed "Buddy" worked, likewise, on a can of Coke. Both stared blankly into the fire, each to his own thoughts.

"Bill." The boy broke the meditation.

"Uh-huh."

"Why me?"

"Why you what?"

"Why did you pick me to kidnap?"

"Because your folks are filthy rich, and I'm filthy broke."

"But there are lots of other people with plenty of money. Why did you pick me out?"

"You were easy to grab."

The answer didn't satisfy, but it triggered another question. "What did you do with James?"

"James who?"

"Our driver. How'd you get the car away from him?"

"Piece of cake," Bill replied; and Buddy noticed for the first time that there was a definite twinkle, almost a boyish look, in the man's deep brown eyes.

"He was a pushover," Bill continued. "I left him in his baggy bloomers tied up in an alley behind a dirty book store, with some porno magazine he'd just bought." The man chuckled at the memory.

Buddy chuckled also, delighted at the mental picture he conjured from the description. "That's neat," he said. "I hate that guy."

"Good," Bill replied. "Now I don't feel so bad."

"But I still don't understand why me."

The man looked at his more-or-less-free prisoner, carefully calculating what to say without revealing too much, and replied, "Because your old man's a bastard."

For some reason, Buddy didn't seem inclined to protest the declaration. He waited for elaboration.

Bill continued, "You are probably not aware of this, but your father and his company are screwing everyone in Houston. Everybody who pays a light bill or a gas bill—and that means everybody—is having it stuck to them by none other than the eminent Mister Hamilton Robert Caine, Senior."

The boy wondered how Bill knew the middle name.

"Since your esteemed father ascended the throne of Texas Consolidated Utilities Corporation, light bills have quadrupled in the city of Houston." He was getting warmed up now.

"But it wasn't enough to put the squeeze on the light bills. That fuckin' company, under your daddy's leadership, went out and bought the natural gas company that serves most of Houston and a great hunk of South Texas—the same company that was, and still is, under contract to supply *all* of the natural gas to fire the Texas Consolidated generating stations. How that one ever got past the state utility commission I'll never know— except that I do know, as an absolute fact, that your father has at least three of the commissioners in his pocket. They're on the take.

"So, now that he's got the electricity and the gas, he can screw everybody comin' and goin'. He jacks up the price on the gas—which is ridiculous, because there's an oversupply of natural gas in South Texas—then the utility commission, and the damned governor, and every-damned-body-else lets him get away with using that artificial price jump to hike the price of electricity.

"Shall I go on? Shall I tell you about the coal mining operations in Wyoming that are now owned by Texas Consolidated . . . and their contracts to supply the new coal-fired generating stations in Houston?

"No, there's just too much. You father's a first-rate bastard; and grabbing off his kid for ransom, I figured, was one way I could make him squirm—one way I could hit him personally, right in the pocket book. And that's the only thing he cares about. Not to mention the fact that I'm desperate for dough myself."

"Do you know my father?"

"No," Bill lied, "but you don't have to know him to know that he's a first-class bastard."

"What about my mother?" the boy wondered, realizing that this episode would have a devastating effect on her. "What has she ever done to you?"

"Don't you worry about your mother, kid," Bill replied. "The minute she gets back from that Pacific bunk-hopping party they've gone on, she'll turn this whole thing around into a personal triumph, a mantle of personal glory to wrap herself in. She'll get reams of publicity; and she'll love it."

The newly noticed eye-twinkle was becoming an almost fero-cious gleam. "I can just see her now," he continued, "being interviewed by hordes of the little television trained seals with their cameras and their microphones, asking inane questions like, 'What was your first reaction when you learned your son was kidnapped?' And she'll play the distraught mother routine to the hilt.

"All the gossip columnists will vomit out yards of sentimental literary puke about the poor, dear lady. And she'll eat it up. She'll probably order a whole new wardrobe in black, to look more like the lady in grief, and to have it on hand for mourning just in case you turn up dead. Don't worry about . . ."

"My mother's a bastard, too," the boy interrupted, stunning the man into silence.

At some length, Bill asked, "What made you say that?"

"Oh, never mind," the boy replied. He didn't want to think any more about the parents who didn't act like parents, and neither did he want Bill to supply him with any more reasons to dislike them. Besides, he was hungry. Holding up his two-wiener roasting stick, he asked, "When can we eat these things?"

"Like right now," Bill replied, considering also that there had been quite enough Serious Conversation. "What'll you have, ketchup or mustard?"

"We got buns?"

"We got buns."

"How about ketchup on one side and mustard on the other?"

"How about you fix it yourself?" the man responded; and together they walked into the trailer.

Emotional trauma, and there had been plenty of late, had done nothing to diminish the boy's appetite. He consumed four hot dogs, three servings of the sweet-doctored pork and beans, two cans of Coke, and a mound of potato chips. Day had slipped into evening, and the man was breaking out the marsh-mallows for their turn at the end of the yaupon sticks when something cut loose in a nearby tree. It was the same rattle-chatter that had worried the boy in his half-sleep the night be-fore.

"What's that noise?" he asked.

"That's a squirrel," Bill replied, just as a similar chatter broke loose from another direction. "And that's another one."

"They surely do sound weird," Buddy said. "Can you shoot them at night?"

"It's not legal, and you can't see them anyhow. I'll guarantee that you'll wear out a full set of flashlight batteries and you still won't be able to spot one at night."

From quite a distance came another sound, as the forest's nocturnal creatures began to stir. It sounded like the whinny of a horse, getting closer with each of several calls. Buddy shot a startled glance over the toasting marshmallow at the face of his captor and woods guide in the flickering firelight. "What's that?"

"Horse-bird," the man replied with a smile. "The first time I ever heard one of those suckers I thought Pegasus had come back to the East Texas woods. I knew it was a horse, but I also knew the damned thing was up in the trees somewhere."

"Horse-bird . . . bull!" the boy exclaimed.

Bill smiled. "No, it's really a screech owl; it just sounds like a horse. I suppose you heard that big owl right outside the trailer last night."

"I surely did. He scared the socks off me," Buddy said.

"That was what they call a great horned owl."

"I know that," the boy bragged, "but it took a while for me to realize it."

Suddenly, an ungodly commotion broke loose. Startled, both man and boy glanced around to find Brutus at full gallop, hot on the trail of a hapless armadillo. The strange-looking, armor-plated creature was scurrying with all its might to avoid capture by the big dog, and making the weirdest noise that Buddy or Bill had ever heard. It was an undulating whistle, like a water-logged electronic police siren.

Darting and dodging, the armadillo ran directly at them, and Bill and the boy had to lift their legs to let it run under—otherwise, there would have been a collision. As it scurried under Buddy, he reacted with a well-timed kick that sent the harmless creature tumbling. The dog, intent on the chase, ran squarely into Bill's legs and knocked him sprawling, with his lawn chair landing on top of him. By that brief intercept of his pursuer, the terrified armadillo was able to escape and disappear into the night. Brutus, once recovered from the crash, went sniffing unsuccessfully after.

The man came up laughing; and the boy laughed even harder. They laughed and they laughed, uproariously—a perfect release for the tensions that had held sway in both of them, tugging this way and that, since the afternoon of the day before. Enjoying the laughter for its own sake, they laughed some more.

"Great kickshot, kid," Bill chortled, with tears streaming down his cheeks.

"You made a super bodyblock yourself," laughed the boy. "Did you break anything?"

"Oh, shut up and eat your marshmallow," Bill exclaimed in mock anger. He gathered himself off the ground and straightened up the fallen chair. "Mine's down here in the dirt somewhere." And he began to search, on hands and knees, for his fallen yaupon spear.

"I thought you and Brutus looked great together," Buddy chided.

"And I think you're a little turd," Bill replied. By now, they could both barely manage a chuckle; they had been laughed out.

Shortly after the last marshmallows had been consumed (score: Bill 2, Buddy 5) and after such a strenuous day for them both, neither man nor boy required argument to be convinced that it was time for bed. Inside, the trailer had been cooled down to a tolerable temperature; and Bill surprised the boy with a toothbrush he had purchased for him while at the grocery store.

"Here," he told him, quite paternally, "go brush your teeth and wash your face in the sink. You look pretty filthy; we'll get a bath tomorrow."

The boy obeyed, then Bill did the same.

"Take off your filthy clothes now and get into bed," the man told him. "I've gotta put your bracelet back on you."

More than a little crushed, the boy asked, "You mean the handcuffs?"

Bill nodded. "I'm sorry, but I just have to do it this way."

It hurt the boy that the man who could almost be his friend lacked the faith in him to discard the cuffs completely; but considering the freedom he had enjoyed for the past several hours, and the fantastic experiences during them, he made no protest.

Buddy made a quick trip to the tiny bathroom and returned to discover, for the first time, where his captor slept. It was an overhead bunk, almost as big as a full bed, that the man pulled down from the upper corner at the front of the trailer, above the small couch—a cozy arrangement.

Bill removed his shirt and cut-off jeans and placed them on the couch below his bed. Buddy watched, then followed suit and stripped once more to his briefs.

Bill looked him over. "Boy, you are a sight," he said.

He was right. The boy had red-line scratches on both legs and both arms from the afternoon's excursion through the brambles. There was a double line of dirt in the wrinkles inside each elbow, and a similar pair on the lower neck. His hair was a mat, its former golden hue now greatly subdued. Both knees were black smudges, and his calves below them were flecked with dirt, bits of crumpled leaves and other forest-floor debris— quite a contrast to the spick-and-span preppy of the day before. But that one had only grunted, "Hullo." This one smiled broadly—visibly weary, but radiant through the accumulation of grime.

"Go back outside," the man ordered, "and brush off as much of that crap on your legs as you can."

Buddy complied; and when he returned inside the trailer, the man handed him a damp paper towel. "Now see how much of that you can get off your knees with this."

The boy did the best he could, drying the wetted spots with another paper towel, then stood in the middle of the trailer, looking pleadingly at the kidnapper. His eyes, as before, mutely telegraphed a message—which was duly received.

"Uh-uh," Bill grunted in denial. He wished for all the world that he did not have to bind the boy to his bunk again, but he felt compelled to do so. After all, "Buddy" or not, the boy could be conning him, just waiting for an opportunity; and asleep, he would be easy prey. It was no different than putting a loaded gun in his hands. "Come on now," he said, "crawl into bed."

Resigned and without protest, the boy did as he was told; and Bill snapped the handcuffs around his right wrist and onto the steel pole.

"Life sucks and then you die," Buddy observed, quoting some eminently forgettable modern sage.

"What's that?"

"Nothing." And with his feet and his one free hand, the boy fished-up the light blanket that lay crumpled at the foot of his bunk, in the unlikely event that it might be needed during the night.

Bill reached across his own bed to place a pistol in the corner, within reach. Buddy saw it, and thought it looked to be different than the one he had worn earlier, but he couldn't be certain. Then the man in his skivvies climbed into his fold-up sleeper and switched off the battery-powered ceiling light. Darkness took over the trailer.

In spite of his pique over the handcuffs, the boy felt compelled to comment on the day. "Bill," he called.

"What?"

"Thank you."

"Good night, Buddy."

"Good night, Bill."

▼ ▼ ▼ ▼ ▼ ▼ ▼ ▼ ▼ ▼ ▼ ▼ ▼

6

As he stretched out anchored to the bed, events of the day danced in vivid Technicolor through the boy's mind. In all likelihood, Camp Rio Alto might never return again to his preslumber mental ramblings. Vignettes of group swimming, group crafts, group dining—group everything—were replaced by luminous recollections of mountain lion tracks . . . the chill of the creek-tunnel where they were found . . . the thin, deadly fangs in the white maw of the snake . . . and Bill's incredible shooting. The campfire scene was replayed, also, with the mounded pile of pine needles blazing and smoking, their flames licking at the kindling; and the last brightly glowing coals that toasted the marshmallows—amulets of flame that could mesmerize a person into a trance. He chuckled inwardly, recalling the incident with the armadillo—the uproarious tumult, the solid whop when he kicked the side armor of the little beasty, and the hilarious collision of big, funny Brutus and Bill.

And Bill!

How could he figure out that man? How could he understand the relationship between them? From early that morning, when the two were depriving the dead squirrels of their skins, his apprehensions and hatred of his captor had shifted toward ambivalence. The boy remained a prisoner, attested undeniably by the cruel bracelet he was forced to wear to bed; yet for the several memorable hours previous, he had been free—free to do almost anything except run away. And now, the boy realized, he was no longer at all interested in running away. Why not?

That man he called Bill had brought him into a fascinating new world of nature's own construction. The antithesis of the artificial, cultivated city life to which he was accustomed, it was down-to-earth, real, gutsy, and exciting. From loathing and dread, the fifteen-year-old's condition had been inexplicably transformed into warm companionship and good, earthy fun—in the space of a single day!

But how, he wondered, could it have happened so quickly? Was it because either boy or man had changed into something he had not been before? He was certain that wasn't likely. Whatever was or was not likely, there were no answers available that night.

As sleep began to descend on the boy known as Buddy, he pondered: Who is Bill? Why had he chosen him to kidnap? What would become of the man? What would become of either of them?

The night sounds were in full chorus all around, no longer frightening, when that single, curious sentence surfaced and replayed in his memory:

Now you just sit tight, Buddy Boy, and everything will be all right.

He tried desperately to concentrate. What was it? Something deep inside was trying to get remembered, but it was having a difficult time getting out. Whatever it was, it wouldn't make it out that night; the boy was sound asleep.

▼ ▼ ▼

Buddy was not alone in his mental meanderings; Bill's mind was racing, as well. He reflected over and over on the boy's curious statement: "My mother's a bastard, too." Why would the kid say a thing like that? Surely he wasn't physically mistreated at home; more likely, there was some deep hurt, or resentment, that had been festering in him for a long time.

His mother was beautiful, there was no doubt about that. She was queen of the Houston jet-set society clique, and the darling of what Bill considered to be journalistic abominations—the gossip columnists. One such had once pontificated in print, "Melanie Caine *is* Houston society."

Recalling that little tidbit made Bill want to puke. He had seen her falling-down drunk—vomiting, cursing, and ripping off her delicate lace panties to stuff into the face of a defenseless man who had deigned not to succumb to her blatant sexual enticements. To make the episode all the more distasteful, it had taken place on her husband's company airplane (without the husband) en route back to Houston from some self-indulgent jaunt to Los Angeles—at company expense, of course.

But surely, Bill reasoned, nothing like that had ever been exhibited in front of the boy.

Yes, the kidnapper had indeed lied to the boy when he told him he did not know his father. Bill was one of the pilots on that airplane!

For two years, he had been on the payroll of Texas Consolidated Utilities' Transportation Department as what they called a junior pilot. The title itself was demeaning. The only thing it meant, in reality, was that there was only one senior pilot in the group of four employed by the company. As a consequence, the rest were shamed with the title of "junior."

Bill wondered about all the pent-up hatred he had spewn at the boy earlier with regard to his father. Had he revealed too much personal knowledge? He hoped not. If he had gone too far, Bill knew, it was almost as though he could not contain himself—because he had actually witnessed some of the esteemed Mr. Caine's corporate shenanigans; he knew about them first hand.

Bill had seen and known of deals cut in the cabin of the airborne Gulfstream that no decent jury in the world would dismiss as anything less than criminal. As the company expanded from a mere electric utility into natural gas transportation and sales, oil and gas exploration and production, and, finally, into coal mining and transportation, Bill had overheard plans hatched and strategy drawn that cut the corporate throats of companies unfortunate enough to have become acquisition targets for the crushing tentacles of Texas Consolidated. He had gone so far as to plant a hidden microphone in the cabin of the airplane, allowing him and the other pilot to listen-in through their headphones in the cockpit. Yes, he knew whereof he spoke with regard to the nefarious Mr. Hamilton Caine.

Bill had even had the boy on the plane with him once; but that was about five years previous, so he would have been barely ten at the time. Also at the time, Bill's hair had been cropped much shorter, and he had not worn a mustache (company policy). Besides, the plane was full of people, returning to Houston from a pre-Christmas shopping spree in New York City—much too much distraction, he believed, for a kid of ten to remember a junior pilot. Bill could recall only one personal contact: he had helped the boy get latched into his seat belt.

▼ ▼ ▼

Buddy did not hear the jingle of the small alarm clock that sounded at five o'clock the next morning, but his olfactory senses had already begun to register the aroma of frying bacon and percolating coffee when the hand on his bare stomach awakened him. Bill was kneeling beside him; it was still dark outside.

"Want to go do a little squirrel hunting?" the man asked.

The boy squinted and blinked his way into wakefulness. "Can I shoot?"

"No, but you can be there, anyway, if you can learn how to sit quiet and be very still."

"Sure, why not; but you'll have to take this thing off," Buddy said, half-petulantly displaying the handcuffs.

The man already had the keys in his hand; and in short order, the boy was freed once again.

"If you need to take a leak," Bill said, "go outside. This trailer doesn't have the world's supply of water or sewage-storing capacity."

"What if I have a sit-down job?" the boy asked, recalling Bill's euphemism of the day before.

"We'll save the indoor facilities for that."

Buddy climbed out of his bunk and walked out the door to comply with the new sanitation code. He was greeted there by

Brutus, hoping for a romp; but the dog had to settle for a quick pat on the head and a tug at one ear.

Never before in his life had the boy even imagined anything akin to what he was doing—walking outside alone into a dark wilderness, in nothing but his underwear, to go pee on the ground. With the crunch of leaf-debris beneath his bare feet, he felt suddenly less like a boy and more like a man. Boys don't face the mysterious night alone. He knew that out there in the darkness, somewhere, was a large, carnivorous beast capable of crushing his spine with a single bite. Yet the realization brought no singular apprehension, it only contributed to the overall sense of awe that the night woods presented before him. It triggered a shiver that started at the base of his spine and rippled all the way up to his shoulders—a totally delicious feeling.

Overhead, four hundred zillion stars were playing peek-a-boo through the leaves that sheltered the hideaway. Once or twice, at Camp Rio Alto, he had seen a sky full of stars similar to that, but in the city-lighted skies of polluted Houston, never.

Bill now had a gasoline lantern burning inside the trailer instead of the much weaker electrical fixtures, no doubt to conserve the trailer battery; and enough light spilled through the windows and doorway to illuminate the creek beyond. Buddy felt a compulsion to get closer to it, to venture farther into the darkness on his own, in his now almost completely primordial state.

His toes tasted the bank sand and were massaged by it in return; and they craved more. Almost with a mind of their own, his feet carried him onward, refusing to stop until they felt the shock of the frigid creek water. But that, too, felt good—a strangely sensuous pleasure that the youth could not begin to describe nor to understand. No one feels through his feet; but at the moment, Buddy was doing exactly that—feeling the sandy bottom of the creek, feeling the rush of water now lapping at his ankles, and feeling a new toehold on life. It became an initiation, an auto-baptismal into the realm of nature's own truth and reality, stripped clean of the artificial trappings of the city world he had known.

Enjoying a heady sense of exaltation that was like a lung-

filling breath of mountain air, he waded farther into the creek
until he stood knee-deep near the center. The water was cleansing, purifying; and its urgent flow seemed somehow to coalesce
the crosscurrents of emotions stirring deep within him into a
sensation of kinship with the dark universe around him. He felt
alone with God.

No one in his immediate family had ever had much to do
with religion, except for an occasional, perfunctory attendance
at church just to maintain appearances; but The Spirit had
never visited the boy.

Now, standing all but naked in God's own secret place, his
lower legs numbed by the rush of the chilled, deep-woods holy
water, he reared his head back as far as it would go, until he felt
the muscles tighten in the small of his back. He couldn't say
why, except that it felt good, but he raised both arms skyward,
fingers outstretched, as if to try to grasp a piece of the distant
firmament and pull it down around him.

"Are you praying for deliverance . . . or acceptance?" Bill
was standing on the creek bank behind him.

The boy gave no answer. He turned away briefly, attempting
to force his eyes to penetrate the darkness upstream, perhaps to
grab a piece of it and take it in with him; then he splashed his
way back out.

"Breakfast is ready," the man said; and they walked together
back to the trailer.

Bill was now wearing his cut-off jeans, so Buddy followed suit
and donned his own incredibly dirty ones. Shirt and shoes,
though, still seemed inappropriate.

"You drink coffee?" the man asked.

"No, but I'll try some."

The camp cook already had a cup of milk warming on the
stove. He poured a small mug a third full of hot, black coffee,
filled it the rest of the way with the hot milk, then stirred-in two
large teaspoonfuls of sugar. "Try this," he said. "The coonasses
in Louisiana call it *café au lait*."

Buddy sipped on the steaming brew and liked it. It tasted a
trifle bitter, but at the same time sweet, and soothing. "I never
tasted coffee before," he said.

"Bet you never stood half-naked in the middle of a creek and stared at the stars before, either," Bill said.

"No, not that either." And Buddy sensed a realization that the two distinctly different pleasures were connected, some-how—integral parts of some yet unfathomable whole. And it was good. Whatever it was that was the then-and-there, it was good. He belonged to it. And he was eager to get on to whatever came next.

Before sitting down, Buddy grabbed a towel that was hanging inside the bathroom cubicle and dried his blue-cold legs. Then he took the unused blanket from his bunk, sat down at the dining table and wrapped the blanket around his legs. "They're frozen," he said.

Breakfast was crisply fried bacon, skillet toast, and eggs cooked grease-free, sunny-side up. The boy had not been questioned as to how he would like his eggs—or even whether he would like eggs at all—but he accepted what he was given and ate heartily.

After the dishes were stacked, the man shucked his cut-offs and stepped into the camouflage pants he had worn the morning before. Tossing the boy's raunchy shirt to him, he said, "We've got to figure out some way to hide you." He went to the small trailer closet and extracted a flimsy, smock-looking garment made of camouflage netting. "Here, try this on."

The camo outfit fit the boy like tube socks on a rooster, but it did hide a large expanse of skin and the brightly colored designer shirt.

"We'll have to do something about those legs," Bill said. "The way the squirrels will see it, they'll practically glow in the dark. Here, smear some of this on them," and he handed Buddy the two-color set of green-and-brown makeup he had worn on his face the morning before.

"My face, too?" the boy asked.

"Especially." And the man grabbed a fingerful of each color to obliterate his own countenance.

Fortunately, the camo smock that swallowed the boy had a hood to cover his glistening blonde pate. With his face and legs now smeared, indistinguishable, he was ready to disappear into the bush.

"You're beautiful," Bill teased. "Now let's go see if you can sit quietly and watch the woods come to life."

Bill opened the closet door again and took out a double-barreled shotgun. It may or may not have been there all the time, Buddy thought, but he had no way of knowing. It looked to be all business.

"Is it loaded?" the boy asked.

"No, but it will be when we get there," Bill replied, as he revealed a handful of twelve-gauge shotgun shells.

Picking their way with a flashlight, the hunters walked as quietly as they could; but with the layering of leaves on the ground beneath them, they might as well have attempted quiet walking on a sea of fresh potato chips. As they proceeded to a spot about seventy-five yards from the trailer, the first shading of predawn light was beginning to chase the stars from the cloudless sky. Bill touched the boy, indicating a halt to the hike, then sat gingerly down on the ground and leaned against the trunk of a large oak tree.

The man whispered, "You sit opposite me, on the other side of the tree. As soon as you can just barely see, start searching up in the trees. You probably won't see one until it moves; but if you do, reach around and give me a tug. Don't say anything, just point slowly to where you see him; and no big motions. Okay?"

"Okay," the boy agreed, and he settled-in against the bark of the tree.

Slowly, the light came; and the squirrels didn't. Buddy didn't really know what to expect. He had seen plenty of squirrels in Houston city parks—fat, thoroughly tame, and begging for handouts. There were squirrels aplenty in his own tree-bedecked River Oaks neighborhood as well—wilder than the ones in the parks, but still quite accustomed to having people around. One certainly didn't need camouflage face paint to get close to any of those. He had a feeling, though, that the creatures of the wildwood might be different.

Different they were, indeed. The first glimpse the boy got of one was nothing more than a movement, a blur up high in a tree some thirty yards away. Trying hard to focus on it in that dimmest of light, he finally caught sight of a wispy little creature that seemed to fly among the tree limbs and branches above. It floated along, collecting footing, leaping from and alighting onto what appeared to be virtually nothing; and it continued to do so from one tree to another, as if there were no trick to it at all. Its grace was astounding, to the extent that the boy, in his fascination, almost forgot his reason for being there.

Reaching around the tree trunk, he touched Bill on the arm and tugged his sleeve. As the man leaned around, Buddy pointed the direction of the fleet, tree-borne will-o'-the-wisp and whispered, "He's right up there. See?"

Bill didn't see, for a moment; then the animal's movement against the ever-lightening sky gave his position away. Bill leaped to his feet and swung the big shotgun into the trajectory of the fleet little bushy-tail, just as he would for a flying game bird, and quickly touched off the left barrel.

BUH-LAM! The shot shattered the morning stillness and echoed through the woods. Buddy watched the squirrel recoil from the impact of the shot load and tumble down. It bounced off several tree branches on the way to the ground and landed on the heavily cushioned forest floor with a clump.

"Awesome shot!" the boy yelled, unable to fathom how such a performance could be accomplished. "Totally awesome."

"Go pick him up," Bill said. "Just keep your eyes glued to the spot where you saw him go down, and you'll walk right up to him."

Buddy tried to do that, but he stumbled over a vine, fell to the ground and lost sight of the location.

"Nice going, Grace," Bill chided, and joined him in the search.

The downed squirrel was not difficult to locate—a clump of gray fur against the mottled yellow and brown of the leaf-strewn turf. Bill allowed Buddy the honor of collecting the prize, which the boy hoisted with obvious pride and at least a sense of shared accomplishment. In the still-dim light, he curiously examined the prey for bullet wounds, locating at least a half-dozen spots where the limp body had been penetrated by the shotgun pellets.

"You got him pretty good," he told Bill.

"Yeah," the man replied. "Now let's sit back down and be quiet, and maybe we can get another one."

They returned to the same tree and resumed the back-to-back position in which they had sat before. Presently, Buddy caught sight again of movement up in the trees, and he reached out once more to tug at Bill's camouflage jacket sleeve. As he pointed to his sighting, the subject creature let out a loud, raucous, "Caw, caw!" and flew heavy-flappingly away.

"We're not interested in crows this season," Bill whispered.

"Sorry."

The gray pallor of predawn was now completely gone, and directly in front of the boy, a distant, flaming orange ball peeked out between a pair of loblolly pine trunks and shot tentative shafts of gold-tinted radiance through the forest. Almost simultaneously, the previously light dew that had dampened the pair's posteriors congealed into mist, then rose up from the ground and took up temporary residence among the tree limbs.

The boy's eyes drank in deeply the spectacle of the sunrise, absorbing its majesty. It was as inspiringly beautiful as the scene with the lion tracks had been frighteningly exhilarating the day before. He wished that, somehow, he could keep it, just as it was—encapsulate the moment, clasp it to him and hold on to it forever. But the sunrise never waits; and as quickly as the mists had risen up among the tree branches, they were captured by ministers from the blazing celestial orb and instantly spray-painted by their refracted rays. Buddy watched in slack-jawed wonderment as the morning mist became a pink cloud, floating above him. He had to share it.

"Look," he whispered, reaching around the tree once again to touch the man on the arm.

"Where?"

"Look up in the trees."

Anticipating another squirrel, Bill looked, but noticed nothing.

"Isn't it neat?" Buddy asked.

At length, the man did notice—not only the marvelous display being performed by Mother Nature and the East Texas woods, but also the expression of pure awe that was written all over the face and in the luminous eyes of the captive boy. *That look alone,* he thought, *is worth the price of admission.*

The boy was not without company in experiencing a new assortment of wonders. To a childless bachelor, a teenage kid can be a source of wonderment in himself—particularly with regard to language. To adolescents of the day, as Buddy continually demonstrated, a modestly successful example of the most mundane effort, activity, or experience of any sort rated the virtually obligatory superlative, "awesome." Something even slightly in excess of that became "totally awesome." One step beyond "totally," and nothing could be exceeded; it was "to the max." Yet, there sat that obviously intelligent youngster, educated in nothing but the finest of schools and apparently well-read for his age, staring in open-mouthed amazement at what truly was an awesome display in one of the world's finest natural showplaces; and the best he could do to articulate his delight was to label it "neat."

What must it be like to be a parent? Bill wondered to himself. *I guess maybe it's neat.*

Aloud, he concurred in his bemusement, "Yeah, neat. In fact . . . totally."

The next sighting was Bill's turn. Two fleet little furry phantoms came flying among the tree limbs from off to his right. As though it were an established pathway, the second appeared to take precisely the same route, alighting on exactly the same twig as the first, and scurrying along the same branch before springing away to the identical limb of the next tree—or so it seemed. Bill reached around the oak trunk to alert Buddy to the activity, and they both watched as the brace of bushytails gambolled an aerial expanse of thirty or forty yards from the hunters' right to their left.

When he felt comfortable with the shot, Bill rose to his feet, settled the shotgun sights ahead of the trailing squirrel, and touched-off the right barrel. Recovering quickly from the recoil of the big shotgun, he resumed his swing in the same, continuous movement, put the front bead sight ahead of the other squirrel, and fired the second barrel. The two arboreal acrobats ("nothing but rodents, just like rats," Bill remembered) hit the ground within fifteen feet of each other.

"All *right!*" the boy exclaimed, as he sprang to his feet to go retrieve the quarry.

"Is that good enough?" Bill asked, braggingly.

"Totally good enough! Absolute good *enough!*" the teenager proclaimed as he ran back to the tree with well-taken game in each hand and an enormous grin across his face.

He dropped back down into his original position against the tree, ready for the next episode; but Bill remained on his feet.

"Come on," the man said, "that's enough for now. We have as much as we can eat at one sitting, and there's no use being greedy."

"Can't I please try shooting one?" the boy pleaded.

"No."

"Why not?"

"You know why not," Bill said, extending his right hand to help the boy up. "Besides, that's as many as I want to mess with cleaning right now."

Since he had no choice, Buddy acquiesced.

▼ ▼ ▼

There was little choice in room B-22 at the Federal Building in Houston that Thursday morning, either. Special Agent in Charge Henry Wilson continued to exude confidence in the presence of the special task force he had assembled; but he privately despaired at the paucity of clues. There were no fingerprints, no written message—not even the classic movie one with words cut out of a magazine and pasted together—and no apparent trail to lead investigators to the whereabouts of the kidnapper and his captive. Nothing positive, just a lot of question marks.

And the case was getting cold. Cold and old.

There had been several telephone calls, in the beginning, from people claiming to have the Caine boy, and each of them had been tape-recorded at the police station, as per usual procedure. All but one of them had been dismissed as hoaxes. But not one—not a single one—had come in since the special command post had been set up in room B-22; the red telephone instrument tapped directly into the Caine mansion had not brought a single ransom demand, just the usual assortment of family calls and computer-generated solicitations. The black phone, hooked up directly to the HPD dispatcher's desk, had not jingled even once. Wilson knew that in a case such as this, no news could definitely be bad news.

Worse yet, perhaps, was the fact that the parents of the missing boy had still not been contacted; but it was now only a matter of time. Wilson and his task-force team now knew for certain the identity of the sailing ship upon which the Caines must now be cruising somewhere in the South Pacific; and the Coast Guard in Honolulu was broadcasting radio messages every half-hour in attempt to contact them. So far, to the best of Wilson's information, they had not yet been able to do so.

"So what in the hell do we have?" he asked Liddell Peters. Two other task-force members, normally assigned to the command post, had just departed on a short-term investigating foray, leaving Wilson and his chief assistant alone.

"What do you mean?" Peters replied.

"It's been almost two full days since the Caine kid was snatched, and what have we got? Mighty god-damned little."

"I agree, chief. All we've got is the composite drawing the chauffeur gave us, and the voice analysis; and I'm afraid that's not very much."

"Maybe it isn't," Wilson noted, nervously drumming his fingers on a desk. "But maybe it is. How much have we done to try to put the two together?"

Peters didn't answer. He had removed his glasses and stuck the tip of one of the stems into a corner of his mouth. He had melancholy green eyes, set deep beneath an unruly outcrop of thick, brown eyebrows. Wilson knew that in that posture, the agent had shifted into his pensive mode.

The only thing really worth ruminating on was the voice analysis. Wilson had taken the tape recording of the only telephone call that seemed legitimate—the one in which the caller had announced in gangsterese that "they" had the Caine kid and he was all right—and had it digitally reproduced. Then it was sent to FBI headquarters in Washington over a fiber-optic line for the voice to be electronically analyzed. From that, a personality profile had been derived.

The results were interesting, if not surprising. In the first place, the caller was obviously using a phony dialect, intended to disguise his real voice. In that, he had succeeded; but no one can disguise his vocal chords; so Wilson and his fellow investigators had enough vocal description on hand to be certain whether any succeeding calls were legitimate—at least whether they came from the same man. Also, they hoped that by the same voice-analysis techniques, they could learn even more about the kidnapper from the next call. If only there would be a next call.

They were pretty sure, for instance, that the man who called that Wednesday morning was a middle-aged, white male from the southwestern United States—in spite of the caller's attempt to sound like the typical movie depiction of a New Jersey hoodlum. There were indications in the man's voice profile that he might have suffered a slight hearing loss, of the sort that is caused by prolonged exposure to loud noises, such as heavy machinery. Extensive gunfire was another possibility for such a hearing loss.

"I can't get over the feeling," Wilson said to Peters, "that the guy who snatched the kid was somebody known to the Caine family, if not to the boy himself."

"But not the chauffeur, I don't think," Peters replied. "We gave that poor bastard so much hell that I know he'd have spilled if he knew anything at all."

And they had. HPD and FBI investigators, separately and combined, had grilled the hapless Mr. James Jamison unmercifully, and at length; but they had been completely unsuccessful in getting the man to implicate himself. Jamison had broken down and wept; he had slipped into near hysteria; he had shown consuming fear during the questioning—but nothing surfaced through it all to indicate with any surety that the chauffeur had any personal connection with the kidnapping.

His quarters over the Caine family garage had been thoroughly searched, but nothing out of order was discovered other than a rather extensive collection of pornography. The man's porno connection was further established through questioning of employees and regular clientele of Southwest Video-News, behind which the chauffeur had been found stripped, bound and gagged. Investigators could find no regular visitors to the video-porno palace who had any personal relationship with Jamison; in fact, the man seemed simply to have no friends at all. There were a couple of dirty-book purchasers who had been detained, questioned, and found to have minor criminal records; but no connection could be made between them and either Jamison or the Caine family.

"I think you're right," said Wilson. "But we still can't rule out the chauffeur altogether."

"But you still believe it was someone who knew the kid, or at least the family."

Wilson nodded. "Never dismiss a hunch."

"Who, then?" Peters questioned. "Employees? Family friends? I don't agree. I think it was a random grab—somebody who picked out the family from the newspapers or something, and then figured out a way to make off with their kid."

"Maybe you're right," Wilson granted. "But I don't think so."

The Special Agent in Charge rose from his chair in the main room of the command post and headed toward a small adjoining office.

"Where to, Sherlock?" asked Peters, teasingly.

"I'm retiring to my private think tank, my dear Mr. Watson, to try to reason things out. All truly great thinking must be done in private, don't you see?"

"What shall I do if I see a blinding light pouring out from under the door?"

"Just do what you usually do," Wilson replied from the doorway. "Genuflect." He entered the small office and closed the door behind him.

Henry Wilson's good-natured banter belied his true feelings about the case. In reality, he was becoming consumed with it—

that was the kind of investigator he was. If the case dragged on much longer, it could easily become an obsession.

Wilson sat at the lone desk in the undecorated office and stared out the window.

Middle-aged, Jamison said. Anywhere between thirty-five and forty-five, but difficult to pin down any closer than that. He had black, curly hair and a thick mustache. He was of medium height and apparently powerful build. No limps. No visible scars. And dammit, no fingerprints. All there was, was the composite picture.

Over and over in his mind, Wilson silently mulled what few clues he had, unable to escape the notion—even the probability, as he saw it—that the kidnapper knew his victim, if not vice versa. A friend of the family was not a likelihood; but, as any other possibility, it could not be completely dismissed. A former household employee maybe? Jamison's composite drawing had already been checked with the entire Caine household staff, and no one could recognize it. Whoever it was, though, was certainly familiar with the chauffeur's routine.

One of the staff had disappeared—Guillermo Villareal, the gardener. Wilson reasoned, though, that it was unlikely that his disappearance had anything to do with the kidnapping. Most likely, he guessed, the man was an illegal alien, a wetback, and he had simply split when investigators started nosing around the Caine mansion. He would turn up sooner or later, but not likely in connection with the kidnapping of Hamilton Caine, Jr.

From all there was to go on, then, Wilson now began to reach the conclusion that there remained only two major possibilities of personal connection, rather than a random selection, as Peters believed. First, the man might work or hang around some place frequented by the boy, which meant that Wingate School should be considered. Second, the kidnapper could be an employee of the father's company—someone who had a grudge, perhaps, and who knew something about the Caine family life.

As Wilson stared out the window of his private "think tank" in the Federal Building, he noticed for the first time that there was a deeply darkening cloud in the northwest, growing larger and darker by the minute. The people out in Spring Branch were in for a soaking.

And so, he decided, was anyone even remotely connected with the socially and industrially prominent Hamilton Caine family of Houston, Texas—a torrent of probing questions. To-morrow, Friday—as soon as a couple of thousand copies could be printed—Wilson's team would begin circulating the composite sketch of the kidnapper to the faculty and administration of Wingate School. Concurrent with that, a recognition search would have to begin among employees of Texas Consolidated Utilities Corporation. Later, perhaps, all of River Oaks.

Wilson felt that the obvious place to start would be the personnel office at the corporation. After that, then what? Some occupation, perhaps, where an employee might be subject to enough continuous, loud noise to incur a slight hearing loss.

And what, wondered the Special Agent in Charge, might that be? Generating stations? No one there would likely have any contact with the Caine family. Machine shops? Same answer. Drilling operations? Even less likely, for the same reason.

Airplanes? Now that was a thought. Wilson did not know whether the corporation operated its own airplanes, but it was highly likely that it did. Airplanes make a lot of noise. And the Caines—at least Caine Senior—would certainly be flying in them.

In the command-post room with its two direct telephone taps and a massive assortment of the latest state-of-the-art tracing equipment, Liddell Peters sat quietly alone with his own private meditations on the case. He flinched when the door to the adjacent little hideaway office burst open and Henry Wilson reappeared.

"Liddell," Wilson announced. "Get on the telephone to whatever contact you've made over at our missing friend Mr. Caine's corporate empire and find out if they have an aviation department or anything like that. I've got an idea just who our kid-snatcher might be."

▼ ▼ ▼ ▼ ▼ ▼ ▼ ▼ ▼ ▼ ▼ ▼ ▼

7

The squirrel-cleaning chores were performed outside, this time, on a folding metal table the man had fished-out from beneath the trailer. It was heavily rusted, but functional. The boy wondered how much more equipment Bill would pull out from beneath that forest-green portable homestead.

Buddy performed perhaps one third of the skinning chores, with some degree of competence if not speed. He did not look forward to the second operation, but he had to participate, nonetheless. They went inside for the evisceration ritual, where Buddy managed to get more or less covered with blood and gore from his fingertips to his elbows. By now, it was 9:30 in the morning, and the interior of the trailer was already beginning to heat up.

Buddy shucked his filthy shirt and tossed it onto his bunk. "I hope you don't plan to run off and leave me chained-up in this hot-box again today," he said.

"Not today," Bill replied. "We'll just let them stew on your mysterious disappearance for another day, and give your ocean-sailing parents time to get back to Houston."

"It gets hotter than hell in here," Buddy noted.

"I know. Maybe I won't have to do that to you again."

"Does that mean that maybe you will?"

"Don't worry about it," the man advised. "Right now, you're filthy again." Tossing a bar of soap to the boy, he added, "Take this and go down to the creek and wash that mess off your legs.

That ought to cool you off a little." They both had cleaned the woods makeup off their faces before beginning the game cleaning.

"And give this to Brutus on your way out," Bill added, handing Buddy a paper plate laden with the morning's collection of squirrel entrails.

"Guh-ROHS!" the boy exclaimed.

"Shut up and feed the dog," the man ordered, as he began wrapping the morning's game in waxed paper to store in the refrigerator.

Buddy found the creek water on his legs to be every bit as chilling as he expected it would be. A collection of oak and sweetgum leaves, pine needles, tree bark and dirt had become stuck to the grease paint on his lower appendages, providing an even more effective, though messy, camouflage. Washing was not a bad idea, only a cold one; and he hurried with the chore, retreating quickly into the trailer for a towel as soon as he had finished.

"What's the coldest thing in the world?" he asked the man.

"A well-digger's ass in Idaho?"

"Wrong," the kid replied. "It's my legs."

"When I was in school, we figured there was nothing colder than a witch's tit . . . in a barrel of salty ice . . . at the North Pole . . . in the middle of January."

Buddy stared at him, bemused. "You're just full of that kind of stuff, aren't you?" he asked.

Bill shrugged. "You just think you're cold. Wait 'til a little later and you'll get to take a bath."

"In that creek?"

"That very one."

"Bull SHIT!" the boy replied. "Not this kid."

"You ever been skinny-dipping?"

"Sure."

And he had, once. Buddy and three other boys had slipped away from the group at Camp Rio Alto on one occasion, and stripped off for a brief swim, *au naturel*, in the nearby Frio River. They quickly learned how the river got that name (it means "cold" in Spanish) and decided in short order that it didn't take long at all to get all of that pleasure their young bodies could stand.

"No thank you," he said, recalling the incident; and he walked out the door.

Having finished his breakfast repast, Brutus greeted the youth once again with his peculiar demand for attention—sticking his head through Buddy's legs from behind and raising him off the ground. As before, the boy went sprawling.

"Brutus, you old mutt!" he exclaimed; and he reached up from his supine position to grab the big dog's head with both hands and give it a shake. Brutus responded with a lick on the face.

"Where's your stupid Frisbee?" he asked the dog. Impolitely, the dog did not reply.

"There it is," Buddy said, answering his own question as he located the blue tossing-saucer near the tree where he had been chained the day before. "Come on."

After he completed the kitchen chores, the man watched from his trailer doorway as the boy and dog romped. He sensed the restlessness in the youth, the pent-up energy that seems always to be there in a teenager, crying to be expelled; and he felt some of the same in himself. The body's muscles need to be worked. Hunting of any kind is exciting and fun; but something like squirrel hunting, in particular, does nothing to fulfill the body's need for exercise. In fact, sitting quietly huddled against the trunk of a tree has just the opposite effect. The ground dew always manages quickly to penetrate the trousers and dampen the *derrière*; and from there it finds a way, somehow, to permeate the system and settle into the muscles and joints, leaving them aching to be exercised. He had just the remedy.

"Hey Buddy," he said, approaching the boy. "Ever play badminton?"

"Badminton? Sure," the boy replied, recalling indoor activities in the school gym when inclement weather made outdoor phys-ed impractical.

"I think I can scrounge up enough equipment for a game; and if we work at it a little, we can probably clear off a space big enough for a court right here," Bill said, indicating an area between the trailer and the creek bank.

"Sounds good to me," Buddy agreed. "Especially if you want to get your butt beat."

He was thinking of his summer of tennis lessons and tournaments, and how badminton, a sissy game by comparison, would be easy meat for him. He also became aware of what he had just said to the man about "beating his butt." Never, ever, had he felt comfortable enough with an adult to talk to him like that—just as he would to his friends. He enjoyed it. And he was confident that he would beat his butt, too.

"Well, I'll just have to give you the chance and we'll see," Bill replied.

Buddy knew right away where the man would find the equipment for the game—under the trailer, of course. And he was correct, at least with regard to the net and poles. The rackets, though, were acquired from a locked compartment on the side of the trailer. They were gut-strung and tightly held in wooden presses; and the shuttlecocks were feathered, not the cheap, plastic variety found in department stores. The quality of the equipment failed to register on the boy, however. As he had attended only the finest of schools, he was accustomed always to having nothing but the best and most expensive equipment. It didn't occur to him that gut-strung rackets and feathered shuttlecocks were not the sort of things one might expect to find in the average trailer in the woods—they were indicative of someone serious about the sport, not the casual birdie-plopper. But the kid was young, and he still had plenty to learn.

Preparing the badminton court required over an hour's work from both man and boy. Bill located a set of instructions indicating the proper dimensions for the court; and they stepped them off, as best they could, to regulation. One boundary was established adjacent to a foot-wide tree trunk, and the others fell more or less naturally into place. A small holly tree was chopped down and its stump removed in what would be one end of the court, then a clump of unidentified brush was whacked away by axe and machete from the other end. Next, the entire area had to be raked relatively free of fallen leaves, branches, twigs, pine cones, and assorted forest debris.

At length, the two workmen managed to lay out a court as close as possible to the requisite twenty feet by forty-four feet, and Bill outlined the entire perimeter with Day-Glo orange surveyor's tape—the kind used extensively in the forest for marking trees to establish cutting boundaries, property lines, and so forth. Buddy found it not the least surprising that the man just happened to have a roll of that tape on hand—no more so than the fact that he had a hoe, shovel, rake, badminton poles, folding table, etc., etc., etc., stored beneath that trailer; or that he had, no doubt, a small arsenal stashed away in that wooden locker in the van—and who-knows-what-all tucked away within the trailer itself. Nothing in the line of equipment or impedimenta surprised him any more.

The boy enjoyed doing the work—whacking at the shrubbery with the machete, raking leaves from the sandy turf, and hacking out with a hatchet some stubborn roots that remained poking out of the ground after the cover was removed. He worked up a modest sweat doing so, not realizing that the area in the shade, adjacent to the creek bank as they were, was several degrees cooler than the rest of the forest atop and beyond the banks.

Bill was a heavy sweater. Once again clad in his faded cut-off jeans, he had been shirtless since the hunt. Droplets of perspiration glistened atop his heavy crop of body hair as the two continued the court preparation.

The forest paid little heed to the human activities. Buddy kept hearing a clicking sound in the trees overhead; when he stopped work to see what was causing it, he spotted a pair of male cardinals flitting among the branches. They were bright red from the tips of their sharply pointed crests to the ends of their flaring tails. *Pretty birds*, he thought silently, *but not much for singing*.

Aloud, he asked, "What kind of trees are these?"

"You mean this one?" Bill responded, pointing upward.

"Yes," the boy replied.

It was the one with the mottled gray-and-green bark—the one

that had a matching, larger example across the creek; and the two, combined, provided most of the canopy that hid the campsite from above, but managed to reveal the stars from below.

"Beech," Bill told him. "That one over there," he said, indicating the larger one that half-tumbled down the creek bank, "is a beech. This smaller one here is a son-of-a-beech."

The boy grimaced, protesting the grown man's pun. "Gimme a break, will ya?" he pleaded.

"Shut up and work," Bill replied. "You'll get your break when you get that badminton racket in your hand. Then we'll see who's the breaker and who's the break-ee." The game of psyche-out had begun.

"Hah!" the boy exclaimed, confidently undaunted.

"Yeah, hah," Bill echoed.

When the job was done, Bill went into the trailer to retrieve yet more equipment. He removed his left sneaker and squeezed his foot into an elastic ankle support. Then he strapped a wide band around his right forearm immediately below the elbow.

"What's that for?" the boy asked.

"I'm not fond of tennis elbow."

"Is that all now?" the boy teased. "Are you completely dressed? Sure you don't need to put on a steel jock strap?"

"No, but we'll see. I need all the help I can get."

"It won't be enough, I promise you," the youth swaggered, indicating that psyche-out is a two-way street.

The two players managed only a little back-and-forth pinging of the shuttlecock before they found themselves unable to accomplish anything on the court. Big, playful Brutus was a major problem. He insisted on joining in the game—biting at feet, barking, chasing the feathered birdie, and generally making a nuisance of himself. What angered Bill was that he refused to mind when ordered to go guard the house, to obey the "stay" command, or anything else. He wanted to play. With visible disgust, but not without understanding, Bill dragged the big dog back to the trailer and handcuffed his collar to the same chain and tree that had tethered the boy. Brutus barked, whined, and otherwise complained for a while, but he finally gave up and went to sleep.

Back to the badminton again, Bill and his new woods-buddy began to ping the bird back and forth across the net in earnest—but lightly, easily. Shots from both sides were prone to be lofted rather softly from about mid-court to the base line, with neither of the soon-to-be combatants attempting anything fancy or particularly serious. Buddy tried to exhibit a little fast-on-his-feet work a few times, but it was mostly all for show; and never once, when he tried it, did his shot land properly in the opposite court. Bill made no such display; he simply managed, most of the time, to get under the falling shuttlecock and return it back to its sender—but never with any particular authority. His doing so seemed to set the pace of play.

After ample warm-up, they agreed to ping for serve. One hit for each letter: P-I-N-G . . . and Buddy won. His serve.

Before beginning service, they read aloud some of the rules from the instruction sheet, redefined the mid-court service lines, which had been inscribed only with a shoe heel dragged across the sandy soil, and started the game.

"Just be kind," the man pleaded, spinning the racket in his hand. "Remember that I'm only a creaky old fart."

Buddy smiled. His moment of retribution had come.

The youth's initial serve, still soft and tentative, came down near the middle of the service court, where Bill sidestepped and took it with his forehand, sending the feathered projectile down the line and deep into the opposite side of the court from where Buddy had served. The kid raced athletically to return it, and just managed to catch it with a desperate backhand swing that lofted the birdie lazily and barely across the net. The man was at the net, waiting.

ZING! Across the court it went and into the ground like an arrow from a crossbow. Buddy saw it, all right, but he would have had to have arms twelve feet long even to hope to return it. Surprise shot. Bill's service. Boy's turn to make a nasty return.

The man's first offering just barely cleared the net and dropped lazily, but hastily, toward Buddy's feet. Easy shot. He picked it up with the tip of his racket and sent it straight into the net. Point, the man.

Bill's next service, from the opposite side of the court, lofted far back toward the corner. "Out!" the boy called, prematurely. Then he watched helplessly as the bird dropped to the ground within six inches, either direction, inside the absolute corner.

Two to nothing.

Buddy began to see the light. The man was certainly not playing anything like he had been during their practice pinging. But the kid had never really been hustled before, and he still didn't realize just how badly he had been stung. Not until the score reached seven to love did the boy begin to comprehend that he had been bamboozled by a superior player—never mind all the straps and bandages—and that he had better start putting a lot more into his shots if he was going to survive the game without being skunked.

Finally, after Bill had run his string to nine-zip, he managed to miss a shot—a back-court zinger that fell just beyond the base line.

"Okay, you 'creaky old fart,'" the boy hollered with mock petulance. "Now it's my turn. You thought you were going to shut me out, didn't you? Well, nobody's ever done that yet."

He gave the birdie a resounding underhand whack and sent it screaming across the net—easily three feet out of bounds. Now it was Bill's serve again, and he ran a string of four more successive points until Buddy actually made a shot, catching Bill running crosscourt and placing it behind him. Unfortunately for the boy, points are scored in badminton only by the server.

"Congratulations," the man said. "You finally learned the name of the game."

"What's that?"

"Put it where they ain't."

"Yeah," the boy replied. Now it was his chance to serve again, and he could start piling up points.

ZING! WHOP! The man's return caught the boy stingingly on his right thigh.

"If you're trying to de-nut me," Buddy said, "you missed."

"Next time," Bill replied, whereupon he resumed service and ran out the game: fifteen to nothing.

"Still think it's a game for sissies?" the man asked as they crossed over to change courts.

"I never said it was."

"No, but you thought it, didn't you?"

"Yeah, I guess. How'd you ever learn to play like that?"

"From my wife."

"You're married?"

"Used to be. She played on the women's varsity team in college."

"You got any kids?"

"No kids."

"How long ago was that?" the boy asked.

"That I didn't have any kids? Two days ago. Now I've got my hands full of them."

"No, I mean since you were married."

"Too long to remember," Bill replied. "Not long enough to forget."

"Well, you've got your hands full now for sure," the boy said. "Just serve that stupid bird and you'll find out."

"Loser serves," Bill told him, and he tossed the shuttlecock across the net.

The second game, again, was no contest. Bill did manage to slip-up once and allow the boy to score a point; but it was the only one. Final score: fifteen to one.

By then, the sun was high. The forest heat and stifling humidity had settled into severe oppression, and both man and boy were covered with sweat.

"Okay, kid, enough lessons for now," the man said, rubbing it in. "Let's have something to drink and start thinking about lunch."

"Good idea," the boy concurred. "But I want a chance at a rematch."

"You've got it. Now be a good loser and go inside and get us something to drink. I'll take a beer; you can have whatever you want that's there."

"Can I have a beer?"

"Beer my ass. How old are you?"

"Thirty-nine."

"Well, I guess that's old enough. How about we split one. Get two, and you can drink a half."

"Good as done," the boy replied.

They moved their chairs down to the creekside to take advantage of the cool air radiating from the flowing stream. Then both slumped down with their legs stretched straight out to sip their beers—hot, tired, thirsty, and from all outward appearances, happy.

Bill could feel the heat radiating from his own forehead, and he stooped down to the creek, picked up a handful of the chilly water and spread it across his brow. Then he pulled off his shoes, pocketed his ankle support, and dug his feet sensuously into the damp, cool sand. Buddy did likewise; but soon he got a better idea. He got up from the chair and waded quickly across the creek to the other side, where he sat down against the high bank with the cooling sand not only on the bottoms of his feet, but also the backs of his legs and his bare back.

"That feels good," he said, taking another sip of his very first all-to-himself brew.

"You sit there and drink all that beer, you twirp, and you'll never get up," the man said.

"So why should I want to get up?"

"You got me. You got any idea what time it is?"

"Who cares?" the boy replied.

"We ought to catch a newscast."

"What will we do with it after we catch it?"

"Smartass!" Bill said. "You're starting to talk like a drunk already."

"Let's don't listen now," Buddy said, somewhat to Bill's surprise. "Let's just sit here and cool off. If we miss one now, there'll be another one later. There's always a damn newscast."

"Yeah, always," the man agreed. He didn't really want to destroy the moment either.

Bill found it downright incredible watching that kid—that young, teenage kid; that boy whom, only two days ago, he had captured in a sack and brought kickingly to those woods; the soon-to-be man-child who doubtless once wished that he could kill his abductor, now stretched out contented as a milk-fed puppy, wallowing in the creek sand and drinking the kidnapper's beer.

The boy was to be his meal ticket, his grubstake. As evil a thing as kidnapping for ransom was, Bill felt that Buddy's disgusting parents deserved it; they could afford it; and the ransom money that the boy, himself, had demanded to be doubled, would buy the man a new start: a ticket to Alaska and one more final grab at life's brass ring.

For years, he had dreamed the seemingly impossible dream of flying the Alaskan bush; of buying a good amphibious float plane to ferry well-heeled hunters and fishermen into the wild back-country—the majestic mountains of the Brooks Range, perhaps—and to be free.

He had come close. After he quit in disgust and left the tightly structured existence of Texas Consolidated Utilities, he found his way to southern Louisiana and ended up doing the next best thing. He did have his own business operation and his own amphibious Cessna float plane, flying out of the booming little oil town of Lafayette. He was making good money ferrying oil company officials, tools and equipment to the many drilling barges operating in the swamps, bays, and bayous of the soggy, oil-and-gas-rich Louisiana coastline.

It was a good life—not the Alaskan bush, that could come later—but a good life. No one ever made any terribly stringent demands on him. If the weather was bad, he simply didn't fly. Trips were never arduous—generally forty-five minutes to an hour at the most.

The bayou and swamp country that covers the entire coastline of southern Louisiana was mysterious and compelling. He was frequently required to make delivery flights just after daybreak—always arriving at the drilling locations when that waterlogged terrain was obliquely lighted with the first rays of the sunrise. From the air, it was like a delicate lace border on a fancy quilt, etched in satin and rimmed in gold, and he never tired of seeing it.

For him, as for almost anyone then connected even peripherally with the American oil and gas industry, those were heady times. As the petroleum price-per-barrel skyrocketed, the oil companies virtually threw money away, and everybody in the business got fat on it. For the man now called Bill, that meant frequent charters in and out of the swamplands, as well as regular assignments for specific drilling contracts under which he worked on retainer.

It also meant heavy debt, as Bill, like everyone else in the business, was betting on the come. His plane was heavily mortgaged, as was the house in which he lived—everything. When the bottom fell out of the oil business, many small operators such as he quickly went under.

Virtually everything of Bill's went to foreclosure, and he ended up back in polluted Houston again, lucky to land a part-time job with an aerial charter service. Part-time, in that instance, meant that he got paid only when he was called in to fly, but that he was on call all the time—twenty-four hours a day, seven days a week. It was only an existence.

He had hatched the plan to kidnap the son of his former employer one middle-of-the-night as he lay in bed, unable to sleep, mentally laboring to avoid self-pity, and desperately searching for a plan, a scheme, any kind of idea that might turn him into his own man again—something to give him one more shot at the Alaskan bush.

For weeks, thereafter, he studied the Caine family habits, quietly shadowing their limousine as it carted the kid to and from his tennis and other summer activities; but there was not enough routine about it to make an attempt at snatching the kid anything but a wildly reckless maneuver. As such, it was far too risky. Then came school and the always predictable routine of that weird chauffeur; with that, the otherwise despicable act of kidnapping became a simple matter of planning.

And now, there he sat—his grubstake, his captive—drinking the man's own beer and quietly crapped out on the bank sand of a nameless creek in this harsh, but beautiful, Big Thicket country that the man had known and loved so much for so many years.

And was the boy really any longer his prisoner? Not hardly. In fact, it occurred to Bill that the situation might be just the opposite. He found himself trying to think of ways to amuse the youngster—to show him things about the woods, to demonstrate, to teach. And he enjoyed doing so—far beyond anything he might previously have imagined. Silently, he reflected, *What a stupid way for a kidnapper to act.*

As for the object of the kidnapping, young Buddy was now out of it. Added to fatigue from the physical strains of the day—the unexpected early rising, the tension and excitement of the squirrel hunt, the heavy work of clearing the badminton court and the strenuous activities of the games themselves—his relaxed position and the half-can of beer that he had managed to consume had put him away. He was asleep, sitting up.

▼ ▼ ▼ ▼ ▼ ▼ ▼ ▼ ▼ ▼ ▼ ▼ ▼

8

Shafts of pink, gold, and orange pierced a skinny line of fluffy, purple-gray cloudlets that traced lazily along the eastern horizon, as dawn began to break across the gently rolling waters of the South Pacific. Somewhere southwest of Acapulco; somewhere northeast of Tahiti. Somewhere out of the grasp of the mental and emotional tugs-of-wars that plague the practitioners of modern American civilization, and far removed from the minute-by-minute exigencies of corporate and household command.

There was no trace of the glory of the sunrise, though, in the master stateroom of the *Heavens To Betsy*—a two-masted sailing yacht rigged at the time with nothing but a shortened mainsail and a lazy jib, to ease its passage smoothly through the night in unhurried quest for that pinpoint of wave-tossed real estate enshrined forever in romantic memory with the escapades of Fletcher Christian and Paul Gauguin.

Curtains and blinds, tightly drawn, had assured the waste of that glorious dawn so effectively that it might as well have been midnight. The actual midnight just past, on the other hand, would probably be considered to have been far from wasted by the occupants of that gently rolling nautical pleasure palace—as soon as they were able to remember it.

An urgent rapping on the door was as welcome as the announcement of doomsday to those ensconced in the stateroom's satin-sheeted, king-sized bed.

"Mr. Hawkins, sir; it's Captain Twiney."

Oliver Hawkins, owner of the *Heavens to Betsy*, as well as president and chairman of the board of a modestly huge insurance company known as Gulf Crest Life and Endowment, struggled mightily to surface through the fog of his personal, morning-after hell.

"What? Huh?" he demanded of the insistent knocker.

"Captain Twiney, sir," the voice beyond the door repeated. "There's an urgent radio message."

With all the grace of a pregnant pachyderm, the bulge-bellied Mr. Hawkins struggled his naked body across that of the lady in bed beside him.

"I'm coming, hold on," he mumbled, pausing momentarily en route to confirm the identity of his bed partner. Until then, he was not terribly sure.

Mrs. Hamilton Robert Caine, so thoroughly enshrined in the Houston social pages as Melanie, attempted to bury her uncustomarily uncoifed blonde tresses in a mound of pillows to escape the serenity-shattering cacaphony that had erupted around her. A grunt was the only audible extent of her complaint. It was, that is, until the stateroom door opened on the portly presence of her still-naked host, blasting the motel-room darkness of the master cabin with a shattering shaft of sunlight.

"What in the hell is going on?" the lady inquired.

Hushed whispering at the doorway was the only reply.

Groping his way back into the cabin through the hangover fog that clouded his brain, Oliver Hawkins struggled into a pair of boxer underwear that clung precariously below the precipice on the downward swoop of his enormously distended abdomen, atop the scruffy-haired menace of his groin. Then he sat gingerly onto the foot of the bed.

"Oliver?" Mrs. Caine questioned before memory or reason could function. "You here? Where's Hamilton?"

"Damned if I know," her host replied. "I guess he's in your cabin with Betsy. You'd better wake up."

"What is it?" the lady asked, sensing finally that there was something unpleasant afoot.

"There's been a . . ." Hawkins stammered, haltingly. "That is, your son . . . Ham Junior . . . he's been kidnapped."

"Of all the crap!" she screamed in a sudden fury that spoke more of discommodation than motherly concern. "What do you mean?"

"That was the captain. He just received a radio message from the Coast Guard in Honolulu. Someone—a man—tied up your chauffeur, stole your limo and kidnapped your kid from school. They're demanding a ransom of two hundred thousand dollars."

"But how can *we* do anything about it? We're in the middle of the god-damned ocean."

"They can send an amphibious plane if we ask them to. I'm supposed to go radio them back with instructions and our position."

"Better go get Hamilton first," she replied. "He'll be furious."

He was more than furious.

"That little pain-in-the-ass!" the father exclaimed, as the ocean-cruising foursome—Hamilton and Melanie Caine, Oliver and Betsy Hawkins—discussed the unwelcome news over coffee and Bloody Marys, gamely battling with hair-of-the-dog, the morning-after effects of copious quantities of margaritas and piña coladas the night before.

Caine's temper, which had been only seething, was now beginning to flame. "He insisted on giving us a hard time before we left . . . and now this." Then to his wife, as if attempting to put the blame on her, "He was nothing but a biological accident that never should have happened in the first place."

"Don't give me that," countered Melanie Caine, testily. "You were all full of that son-and-heir crap at the time, if you would just be honest enough—for the first time in your life—to remember."

"Trouble is all he's ever been," her husband continued to steam. "Always bugging me about every god-damned thing imaginable. Why don't we do this? Why don't we do that?" Addressing the host and hostess, he added, "He even wanted to go running off to the ranch of somebody we don't even know as soon as we left town. And now he's screwed-up the only decent vacation we've had in years."

"Come now," Oliver Hawkins interceded, "you can't really blame this on the boy. It isn't like he's personally responsible for getting himself kidnapped."

The cabin boy, a seventeen-year-old Mexican youth named Miguél, who had been signed on in Acapulco, timidly interrupted to decant fresh coffee into the cups, warming the residue that had been mostly ignored in favor of the tongue-biting Bloody Marys. The poor kid was embarrassed beyond description over the goings-on of the night before, and he didn't know how to handle it.

It was sometime in the middle of the evening of heavy drinking and indiscriminate sex play among the older folks, that Melanie Caine had managed to waylay the boy, as he dutifully tended to their service wishes, and drop his crisply starched, white linen uniform trousers down around his sneakers. As he stood frightened and uncomprehending beside her, she was fondly fondling the rapidly swelling bulge through his white cotton briefs when the owner of the vessel called a halt.

"On my ship," Oliver Hawkins proclaimed, "you don't screw around with the help."

Fearing a repetition, Miguél quickly finished his coffee-warming task and retreated to the corner of the bar to await further orders.

"Well this is not the time or place for any more recriminations," Betsy Hawkins announced from a mascara-smudged, lipstick-smeared countenance beneath a tangled mass of heavily dye-rinsed, strawberry blonde hair. "You've got to decide what you're going to do and get to doing it. If they said they would send a plane, then you've got to have them send a plane. You've got no other choice."

"Maybe we can get this all wrapped up quickly once we get back to Houston," Melanie Caine reasoned. "Then we can fly out and rejoin you in Tahiti."

"Yeah, maybe so," her husband agreed, as his anger finally began to recede. "But it might not be all that easy. What if the kidnapper reneges on the deal? It could drag on for days. We might not be able to get back in time."

"I can't believe what I'm hearing," the corpulent Mr. Hawkins observed. "Here your only child has been kidnapped, and you two are talking seriously about simply flying back to Houston, paying off the kidnapper, and then flying back to Tahiti . . . business as usual. Don't your son's feelings mean anything to you?"

His question was met with silence; and none of the four noticed the sneer on the face of Miguél as he stood statue-still at the end of the bar.

It was a good five hours later when the sleek-hulled Coast Guard amphibian lifted off and winged away from the now gloom-enshrouded *Heavens To Betsy*. On board the plane, the distraught mother was worrying intensely about what she would wear to the first press briefing upon their arrival; and the overwrought father was hoping against hope that the kidnappers would not raise the ante before he and his wife could make it back to Houston.

▼ ▼ ▼

The big dog, Brutus, was obviously happy when his master stooped down and unlocked the handcuffs to set him free from the chain that bound him to the tree. When Bill stood, the dog reared up on his hind legs and placed his big paws on the man's chest.

"Got a kiss?" Bill asked. The dog responded with an enthusiastic licking of his owner's face and a barked plea for a play-tussle.

"No, I can't play now, Brutus, I've got to put some lunch together. Go wake up the boy," he said, pointing to the snoozing young person across the creek. "Go get Buddy."

The dog wagged his tail excitedly and barked his approval of the idea; he didn't know what it meant, but he received it enthusiastically, nonetheless. Not knowing what else to do, Brutus reared back on his hind legs again, pawed the man on the chest and barked. Then he looked Bill directly in the eye and stuck out his tongue. That was the dog's way of asking, "How about something to eat?"

"No, you're not going to get lunch, you greedy old hound-dog," Bill said. "You had a good breakfast, what more do you want?" With that, he affectionately massaged both sides of the dog's head; then he pushed him away and walked into the trailer.

While Bill was inside, the huge canine did locate the boy, and anointed him into wakefulness with a big and proper tongue-bath across the kid's entire face.

"Ptooey! Yuk! Brutus, you big, gross, dumb, dodo-head!" the boy yelled, fending off the offender.

Brutus considered the boy's pronouncement to be a compliment, so he lunged after him to administer another anointment.

"No, dammit! Now quit!" Buddy jumped to his feet in self-defense, raining sand from his entire backside as he did so.

Brutus responded with a loud, bass bark, trying to entice the boy into play.

"Oh go away, will you?" the boy pleaded, still trying to shake from his head the remainder of the nap that had been so rudely and abruptly halted.

He bent down on the creek bank, picked up a stick and tossed it upstream as far as he could. "Go get it, you hairy beast!" The dog went splashing after, and the boy ran to the trailer for protection.

"What do you say, Sleeping Beauty?" greeted the man as he stepped out through the trailer door with the portable radio in his hands. "Is Brutus getting you down?"

"He had me down, but I got up."

"Well, get back down again in that chair over there," Bill said, pointing toward the folding table with the two lawn chairs now adjacent, "and let's have a bite of lunch."

A loaf of bread, a jar of sandwich spread, several packages of lunch meat, sliced cheese, a bag of potato chips and two cans of Coca-Cola were already on the table.

"I got you a Coke," Bill said, "unless you'd rather have another beer."

"I don't like beer," the boy confessed.

"Good thinking."

While his house guest dug into the sandwich makings, Bill tuned-in the same Houston radio station as before. He had to endure seven and one-half minutes of rock music, which the boy seemed to enjoy and the man quite obviously detested, plus three minutes and fifteen seconds of radio commercials. Finally, the station launched into canned teleprinter noises, garbled Morse code and gushy hyperbole to preface the proud pronouncements of its adenoidal newscaster:

Good afternoon ladies and gentlemen.
Tropical Storm Elizabeth is now reported to have winds in excess of sixty miles an hour, and the National Weather Service says conditions are favorable for the storm to develop into the season's third hurricane.

"How do you like that, kid?" Bill interrupted. "Already you've been pushed out of the lead story. You see how quickly they forget?"

The storm, which popped up unexpectedly as a tropical depression in the Gulf of Mexico Tuesday night, has now intensified, with winds reported at sixty-three miles an hour near the center.

Meteorologists at the Weather Service say that conditions are favorable for the storm to intensify further, but that steering currents are weak, and there is no predicting which way it might head before making landfall. Elizabeth is now located about one hundred and seventy-five miles south of Morgan City, Louisiana. A large band of heavy rains has already begun to pelt the Louisiana coastline. Gale warnings are flying along the entire Gulf Coast from Brownsville to New Orleans . . . and a hurricane watch is in effect.

The Houston Police Department, meanwhile, aided by the FBI, is still waiting for the kidnapper of young Hamilton Caine, Junior, to drop the other shoe. The son of a prominent Houston industrialist, young Caine was kidnapped as he left the exclusive Wingate School, off Memorial Drive, on Tuesday.

HPD Detective Sergeant Wesley Price says the department has received a number of phone calls from people claiming to have the boy and demanding ransom. Price said it's not unusual to get a lot of calls on a case like this, but most of them are hoaxes. He said a lot of kooks want to get their names in the paper and their pictures on television . . . and some even think they can get away with a bundle of ransom money. But according to Price, police believe that only one call came from the real kidnapper . . . and he has not called but once.

Authorities are not saying anything for the record, but it is known that they are privately expressing fears for the fifteen-year-old boy's life. They seem to be afraid that the kidnapper may have given up the whole idea because he could not reach the boy's parents for the ransom demands . . . and he may have killed the boy to avoid detection. They say the longer they go without hearing from him, the more they fear the worst.

Meanwhile, the boy's parents, Mr. and Mrs. Hamilton Caine, Senior, are on their way to Houston. The couple had been on a sailboat cruise in the South Pacific—on their way to Tahiti—when their son was kidnapped. We have information that an amphibious airplane has just been dispatched from Hawaii to pick them up. They will be flown back to Hawaii and from there, back to Houston. They are expected in sometime tomorrow.

Well, the Astros took another pounding in the Dome last night . . .

Bill clicked off the radio. "There you have it, kid. Your folks are on their way to save you from the clutches of the kidnapper—if you are not already dead—and we may have a hurricane coming. What else have you done for excitement lately?"

"I got licked in the face by a big, dumb dog."

Perfectly on cue, the canine so described reached his dripping-wet head over the arms of the folding chair and dropped a wet stick into the boy's lap.

"Does that mean we're engaged?" Buddy asked Brutus. The dog responded with a loud, enthusiastic bark.

"Now don't get too carried away there," Bill admonished. "He's already taken."

"Well, I wish he had 'taken' his wet, nasty body somewhere else while I'm trying to eat."

"You shouldn't have too much criticism of nasty bodies," Bill noted. "Have you taken a good look at your own lately?"

"Well . . . who cares?"

"Certainly not Brutus." Pointing to his side, the man commanded, "Now come over here and SIT DOWN!"

Reluctantly, the huge, playful beast obeyed.

"It looks as though I figured it about right," Bill said. "The news guy said your folks should be back in Houston some time tomorrow. That's Friday. They'll get the word that I'm demanding all that money for their precious child, and your esteemed old man can start getting it together. I'll give him a personal call on Saturday; and, with any luck, you can be back in their loving arms by Monday night."

"I wish they'd stay gone a month," Buddy said.

"I don't think I could afford to feed you for a month," Bill replied, as he watched the boy bite into his second sandwich.

"We could make do. You'd just have to shoot a lot of squirrels. Or I would, maybe."

It was obvious to Bill that Buddy now felt comfortable in his situation. After all, who can relax and fall asleep on a creek bank if he's up-tight and apprehensive—even if he does get knocked out by a half-can of beer?

But oh, what a mess that short nap had made of him. If he had not been a study in dishabille beforehand, he certainly was now. The washing he had given his legs after the squirrel hunt had been perfunctory, at best; but the lower limbs were clean enough to reveal, once more, the scratches inflicted on their hike to find the cougar tracks the day before. His once-white leather shoes were hopelessly smudged; and without the label on the right hip pocket, the manufacturer would never recognize those cut-off designer jeans.

His face looked just like that of any other kid—usually a younger kid, perhaps, but any kid who had played hard in a dirt pile and had been given an order to wash his face before coming to the table. There was an oval of semi-cleanliness outlined by the corners of his eyes, the middle of his forehead, his sideburns and his chin. The rest was pure smudge. His crowning glory, that shock of golden-blonde hair, was like a haystack that had been massaged by an egg beater. Although it appeared not to have been combed in a month, it had actually been only two days; but playing dirty in the woods seems to accelerate that sort of thing.

But that was just the front of him. A coating of sand from the creek bank was stuck to his entire backside, from the crown of his head to the inside of his knees. As Bill saw it, a bath was not only advisable, it was mandatory (not that Bill wasn't in need of one, himself).

"Kid, I hate to tell you this," he said, "but there are no two ways about it. You've got to have a bath, like it or not."

"I don't think I like it too well. I never was fond of freezing to death."

"You won't freeze to death. In fact, once you get used to it, you'll probably have a ball."

"Thanks a lot, but no thanks."

"Okay, let's put it this way," Bill explained. "You are covered with sand, and that stuff won't dust off. It has to be washed off. I damned sure don't want it in the trailer." The man realized, all of a sudden, that he was sounding just like a parent.

But he continued. "You've played hard and sweated hard, and so have I; and let's face it, fellow, we're both beginning to stink. Also, those cute little red skivvies of yours are probably getting pretty rancid by now; they need to be washed just like the rest of you. Besides, if I deliver you back to Houston looking like that, they'll lynch me, for sure.

"Now, as soon as we finish lunch—if you ever stop eating— I'm going to go take a bath in the creek. And so are you . . . if I have to pick you up and throw you in, and scrub your filthy hide myself."

"You're not supposed to go swimming right after a meal," the boy argued, "it gives you cramps."

"That may be so if you're out in the ocean somewhere, or trying to swim a mile across a lake. But I don't think you'll have any trouble saving yourself if you should suddenly become cramped-up in a creek fifteen feet wide."

"Is it deep enough to swim in?"

"There's a pool right out there," Bill said, pointing, "where it's about chest-deep; and it's long enough to swim twenty or thirty feet. It's refreshing, too. Look at you; you're not only filthy, but you've got sweat dripping off of you just sitting here. It's probably ninety-five degrees here in the shade. A swim will cool you off."

Buddy made no reply, as it was obvious that any future argument would be futile. He resorted to a guile that is innate in the psyches of all children from infancy to adulthood—to let his attention be distracted and his mind to wander. Sometimes, with luck, such a maneuver can result in a successful change of subject.

The youth tilted his head back to watch a large mass of voluminous white clouds racing hide-and-seek across the blue sky above the lacework screening of the trees. He wondered in which direction they were headed; and in which direction, in fact, he was headed—he and that man who had captured him and was now insisting on freezing him to death.

"Which way are those clouds going?" he asked the man.

Bill looked up. "Roughly north," he replied.

"They surely are going fast."

"I suspect that storm out there might have something to do with that."

"Are we going to get a hurricane?"

"Who knows? It's not even a hurricane yet. The news guy said it can't make up its mind which way to go. And the way those things do sometimes, that mother could fiddle around out in the Gulf for another week before it moves inland. What we *are* going to get is a bath. Now come on, let's put this stuff up and get at it."

Buddy made no reply. He was holding out hope, perhaps, that some *deus ex machina* would swoop down and save him from that frosty fate.

It didn't happen. After the lunch makings were put away, Bill brought out two towels, a bar of soap housed in a yellow plastic container, and a length of insulated telephone wire, and he placed them on the rusty metal table.

"What's that for?" the boy asked, indicating the wire.

"Clothes line, to hang up our undies."

Buddy couldn't help but smile. To hear that grizzled guy who hunts wild animals for breakfast and knows all about lion tracks and snake fangs refer to his dirty shorts as "undies" was too humorous to take without a smile, which was probably the reaction intended.

Bill climbed the bank beyond the trailer to string the wire between two pine saplings that were in the sunlight, about ten feet apart. When he returned to the trailer site, he walked over to the table and sat down on a chair to remove his shoes. Then he took off his cut-offs and his briefs, took the underwear and the soap in hand and walked naked down to the creek.

"Come on," he said, "unless you want me to come after you."

The man draped his laundry-to-be on a small yaupon bush near the creek bank and started slowly, cautiously, into the creek.

"C'mon, Buddy. The toughest part is getting in. Once you get used to it, it's no problem. And the best way to do that is all at once. *Banzai!*" And with that, he dove head-first into the small pool.

"WHOOO!" he yelled, as he came back up and onto his feet. "I won't shit you, kid, it's cold. But it feels good. Now come on in and toss me the soap. I left it right there by that bush."

Buddy strolled to the creek bank, stared at his captor in the water that he now considered to be no less chilling than the polar ice cap, and contemplated his situation. He was backed into a corner and he knew it. Childhood modesty didn't really enter into his decision; there had been enough group showers at summer camp and in the school locker room following tennis and gym classes to have allayed all that.

Expelling a deep sigh, for effect, he declared, "Oh well, what the hell!" Then he removed his shoes, jeans and underwear, with which he further decorated the creekside yaupon bush, and started tentatively into the water.

"Way to go, kid," Bill said. "Now wait just a minute before you come in and let me check it out."

"For what, snakes?"

"Yeah. And alligators. And maybe hippopotami," the man teased, "but mostly for tree limbs." He began cautiously to wade around the perimeter and criss-cross through the middle of the small creek-pool-cum-bathing-and-swimming-hole.

Buddy waited until Bill declared, at length. "It's okay, no trees. Now come on in. Remember, the best thing to do is dive in head first and get your whole body wet at once."

Easier said than done. As diving in was obviously unthinkable, Buddy inched gingerly into the water one cautious step at a time, prolonging the agony. The boy had been in the creek as deeply as his knees before, and had gotten used to it with no great difficulty; but the deeper he immersed his reluctant young body into the frigid water, the colder it seemed to get. Bill watched with his now-familiar wry, half-smile.

"No guts, huh?" he teased.

"I'm trying." The flowing stream was now lapping at the bottom of the boy's crotch.

"You get past that," the man said, pointing, "and you've got it made. But believe me, the best thing to do is just to plunge in the rest of the way and swim, to get your blood circulating."

Acceding, finally, the boy took a breath, held it, dove in and swam toward the man—thrashing frantically with his arms and legs in order to give them the most circulation-inspiring movement possible in the shortest distance. He surfaced right in front of Bill.

"Whoo-*EEE!*" he yelled. That *is* cold! Anybody for a tall, blonde Popsicle?"

"I knew you'd like it," Bill said, matter-of-factly. "Now swim around and get used to it."

Once having overcome his reluctance and the initial shock of the frigid water, it didn't take long for the boy to get fully into the spirit of things. Brutus, on the other hand, needed no coaxing at all. In short order, he had plunged in and dog-paddled his way to the frolicking boy—although he was not quite certain what to do when he got there.

Buddy solved that quandary by dashing out onto the bank, picking up a small stick and calling to the dog, "Come on, Brutus, go get it!"

Brutus got out onto the bank, shook off a small rainstorm, and waited for the boy to throw the stick. As soon as he did, Buddy dove back into the creek-pool and swam underwater until his hands touched the sandy bottom on the opposite side. Standing up, dripping, in water barely knee-deep, he glanced down at his much-contracted genitals—victims of the chill bath.

Laughingly, he observed, "My balls have disappeared."

"I lost track of mine about five minutes ago. At last report they were about here," Bill said, clutching his Adam's apple.

"Oh, oh!" the boy exclaimed, as Brutus came swimming to him with stick in mouth, and he dove back in for another underwater excursion. Brutus swam after him, puzzled, and watched to see where the boy would surface.

As the youngster continued to romp with the dog, Bill waded out of the creek, plucked their underwear off the yaupon bush, took the white bar of Ivory soap out of its plastic container and sloshed back into the not-too-sanitary-looking water. He then began methodically to work up an effective, if mediocre, lather for the two campers' laundry.

Watching the operation, Buddy asked, "Won't they take a while to dry?"

"Most likely not too long in this heat. That's why I put the clothes line up there in the sun."

"What'll we wear 'til they're dry?"

"Haven't you ever gone without underwear before?"

Buddy shook his head.

"First time for everything," Bill said.

Buddy picked up a handful of water and let it trickle through his fingers back into the creek. "This water isn't as dirty as it looks from up top. How come?"

"It's not dirty at all," Bill told him. "It's just discolored. All of the water in this creek comes from underground springs—that's why it's so cold. It's probably crystal clear when it reaches the surface from down below; but then it moves along in little streams, filtering through decaying leaves, tree bark, and all the other forest litter, and it gets discolored . . . sorta like making tea.

"The same kind of thing happens to water at the paper mill over on the Neches River. They use it in the paper-making process; and when they're through with it, they run it through all kinds of filtration plants, aeration pools and all that good stuff, until it's as pure as a virgin's kiss. But it's stained brown, a lot like this creek, and there's no way they can get that color out. They call it liquor."

"How come you know so much?" the boy asked. "Do you live around here?"

Bill shook his head. "You pay attention now and then, and sooner or later something's going to sink in."

With their skivvies now clean enough for most civilized people, Bill waded out of the water and ascended the bank behind the trailer, to hang them on the telephone wire. As he departed, he tossed the soap to the boy; but Buddy was not prepared to catch it, and the bar of Ivory splashed into the water. It surfaced promptly, then began to float away in the current.

"Check it out!" the boy exclaimed as he rescued the bar before it could get too far downstream. "It floats. I never saw soap that floats."

"It's also biodegradable, or so they say," Bill replied as he splashed back in, "and that makes it just about perfect for bathing in a country creek. What you need to do now is rub the soap over your nasty hide from top to bottom. And be sure to get your hair good and clean."

There I go, he reminded himself, *sounding like a parent again.*

As boys will do, Buddy became a mass of suds from head to toe in short order. "How's that, coach?"

"I guess it will do for starters. Now you can rinse it off . . . and hand me the soap."

Playfully, the boy offered the soap bar in a mass of suds with his outstretched hand and squeezed hard. The soap shot forward and plopped into the water, short of its target. Bill made a disapproving grimace and stooped to pick it up, as Buddy splashed back into the creek to rinse away the suds.

When he surfaced, he found Bill just beginning to disappear under his own body-load of suds. It was exactly the opportunity that the boy had been waiting for.

"I've got to visit the bathroom inside for a minute," he told Bill, then he splashed out of the creek.

The idea seemed altogether logical to Bill, who then proceeded with his bath. He took no notice whatsoever when the boy strolled back up to the trailer, picked up a pair of cut-off jeans from the metal table and walked inside. All of that was innocent enough—except that the jeans the boy retrieved were Bill's, not his own.

Buddy watched through a trailer window, waiting for an opening, while he thrust a shaking hand into the right-hand pocket of Bill's cut-offs and fished-out the man's key ring. When he saw Bill sink into the creek for a rinse, Buddy knew that it was now or never. Quickly, he was out the door and running with all possible speed toward the van, hoping with all his might that the back door would not be locked.

Luck was with him, it wasn't; and the boy hastily entered and closed the door behind him. When he looked out the back window, Bill was on the bank again; and Buddy's heart leaped into his throat.

Without even so much as a glance toward the trailer, the man stooped down, returned the bar of soap to its yellow container, and splashed back into the creek for a final rinse. To Buddy's good luck, there were only a half-dozen keys on the ring, and just two of them had the same name printed on them as the brand of the lock on the wooden chest that Bill had called a "big boy's toy box." Fumbling, nervous, he soon had the lock removed and the lid lifted; then he stared wide-eyed at the contents. There were two pistols in holsters, a pair of zippered cases that probably held other pistols, the big double-barreled shotgun that had been used on the squirrel hunt, three other long guns in cases that Buddy guessed were probably other shotguns or rifles, plus boxes and boxes of ammunition. There were also assorted targets, cleaning equipment, and other gadgetry which the boy couldn't begin to guess what they were.

He recognized one of the guns in the holsters as the pistol with which the man had shot the snake the day before. It was a single-action revolver, the type which the boy had seen used often enough in Western movies and on television to be able to figure out how it worked—at least rudimentarily.

Buddy opened the van door slowly and stepped out with caution, gun in hand. As he left the van, the kidnapper was bent over, swishing out the last suds from his hair; but the miscreant youth had managed to take only two cautious steps toward the creek when the man in the water abruptly halted the rinsing operation and raised to full height. He quickly became aware of the boy's stealthy stalk toward him.

Buddy had hoped to approach the bathing area unseen; but with his guile now obviously detected, there was no other option for him but to gut through it and walk directly to the creek. Although the rest of his slender young body remained naked and vulnerable-looking, his face was cloaked in a display of jut-jawed determination and firm resolve.

"Okay, Mister Hot-Shot Pistol-Shooter," he called as he neared the man he called Bill. "I've got the gun now."

Hoping that he was doing it right, he pulled back the hammer and heard the cylinder rotate with three clicks before it stopped—fully cocked and menacingly ready to fire.

9

Disappointed and hurt, if not terribly surprised, Bill knew that he had obviously made a grievous mistake in allowing the captive boy the freedom that he had so openheartedly given him. He had been correct in his initial reservations—he most definitely should have kept the kid in handcuffs and on the chain. He even remembered his thoughts, way back there, that Buddy could have been conning him, just waiting for his chance. And the little rich bastard had done it. He'd pulled it off. He had outwitted his kidnapper.

He had certainly played it cool—Bill had to give him credit for that—and his devious, now obvious, guile had worked to perfection. The kid had softened him up.

Bill didn't know which to be most—hurt or angry. His pride was hurt, without doubt, and so were his accursed feelings; but he was angry to the point of being furious—angry with himself. He was angry with Buddy, oh, yes—who could avoid being angry when someone whom he has befriended, and treated kindly, has turned on him? But he was even more angry at himself, at being so soft that he allowed it to happen. He had let the boy charm his way into his affection, and had dropped his guard.

But he mustn't show any of that now. Coolness was the only way out.

Bill responded to the threat by dropping back into the creek pool for yet another, unneeded rinse. When he surfaced, he shook the water from his hair, and in a continuing deliberate, studiedly casual manner, wiped it away from his eyes. Then he glared at the unclothed, pistol-wielding youth.

"Do you have any idea how silly you look?"

"I don't care," Buddy replied, as he elevated the barrel of the gun toward the sky and pulled the trigger.

The pistol barked, satisfyingly, but so loudly that it hurt his ears. As quickly as he could fumble his way through it, the boy recocked the gun and fired it into the air again. And again. He continued doing so until, on the sixth attempt, the pistol made only a click; and his ears rang.

So earnest was the youth in his determination that he half-screamed his pronouncement, "Now will you please believe that I don't want to kill you and teach me how to shoot? Please?"

From his waist-deep position in the creek, Bill replied with well-disguised relief, "My daddy taught me never to argue with a man with a gun in his hand . . . especially if he's blonde-headed, blue-eyed, and buck-ass naked."

"You mean you *will*?"

"I was planning to anyway, tomorrow."

"Hot damn!"

"Now don't get carried away," Bill admonished. "Take the gun into the trailer and put it on the bed. Then get your sneaky butt dressed."

Bill didn't know whose "sneaky butt" should be whipped— the boy's, or his own.

▼ ▼ ▼

That afternoon, Bill made good on his promise to give Buddy a second chance on the woodland badminton court, only this time he took pity on the youth and intentionally muffed enough points to let Buddy win one game outright and come within a sudden-death tie breaker of winning a second. Unaware of the charity, the boy relished his revenge upon the man whom he now delighted in calling a "creaky old fart."

The strenuous activity of the badminton brought a fresh crop of heavy sweat to both combatants—enough to necessitate another bath in the creek. Following that, Buddy learned what Bill already knew—that the chill of the creek bath would remain with them for hours if no more heavy physical labor was undertaken.

Then it was fire-building time again; and for this occasion, Bill delegated the chore entirely to his young charge, with the only instructions given him being to scrape away the past night's ashes and unburned residue before putting the ingredients into the fire hole. Buddy enjoyed the responsibility and went about it with zest, even fending off his teacher when the man offered to assist in breaking up the larger pieces of wood.

"Okay," Bill allowed, "just this: if you're going to use the axe to chop up any of the big chunks, put on some safety glasses. There's a pair in that locker you broke into in the van. You go whacking that thick stuff with an axe and there's no telling which way the pieces are going to fly—like into an eye, for instance. You wouldn't want to mess up your shooting eye before you get started, would you?"

Enough said; the boy proceeded quickly to the van. Aside from the well-presented case for getting the safety glasses, he was happy to have the opportunity to rummage around in that goodies-laden wooden chest.

"Do you think you can teach me to shoot as good as you?" he asked on return.

"As *well* as I," Bill corrected.

Chagrined, Buddy asked, "What the hell are you, some kind of goddamned English teacher too?"

"You never know," Bill replied, doing his best to imitate the countenance of Mona Lisa.

Buddy shook his head and half-muttered, "Damnedest guy!"

He did a commendable job building only his second campfire. As this, too, was to be a cooking fire, he followed the man's instructions to use only hardwoods; and after due deliberation and careful construction, he had a nice fire blazing.

"Why in the hell we need a fire in weather like this is a mystery to me," Bill observed.

The younger camper noted, "Well, if we get too hot, we can always go jump back into the creek."

"You surely did change your tune about the creek in a hurry," Bill noted.

Buddy looked up and nodded a smiling agreement, then returned to his task of putting the fire makings together, while Bill busied himself cleaning a small four-legged grill which he had retrieved, like so much else, from beneath the trailer.

"We've got to use lots of heavy stuff and let it burn down to thick coals this time," he told the boy. "We're not just going to roast weenies, we're going to cook them squir-rulls."

"You mean barbecue them?"

"Sure. Why not?"

"Whatever you say, chief."

Bill smiled his half-twisted, half-quizzical visage once again. "My, isn't the kid in good humor?"

"Yeah," the boy replied with a wrinkle in the corner of his mouth highlighted by the dark shadow of early teen mustache above it. Bill noticed that there was also a slight twist to the boy's head, in addition to a growing sparkle in his eyes.

Behind the boy, the campfire flickered; while in front of him, the waning sun set the very air aglow with a pink-orange blush that permeated the entire camp—man, boy, dog, trailer . . . everything.

Buddy was quick to notice. "What a weird light," he said. "It feels like something magic is happening."

Bill silently agreed that the boy might easily be right. The sunset glow added an almost unearthly dimension to what was a palpable warmth now radiating toward the kidnapper from the captive kid. He felt engulfed, basking in a glow of newfound admiration . . . of trust . . . and of respect. Easily, Bill feared, he could grow to like it.

▼ ▼ ▼

Day was ending in another quarter of the world as the giant Boeing 747 lifted off from the island of Oahu, leaving the swaying palm trees and shimmering grass skirts, the endlessly rolling surf and the overpriced hotels to revel in their own, individual manners in the glory of the Pacific sunset.

For the expensively dressed, middle-aged couple in the

cushy, lounge-chair seats of the first-class section, home was still a long, exhausting way off. They would stay the night in San Francisco and be whisked away on the corporate jet early the next morning. Even if they could have booked a straight-through flight from Hawaii to Houston, it would simply have been too arduous. Since their unpleasant awakening at the un-godly hour of dawn that morning, the day had already been almost too physically and emotionally trying to bear. Indeed, they had been catapulted from a relaxed, whisper-quiet, nau-tical idyll of at least two centuries past into the hurried, harsh, screaming-jet realities of the late 1980s—and all of that, for each of them, with a roaring hangover. Without doubt, life was cruel.

Neither of them felt like talking; but several important areas of consideration needed to be discussed before they confronted the ordeal awaiting them the next day in Houston, Texas.

It was Melanie who spoke first. "I think it's only proper that you should be the spokesperson when we first meet with the press, don't you?"

Her husband thought momentarily about challenging her unisex "spokesperson," but decided against it. Instead, he sim-ply nodded his agreement.

"Later, I'm sure," she continued, "there are bound to be per-sonal interviews with both the television and newspapers, and I suppose we'll both be doing those on our own."

"I suppose so," Caine agreed. "But with any luck, none of that will be necessary."

"You're not implying that we should avoid personal inter-views, are you?"

"No, my darling of the society pages, I am not implying any-thing of the sort. Far be it from me to deprive you of your hour of glory."

Testily, as she had done all day, the mother of the kidnapped youngster snapped back, "Sarcasm does not look good on you."

"Nor you either," her husband replied. "I suggest you start practicing up on your grief posture. That's probably the way you'll want to play it when we get back home."

"Well of course I'll be grieving. I'm grieving right now, aren't you? Our son has been kidnapped, for heaven's sake."

"Try keeping that in mind; and let the professionals worry about the press."

"What does that mean?"

"It means that when I called from Honolulu, I left orders for our public relations people to handle all that stuff. They will have a news conference set up at the airport when we arrive . . . in our own hangar . . . under our control."

"Oh. Well, I hope they take the precaution of having the *right* reporters there," the lady worried.

"Heaven forbid otherwise."

▼ ▼ ▼

The cooking fire there at the creekside had dwindled into glowing coals. The woodland dinner of barbecued squirrel, steamed rice and a canned vegetable had been consumed by the trio of man, boy, and oversized dog. The yaupon wiener-roasting spears had been pressed into marshmallow-toasting duty once again, and Bill was sipping pensively from a half-glass of bourbon. Overhead, beyond the quite-dark night, another brilliant display of celestial beacons was trying to infiltrate the slightly rustling tapestry of leaves overhead. The evening had slipped quietly into night, and the mood was pensive, meditative—a time given to personal, private reflections.

It might have been that the quiet thoughts of the two campers were on each other when the man glanced up to find the boy gazing intently at him. Self-consciously, both hastily shifted their stares back into the depths of the glowing coals; but for Buddy, at least, the thoughts would not change. The inexplicable kindness in the man's eyes continued to dance in his mind.

Shifting his thinking, Buddy tried to recall the color of his father's eyes, and he was puzzled by the realization that he couldn't do so, he didn't know their color. As he stared directly into the glowing coals, he could still feel and see Bill's quickly averted gaze—the warm, dark, puppy-brown eyes of his kidnapper; but try as he would, the boy could not visualize the eyes of his own father. He was further puzzled to think that he wished that he could. Better, he thought, to concentrate on the subject at hand.

Buddy finished off his fourth toasted dessert from the end of the yaupon spear and broke the silence. "Bill."

"Mm?"

"I love it here."

"Me too, kid. I love it too."

For both of them, that seemed to say it all for the moment, and each slipped back into his own, private, fire-staring meditation.

So quiet was their mood that one could likely have heard a daydream stirring when, with the startling suddenness of a thunderclap crashing out of a cloudless sky, their tranquil scene was ripped wide open by the most heart-stilling, sphincter-shrinking, wild animal scream native to the North American continent—or maybe anywhere. It lingered on a steady note for a long few seconds, then tapered down to a thunderous silence.

Buddy froze, transfixed, while Bill leaped to his feet and dashed for the back door of the van. He fished quickly into his armament case, snatched his .45 caliber automatic from its holster, grabbed a large, six-volt flashlight, and attempted to dash back out the door. But that was impossible; the exit was blocked by the catatonic posture of a blonde-mopped kid with eyes that were now pie-plates of pure terror.

"Wh-what was it? What **WAS** that?" the boy stammered.

"Let me out, get out of my way!" was the only reply. When the terrified boy stepped aside, Bill raced out into the night, shining the light in quickly sweeping arcs around the perimeter of the campsite and into the trees. The beam landed on Brutus; and Bill could see the hair on the back of the dog's neck standing straight up as he emitted a deep, low growl. Buddy remained on the trailer doorstep.

"I don't see him," Bill said. He returned back to his fireside chair, sat down, and placed the big pistol in his lap. "Keep your eyes open, Brutus."

"You don't see what? What was that noise?" the boy demanded.

"That, my little buddy, was our friend who makes the big paw prints in the sand."

"**THE COUGAR?** That was the **COUGAR?**"

"The very one," Bill replied. "Or one of his relatives."

"What will he do? Sh-shouldn't we go into the trailer? He sounded like he was right here with us."

"You can go into the trailer if you like, but I don't think he'll bother us . . . especially not with Brutus here."

"Can Brutus whip a cougar?"

"Most likely not, but the cougar doesn't know that. They're mostly shy by reputation, anyhow, and as scared of dogs as any other cat."

"That thing didn't sound too shy to me," Buddy argued.

"Oh, most likely he was just bitchin' at us, because we're here."

"Well he sure made his point."

"Yep. He certainly did do that. That was some kind of scream, wasn't it?"

"Holy shit!" the boy exclaimed, sinking finally into the chair next to Bill. "That really freaked me out!" There was a serious, sober and concerned look on his face that Bill had never seen before.

"That's the first time I ever heard one," Bill said. "And you should consider yourself privileged, kid. I doubt that many people in this country of ours will ever be hearing the likes of it again."

Excited by the event, Bill turned analytical. "I've read about them and what a horrifying noise they can make; and I can tell you, after that one, that there's no way that anyone can describe just how hairy a sound that really is. Some say it's like a woman screaming. Not that one. That was like a high-voiced man with lots of vocal strength—an operatic tenor, maybe—in mortal terror . . . like he's just about to get hit by a train. No, that was no woman's scream; that had balls to it . . . in large quantity."

Buddy suddenly connected. "The first night I was here I heard something in my sleep. It sounded far away; but I was so deep asleep that it didn't register, and I forgot about it. But I think that's what it was. I heard him before."

Smiling wryly again, Bill asked, "Do you still love it here?"

"I think I'll love it a lot more after I learn how to shoot," the boy replied, in dead earnest. "How long do you think it will be before the hair stops standing up on the back of your neck?"

"Maybe by morning," Bill replied, "if you sleep on it hard enough. What I need now is another drop of nerve medicine," and he reached for the glass of whiskey, of which he had absolutely no recollection setting down on the metal table.

"Can I have some too?"

"No, you can not."

"Just thought I'd ask."

In very short order, the boy began to realize just how tired he really was. It had been a terrific day, but his young body now called for rest. "When do you want to go to bed?" he asked.

"I think it's a pretty good idea right along about now," Bill replied, as he slugged down the last few sips of bourbon. "We've got to straighten up, first. Do you want to clean off the table and take the dishes inside, or would you rather go up and get our pajamas off the line?"

"Up there?" Buddy asked, glancing into the lion-infested darkness above the trailer. "I think I'll take care of the dishes."

"Good thinking," Bill said, as he took the .45 in hand and headed off to retrieve their creek-washed skivvies.

Kitchen duties received a short shrift that evening. In the woods, dirty dishes can always wait until tomorrow. It wasn't long before the two companions had brushed their teeth and slipped into their clean underwear.

"Do I have to wear the bracelet tonight?" the boy pleaded.

"No bracelet tonight . . . or ever again."

Buddy gave his friend a thumbs-up signal and plopped into his bunk. Bill was not far behind in his fold-down bed, and soon the trailer was in darkness—darkness and plenty of heat. The weather seemed to be growing progressively more overbearing by the hour. Outside, it was not so noticeable in the cooling effect that constantly emanated from the nearby creek; but inside the trailer, with its scant few (and small at that) windows, the air was heavy . . . humid . . . hot . . . and oppressive.

"Let me know if you need another blanket," Bill said.

"Yeah, sure will."

"We can haul our mattresses outside and sleep under the stars, if you like."

"Thanks a lot," the boy replied, thinking of cougar screams and the like, "but no thanks."

"Probably too many mosquitoes, anyhow. Right?"

"Yeah . . . mosquitoes."

There were no mosquitoes inside the trailer, though. Nor cougars. Just a couple of very tired, but uncomfortably warm guys. Buddy promptly convinced himself that even his abbreviated little bikini briefs were too much clothing to bear; so in the spirit of Camp Rio Alto, and a rollicking part of the just-ending day, he slipped them off and stuffed them into a corner of the bed.

What the heck, he thought, *Bill won't care.*

Bill had his own problems—recurring ones. As he lay motionless on his suspended bed in the stifling heat, he felt a rivulet of sweat trickle into the pouch of his newly washed briefs. And he thought of Louise.

Futilely, he wished that he could stifle his thoughts, as he began to recall when the sweat-trickling sensation had been reversed, top to bottom. He was belly-down, with Louise beneath him, and similar rivulets of perspiration trickled from his love-steamed body onto that of his pretty young bride.

It was July, and they were camped a dozen or so miles up the beach, north, from the overstuffed condominiums and pretentious resort hotels on South Padre Island, off the southern tip of Texas.

July . . . and the hot, steady breeze off the Gulf of Mexico flushed through the too-high mesh window on one side of their tent and out the other, providing essentially zero cooling effect for the young married couple writhing sweat-soaked atop an air mattress on the canvas floor.

July . . . and droplets of water collected on the mesh windows as that humidity-laden hot breeze passed through, while the whistling of the wind and the roar of the surf combined to drown the sounds of passion inside the tent.

Vividly, as in a dream, Bill could see himself, the young

husband, raise his supple body to maximum possible extension. When he lowered, it was at times slow and deliberate, and at other times sharp and quick. And his pounding *huevos* dripped sweat.

And they would hurt—just as, now, they were beginning to ache in their sweat-soaked cotton cocoon in his creekside trailer in the woods. Only the present ache was not from pounding, but from unwanted excitation and deprivation.

Louise, he thought wistfully, *how that woman could screw.*

It had been a glorious time, that camping trip to the island. They made love so much that he didn't know whether he would have the strength to break camp when it came time to leave.

Inside the tent. In the heat. In July.

But outside the tent—oh yes, they did it outside, as well. Vividly, again, Bill could see the two of them rolling around, coupled in complete conjunction atop the wet sand at water's edge—with occasional ripples of the surf, in its dying gasps, lapping at their toes and ankles. Then they lay drained after it was over, until the incoming tide forced them away from their sunburning, supine repose and into the water for a bracing skinny-dip in the surf.

Yes, by God, Bill recalled to himself, with increasing pain, *we even did it in the surf! Now that took concentration.*

He agonized, *Yes, oh yes. She could never make it as a wife; but oh, how that woman could screw.*

In fact, the auburn-haired lady did it so well, and with such aplomb and obvious enjoyment, that the pair continued having sex together even after their divorce. That no-strings-attached activity continued for nearly two years after the final decree, until that night in October, Bill recalled, when he stood forever ringing the doorbell at her apartment with a bottle of *Pouilly-Fuissé* in one hand and a single red rose in the other. But the doorbell was never answered. He later learned that she had run off with a rock band—not just one member, the entire band.

Rolling over onto his stomach, in effort to stifle the pangs of celibacy, Bill pleaded to himself, *Memories, please go away.*

But the maneuver did no good at all, and the plea fell on deaf ears. Instead of the surcease for which he longed, his nocturnal reminiscences shifted into high gear; and that meant the most bittersweet memories of them all: Marie-Claire.

Delicious. That was the only word the now-anguished man could come up with when thinking of Marie-Claire. It was not the right word, because it said nothing of their love, nor of the emptiness after he had gone.

She was petite. Dark, like Bill. With straight, raven-black hair and a slender, delicately sculptured face that was dominated by the most hauntingly beautiful pair of dark, sensitive-brown eyes in the entire history of the universe.

Marie-Claire. She was uneducated. Uncultured. She would be totally out of place on a gentleman's arm at the symphony or the opera. She wouldn't have had the slightest idea what to do with a finger bowl or a dessert spoon. But her love was as real as the poverty of the southern Louisiana swamp country from which she had sprung, and as unbridled as a busload of high school football players turned loose in the New Orleans French Quarter.

Marie-Claire. Brought-up near the tiny community of Breaux Bridge, she had migrated to the larger town of Lafayette at a tender, fragile, sixteen years of age to make it the best she could—because, indeed, nothing could have been much worse than the wrenchingly poor, inclined-to-incest, catfish-and-cornbread existence from which she came.

The girl from Breaux Bridge had landed a job waiting tables at the *Mon Cher* Cajun restaurant, and it was there that he had found her. And she had found him. And together they had found a bliss, the likes of which the airplane pilot from Houston had seen only a hint of in his short and unfulfilling marriage.

As his independent float-plane flying business had grown and prospered there, in the heyday of the petroleum industry, so had their love affair. Living together in a comfortable, but somehow fittingly ramshackle little cabin not far from the Lafayette airport, the lovers shared each other's lives and passions, never demanding any kind of commitment or promise beyond the pleasures, the boundless love, and the always-intense lovemaking of the moment.

She worked until ten o'clock or later every night—flirting, he knew, with everything in pants that entered the restaurant. She considered it part of her job. But Bill knew that in spite of all that, and whatever may have transpired before they met, she saved herself for him. Her love was his alone.

Twice, sometimes three times a night, she wanted his loving. Being from the bayou country, she was firmly convinced of the power of raw oysters to increase a man's sexual prowess. Therefore, almost every night, she would bring home with her a pint of shelled oysters and a container of the tangy, hot, red-sauce from the *Mon Cher.*

Playfully, one night, she reasoned that if oysters, ingested, could increase sexual productivity, then their residue, applied topically, should perform equally as well—thereby doubling the desired effect. Thus was born the most glorious, decadent, and delicious love ritual the man now known as Bill had ever experienced.

He wanted not to think about it, lying sleepless there in the woods and unable to do anything about the emotional swelling that the recollection always brought within him; but he remained helpless in the onslaught of rapidly unreeling memory.

After she had hand-fed the oysters to him, Marie-Claire—fragile, delicate love-partner that she was—took a handful of the oily liquor from the cardboard pint and massaged it generously onto, into, and around her lover's genitals. Then she licked off the oyster residue, sending him as close as anyone ever came into absolute ecstasy.

Bill's loving response was to devise "The Annabel Lee." Marie-Claire was always moved by the beauty of the Edgar Allan Poe classic, and she never tired of hearing him recite it—though she never heard the poem in its entirety.

"It was many and many a year ago," he would recite, then plant a kiss gently on her neck.

"In a kingdom by the sea" . . . kiss on her right breast.

"That a maiden there lived" . . . kiss on the left breast.

"Whom you may know by the name of Annabel Lee" . . . and he'd kiss her gently on the navel.

As he moved through the verses, he moved his kisses, likewise, onto all parts of her body—from the top of her twisting head to the tips of her tingling toes.

> And this maiden she lived with no other thought
> Than to love and be loved by me.
>
> I was a child and *she* was a child,
> In this kingdom by the sea,
> But we loved with a love that was more than love—
> I and my Annabel Lee—
> With a love that the winged seraphs of heaven
> Coveted her and me.

But he never finished the poem. He feared that the delicate, emotionally fragile Marie-Claire—whom he, too, loved with a love that was more than love—could not handle the tragedy of the wind blowing out of the cloud by night, chilling and killing Annabel Lee. So he simply never got that far. Thus, to her, it remained a beautiful love poem—nothing more.

By the time he reached the point where the winged seraphs of heaven were doing their coveting, his kisses had reached the velvet-smooth inside of her thighs, and his own beautiful, young love-mate was writhing in anticipation of the feature activity.

And he missed her. Lord, how he missed her!

It was no wind blowing out of a cloud, but the ill economic wind that blew about the demise of the oil and gas industry—as he and thousands of others had known it—that brought a halt to his brief, passionate life with Marie-Claire. Bankrupt and near destitution, foreclosed-on and evicted from the lovenest of his home, he simply disappeared one night—no longer able to face his fragile, sweet, beloved as a failure. And he hated himself ever after for doing it.

As he stared into the darkness of the trailer, the veil of sleep at last began to cloud-over his troubled consciousness; and his receding thoughts whispered silently, from the long-felt loneliness within him, his own paean to performances past:

Marie-Claire, from Breaux Bridge fair
I kiss your eyes, I kiss your hair.
I search for some new place to kiss you,
Marie-Claire, how much I miss you.

When sleep finally overcame, it found the loving-starved kid-napper with his pillow clamped tightly between his thighs, and his mind entwined in doggerel.

▼ ▼ ▼

In his bunk across the room, Bill's young captive had no such reminiscences to trouble him. His were only the vestal begin-nings of the urges that racked the mind and body of his former captor, and they gave the youth no problem that sultry night. His mind was filled with excitement of a different sort.

As he lay waiting for sleep to come, Buddy reflected on the day . . . and what a day it had been! What sights he had seen; what sounds he had heard; and what fun he had had!

Reconstructing the day chronologically, he remembered the pink cloud that had floated above them as they sat leaning against the oak tree that dark and early morning, getting their rear ends soaked with dew . . . the squirrels floating, sailing, flying through the trees. He recalled the physical shock as he plunged for the first time into the chill of the creek. What a gang of fun it had been running around naked, free, unin-hibited—wild as a savage. What a good sport Bill was. What a heckuva guy to be in the woods with. And what a helluva fright when that cougar let go with its scream; and how cool Bill was in response. Buddy felt that with anyone else around, he would have run into the trailer, locked the doors and windows, crawled under the bed and stayed there for the next week. Only with Bill did he feel safe.

Yes, what a day it had been; how could he ever top it? Easy. Tomorrow, Bill was going to teach him to shoot.

Hurry up sleep and hurry by night, this boy can't wait until tomorrow.

10

"Come on yourself," the man mumbled aloud. He had been deeply asleep, and was awakened by his own muttering. Straining to clear his head, he recalled that in his sleep—perhaps it was a dream—someone was hollering, "Come on!"

As his eyes began to focus, Bill realized that it was full daylight outside. His sheets were damp with sweat from the long, hot sleep. If the weather had ever cooled during the night, any pleasantness was rapidly slipping away—at least inside the trailer. He glanced over at the boy's bunk. Empty.

That recognition shocked him into full wakefulness, and he jumped out of his suspended mattress onto the trailer floor, grabbed at his watch on the couch-side table below, and found that it was almost eight o'clock. He had grossly overslept!

Bill quickly pulled on his cut-off jeans, slipped into his sneakers and stepped out the door. The weather was a little better outside, though not terribly much.

But where was the boy? There was no sign of Brutus, either. The dog would normally have been stretching and waddling up, waggle-tailed, for a morning greeting; but now, there was no sign of him.

Ultimately, he heard a faint call. "Brutus . . . come on!" It was the same "Come on," to which he had replied in his sleep, coming from somewhere in the vicinity of the creek; but neither boy nor dog were in view. Walking down to the water to investigate, he heard Buddy's faint voice once again—unintelligible this time, but definitely from upstream.

Bill had to round two bends in the stream before he located them. Clad in his cut-offs and once-white leather athletic shoes, Buddy was sitting against a sweetgum tree adjacent to the creek bank, tossing the spine-encrusted seedball droppings from the tree to Brutus and trying to entice the dog to retrieve them. But Brutus, as much as he loved the retrieving game, was having nothing to do with the tosser's multiple-needled sweetgum balls.

Bill called to the boy, "What in the bloody hell do you think you're doing?"

At the call, Brutus ran to his owner for a morning pat.

Buddy answered, holding up one of the sweetgum balls, "Mostly nothing. Brutus doesn't like these things."

"Do you realize how easy it would be for you to get your precious little ass lost wandering off alone like this?"

"I guess I didn't really think about it," the boy replied.

"Well, you'd better start thinking about it. It just wouldn't fit into my plans at all to have to bring out a search party to find you."

Buddy could see that his friend was genuinely concerned. "I'm sorry," he said. "I was just goofing off. I didn't mean to worry you."

The surrogate father continued to chastise. "Well don't do it again. You don't know what you're doing in these woods. You could have wandered just a couple of dozen yards away from this creek and been totally lost. I don't know whether you have a good sense of direction or not; but look up, there's no sun to guide you. Get out of sight of the creek and you'll get so totally confused that you could wander around in circles for a week and never know where the hell you were."

"There was sun when I came out here."

"How long have you been out?"

"I don't know. I kinda feel like time doesn't mean anything right now. And I like it."

"Was the sun up when you left the trailer?" Bill asked.

"No. I wanted to see it rise again. That's why I came out."

Bill couldn't help himself. Reaching out and tousling the

boy's tangled blonde head, he said, "You're a helluva kid, you know it?"

Still seated against the tree trunk, the "helluva kid" looked up at the man whom he now wanted to please—whether either of them knew it or not—more than anything else in the world. "Is that good or bad?"

Bill recognized the ambiguity of his comment. He relaxed a little, smiled and replied, "I guess that depends on the circumstance."

Buddy smiled back; he didn't really need an answer. "You're not pissed-off with me?"

Bill had been more upset at finding the boy missing than he cared to admit. With Buddy's unexpected show of contrition, he was moved to an even greater depth of feeling than he was willing to allow; and he had to act quickly to stifle it. His best antidote was mock gruffness.

Offering his hand to help the youth off the ground, he half-growled, "Come on, you little shit, you've got a lot to learn."

"Like what?" the eager pupil asked as he jumped to his feet.

"Like . . . like . . ." The man was fumbling, perturbed by the tug-of-war of his own emotions. "You just don't go off in the woods without a knife. It's a cardinal rule. Carrying a pistol is not a bad idea, but a knife is a must-have."

It was weak, but it was the best he could think of to say.

"But I don't have a knife."

"Come on, we'll fix that right now."

"All *right*!" the lad agreed; and they started walking the creek bank back to camp.

"Aren't you hungry?" Bill asked en route.

"I guess you could say so."

"Well, I darned sure am. And if I don't get some coffee pretty soon, I'm going to turn to stone. Do you want your name in the pot?"

"What pot?" The boy didn't understand the expression.

"The coffee pot. Do you want some coffee?"

"Sure, sure I do. And some bacon . . . and eggs . . . and pancakes . . . and waffles . . . and fried squirrels and gravy . . ."

"For a guy who was noncommittal about breakfast, you surely dreamed up an appetite right quick."

"Whatever," the boy responded, with equal noncommittance.

Back at the campsite, Bill led the way immediately to the green van and into the now-unlocked equipment box.

"One knife for a punk kid," he announced. "Coming up." He extracted a moderately long, black-sheathed weapon from the foot locker and told the boy, "Unfasten your belt and pull it out. Do you want to wear it on your right side or your left?"

"I don't know, I never wore one before. What do you think?"

"I think the left; you wear your pistol holster on the right."

That settled, Buddy threaded his belt into the loop of the knife sheath and back through the remaining belt loops of his pants, buckled his belt, then extracted the sharply edged instrument with extreme care.

"Awesome knife!" he exclaimed.

The blade was six inches long, hollow-ground and slender, with a gently curving upsweep to the tip that started an inch and a half back from the point.

"Truly awesome," he continued. "How come you don't wear this one? Man, this is cool."

Bill extracted his ever-present knife from its sheath at his waist. "This one is just handier," he said, "because of the folding blade. When it comes to actually using the knife, I prefer the one you have. It's lighter, and I think it holds an edge a little better. But it's so long, hanging from my belt, that it gets in the way when I'm sitting down—driving a car, in a chair, on the ground, whatever. My trusty fold-up here is just handier."

Examining the now-unfolded, folding model proffered handle first by the man, Buddy decided, "I like them both."

"So do I. Later on, maybe, I'll show you how to take care of them. For right now, just hang onto it. Keep the flap snapped and don't play around with it. It'll cut your finger off quicker than you can say 'ouch.'"

Inside the trailer again, Bill was putting the coffee pot on the stove as Buddy, predictably, completely ignored the admonition not to play with the knife. The man knew better, of course; it is an absolute impossibility to hand a kid a beautiful, shiny implement like that and expect him to keep it in its sheath, unfondled.

Seated at the dining booth, Buddy cautiously ran his index finger along the top side of the blade and asked, "Why is it curved like this?"

"That's for skinning. That one is a general purpose knife, really. An actual skinning knife—that is, one that's made for that purpose only—is almost totally curved, because you have to make a curving motion with the knife as you draw it along the skin next to the meat. If the blade were straight, you'd have to just hack at it; and that ain't too neat."

"I have a friend who has one that's probably twice this big. But it's all dull-looking, and not nearly this sharp. He calls it a 'survival weapon.'"

"I bet it has a serrated edge on top, and maybe a compass in the handle?"

"Right."

"Yeah, I'm familiar with those," Bill noted. "They're nothing but jerk-off toys as far as I'm concerned, for people who want to fantasize about jungle survival, hand-to-hand combat, and that sort of crap. They might be okay if you have to go one-on-one with a Bengal tiger, but the tiger would still win. And I'd hate like hell to have to gut-out and skin a deer with one."

Buddy chuckled, noting to himself that Bill did have a colorful way of explaining things. "Wait 'til I tell him his knife's a jerk-off toy," he said. "You should have been a teacher."

"Spare me. Now make yourself and that knife useful," Bill said, handing Buddy a tube of packaged ground sausage from the refrigerator. "Slice off a half-dozen or so chunks of this, peel off the covering and put them into the skillet. Then you may have the honor of tending to them while I make pancakes."

"Sounds like a deal to me." And the boy set out earnestly at his assigned task.

Buddy had never enjoyed breakfast more. Preparations over the propane stove quickly overheated the tiny trailer, so they moved outside to the rusty metal table to eat. It would be unkind to report the quantity of pancakes that the boy consumed (something on the order of eight or ten—but they were small ones, after all) along with great slatherings of heated, maple-flavored syrup, four pieces of sausage, a large glass of milk, and a bracing, hot cup of Bill's *café au lait*.

During breakfast, the pair could almost feel the weather growing more leaden by the moment. Even as close as they were to the constant cooling that radiated from the creek, they could feel the atmospheric squeeze play from the heat and humidity, as though the two of them were caught inside a giant hydraulic pressure cylinder. In addition, the air was deadly still. Bill recognized the weather syndrome.

"I'm afraid somebody around here is going to get that storm," he said.

"How do you know?" Buddy asked.

"Can't you feel it? Feel how still it is. I bet the barometer is starting to fall off the scale."

"I guess it is a little stuffy. Does that mean we're getting a hurricane?"

"No, but we're getting a good chance at it. We'll check the radio in a minute and see what they have to say. Maybe they'll also tell us if your folks got back to town."

Buddy preferred not to think about his ultimate return to Houston. Changing the subject, he asked, "When am I going to get to shoot the guns?"

"After we clean up the dishes, Buddy; so let's get after it."

There was no radio news broadcast to be had while the clean-up chores were in progress. The time was twenty minutes after ten, and Bill figured the next pronouncements would probably not be until eleven; and he'd be damned if he would listen to that irritating so-called music until the hour. While brushing his teeth, he noticed in the bathroom mirror that he was badly in need of a shave; and he said so to his eager-to-go-shooting young companion.

"Come on now," Buddy pleaded, "I don't want to have to wait for you to shave."

"Okay, I'll make you a deal," Bill said. "I won't shave now if, when I do, you'll do something about that crop of peach fuzz

along with me." He rubbed a finger across the heavy shadow
above the boy's upper lip.

Buddy was delighted to be noticed. "Whatever you say,
chief."

"Okay, sport. Now what do you want to shoot—rifle, shotgun, or pistol?"

"All of them."

"Okay, I asked for that. What do you want to shoot first?"

"Whatever you say, chief."

"Seems to me I've heard that somewhere. Well . . . shotgun
is the easiest, but it might knock you on your ass and make you
gun-shy forever. Pistol is unquestionably the most difficult; so
that means we're going to start you off with a .22 rifle. That
sound good enough?"

"Whatever you say, chief." Buddy could not resist running
that line by one more time.

"Shut up, you sound like a broken record."

▼ ▼ ▼

Every man should have the opportunity to teach a youngster
how to shoot. Bill soon learned that there is very little that is
quite as rewarding as to witness the thrill—actually to experience it with him—when a kid first cracks off and pops a half-
dozen tin cans with a .22 rifle at a dozen yards or so. Soft drink
and beer cans have a most satisfying way of jumping off the
ground, particularly if they are hit a trifle low, and they never
fail to delight a kid when they do so. Buddy proved quite adept
at the shooting game, which brought even more delight to his
teacher.

The rifle that Bill had selected was nothing less than perfect
for the purpose. It was a replica of the pump-actioned
Winchesters that had been used for decades in shooting galleries
around the world, with literally millions of rounds of ammunition having been expended down their abbreviated barrels. The
rifle had an exposed hammer, so that an inexperienced youth
could tell exactly whether or not it was cocked and ready to
shoot; and it held fifteen rounds of long-rifle ammunition in its

magazine tube, providing plenty of highly entertaining rapid fire by a simple, short, stroke of the pump after each shot. Purchased to fit Bill's former wife, the rifle was short enough that a child smaller than Buddy would have no trouble handling it, yet not too small for a grown man to shoot with accuracy and pleasure. Young Hamilton Caine, Jr., fell immediately and everlastingly in love with it.

Bill explained the rudiments of sight picture, breath control, and trigger squeeze, taking care all the while not to make the lesson sound like a science lecture. Those fine points could be stressed in more detail later on, when they got around to handling a pistol. The important point, at the beginning, was to let the kid have some success in the shooting, and to have some fun along with it. Buddy did both—in spades.

From just popping cans in front of the trailer, the shooters moved down to the creek for a little more serious exercise with targets, which Bill placed across the stream so that the creek bank would serve as a safe bullet backstop. As do most kids, Buddy preferred plinking at the cans. Targets are too unyielding. They tend to blare a shooter's poor shots back into his face, pointing a finger and clucking, "shame on you." Besides—they never, ever, jump off the ground when they are properly hit. With a tin can, a miss is a miss—no finger pointing. And even a poor hit can send one careening away proclaiming to the world that it has been mortally wounded.

Bill insisted, nonetheless, on at least a modest quantity of pure target work. How else, he explained, can a shooter know where his shots are really going? It was with targets that the instructor demonstrated the various shooting positions—prone, with legs spread widely apart, kneeling and sitting.

To Buddy, as with most kids, it was all fun; just as long as he was allowed to shoot a lot—with not too much emphasis at the moment, thank you, on doing everything exactly right.

"I shouldn't do this—and I won't allow but a little of it—but here," Bill said, tossing a beer can into the flowing creek. "Try to sink it."

Delighted to oblige, Buddy pumped bullet after bullet into and in the vicinity of the can as the current carried it downstream. It sank satisfyingly out of sight after the third or fourth hit.

"Try not to step on that the next time you go swimming," he told the boy. "Let's go farther downstream and you can try a couple more."

After two more cans were scuttled, to the future disgust of whoever might be so unfortunate as to tread on them, Bill declared a halt to the can-sinking and forced his pupil to try some more difficult targets—twigs and sticks, floating.

Of those, Buddy hit a few and missed a lot, as was to be expected. His instructor, naturally, had to show off a bit, and he managed to break in half a small tree-stick—maybe five inches long and about as big around as a man's ring finger—with a few rapidly pumped rounds of fire as it floated quickly by near the middle of the stream.

As they searched the banks for suitable target material, a peculiar-looking tree caught Bill's eye, and he motioned Buddy over to look at it. It was a rather small specimen, with a trunk only about six inches in diameter. Its entire surface was dotted with knobby protuberances, most of which were topped with sharply pointed, clawlike thorns.

"Have you ever seen one of these?" he asked the boy.

"No, but I'd sure hate to bump into it in the middle of the night," Buddy replied, fingering one of the vicious-looking claws. "What is it?"

"It has a proper scientific name that I don't remember, but the Indians used to call it a toothache tree."

"Toothache tree?"

"Right. That's because it has a built-in pain killer in its bark. Have you ever had a dentist deaden your gums or a sore tooth with Novocain?"

"Yeah, it feels weird."

"Well, a bite of this bark will do the same thing." Bill took out his knife and sliced off a small piece of bark, carefully scraped away the outer portion, and handed it to Buddy. "Here, stick this in your mouth next to your gum and suck on it for a bit. You'll see."

At such a suggestion two days previous, Buddy would likely

have responded with an alternate proposal as to just where the man could stick his hunk of tree bark. But by now, he had become so enamored of his captor's woods prowess that he would probably have spread moose dung on his lips to prevent sunburn if Bill had told him to; so he did exactly as the man said.

Presently, the boy exclaimed, "Wow, I don't believe it! The whole side of my face is going numb. It really is a toothache tree."

"Paleface boy learn quick. Now I hit you in mouth and you no feel it. Okay?"

"Not okay. But man, that blows my mind! It's just like that stuff the dentist gives you, only he uses a needle."

"There's a legend that the toothache tree can do something else, too; but I can't swear to that," Bill said.

"What's that?"

"Well, according to the legend, there were two Indian tribes way back there—both of them large and powerful—that were having it out in a long, drawn-out war over some kind of territorial dispute or something. Two large war parties—one from each of those two proud, fierce tribes—met somewhere around here in the Big Thicket. Could have been right here where we're standing, because it's said they came together on the banks of a small stream.

"They were all sneakin' through the woods, silently knocking each other off with arrows and spears as the war parties of each tribe picked their way carefully through the thicket. The young son of one of the chiefs, too young to be a brave, caught an arrow right in the gut. He was just a kid, no more than eleven or twelve years old. Well . . . that arrow came from the bow of the other chief, and he was overcome with compassion when he watched his enemy chief pick up the dying boy and carry him to the stream to commit him to the Great Spirit. Watching all this, the chief who had shot the arrow threw down his bow and his spear and stepped out of his hiding place.

"With no weapons, he knelt at the side of the boy, who had been placed right alongside one of these claw-covered toothache trees. The chief broke off one of the claws, put it between the fingers of the dying boy, and held it firmly—while he used the claw, in the boy's hand, to cut his own wrist. Then he held his bleeding wrist against the arrow wound he had inflicted in the boy . . . you know, the old ceremonial bit about making him his blood brother.

"But the claw of the toothache tree did more than that. As he knelt there on the creek, not just the blood, but the entire spirit—the soul—of that chief flowed into the body of the boy. The chief, himself, died right there; but the boy lived, and it ended their fighting forever. With not only the blood of the other chief, but his spirit as well, the boy grew up to be the greatest chief of them all, as head of the two combined Indian tribes.

"And so the legend goes that if you break the skin of another with the barb of a toothache tree, you will capture his spirit; and the two spirits—your two souls—will live forever as one."

The boy stared blankly at the storyteller, who sensed that old Indian legends, somehow, are lost on the younger generation.

Rubbing the side of his face, Buddy asked, "When will I get some feeling back into it?"

"Oh . . . maybe by Christmas."

"Thanks. I can hardly wait."

"Let's go back to camp, now, before you shoot up all my .22 bullets. I didn't have but five hundred to begin with."

On the way back, Buddy collected the targets that he had drilled from across the creek and asked, "Can I keep these?"

The two exchanged glances and both realized, simultaneously, that there was no way the boy could retain a memento of their stay together. Their relationship would have to be broken off completely, and the time at which that must happen was rapidly approaching.

Again, just as they had done on that long-ago afternoon when Bill released his captive from the handcuffs and the chain around the tree, their eyes reflected tacit, mutual understanding and agreement. Buddy blinked rapidly a couple of times and bit his lower lip; but neither spoke. Bill shook his head, put his arm around the boy's shoulders and gave him a quick squeeze; and they walked voicelessly back to camp.

Agent Owen Verlin did not like airplane hangars. That was not entirely unreasonable, because he didn't like airplanes, either. Not looking at them; not standing beside them; and especially not flying in them. They frightened him, and there were no two ways about it. He had managed to mask his fear throughout his entire eleven years of service with the FBI; but he still was unable to keep it from himself.

Having just endured a flight into Houston from the New Orleans office, to aid in the now nationally known kidnapping case, he was back among airplanes again, in the Houston Intercontinental Airport hangar of Texas Consolidated Utilities Corporation—headquarters for that company's aviation division. His mission was to question everyone there, to determine whether anyone recognized the composite drawing of the kidnapper, as recalled by Jimmy Jamison. But there was no getting out of that hangar too soon, as far as Verlin was concerned.

It was to no great surprise that he found no one who could recognize the picture. If the kidnapper had been an employee of that department, he learned, it would not likely have been within the past three and a half years, since that was the longest tenure of anyone there—at least among those he interviewed. Blame it on Verlin's deeply ingrained aerophobia; but if the truth ever came out, it would show that he missed a couple of mechanics who were chasing elsewhere after parts, and another employee who was deeply enmeshed in the supply room at the time of the agent's visit. The three, together, had a total of twenty-five years of service in the same location and positions. Among them, they knew everyone who had come and gone within that hangar's operations for the last ten years at least—including all the pilots. They lasted in their jobs, undoubtedly, because they never encountered the president of the corporation.

Except for those three, however, Verlin's information and analysis were correct, which is why he later reported to Henry Wilson that no one stayed in the Texas Consolidated aviation division for very long, because everyone in the place appeared to hate the esteemed Mr. Hamilton Caine.

"Furthermore," Verlin told Wilson, "the feeling seems to be prevalent throughout the company."

"You mean downtown, too?" Wilson asked.

"Absolutely. That's where I started."

"Then the grudge theory isn't such a bad one after all?"

"Not a bad theory, no," Verlin replied. "Certainly wouldn't be hard to find one—sorta like trying to find someone in Poland who hated Hitler."

"But someone with a hearing loss, like from constant noise of heavy machinery. Like airplanes."

An uncomfortable feeling came over Verlin. Wilson had said the magic word, "airplanes"; and he could see himself being sent back to that airport hangar, which was where he decidedly did not want to go. Maybe, he thought, he could weaken that theory.

"How the hell could they determine the guy had lost his hearing from just a few words over the telephone in a phony accent?" he asked.

"A *slight* hearing loss was all they said," Wilson replied.

"Okay, then, a *slight* hearing loss."

"Who are we to argue with the wizards in Washington and their omniscient, omnipotent computers? They detected something in the vocal timbre, I guess—hell, I don't know. Maybe it was a wavering of some sort; maybe it was pitched a little loud, with a little more punch from the diaphragm than from someone with normal hearing. One guess is that it could have shown an abnormal level of irritation on the vocal chords, as if the guy forced the volume of his speech. You know how it is with people who are hard of hearing. They seem to shout all the time.

"I remember going to a convention of the National Rifle Association one time," Wilson continued. "There was a big exhibit hall there to show off all the latest in shooting equipment and the like; but there was something sort of strange about the atmosphere that I couldn't put my finger on right away. Finally, I realized what it was—those people there, most of them old-time shooters, were all shouting at each other. At least it sounded that way to me; to them, I suppose, it was normal."

Verlin got the idea. "You mean they were shouting because they were all hard of hearing."

"Exactly."

Inwardly, Verlin breathed a sigh of relief. He had found the out that he was looking for—something to get away from the idea of airplanes. "Well isn't that the other possibility they mentioned in Washington for the hearing loss? Frequent gunfire?"

"That's right."

"Maybe then," the airplane-wary agent from New Orleans interjected, "maybe we ought to check out every cop in the Houston PD and see if any of them knew Caine. According to what I found out, to know the man is to hate him."

"Who else shoots a lot?" Wilson questioned.

"Oh, about half the hunters in Texas, I'd say."

"But as a profession?"

"FBI agents?"

"Never mind us. Who else?"

"Security cops, maybe?"

"Right," said Wilson. "Get back with Texas Consolidated and check out their security people."

Wilson could now feel the excitement of the chase swelling inside him. He was beginning to bear down; and he enjoyed it. People who shoot guns, he silently agreed, were certainly worth checking into; but an unextinguished signal flare, deep within the recesses of his analytical brain, would not allow him to dismiss, completely, the idea of someone connected with airplanes.

▼ ▼ ▼

As pistols can be quite loud, even the small-calibered variety, the man who was at home around both airplanes and shooting (and had unknowingly suffered a slight hearing loss as a consequence) delved into his copious foot locker and fished out protective ear muffs for both himself and his neophyte young shooter. Then he put on quite a show using the .22 caliber six-shooter—the one with which he had dispatched the snake in the tree, and which Buddy had filched the previous afternoon.

Starting with the unholstered weapon at his side, Bill demonstrated to Buddy how he could raise the gun, cock and fire it either from the hip or at chest height (the latter he called "point-and-shoot") without even taking aim, and knock down at least five out of six drink cans with impressive regularity.

After a few rounds of showing-off, he demonstrated how the particular sidearm he was using could be converted from shooting normal .22 caliber ammunition into use of the longer and much more potent .22 magnum bullets. All that was necessary was to swap the bullet cylinders.

To cap the show, he made that conversion and inserted some bullets with strange-looking blue plastic projectiles on the end. Buddy didn't get a good look at them, but he did notice that they were different. Bill then asked the boy to toss a can into the air. He did, and it was promptly sent zinging away with one shot from the now louder-voiced handgun.

Half-yelling, in order to be understood through the hearing protectors, the ever-observant youth asked, "Is that some kind of special bullet?"

"You learn quick, kid. Yes, it's snake shot." Bill removed the ear muffs, extracted one of the cartridges and handed it to Buddy.

The kid removed his muffs, likewise, examined the blue plastic tip and noted, "It's full of little tiny BB's."

"Not BB's," the man explained. "They're about a number twelve shot—much smaller than BB's—and one charge of these is just right for wasting a snake at three to five yards. You get much farther than that and the pattern disperses too much to be effective."

"Is that what you shot that snake out of the tree with?"

Bill nodded.

"I bet it's also what you used on that running mouse. You're a cheat."

"Wrong, oh righteous one," Bill defended. "When it's you against the world, you utilize every advantage you can get hold of."

"Especially if you want to show off and impress somebody. Right?"

"Well, maybe—but most especially if there's a snake dan-

gling out of a tree right in your face or coiled at your feet ready
to strike, and you need to get off a shot that's gonna knock him
on his ass in a hurry. That's why I carry two of these shells up
front in the cylinder. Then they're followed by three hollow
points. One of these .22 magnum hollow points," he explained,
handing an example to the student, "will blow a good-sized
hole in any snake's head. It'll also collect a cottontail or a squirrel for supper, if you're good enough to hit one. And, if you had
to, it could make a good-sized man wish he hadn't messed with
you . . . even though it's still a measly little .22 caliber bullet.
So that's why this gun is what I usually carry in the woods, with
the magnum cylinder—two snake shot up first, and then three
hollow points."

"But I thought it was a six-shooter."

Nodding to the boy's perspicacity, Bill went on to explain the
safety aspects of carrying the venerable weapon—a replica of the
ubiquitous six-shooters that have been authentic and standard
carry for good guys and bad guys alike in every western movie
ever made—with an empty bullet chamber aligned with the
barrel. He noted that if such a gun were accidentally dropped
with a live bullet in position, the result could be an unplanned
and most unpleasant discharge.

"Let one of these fall on the hammer," he said, "and it might
very well go off and turn you into a permanent boy soprano."

Buddy reflected for a moment on the possible point of bullet
impact that could inflict a wound with such consequences,
smiled and shook his head. "I still think you should have been a
teacher."

"Well, let's see just how good a teacher I am. Let's see if I'm
good enough to teach a twirp to shoot a pistol."

"This twirp can shoot anything," Buddy bragged.

"Shooting is one thing. Hitting what you aim at is another."

With ear muffs back in place, the boy began to learn how to
do exactly that, under the careful and patient tutelage of his
woods professor. Buddy showed an innate capability with the
weapon, just as he had done with the rifle. Putting into practice
Bill's admonition to hold the pistol steadily in his right hand,
with his left hand cradling the gun butt below, and focusing his

vision on the front sight, as ordered, Buddy concentrated on squeezing the trigger.

"Remember," Bill coached, "you don't 'pull' the trigger. Never jerk it. You should squeeze it, ever so slowly, so that when the gun goes off, it should actually be a surprise."

The first time the boy was able to accomplish all of those instructions at one time, the bullet blew a beer can a most gratifying three or four feet into the air.

"Wahoo, I'm the Sheriff of Dodge City!" the new shooter exclaimed. He recocked the gun and repeated the performance. "Wahoo!"

Bill applauded with a broad grin and yelled above the sound-deadening ear muffs, "You're a natural, kid."

The pupil turned to his master with a blissful combination of grin and grime. His face was ear-to-ear smile; and his body was neck-to-knee debris—an effect accumulated from lying belly-down on the sand for his prone rifle-shooting lessons. Bill had thought too late to spread a ground cover for that exercise; but no matter, bathing had become a sport of its own.

What a kid this is, he thought, while sharing the boy's joy of accomplishment. *Probably never been really body-dirty before in his whole, sheltered, River Oaks life.*

While the man studied the blissful mess of a teenager, something entirely different riveted his attention.

"Come here a minute," he said. "I want to see something. Wait! First, hold the gun up, point it at the sky, with your finger off the trigger."

Buddy complied with the shooter-safety order and walked proudly over to his instructor.

Bill looked closely at the boy's chest, dusted away a small portion of sand and forest-floor debris and said, "That's what I was afraid of."

"What?"

"You've got a tick."

The boy jumped, grabbed at his chest and exclaimed, "Where?"

"Now just take it easy, it's not going to kill you. But give me a chance and I'll try to take it off cleanly, if I can. Give me the gun."

Buddy handed over the pistol and asked, "So how do you do that?"

"I'll show you in a minute," Bill said. "First, go take a quick swim and get all that sand and junk off your front." Touching Buddy's chest adjacent to the attached parasite, he said, "That bugger is right here. Now you try to wash off everything around it and don't—repeat, do *not*—scrape the darned thing off. That'll pull off the head for sure, and you'll be stuck with it. Now you go on and jump in the creek while I get things ready to operate in the trailer."

"Operate?"

"Go on."

"Yes, sir. Anything you say sir." With that, the youth stepped into the trailer for a towel, strolled down to the creek and deposited the towel and his clothing on the yaupon-bush dressing table. Then he tiptoed tentatively into the icy creek, took a deep breath and dove into the pool. "Holy shit!" was the last thing Bill heard as he entered the trailer.

Now clean-fronted, semi-dried and re-dressed, Buddy stepped into the trailer to discover Bill heating the point of an ice pick over the kitchen stove.

"What's that for?"

"To try to get the tick to back out of your thick skin without getting his head pulled off. Now lie down on your bunk."

"Get him to back out?"

"I said try. Sometimes it works, and sometimes it doesn't."

"If you're going to brand me with that thing, I think I'd just as soon have the tick."

"I'm not going to brand you; and you might still have the tick anyway, but I'm going to try. So lie down on your back and shut up."

Buddy complied, reaching down to the now easily spotted creature on his chest and gently rocking it back and forth. The bug's head was completely imbedded.

"Stop messing with it," Bill exclaimed, approaching with the red-hot ice pick. Let kindly ol' Doctor William here perform his magic act. The theory, Grodie One, is that if you can get some concentrated heat right next to the little tickie-poo, without frying him, it will force him to back out of your precious skin; then you can just pick him up and squash him." With that, the woods doctor sat on the bed next to the afflicted patient and leaned in slowly, cautiously, with the ice pick.

"What if he doesn't back out?" Buddy asked.

"Then you do just like you'd do on old Brutus out there and pull the son-of-a-bitch out. That'll probably pull off his head; and you'll have an itchy spot there for maybe a couple of months. No fun."

"I'd be happier if you got him out."

"I'm trying. Now just be still."

Inching the heated instrument ever closer to the implanted varmint, Bill attempted to hold it in a steady position, adjacent to the insect's reddish-brown body. "Come on you blood-sucker, back out."

Nothing.

"Well?" the boy asked.

"Not so well. I think I cooked him. He's not budging a budge. I guess he's dead . . . but his spirit lingers on."

"You mean in me?"

"Yeah."

There was a slight, but audible "snap" as Bill plucked out the odious creature; then he offered it for its host animal to inspect. "I think you've kept his head for a souvenir."

"Will I die?"

"Undoubtedly, yes. But I'll give you a few years or so yet. And whatever kills you, it won't be this tick."

Having taken a small toilet kit from the trailer's chest of drawers before the operation began, Bill removed a bottle of camphor-and-phenol medicine and dabbled a fingertip application to the affected area. "This should stop infection and help the itching some. We'll put on some more at bedtime."

"Have you ever had a tick?" Buddy wondered.

"Yes, I've had my share. They're no big deal. Mostly all you can get from them is Rocky Mountain spotted fever."

"Oh gee, that's very comforting," the victim said, arising from the bed. "Is there anything else?"

"Well, yes. One more thing. Better pull down your pants and check for chiggers."

"How do I do that?"

"Just look for a bunch of little red spots. Then you'll know."

Buddy was already looking; and he didn't like what he found. A sprinkling of at least a half-dozen red bumps dotted his lower abdomen. They were beginning to swell; and likely because he now knew they were there, they started to itch, too.

"Oh, shit," he exclaimed. "What do I do now?"

"Relax," Bill advised, "I've probably got 'em too."

Bill reached once more into the medicine kit and took out a bottle labeled, "Chig-Off." He unscrewed and removed the cap, which had a glass-rod applicator attached.

"Here," he said, handing the medication to the boy. "Put a drop or two of this on each one of those spots. It'll kill the little red bugger inside and help relieve the itching."

Buddy didn't appreciate his insect infestation one bit. "Man, this sucks," he announced in disgust, as he twisted to inspect for additional incursions on his back side.

"Be sure to check down among your family jewels," Bill advised, "and put some of the stuff on if you've got 'em there. An itchy crotch is bad enough, but a chigger bite on your ding-a-ling will drive you bats."

After a few applications of the thick, colorless liquid, Buddy announced, "It stings."

"Yeah, but not all that bad; and it's stinging that little red bug buried under your skin a lot worse. That's probably like a lot of other medicine," Bill said. "It seems like the manufacturers put something in them to make them sting or taste bad; otherwise, you'd think you were getting cheated."

When he finished his medication, the boy handed the vial and applicator to Bill, so that he could anoint his own newly discovered cluster of incursions.

Buddy asked, "Didn't you say something about the less clothes you wear, the less chiggers?"

"It seems to work out that way," Bill replied.

"Then piss on it," the boy announced in continuing disgust, as he stepped out of his cut-offs, pulled off his underwear and tossed it onto Bill's still-unfolded bed.

"You're starting to sound like a real outdoorsman now," Bill said. "Better go outside and give yourself a good coating of bug spray. I'm afraid we haven't been attending to that little chore like we should have."

"Either that or it doesn't work worth a shit." Buddy did not wear chagrin lightly.

"Damned sure won't work if you don't use it." The adult followed the boy's lead and tossed his own briefs onto his bed.

While Bill attended to his medicinal ministrations, Buddy went outside to apply a coat of insect repellent. Brutus bounded up for a greeting; but he quickly retreated, barking, when the boy began to spray from the aerosol can onto his two-toned torso. Whichever it was—the odor, or the hiss from the spray can—the dog didn't like it. Bill soon joined them and spray-painted himself, likewise; then both went back inside the trailer to dress.

A touch of good humor returned to the boy as he stepped bare-bottomed into his ragged-leg, former designer jeans. "Maybe if we didn't wear anything at all, we wouldn't get any damned chiggers."

"Can't do that if you want to shoot some more."

"I surely do."

"Then you need belt loops for the holster; and pockets for bullets. Skinny-shooting is out."

"And skinny-dipping is in. Right?"

"Absolutely," the man declared, as he straightened his bed sheets and folded the pull-down sleeping facility back into its hideaway position over the couch. "You like that business, don't you?"

"I like it all," Buddy declared. "I like the swimming, even if it does freeze my balls off. I love the shooting. I like exploring in the woods, too. It's the best kidnapping I ever had."

"I hope it's the last."

"Well, that depends on who does it," the captive youth announced; and he strolled out the trailer door.

▼ ▼ ▼ ▼ ▼ ▼ ▼ ▼ ▼ ▼ ▼ ▼ ▼ ▼

11

Without knowing it, two heavily charged egos were priming themselves for a confrontation, as the parents in the most celebrated kidnapping case in many a decade taxied to the company hangar at Houston Intercontinental in the Grumman Gulfstream jet. Henry Wilson, SAIC at the Houston office of the FBI, had by now shifted into case fixation mode—supremely confident and poised, ready to pounce upon his silent, unknown adversary at any moment; while Hamilton Caine, Sr., aggrieved parent known by all who knew him as industrial horse's ass extraordinary, was primed and ready to start throwing around his weight and looking for a scapegoat. The horde of news media representatives gathered for the event had no inkling of this, of course; all they had was the latest and most dramatic episode in a fantastic story: a boy kidnapped; the parents—kingpins of business and industry and darlings of society—far away at sea; the kidnapper unheard-from since the day after the kidnapping; and now, the return of the parents.

Members of the media who knew anything about the Caines were cynically making bets among themselves as to which would happen first—whether Melanie would overflow with copious tears for the benefit of the cameras, or Hamilton would start barking orders. As it happened, neither was the case.

The age-old dictum, "ladies first," gave Mrs. Caine the first shot; but instead of turning on the faucet, as many of the media people had expected, she assumed a Brave Lady, Stiff-Upper-

Lip posture. And instead of barking orders immediately upon disembarking, Hamilton, Sr., allowed his personal army of sycophants to coalesce around the two of them. Then it was time to bark.

"Who's in charge of the investigation here?" he demanded immediately.

That seemed to be the signal for the news phalanx to advance.

"Mrs. Caine," yelled a young lady running forth armed with a battery-operated cassette recorder and a brand new journalism degree, "what was your first reaction when you found out your son had been kidnapped?"

"Mr. Caine," yelled another, "do you already have the ransom ready?"

Almost simultaneously, someone else questioned, "What do you make of the fact that your gardner has disappeared?"

And as if by spontaneous combustion, there was exactly the sort of uncontrolled bedlam that the public relations staff of Texas Consolidated Utilities had labored so hard to avoid—complete with a lot of pushing, shoving, and generally poor behavior.

"Ladies and gentlemen please . . . PLEASE!" implored Caine's vice president for public affairs. "We have tables set up inside, your cameras and lights are all there. Now kindly give Mr. and Mrs. Caine a moment to catch their breaths. All of your questions will be dealt with in due time."

That seemed to calm the unruly gathering, which began slowly to retreat back into the hangar.

"His name is Henry Wilson," someone replied to Hamilton Caine's question. "He's head of the local office of the FBI. That's he over there," he added, pointing. "The fellow in the tan suit."

As Melanie Caine headed for the interview setup, her husband made straight for the man in the tan suit.

"I'm Henry Wilson," the agent said, offering his hand.

"I know who you are," Caine barked, without accepting the handshake. "What I want to know is what are you doing?"

Quickly sizing up the situation, a Texas Consolidated employee, with more presence of mind than he was paid for, ushered the two into a private office, out of sight and sound of the assemblage in the hangar. That suited Melanie Caine perfectly; she had the news media all to herself.

"We are doing everything we possibly can at the moment," said Wilson.

"Well obviously that's not enough." Caine had found his intended scapegoat, and he was zeroing in.

Undismayed, Wilson replied, "And just what might it be that you would consider 'enough'?"

"You could have found my son by now, that's what!"

"As I said," Wilson replied, maintaining the polite approach, "we are doing the best we can under the circumstances. But, as you are probably not aware, the kidnapper is keeping himself extremely scarce."

"That doesn't make a good god-damn. I expect one helluva lot more from you than that. And you can expect to have your ass severely fried just any day now if you don't come up with something better."

"Meaning what?" Wilson had taken just about all that he could tolerate.

"Meaning that I am not without very close connections in very high places, and unless you get this mess cleaned up in very short order, you could find yourself reassigned to checking suitcases in some chickenshit little border town."

"The Federal Bureau of Investigation does not check suitcases, *Mister* Caine." Wilson had had it. "And if you would only give us a chance, you will find that we are very close to doing that which you are so inappropriately demanding."

"Now don't you go censuring me, you penny-ante bureaucrat," Caine retorted.

"I only calls 'em like I sees 'em. And the way I sees 'em right now is that we don't even know for sure whether your boy is even alive anymore. It is my considered professional judgment that he is, and that the kidnapper knows you have been out of town and is waiting for news of your return to make another contact. Further . . ."

"Further my ass," Caine interrupted. "Let me tell you about

further. The 'further' is that Arthur Lambert, who is a special assistant to the chief of staff in the White House, is a personal friend of mine . . . and also that I personally contributed heavily to the campaign of the president who sits in that big chair in the oval office at that big white house. And that I'll have your incapable head on a god-damned platter in very fuckin' short order unless you get some concrete results . . . and I mean *pronto!*"

The horns of the scapegoat did not fit well on the balding head of Henry Wilson. Smiling quietly, he reached for his billfold, extracted a business card and handed it to his tormentor. "I can be reached at this number any time, Mr. Caine, night or day. We have a tap on the telephone at your house, also night and day. When the kidnapper calls—and I feel sure he will—we'll be on him like a cat on a mouse. In the meantime, I must tell you that the esteem in which your company employees hold you is obviously quite well deserved."

"What do you mean by that?"

"That you are a consummate horse's ass!" Then he walked quietly but purposefully out the office door.

▼ ▼ ▼

The man with the mustache—kidnapper, woods guide, shooting instructor, badminton hustler, doctor, cook, and general companion to overprivileged city boys in the tough East Texas woods—had a full schedule of events planned for that Friday afternoon in their secluded, creekside campsite. In his additional role as activities director, he had promised himself and his young guest that after lunch, the eager new shooter would have the opportunity to try his hand at firing the big, authoritative, and often intimidating .45 automatic pistol. He could also get a few shots with the lighter of the armorer's two double-barreled shotguns—a beautifully slim little 20-gauge, made in Spain.

The remainder of the day would not be entirely shooting, however. Bill told Buddy that he knew of a big magnolia tree a few hundred yards upstream from their camp where a family of wood ducks was nesting—at least they had been when Bill discovered them a few weeks previously.

Bill tried to explain the unbelievably ornate coloration of the male wood duck to his youthful charge, but his powers of recall and description would never pose a threat to Roger Tory Peterson.

"When I first found them," Bill said, "there were what looked to be three or four babies poking their heads out of a nest in a big hollow place in that old magnolia. I don't remember whether it was the mother or the father that was bringing in some kind of food to them; but both of the parents were around, I do remember that. Like most female birds, the mother was quite plain-looking; but that daddy wood duck—you'll just have to see him to believe it."

"Can we go there first?" Buddy asked, surprising Bill with his interest in nature study above shooting. In fact, the way the boy had burned up ammunition that morning, Bill would have been surprised at his being interested in anything above shooting.

"Right after lunch; we'll go have a look."

The luncheon menu was what Bill described as S.O.T. (Same Old Thing). That meant sandwiches, chips, a Coke for Buddy and a beer for Bill. Buddy begged a few sips of beer and said that if Bill would allow him, he wanted to try a can again with supper, but he was afraid that he would be too sleepy if he had one now, with lunch. Bill promised that he could.

The noontime radio newscast, from the Houston broadcaster that Bill designated station K-R-A-P, brought a mixture that was indeterminate as to whether it was good news or bad, as far as the weather prognostication was concerned, and a moment of high hilarity with regard to the now-famous River Oaks kidnapping case.

Undoubtedly the biggest laugh of the day, the latter was the outcome of the airport news conference, when Mr. and Mrs. Hamilton Caine arrived back in Houston from their South Seas sojourn to confront the unpleasant realities of a missing child and ransom demands from a now totally silent kidnapper. It was right on schedule, just as Bill had expected.

What was not expected, although it might should have been, was the comedy twist provided by the boy's Poor Distraught Mother, with her recorded plea to the kidnapper. The radio station played it in its entirety:

I want to say this to the man who has taken our baby: Please. *Please* Mister Kidnapper, bring him back to us. We'll do anything you ask. We'll pay your ransom, whatever you say. We won't call in the police. I don't know who you are; maybe you are a parent yourself. If you are, surely you can imagine what a terrible thing this is that you have done to us. Surely you must realize the torment of not knowing where your child is . . . whether he is alive or dead . . . whether a mother might ever see her baby again. Surely you can understand the torment of a father not knowing whether or not he'll ever get to see his son grow up to become a man. If you can't picture this, Mister Kidnapper, just try to understand that whatever you want, we'll give it to you. Only please . . . *please* get in touch with us. We're sitting here waiting . . . longing . . . and hurting. We have just learned that there is a hurricane blowing out there, and we have no way of knowing whether our boy will be safe.

The newscaster allowed the recorded message to linger long enough to hear the mother's impassioned plea trail off into what sounded like a well-rehearsed sob. And then a sniffle. The effect, intended to be heartrending, brought tears of laughter, instead, to both man and boy in the kidnapper's camp.

Struggling to talk through his snickering, Bill asked, "Can't you just see her? I just wish we had a television set; that was priceless."

Not forgetting that the boy, himself, had said of her, "My mother's a bastard, too," Bill added, "Have you ever heard anything so patently phony in your life? How does it feel to be called a baby?"

Guffawing, the boy replied, "Dah-dah, goo-goo," and began to suck his thumb.

"She's in for a surprise the next time she goes to change your diaper," Bill remarked.

"Dah-dah, goo-goo, baby's got a big one."

"Watch out, baby, Mama might like it too much."

Locker-room humor comes readily to nasty little boys on a camp-out.

On the more sobering subject, the newscaster told his Houston audience they could rest relieved that Elizabeth—now a full-fledged hurricane with top winds approaching one hundred miles per hour—had shifted to a course that would indicate land-fall, some time that night or early evening, in the vicinity of Lake Charles, Louisiana—at least one hundred miles to the east of Houston. Scattered showers and a few gusty winds were about all that "Houston-Town" could expect from her.

That was good news for Houston—but not so good for hideaways camping creekside in the Big Thicket woods; because they, too, were a considerable distance east of Houston.

Bill explained to Buddy, "We're far enough from the coast that we won't get the full brunt of it no matter where it decides to come in. If it stays east of us, we might get some rain and some wind, but it takes a helluva wind to get through these trees down here where we are. But then, a hundred miles an hour *is* a helluva wind.

"But as long as it stays to the east, we should be all right. The worst thing about a hurricane, except for rising water for people right on the coast, is the damned tornadoes that pop up on the northern and eastern sides of the storm. Those are the nasty sides. The western edge, which is what we might be on, is what they call the 'dry side.' It can be bad, but not anything as bad as the eastern side—and the center, of course. I think the most we have to worry about is maybe a tree falling over on us, as long as the creek doesn't get too high. But if we get too much rain, we'll just have to haul-ass out of here."

"Where would we go?"

"Good question. We might could find us a motel somewhere if it's not too late; but I imagine most of the motels anywhere near here are probably full-up already with people that have evacuated from the coast. If it comes to it, we'll probably have to just throw a mattress into the van and sleep in it somewhere. The worst part of that is that we can't show your pretty face anywhere; your picture has probably been on every TV news broadcast and in every newspaper from here to Kingdom Come. Somebody is bound to recognize you. Of course, that would make it a cinch for you, if you still want to get away."

"Bill, I don't want to get away. I want to stay with you."

Doing his best to sound uncaring, Bill replied, "Can't afford you. Besides, you don't fit into my plans . . . 'Baby.'"

The well-aimed loaf of bread caught the teasing, shave-needing Despicable Kidnapper full in the face.

As they straightened up after lunch, it became more and more obvious that a radical change was definitely afoot with the weather. The sun had not been visible since the boy had taken his much-criticized solo excursion up the creek that early morning. The day's leaden atmosphere had lost nothing in the way of heat, but the deadly stillness had given way to occasional, heavy wind gusts that kept tossing the treetops above them into counter-rotating convolutions, while the gray sky overhead boiled with cloud shadings that ranged from painfully bright to ominously dark. Due to the height of the trees and the density of the woods around them, little of this meteorological turmoil was felt on the ground; still, it was quite a show that was going on above.

Bill felt no compulsion to panic, or even to worry, overmuch; and the angry, unsettled atmosphere tended to add an extra element of excitement to the planned exploratory trip upstream.

Because of Buddy's excellent showing with his first pistol-shooting lessons that morning, Bill did him proud by allowing the youth to wear the .22 caliber pistol in its holster on his hip. Threaded through by his belt, it hung neatly balanced on his right by the "awesome" hunting knife on his left. The handgun was loaded with Bill's standard woods carry of two snake shot and three hollow-point, magnum bullets, along with the mandatory empty chamber. Thus outfitted, the golden-topped kid tried to fashion himself as every bit the seasoned outdoorsman.

Just to make certain that the explorers would be well protected come-what-may, Bill strapped on the Army .45. "You take care of the snakes," he told his buddy, "and I'll handle the bears."

Brutus, poor soul, was commanded to stay behind and guard

the house. The guys would hardly be able to sneak up on any wood ducks with the big pooch lumbering noisily ahead of them.

A set of a half-dozen relatively fresh deer prints, running parallel to and then crossing the creek, were the first bit of engrossing evidence to come under the woodsmen's scrutiny as they began their nature hike. They were two and a half, maybe three inches in length; and the guide declared them to be nice ones, very nice ones indeed. The cloven-hoofed tracks were widespread at the tip, which Bill explained indicated that the animal had been running.

"You see the way each half of the print comes to a kind of point?" he asked the boy, who nodded understanding. "Some people will tell you that indicates it's a buck. Well, don't ever buy any swamp land in Florida from those folks, because it just isn't true. I shot a doe once that had the nicest little pointed toes you ever saw."

"Why would you shoot a doe? I thought big macho hunters only shot huge bucks with lots of fancy horns to hang on their wall."

"To tell you the truth, Buddy, it took me a long time to decide that I would shoot a doe if I got the opportunity. God knows, I'd passed-up shots at literally hundreds of them."

"So what changed your mind?"

"They eat good—better than any horny buck with his neck all puffed up from sex fever and adrenaline shooting through his veins. But more than that, I became convinced that hunters, at least in some areas, have got to keep the deer herds thinned down, or they'll literally eat themselves out of house and home; and one of the best ways to do that is to cut down on the female population."

There was a blank look on the boy's face, indicating either that he did not understand, or that he did not want to be bothered at the moment with a conservation lecture. Bill dropped the subject.

Not far from the deer prints, there was a set of raccoon tracks, easily identifiable in the damp creek sand by their elongated toeprints. But what interested Buddy more than the wildlife spoor, at the moment, were the tracks made by the dog, when he had accompanied the boy on his previous jaunt up the creek that morning. Brutus was a large dog, and thus made large tracks in the sand. But it wasn't the size, so much, that held the boy's interest.

"They're just like you said," he observed. Touching the tip of one of the prints, he said, "You can see right here where the claws were. But those cougar tracks didn't show the claws."

"What do you think," Bill asked, "would you like to see some more fresh cougar tracks?"

"Yeah. That would be neat."

"Then let me ask you this: would you like to hear him scream again? Up close?"

Buddy thought for a long moment before replying. "Yeah, I really would. That was the scariest thing I ever heard or saw, but I would like to hear it again. It was so wild, so . . ." He was struggling to find the words to express his feelings. "So much a part of this place. Yes, I would like to hear it again; so I could listen to it closely, and maybe remember it better. It would scare the hell out of me just like it did before, but I think it would be really neat."

"Okay, then, how would you like to see him—right up there somewhere?" Bill asked, pointing toward a nearby bend in the stream. "What would you do if you saw that big, slinky son-of-a-gun sneaking through those bushes, or maybe crouched on one of those big limbs up there? Would you like that?"

"I'd probably piss in my pants," Buddy replied, with total honesty. "But I would like to see him. I would like to see how big he is. You still got that forty-five?"

"I've got it."

"Then I wouldn't be worried. What would you do? Would you shoot him?"

"Now you're putting me on the spot," Bill replied. "I feel exactly the same as you do that he belongs here; and maybe I should just let him stay. But at the same time . . ."

Now it was Bill's turn to struggle at expressing himself; perhaps he was wrestling with his decision.

"I don't know. I guess . . . I guess I probably would shoot

him. He'd be just too good a prize. Boy, he'd look great mounted and kinda crouching on top of a mantle—if I had a mantle. But it's more than that. The hunter's instinct is strong. So is the survival instinct; and you've gotta admit, a big cat—now we're talking mountain lion, Buddy . . . panther . . . carnivorous predator—a big cat like that curled up in that tree up there would probably push that little trigger inside, and I'd most likely have my gun out and leveled down on him before I could even think about it. It's just instinct . . . instinct and training."

"What kind of training?" the boy wondered. "You mean the Army, or something like that?"

"Well, the Army teaches you that, they surely do; and the police teach it even better. But hunters—or maybe I should say shooters, there's a distinction—can teach themselves. I sorta did myself, and I got to be pretty quick. Of course, quick doesn't mean a damned thing if you're not accurate to go with it; but I guess I could pot a cougar out of a tree at not too great a distance."

"And you would, too, wouldn't you? I mean, if you had a chance."

"Yes. Yes, I suppose I would. I might piss in my own pants, too; but I'd give him a quick 185-grain hollow-point somewhere in the boiler room and then worry about washing out my britches later.

"But that's all silly speculation. Our chances of stumbling onto that big, bad pussy cat out here in broad daylight run on a probability scale from about zero to none. But we might can catch those ducks napping if we stop talking so much and walk quietly. I think the place I saw them was only about a hundred yards on up the creek."

"Can I shoot one if we see them?" Buddy asked.

"No."

"Why not?"

"In the first place, you probably couldn't hit one. In the second, I don't want to fool with cleaning it. Ducks are hard to clean. And in the third . . . I'd a lot rather just leave them here. We've got plenty of food."

"What about the cougar; would we eat him?"

"Don't be silly. And stop trying to trap me in inconsistencies. We can at least convince ourselves that cougars are dangerous—especially if they're old and toothless. Wood ducks are just pretty. Now quiet!"

The explorers were practically on tiptoe when they rounded the next bend in the creek, doing their best to imitate soft-treading Indians in buckskin moccasins. Bill sighted the tree right away where he had seen the waterfowl nesting on his previous excursion. It was an old magnolia that was trying to slide down into the water even more than the beech tree at their campsite. Its branches were long and slick-looking. Eight feet or so up from the base was a broad hollow in the trunk, a perfect place for a large nest. But there were no ducklings in it.

When Buddy caught sight of the scene he almost gasped aloud. He had thought their trailer campground was pretty; but the sylvan setting before him was beautiful almost beyond belief. There was a magnolia tree, as Bill described, and at its base the creek was quite wide, by comparison to what he had seen. It had taken a sharp curve just upstream from the big tree, creating an apparently deep eddy on the opposite side. Another magnolia tree with a trunk three feet in diameter, just upstream, had given up the ghost and fallen across the creek, forming a natural bridge. Also—unlike all of that section of the woods the boy had seen so far, which was almost entirely tangled thicket—there was a small, natural clearing on the bank opposite the big magnolia and adjacent to the creek eddy. It even had grass.

Sensing the boy's appreciation of the setting, Bill asked, "Pretty, isn't it?"

"It's beautiful," Buddy declared.

Now that was some accolade, Bill thought, never having heard the kid utter anything in quite such ordinary, human superlatives. He figured that it must rank somewhere between "neat" and "awesome."

"I think those trees on the other side of that clearing are dogwoods," he said, pointing. "Along about late March, they'll be covered-up with flowers, before any leaves come out. They're always the first sign of spring in this forest, when the leaves are still off all the hardwoods, and even the underbrush has thinned out for the winter.

"Winter rains, freezes, broken trees and the like have made the woods into pretty much of a mess by that time. Then along come the dogwood blossoms, all white and sorta floating in the air like wispy little ghosts. They remind me of the legend of the phoenix, rising out of the ashes."

Buddy stared in blank amazement at the man—a kidnapper who sounded like a poet.

"Shortly after the dogwoods," Bill continued, "the swamp honeysuckles come into blossom down along the creek."

"What are they?"

"They're sorta fragile-looking bushes. Some people call them wild azaleas. Sometimes they'll get fifteen, twenty feet tall; and when they're in bloom, they're covered with delicate flowers, kinda salmon-pink, that make the whole thing look like your old maid aunt's lace table cloth.

"You'd love it here in the spring," he added, as though the youngster wasn't loving it enough already.

As they continued to survey the scene, a small flotilla of ducks came paddling around the creek bend into the wide-pool area just ahead. There were obviously two adults and four ducklings. Buddy strained to see which was which; but in his initial, headlong view, he could not discern much difference. Then the flotilla took a turn to port, toward the magnolia, and the boy got a look for the first time at an adult male wood duck. Bill had not exaggerated a bit.

The bird's face was unbelievable. It was iridescent, with an almost bizarre pattern highlighted by a large, round, red-rimmed eye. There were brilliant white cheek and chin marks, along with two white stripes that ran laterally more or less parallel from the base of the bill and over the eye, then terminated together in a sort of crest on the back of the head. Bill was sorry that he had not brought along his binoculars, so that both he and the boy could have a better look. He started to make some kind of whispered observation about the male as compared to the female, but he made the mistake of pointing as he did so.

With his movement, the flotilla was quickly airborne, babies and all, and the bird-study session was over.

But not the woodlands study. At the flight of the ducks, Buddy ran ahead to the little grassy clearing. Despite the swirling, contorting, angry sky above them, this was a place of supreme beauty. The clearing occupied a space adjacent to the creek perhaps twenty yards long. At the end opposite the water was a stand of tall, loblolly pine trees, almost totally devoid of underbrush, with a soft, inches-deep carpet of pine needles underfoot. On the upstream side of the clearing stood a huge, gray-barked tree with long-reaching limbs that just begged to have a rope swing strung from one of them, while the grassy plot seemed to speak out softly, "Come and lie down on me."

That sounded like an excellent idea, but it would have to wait. The young adventurer had more exploring to do yet.

The first, and most obvious, detail to study had to be the big, downed tree that lay completely across the creek. Buddy was quickly atop it, staring into the slow-moving stream and its curious, swirling eddy below. It looked deep and inviting—almost mandatory for a youth to dive into from the fallen magnolia.

"Can we swim here?" he asked.

"I don't know why not, but you've got to check it out first. Also, I'd prefer that you take off that pistol before you dive in. It doesn't work too well after it's been drowned."

Buddy disembarked from the tree-bridge, returned to the grassy clearing and carefully removed the pistol and holster from his belt. He laid them gently on the ground and immediately stripped off. Dropping his ragged-bottom jean-shorts to the grass, he pulled off his shoes and sprinted away to explore the new swimming hole.

"Now you don't just go diving in there," Bill admonished. "You've got to get in ever so easy and check out that pool from one side to the other. If you just go run out on that tree trunk and dive in, you're liable to hit another tree down there somewhere and break your neck. So get in there and get wet first . . . get over the chill . . . then I want you to check out every foot of that pool before you dive into it. It also would be a good idea to check around in the trees and along the water's edge to see if there are any snakes before you do anything. But I'll do that. Get yourself on in."

"Are you coming in with me?" the boy asked as he eased into the frigid water.

"I might, after you see if it's safe enough for me. I haven't decided yet."

"Come on," Buddy urged, "it'll be more fun with you."

Having inched his way in almost to his waist, the boy took a deep breath and held it, then plopped quickly into the water to get the initial body chill accomplished and overcome as rapidly as possible—as he had recently been taught. That done, he began tentatively to explore the perimeter of the pool with the excitement and anticipation of the unknown, and of personal discovery. Bill had been with him, yes; but the youthful adventurer maintained the feeling that he had found this enticing new swimming hole on his own, and that he was now going to master it on his own terms.

He did locate a submerged tree branch on the side of the pool nearest the clearing. With some difficulty, he managed to struggle it out and toss it up onto the sandy bank. Finally, having circumscribed the pool—and it was quite a bit larger than the one to which he was accustomed in front of the trailer—Buddy began cautiously to inch his way diagonally across the center. To his delight, he got all the way up onto his tiptoes while there was still a goodly distance to the center of the pool. At that point, almost directly beneath the fallen tree, the otherwise shallow creek would be over his head—perfect for diving.

The eager youth swam, then waded quickly out of the water and made his way back onto the tree-bridge. Bill watched with concealed pride as Buddy paused, selected his spot, then plunged in, head first.

The boy couldn't swim out quickly enough to express his delight. "Come on, Bill, it's great."

"Who said anything about going swimming, anyhow? I thought you were anxious to do some more shooting."

"Well, I am; but we can do that when we get out. There's plenty of time."

"I hope so," Bill said, casting a wary eye at the weather that seemed to be worsening around them. "I hope so."

"Well, come on. Why didn't you tell me there was a diving pool down here?"

Slipping first out of his sneakers, then out of his cut-offs, Bill replied, "Mostly because I didn't know it."

As he laid his pants onto the grass, Bill carefully took the .45 pistol from its holster and placed it on top, to be at the ready. He did the same with the .22 pistol that Buddy had been wearing, then strolled leisurely over to the newfound swimming hole. Buddy was already triumphantly back atop the diving platform.

The boy issued a challenge. "Betcha don't have the guts to just come up here and dive in without getting wet first."

"And I'll bet you're right. My mama didn't raise any total idiots," Bill replied as he began the ritually slow ingress into the chilly water. "Smartass, do you remember just how short a while ago it was that I almost had to pick you up and throw you in to get your sweet little butt into this creek at all?"

"No guts!" the boy yelled, and he dove off the fallen tree again and swam directly to the man. When he surfaced, he did so with a broad hand-splash that doused his older companion with body-chilling spray.

"Little shit!" Bill growled, whereupon he submerged himself. When he surfaced, he had one complete, fifteen-year-old rich kid held firmly aloft, as far over his head as his arms would reach.

Amazed at the man's strength, Buddy yelled in mock terror and utter delight. He became even more amazed as he felt himself tossed high into the air, with no more apparent effort than if he had been a loaf of bread; and he belly-flopped into the middle of the pool.

Swimming out, Buddy found Bill in hot pursuit. He scampered onto the bank and raced to the tree-bridge. Unfortunately, city boys unaccustomed to country swimming holes don't take into consideration the fact that old, loose-bark tree trunks, having once been trod-on by dripping young bodies, have a tendency to get slippery in a hurry.

"Wo-wo-wo-o-o-o-o!" he hollered in dismay, making a singularly ungraceful and extremely splashy, but unintentional, reentrance into the creek.

Bill was atop the tree trunk when Buddy surfaced, sputtering. "Are you all right?"

"No, I drowned!" the boy replied; and he splashed out the other side of the creek, on the side of the tree with the wood duck's nest.

"That's a nice swimming hole you got there, Buddy," Bill said. Then he leaped away from the diving tree, grabbed both shins in a tight tuck position and cannon-balled in, raising a splash that reached all the way across to the boy on the opposite bank.

The two kids had been romping in and out of the swimming hole for a good quarter-hour when the rain began—an unconstant, spurting and spitting kind of rainfall. The creek water was cold—they were accustomed to that; but the wind-driven rain stung their skin like tiny, machine-gunned bullets of ice.

They ran to the grassy clearing, scooped up their shoes, pants, pistols, and holsters as rapidly as they could, and made a mad, naked dash back to the trailer. Brutus gave them a short, welcoming bark, but remained under the trailer where he had retreated to continue his assigned guard duties in less inhospitable surroundings.

Bill ran first to the van, where he grabbed a gun-cleaning kit before completing his run to the trailer. Inside, Buddy had already begun toweling away the water and chill. Bill took the other towel from the tiny bathroom and joined in the ritual; and they both laughed and complained of the unwelcome turn of events, gasping all the while to overcome the breath-robbing dash.

The towels had seen considerable use, and they had never had a really good chance to dry; consequently, there was some difficulty removing the water. Removing the chill was even harder. Their cut-off jeans, soaked by the rain, were laid across the short shower curtain rod in the bathroom to dry as best they could. Both the man's and the boy's underwear had been folded away atop the sheets in Bill's hideaway bed—too much trouble to retrieve at the moment, so they wrapped-up in the previously unused blankets that had been filed away for future reference the past two sweltering nights. Then both sat shiveringly down on the couch and laughed some more.

The dark, heavy clouds that had brought the rain had also greatly reduced the light level in the trailer. Clinging tightly to his blanket, Bill got up from the couch, retrieved the gasoline lantern from storage, and sat down at the dining booth to light it. It would provide heat as well as light for the trailer. Buddy joined him; he had never seen one of those devices lighted.

As the lantern began to hiss, and the fragile, ashlike mantles sputtered into brilliant light, he asked the man, "Well, what do we do now, coach?"

"I don't know about you, Buddy Boy, but I'm going to take a little medication that will do a little warming inside." Then he got up to retrieve his friendly bottle of Jack Daniel's from the cupboard.

"What makes you think kids don't need to be warmed on the inside, too?"

"Well, nothing I guess," Bill admitted. "How about some hot milk?"

No reply was necessary. Buddy's eyes and his ready-to-puke facial expression said it all.

"Oh, what the hell!" Bill said; and he got out a second glass and decanted a small sipping-on quantity of bourbon for the kid. "What time is it, anyway?"

Buddy picked up his watch from the corner of the table (he had taken to leaving it off, just as Bill always did).

"It's three forty-seven."

"Well, hell," the man rationalized, "somewhere off the coast of Newfoundland it's almost six o'clock, and that's damned sure cocktail time for anyone. *Salud!*" And he clicked glasses with the boy.

Buddy felt his first sip of real whiskey burn its way down his throat and singe the lining of his stomach. The effect was unexpected, shocking; but it did live up to its billing—it was warming.

"What do you think?" Bill asked.

"E—ee-fst."

"Burns, doesn't it?"

Buddy nodded his head. "Ye-ast."

His host arose, filled a glass with tap water and handed it to his gasping guest. "Here, little buddy, you need a chaser."

The boy downed the water, urgently, and ultimately managed to survive his initial encounter with the evils of hard liquor.

"I think I . . . took (wheeze) . . . too big a (wheeze) . . . bite," he finally managed to stammer.

The contributor to his delinquency agreed. "I think you did, too. Now take it a little easier. On the other hand, you can just give it up completely, if you want to."

"No, I don't want to," declared the stubborn kid.

"Suit yourself. Then just sip it slow and easy-like. Use a lot of chaser. But don't expect any refills; I don't want you getting sick on me." With that, the man tossed down the remainder of his glass and poured another, to the wide-eyed amazement of his young companion.

"We've got a couple of wet pistols here we've got to get dried-off and oiled," Bill told him. "So let's unload them and get with it."

With the heat-producing lantern on the table beside them, and the Jack Daniel's providing central heat from within, the two drinking buddies warmed up promptly and lowered their blanket-wraps down to their waists.

Buddy watched with fascination, nursing slowly on the bourbon and drinking plenty of water, as Bill disassembled the two pistols. The .22 caliber six-shooter was a simple matter—he pulled out a rod that held the cylinder in place, removed the cylinder, and that was it. He then sprayed the innards with an aerosol can which he explained contained a mixture of both water-displacing and lubricating agents in some kind of silicone base. The exterior of the gun was wiped with a rag-load of the same product.

The big Army .45 automatic was a different proposition. As the man's dexterous fingers started taking it apart, the boy wondered how he might ever manage to get it back together again.

Aware that he was playing to an audience, Bill said, "I understand that in the Army, you have to be able to do this blindfolded."

"And put it back together too?"

"And put it back together too. But I was never in the Army, so I can use both eyes."

"Were you in anything?"

"Yes, I was in the Air Farce."

"The Air *Farce?*"

"Did I stutter?"

"I take it you didn't like it too much."

"No, not too much," Bill acknowledged, applying the lubricant spray to the inner workings of the big sidearm.

"What was wrong?" Buddy wondered.

"Kid, there are just some people who can't necessarily jump just because somebody with one more stripe or a dinky little gold bar yells 'frog.'"

"Were you a flier?"

"Nope. Wanted to be. But it turned out that I had an anatomical abnormality which made me unsuited for pilot training—or for much of anything in the military."

"What was that?"

"You see this nose?" Bill asked, touching the tip of his moderate-sized proboscis and turning to full profile.

"Uh-huh."

"It is physically incapable of fitting into the crack of anybody's ass. And suck-ass is the name of the game in the military." Growing more expansive—perhaps due to the several belts of bourbon—he added, "And in a great deal of corporate life, too."

"But kidnappers don't have to do that, right?"

"Now don't put that too heavy on me, Buddy."

"I'm sorry. You're really a brain surgeon, right?"

"Right. And all my malpractice insurance got cancelled right before I accidentally mutilated this guy on the operating table, so I got desperate for dough."

"What did you do?"

"Oh, I ran off to the Big Thicket where nobody would find

me, and then I came up with the idea of snatching some rich son-of-a-bitch's kid and holding him for ransom."

"I mean, what happened to the guy on the operating table?"

"Oh, him? I sliced his pecker off."

Buddy snickered. "How could you do that being a brain surgeon?"

"Stupid operating room orderlies; they put him on the table backwards."

"Do you know what I think?"

"No, what do you think?"

"I think you're the world's biggest bullshitter," the boy declared.

"Oh you do, do you?" Bill asked, as he began to reassemble the automatic—carefully guiding the barrel back into the slide assembly.

"Yeah, I do."

On the subject of bullshit, an unsettled question had been lingering in the back recesses of Buddy's mind ever since his last day at school. He had been tempted more than once to ask Bill about it; but, each time, he had been put off by timidity. Now, though, it was well established that the two were absolutely straightforward with each other; and if there was ever going to be anyone to whom he could ask such a question, it was Bill. And the timing seemed appropriate.

"Bill?" he began, tentatively. "Can I ask you a question?"

"Did you ever have the idea that you couldn't?"

"No, I guess not."

"Then ask."

"Is it true that boys . . . that boys . . . bleed? . . . the first time they . . . have sex?"

"What do you mean?"

"I mean, you know . . . like girls do when they lose their . . ."

"Their cherry?"

"Yeah." Buddy felt relieved to have it out.

"Where did you ever get that idea?"

"Oh, some guys at school."

"I knew it wasn't from sex education class."

"I haven't taken sex education."

"It figures. Do you want to?"

"Well . . ." The boy groped to reach his honest feelings. "Sometimes yes and sometimes no. I kinda think it would be embarrassing—especially if it's boys and girls together in the same class. And maybe it would all be a drag because of that.

"But sometimes, I think it would be kinda nice if there was someone that I could go to, to ask a question about things once in a while. I mean . . . there's so much bullshit."

"Yeah," Bill acknowledged. "You get a lot of it, don't you?" Buddy nodded.

"For instance," Bill noted, "I'm sure you've heard that masturbation will cause you to go crazy."

"Yeah, like that."

"Well, I never saw any proof of that. The only thing I know for sure about masturbation is that, if you do it too much, it causes little hairs to grow out in the palm of your hand."

Almost unconsciously, Buddy turned up his right hand and looked at the palm. No sooner had he done so than he knew he had been had. His eyes darted back to Bill, and he saw that tiny, twisted little half-smile in the left corner of the man's mouth.

"Gotcha!" Bill teased.

"You're an asshole!" Buddy responded, looking around unsuccessfully for something to throw at that evil old man across the table from him. Then he grinned at the well-executed entrapment and lightly chuckled at the joke on himself; he knew that it had been done in good nature. And he thought, *There's nobody on earth like Bill.*

"No, Buddy," the man said with a warmer smile. "It's all bullshit. The whole lot of it. Whoever told you that about losing your cherry is totally full of it."

"That's what I told him. He's a junior; and he brags so much about getting sex all the time. He treats everybody else in the world like they're total dummies."

"Well, I can almost guarantee you," Bill consoled the boy, as he began to wipe the now-reassembled .45 automatic with an oily rag, "if he goes around talking like that—especially about boys bleeding—that he is not only a blowhard and a liar, but he is most likely every bit as much a virgin as you are."

A huge grin spread across Buddy's face. It did him enormous good to hear that.

But his thirst for knowledge remained unquenched. "What is a 'cherry,' anyhow?"

"Well, as far as boys are concerned, it is nothing but . . . oh, what shall I say? Ceremonial. There's nothing actually physical about it at all, like there is with girls."

"What happens with girls?"

"Buddy, there's a kind of membrane inside a girl's body, called a hymen. It's at the entrance to the vagina—inside what's known in the little boy's world as her pussy—and the first time some horny guy penetrates into there, it gets broken. And she bleeds."

"Does it hurt a lot?"

"You want to know the absolute truth?"

Buddy nodded.

"The absolute truth," Bill confessed, "is that I don't know . . . because I never got one. Every sex partner I ever had, had been down that road before."

Buddy's response was sympathetic. "That's sad."

"Well, maybe it is and maybe it isn't. That depends upon how much of a hypocrite you are."

"What do you mean?"

"I mean that, if you think it's important for guys to get a lot of tail before they get married, but for their brides to be virgins . . . then you're being a hypocrite. Just ask yourself, where are all those virgins supposed to come from?"

"I never thought of it that way."

"But you have thought about having sex a lot, haven't you?"

"Yeah," Buddy admitted, with an honestly candid grin and a blushingly chaste nod of his head. "I really have." The blue eyes were absolutely sparkling.

Bill studied the budding specimen before him with the envy of every middle-aged man for a handsome youth. His shoulders were so broad, so straight, and so disgustingly tanned—setting off in sharp contrast that shock of golden blonde, tantalizingly unruly hair. And with those eyes, Bill wondered, what female on earth could resist him?

The man ruminated to himself, *When that kid finally gets his dipstick wet, he's gonna sweep the field. There won't be a sweet young thing in sight who won't gladly lay down her virtue, along with her luscious young body, with just one blink of those damned eyes.*

"Just don't pant too hard," he advised the youth. "Don't be so eager that you stumble into your first lay-in-the-hay, then come off with a lifelong of trouble along with it."

"What do you mean?"

"I mean protect yourself, kid. Don't let your horniness run away with you so quickly that you get some sweet little gal knocked-up on your first punch. What this country does not need is any more teenage pregnancies. *You* don't need one, for sure. It could screw-up your life; and it's totally avoidable."

"You mean that guys ought to wear rubbers, don't you?"

"That's exactly what I mean—keep your shot load to yourself. If I had any with me, I'd give you one right now, for you to stick in your billfold. That's as important as keeping a quarter in your wallet for a phone call in case your car breaks down."

"Thanks. I'll remember that when I start . . ."

"Driving?" Bill helped him finish the sentence.

"Yeah," the boy replied, with reddened cheeks. "When I start driving."

"Let me tell you this much about sex and be done with it," Bill said. "Sex is wonderful. Even if it's the most casual lay you could ever get . . . even with a cheap whore. For both the guys and the gals, screwin' feels absolutely great. It's tremendous. As you might say, 'totally awesome.' But that's not really what it's all about.

"Sex, between a man and a woman, is the ultimate expression of love. When you pop your rocks off inside the woman you love, your whole . . . everything, your entire being . . . goes with it. That's what they mean when they talk about husband and wife . . . or lover and lover, if you please . . . being united. You are emotionally, at least, welded together. And for just a few beautiful moments, it feels like you are permanently joined physically, as well. The two of you have actually become one. And that, my little pal, is what it is all about."

Buddy looked at his mentor and smiled shyly, in appreciative silence.

"That and one thing more," Bill added. "Love 'em and leave 'em, if you must, but until you are married and eager to have a child, just make sure you don't leave anything inside them but a nice warm glow."

With that, the man picked up the magazine for the auto pistol and began to stuff it with potent-looking, hollow-point bullets.

"Like I said before," the boy noted, "you should have been a teacher. I mean . . . you sure can take a pistol apart and put it back together well."

The man glanced up from his work, satisfied that his lecture had made a worthwhile impression. "I don't shoot it too badly, either."

"I know. I wish I could shoot like you."

"You could, Buddy, if we just had the time for me to teach you."

A quick spurt of rain was lashed against the window beside them by an accompanying gust of wind. The boy's eyes lost their twinkle of anticipation, and they began to show concern.

"Bill . . . what's going to happen to us?"

Shoving the loaded magazine back into the butt of the pistol, the man replied, "Oh, we're gonna ride out this storm. It's gonna be all right. And like I told you before, if the creek gets up too high, we'll just have to haul-ass out of here. Of course, we might get the van stuck in the mud; then we'd be up that other well-known creek . . . without the proverbial paddle."

"I didn't mean that," the boy explained. "I meant us, after this is all over. Will I ever see you again?"

Bill looked away. He made an attempt at looking out the window, but it was frosted-over from the chill of the rain outside and the heat of the nearby lantern. He got up with his blanket-wrap, no longer needed, and walked the few steps to the couch area. Lowering his bed, he fished-out their underwear, then pushed the bed back up, out of the way. He tossed the red bikini to the boy, then pulled on his briefs and sat down on the couch, still silent.

Buddy donned his own skimpy garment, sat down beside him and asked again, "Well, will I?"

Bill couldn't look him in the face. "I don't . . . see how." Too much whiskey, he guessed; he was visibly upset, and he knew it.

"But we could find a way," Buddy pleaded. "Nobody would ever have to know." Thinking even farther ahead, he added, "After I'm sixteen, I'll be getting a car; and then I can come and go on my own. We can go lots of places together."

"Like to jail? You want to go to jail with me?"

"You don't have to go to jail. No one will ever get me to tell who you are. Shoot, I don't even know who you are; how could I tell anybody?"

The man with the mustache thought about Alaska. And flying the bush. He thought about all his plans and dreams—one last grab at the brass ring, that's all he was going to get. And now, one missed step and he's in the federal pen. He knew that they don't hand out light sentences to kidnappers; and the way he'd heard it, even fellow cons in the prison don't treat them too swell, either. There was no other way out; he had to go on to Alaska.

Still unable to look into those eyes, he said, "Buddy, I don't plan to stick around anywhere near Houston. I'm gonna have to clear out."

"Take me with you?"

"Don't be silly; they'd find us in a minute."

"They won't find us here."

"Here is not where I plan to remain, either," Bill replied. "You think it's great now, but you'd get plenty tired of it after a very short time."

"But Bill, we . . ."

The man cut him off. "That's enough, now, Buddy. Look . . . you're upset . . . I'm upset. You've got whiskey in you that you don't know how to handle. I've got a little in me, myself; and it'll do funny things to your brain. Screws up your reasoning. Now let's just don't talk about it any more right now.

"Right now," he continued, managing at last to look directly at his sorrowing young pal, "we've got a hurricane to worry about. We still have to get you back to Houston and into the loving arms of your dear, devoted parents; and I've got to get my greedy hands on their dirty money and not let the FBI get its hands on me. This is not the time to be worrying about whether you and I can ever see each other again."

"Okay," Buddy agreed. "Promise me that you'll think about it later?"

"All right, I promise."

"If I think of something can I talk about it?"

"No. Not now. Just get it out of your mind completely," Bill ordered. "Go look out the window and see what the storm looks like."

Reluctantly, Buddy did as he was told. From the doorway, he said, "It's really not so bad. It's just raining kinda off and on, like it was when we came in."

"Good," Bill said. "I think our lady Elizabeth is going to pass us by to the east. Tomorrow, it'll be all gone and we can go back out and get some more shooting done. We might even be able to before it gets dark tonight."

But they didn't. With such thick clouds overhead, darkness was not a long time coming. The rain remained about the same as it had been when they were driven from their frolicking at the swimming hole, arriving in spasmodic spurts. Occasionally, it would take a notion to pour in heavy, wind-driven sheets, but only for short periods. At other times, the rain would stop altogether; but that was always difficult to determine in the deep woods. An umbrella of trees will rain droplets from their leaves long after the actual showers have ceased. All that is required is a slight gust of wind; and on the outer fringe of a hurricane, there is always plenty of that.

▼ ▼ ▼ ▼ ▼ ▼ ▼ ▼ ▼ ▼ ▼ ▼ ▼ ▼

12

A gust of wind swirling from across the creek shook the trailer—nothing big or especially frightening, just enough to let the occupants know that there was a storm around—lashing a brief torrent of rain against the windows.

Inside, spirits had sagged noticeably. Buddy's fear of losing contact with the closest, best companion he had ever known had infected both of the campers. Even without regard to the spirit-dampening uncertainties of the weather, both were achingly aware that Judgement Day was near for the two of them. As much as they tried to avoid the subject—and they did try, even Buddy—it lay there festering beneath the surface of their consciousness through any topic of conversation. Attempts at forced jocularity fell immediately flat, and both quickly gave up on that idea.

Supper was an equally flat undertaking. Under their burden of emotional strain, neither had much of an appetite, so a warmed-up can of beef stew and a few crackers were more than enough for both; and there remained a goodly portion of that left over for Brutus, to add to his dry dog food.

Even after the supper dishes were cleaned away, almost any conversational gambit was doomed to failure. Each had trouble looking the other in the eye, and though neither intended to be rude, they just couldn't help it.

Finally, as Buddy was standing at the doorway trying to force his vision to penetrate the darkness outside, Bill put a hand on his shoulder and said, "Okay, kid, I'll do the best I can. I'll try to figure out a way for the two of us, somewhere down the line. I promise."

That cheered the boy considerably. He turned and slapped the man on the shoulder. "Deal," he said. "That's a deal."

Bill went to the sink and started to clean out the coffee pot. The way they were feeling, if Buddy had been a grown man, Bill would have thought it a good time for both to get drunk. But the youth had only just had his very first taste of whiskey, so any such thought was out. A pot of coffee seemed like the next best idea.

Buddy continued to stare into the rainy darkness out the window. With his mind at least somewhat at ease, though a trifle dizzy from the bourbon, his thoughts returned to their surroundings. "What the heck is this Big Thicket, anyhow?" he asked. "Is that where we really are?"

"I guess we're as much in the Big Thicket as anybody is in the Big Thicket any more," Bill replied as he put the coffee pot on the fire. "There really is no more Big Thicket as such, only the remnants of it. Otherwise, it's mostly a state of mind."

Waiting for the coffee pot to perk, Bill stepped into the bathroom to make preparations for the first shave he had had in three days. He needed one badly; else, in only a couple of more days, his heavy mustache would acquire the company of a full, black beard.

As the man squirted a healthy offering from an aerosol can of shaving lather into his hand and began to rub it onto his cheeks, Buddy asked, "Was there ever really a Big Thicket?"

"Oh yes, there was indeed," Bill replied. "Estimates vary, but it's said that some time before the 1880's or so, it stretched for a hundred and fifty miles across the eastern part of Texas, in a band at least fifty miles wide."

"What was it?"

"Naturalists like to call it the biological crossroads of America, with various kinds of plants that are native to all four quarters of the country—east, west, north, and south—all in one spot. It still is that, to a degree. But in the beginning, at least as far as white man is concerned, it was mean. Forest, woods—the thickest, densest, toughest kind of stuff you can imagine—with stands of really huge pines and hardwoods, and underbrush and swamps that were damned near impenetrable in spots. According to some of the legends, the place was so tough that even Indians couldn't go into it."

"You mean the cannibal Indians you tried to scare me with?" the boy asked, trying his best to sneer.

"You think I was putting you on?" Bill responded, drawing the safety razor deftly down his upstretched neck. "Well, I was a little bit, at least as far as this century goes. But there used to be some in this vicinity. They were known as the Karankawas. And there still is an Indian tribe not far from here—the combination of two long-ago tribes, the Alabamas and the Coushattas. But as far as I know, they haven't eaten any blonde-headed little city punks lately." He smiled and wiped away the unshaven remains of lather with a wash cloth.

The trailer was filled with the inviting aroma of perked coffee. Bill stepped over to the stove, turned off the fire, then stepped back into the bathroom to rinse his razor under a measured ration of hot water from the tiny lavatory. "Okay, squirt," he said, handing the razor to the youth, "your turn."

Buddy glanced first at the cutting instrument in his hand, then at his own reflection in the bathroom mirror. Rubbing a tentative finger across his upper lip he said, "Okay, coach, give me some of that stuff."

Bill squirted a shot of the canned lather into Buddy's outstretched palm. The boy dabbled a wad of it onto the dark, heavy shadow of peach fuzz above his upper lip and asked, "Should I do it all, or just up here?"

"Might as well go the whole route. Who knows, it might be down to your knees by morning."

"Very funny." And the first-time shaver spread the remainder of his palmful of lather across his cheeks and chin. "Now what?"

"Now yo' takes that-there razor in yo' hand, Bo, and yo' scrapes it acrost yo' face."

"What if I cut myself?"

"Wouldn't be right if you didn't the first time around. This is the first time, isn't it?"

"Yeah."

"Well, you're overdue. So get after it," the man ordered.

Buddy stared intently into the mirror and drew the razor lightly across his right cheek. Satisfied that there was no blood yet, he made another sortie across the other cheek, carefully inspected the results and asked, "What happened to the Big Thicket?"

"Greed. Money-lusting people, not that different from your own dear father, came in and whacked it up and sent the trees to the sawmill. And if that wasn't enough to screw up the landscape, they discovered oil over by Sour Lake; and that brought in another breed of scalawags even worse than the timber barons."

"Ouch!" Buddy exclaimed, having made the inevitable razor nick just below his nose. "Damn, I'm bleeding!"

"That'll teach you to be more careful," Bill said, unsympathetically.

Buddy clenched his jaws, wiped away the trickle of blood with his left index finger, and proceeded with the delicate operation, which he completed with only one more slight nick.

"Good. Congratulations," Bill said as the boy wiped away the remainder of the blood-streaked lather from his now-initiated young face.

Pulling aside the mirror, the shaving instructor reached into the medicine cabinet behind it and extracted a bottle of aftershave lotion, with which he gave his own face a good dousing, then smeared another palmful across the face of the boy. "Welcome to manhood. Any man who drinks straight bourbon whiskey ought to at least be shaving."

"But I'm still bleeding," Buddy noted as he looked apprehensively into the mirror."

"Emergency first aid, coming up," Bill said. He tore off a section of bathroom tissue, dampened it under the faucet, then tore off two small pieces, which he stuck onto each of the boy's razor wounds. Blood dots quickly appeared on each, but there was no more flow.

Buddy looked disapprovingly into the mirror. "How long do I have to keep toilet paper stuck to my face?"

"No more than a week. It'll be healed by then."

With one more inspective glance in the mirror, the youth proclaimed, "Awesome face!" He rinsed the razor as Bill had done, handed it to him, and swaggered out of the bathroom into the couch-entry area. "Totally awesome!"

The shaving gambit had worked; Buddy was in good spirits again. Likewise, by contagion, so was Bill. In a camping trailer, tent, or any small confine, a single case of down-in-the-dumps can infect everyone around. Suddenly buoyed spirits can have the same effect.

"How about some coffee, Awesome-Face?" Bill asked.

"That'll be good. Don't happen to have any cookies to go with it, do you?"

"No, but I betcha we could whip up some toast and jelly." Bill immediately put the skillet onto the range.

Appetites having returned, the spiritual restoration was complete.

Outside, the rain appeared to have stopped, at least for the time being; but the wind continued to kick up a rumpus in the treetops. Although the trailer was rather well sealed, Buddy and Bill could still, occasionally, hear the intense arboreal rustle amid the angry winds whirling above them. Only on rare occasions did they actually feel any perceptible effect from the wind at their level, and that was little more than a rocking of the trailer and an accompanying loud squeak from its underpinnings.

It was highly perceptible, though, when a branch broke off somewhere above and came crashing down on the roof of the trailer.

"What the hell was that?" the startled Buddy asked.

"Piece of a tree," Bill replied, setting down his coffee cup. "Guess it thought it would make a good decoration on top of the trailer."

"Could a whole tree blow over on us?"

"Yep. Guess it could. I've seen 'em blown over before."

"What would happen?"

"Depends upon where it landed," Bill replied. "We could find ourselves suddenly out in the open . . . or else we might just become another legend of the Big Thicket. The kidnapper and the kid . . . disappeared into the Thicket and got swallowed-up in a hurricane. Nobody ever saw them again."

"That isn't funny."

"Want to hear a funny one?"

"Yeah."

"Don't know any. But I know a mysterious one. All the really good Big Thicket legends are mysterious ones."

"Okay, tell me a mysterious one."

"Weird lights."

"Lights?"

"Right. Small balls of light that seemed to float along in space—not up high in the sky or anything like that, but just a few feet off the ground."

"Where was this?"

"Right around here somewhere. I think it was along a road over near Saratoga. That's right; it was a road made out of what had once been a railroad track. People used to come from miles around to go walk, or park their cars, along that road—just to see those balls of light come zipping along."

"When was that?" Boys are suckers for mysterious stories; and what better way to while away a stormy evening?

"I'm not sure," Bill replied, "but I think back in the early thirties or something like that—but then, it could still be there, for all I know. Just a little ball of light, so the legend goes. And it would come zooming along the road. People who were there in a crowd said that it would even dance in and out among them. Nobody ever caught one, or got hurt by one, that I know of."

"What do you suppose it was?"

"I haven't the foggiest. Some folks believed it was the ghost of some Mexican railroad worker that had been decapitated, roaming around and looking for his head . . . or maybe it was his head roaming around and looking for his body, I don't know. But there was also some pseudo-scientific thought from some geologists or some such—folks that were here because of the oil boom—who figured that it was a phenomenon caused by swamp gases. There were a lot of sulphur springs in that area, and the geologists said that they might have contributed. I guess they must have thought it was something like an oversized fart that danced up out of the swamp—some sort of poltergeist swamp-fart."

Buddy snickered. "Do you believe it?"

"You don't know what to believe when it comes to weird things like that, especially when a lot of people have seen it. I never saw it; but I did see a weird light on the trees one time, coming from nowhere."

As if to punctuate the tale, there was a sudden howl of wind outside, and another spurt of horizontal rain lashed against the trailer windows. Buddy felt a shiver run up his spine.

Bill removed the toast from the skillet, handed a piece to Buddy, spread strawberry preserves on his own and continued. "I was sitting on a deer stand at dark-thirty in the morning, waiting for daylight and for some nice, big, eight-pointer to make the fatal mistake of crossing in front of my gunsights. It was dark enough to develop film.

"When you're waiting there like that—you should always be on stand at least a half-hour before first light—you squint and strain, waiting for the light to come, because that's when you're most likely to see a buck sneaking back to his hiding place somewhere in a yaupon thicket.

"So, in spite of the fact that it was totally dark, I was still looking around—every way I could turn my head. There was a little clearing beside me; and I was glancing across that, trying to see into the pine trees beyond, when I suddenly noticed this light shining on the trunks of the trees just past the clearing. It was a shaft of light maybe four feet across, coming from the right, which would have been from the east. There were, I don't know, maybe ten or a dozen trees lit up that way—just like somebody was shining a high-powered spotlight on them, from the right-hand side.

"Now I don't appreciate somebody horning in on my hunting place. I started to switch on my own flashlight and shine it over there toward the east, just to let whoever it was know that I was there and to get the hell away; but that didn't seem like too good an idea. Deer can see spotlights as well as people can.

"So I sat there a little longer, and the light stayed, right where it was. I figured at first that it might have been somebody moving around over there. But the light just stayed. What I figured then was that someone had been moving around, but that they'd set their light down on a tree stump or something— maybe just to adjust their gear, I don't know what—and that's why it stayed shining in that same spot.

"Well, I decided I wasn't going to put up with some fuckin' yahoos right in my lap, so I clambered down from my tree stand and went looking for them. There was just a hint of light in the eastern sky, ahead of the sunrise, so I could see just well enough to grope my way around without my flashlight. When I got down, the light was still there, on the trees; but it had become a little weaker, maybe because I had changed the angle that I was looking at it.

"There was a trail leading north out of that little clearing—I had cut it myself—and a branch from it heading east, right about the spot where that light was hitting the trees. I walked up that trail and took the eastern fork; and when I turned and looked behind me, the light was still there, shining on the trees, from the same direction. And there I was, facing east, looking right to where the light was coming from . . . but Buddy, there wasn't any light over there. Just the tiniest little predawn glow in the sky. No spotlight, no moon, nothing."

"What do you suppose it was?" Buddy was on the edge of his seat.

"Wait, I haven't finished. After I had looked over to the east and found nothing, I went back to my stand, but I didn't climb back into it; I just looked back at that light on the tree trunks. It was, I don't know, maybe eight or ten feet off the ground, and still there. But what I had been looking at all along was tree trunks on the west side of this little trail I told you about. When I got back to my stand, I noticed for the first time that there was a light on a few trees—maybe four or five of them—on the eastern side of that trail, also. But that light was coming . . . from . . . the other . . . direction! From the west! It was like that light glowing on those trees was coming invisibly from somewhere in thin air, up off the ground, and shining in two directions—from the *middle* of that little trail."

"Weren't you scared?"

"Let's say that I was suddenly taken with an urge to hunt somewhere else that morning."

"Man," Buddy said, "that would have freaked me out!"

"It freaked me out, okay. Now, I understand a lot of things. People out alone in the woods . . . in the dark . . . in unfamiliar surroundings . . . might get a little spooky and imagine something or other that isn't really there. But that won't wash in this case. Those were not unfamiliar surroundings. It was my own land. I had camped and hunted on it for over five years, and I was more or less familiar with every tree on it."

"Where was that?"

"Not too far from here, north," Bill replied, pointing toward the creek.

"Do you still own the land?"

"No, I sold it to raise a little cash."

"Do you own this land?"

"No."

"Who does?"

"I haven't any idea."

"Then how come you're here? How did you know about this place?"

"I'm acting like these damned East Texas rednecks have been doing since before they cut all this place over, back before the turn of the century; and they've been doing ever since. I'm using it because I want to; because it suits my purpose. That's the way they do it around here. It's the most lawless place, with the most lawless people in the whole state of Texas. They seem to think that they have the right to do as they damned well please, whenever and wherever they damned well please. So, I'm in Rome, doing as the Romans do."

"Then you really weren't bulling me when you first told me about the people around this place," Buddy said.

"Well, maybe I stretched it a little bit."

Outside, the wind howled again; and the two heard another,

especially strong rustle among the trees overhead. Buddy said, "Well, I still love it here. Maybe when you get all that money from my parents, you can buy another place around here somewhere and I can come visit you on it. Maybe you could buy this place . . . that would be great."

Bill smiled at the kid who was trying so hard to keep something going between them. "Yeah, maybe."

There was another heavy rustle in the trees above them, and Bill decided it was time to investigate the goings-on outside. The off-and-on pattern of the rain, which had continued through the evening, was in an "off" cycle at the moment, so it was a good time.

Picking up the handle of the gasoline lantern, he told the boy, "Come on, let's go out and see what the creek is doing."

There was tree litter all over the ground—broken-off branches and limbs; but somewhat to Bill's surprise, the creek appeared to be in good shape. There was a little rise, but nothing of major concern. The rain had been only sporadic, after all; and Bill explained to Buddy that it takes a constant deluge for a pretty good while to trigger any really significant rise in the creek.

"I don't think we have anything to worry about," he said.

Brutus appeared to be glad of that. Having emerged from beneath the trailer to accompany the two guys on their quest, whatever it was, he was happy to retreat to shelter. In a futile attempt at playing on human pity, he begged to be let inside the trailer; but he quickly gave that up as a lost cause. Nobody enjoys being in close quarters with a wet dog—especially a wet, big dog.

Back inside the trailer, Bill looked at his watch—a little past nine—and asked, "What do you think? Do you want to stay up and tell some more ghost stories, or are you ready to go to bed?"

Buddy had no real preference. Teenagers rarely ever are aware that they are tired until the action ceases and somebody reminds them. "Whatever you think," he replied.

"Well, what I think," Bill said, "is that it's going to be a good night for sleeping; and I, for one, am ready for it."

That seemed to settle the issue. Bedtime was tacitly declared, but only after a few clean-up chores were accomplished. The coffee pot was rinsed and set aside, teeth were brushed, and the toilet-paper bandages were removed from the boy's self-inflicted facial wounds. Bill unfolded his sleeping facility, extinguished the lantern, and both climbed semi-exhaustedly into their beds. The temperature had cooled considerably because of the rain— a far cry from the sweltering heat of the previous two nights— and each of the played-out campers immediately curled-up beneath his light blanket.

Sleep came early to neither of them. Buddy lay in his bunk trying to visualize balls of light floating down a country road and darting in and out of crowds of amused spectators, and pine trees at the edge of a forest clearing illuminated by ghost light. Accompanied by the howl of wind, the tumult of tossing tree-tops overhead, and the occasional, intermittent lashing of wind-driven rain against the front of the trailer, they were marvelous, shiver-producing, bedtime reflections.

Bill's thoughts were more pragmatic. Tomorrow would be the day that he had to return to Beaumont and make another telephone call to Houston, pressing his ransom demands this time to the eminent Mr. Hamilton Robert Caine, Sr., himself; and to make arrangements for the exchange of tousle-topped boy for government-issue greenbacks. He hadn't yet figured out exactly how he was going to do it all—that is, what he was going to do with Buddy while he drove to town.

He dared not take the boy along with him and risk recognition. Yet he hated to leave him there alone in the woods. It would be a lonely three hours or so that he would be gone. His original plan, of course, had been to leave him handcuffed to the bed, or chained outside to the tree as he had done on their arrival at the campsite; but that sort of cruelty was no longer necessary. He could trust Buddy. The problem remained unresolved, as sleep overcame him instead of inspiration.

It was never known how long the two of them slept. It could have been as long as two or three hours, or as short as thirty minutes. Whatever it was, their awakening was abrupt.

Bill was jarred by a sudden, violent shaking of the trailer. It appeared not to be the same as the occasional rocking it had taken from the wind gusts that blew at them from across the creek, but that was difficult to determine through the nether-world of sleep.

When consciousness finally overcame the mental cobwebs, he leaped from his suspended bed and landed with a splash; the trailer floor was covered with water. He reached for the light switch, but the only response was a loud hissing, which must have been the battery or the line shorting out.

Yelling, "Buddy! Wake up!" Bill waded across the trailer floor, shook the still-sleeping youngster by the shoulder and commanded, "Get up NOW! We've got to get out of here!"

As the boy struggled to consciousness, Bill grabbed his hand and said, "Come on, let's go."

Buddy was really not yet fully awake as they exited down the trailer steps in the darkness outside into waist-deep water—but the van was on higher ground. Bill was pulling his young charge toward their only escape route when the boy, realizing his state of undress and the obvious need to get into the van and drive away somewhere, was suddenly overcome by an attack of civilization.

"My pants, just a minute, I've got to get my pants." He tore loose from the man's grasp and waded back into the trailer.

The boy had barely gotten inside when it hit. From out of the darkness, a giant crest of water slammed into Bill with the fury and irresistible force of an oncoming train, and he was imme-diately swept away.

Gasping, struggling to keep his head above the torrent—to hold his breath, to stay alive—he yelled, "Buddy, stay with it. . . !"

Through his struggling, Bill found it all totally unbelievable. He knew about the wall-of-water effect on rain-swollen creeks and rivers; he had even seen the aftermaths of a couple of them—one in far West Texas and the other in Colorado. But that sort of thing happens only in deep canyons and arid loca-tions—dry creekbeds that fill up with a multi-inch downpour and turn into raging torrents. But this was East Texas, the Big Thicket. It was used to lots of rain. The creeks will swell up and overflow, yes; but that wall-of-water business can't happen here. Besides, there hadn't been that much rain.

But it did happen; and there he was, caught in its inexorable rush and struggling to stay alive. And Buddy, the innocent kid for whose circumstance the kidnapper was responsible, was back there where the man had brought him and left him—drowning in the trailer.

Coughing, sputtering, stretching to get a toehold here, a shove-off there—enough to keep his head above the flood—Bill screamed again in anguish, "Buddy!"

"Buh-dee-ee-ee!"

▼ ▼ ▼ ▼ ▼ ▼ ▼ ▼ ▼ ▼ ▼ ▼ ▼

13

Bill managed to develop a sort of rhythmic bodily undulation within the implacable crest of the flood. He kept both legs at half-cock, ready to spring away from a side bank or a touch of bottom, and this worked to propel his head above the flow often enough to enable him to catch an occasional quick breath. He shielded his head between his arms to protect it from the severe blows his entire body was getting as it was buffeted about against tree trunks and limbs, creek banks and other protrusions. Thus riding out the torrent, he hoped, he could keep from drowning.

He was somewhere near the center of the crest when his frail, unprotected collection of human flesh, bones, and thin, tender skin was hurled through an excruciating torture chamber. It was the dense arbor above the creek tunnel where he and his young Buddy had discovered the lion tracks. His body was rapidly extruded through the dense entanglement like a lead bullet down a rifled gun barrel—squeezed, scraped, twisted and distorted every foot of the way. When he emerged, after perhaps seventy-five yards of punishing bristle-brush, his skin was all but shredded, and bleeding from a multiplicity of lacerations. If he could have been seen through the pitch darkness of that terrible night, he doubtless would have appeared more like a zebra than a human, only with red stripes instead of black.

The fury of nature's force failed to be impressed, however, with the man's having survived that one simple torture-tunnel; there remained yet miles of creekbed downstream to be swelled with the hurricane-inspired flood crest, and untold punishment waiting to be dealt to his tortured body in that impenetrable darkness.

Again maintaining his ready-to-spring, crouched position, Bill's feet felt an earthen outcropping and he leaped upward, once more to propel his head above the tide and attempt to grab a quick breath of air. He was himself grabbed, instead.

Having utilized his arms as propelling implements, like a swimmer heading to the surface after a high dive, his head was unprotected when it encountered an overhanging magnolia limb. It caught him in the left temple, and he felt himself begin rapidly to lose consciousness. The blow to the head and incipient blackout occurred simultaneous to the rapid inhalation intended to provide another life-sustaining lungful of air; but he was knocked back underwater by the tree limb, so what he received was a lungful of water, instead.

The bodily control that he had been able to maintain was now completely lost, and he was thrust helplessly onward by the rushing water. Gasping and coughing, Bill struggled to remain conscious . . . to expel the water from his lungs . . . to get more air . . . to stay alive.

In the midst of his battle, he thought of Buddy, back in the trailer, and wondered whether the boy could possibly survive. The thought triggered an intense feeling of fright, and deep remorse, that jolted his entire being like the body-shock from a dose of high-voltage electricity. Coupled with that fright and remorse, though, came a profound sense of determination.

I will make it through this! he told himself as he continued his pell-mell advance. *I will survive and get Buddy out . . . if only he can manage to keep himself alive.*

Bill's feet touched ground, tossing him into a somersault. Although barely conscious, he was able, by reflex action, to form his right arm into a crook in hope of grasping onto something that could halt his helpless flight downstream. Another overhanging limb stuck his head a glancing blow and lodged in the crotch of his arm, jerking his headlong surge to an immediate halt. It was the break he had hoped for.

Forcing himself to summon all the strength within him, Bill

lifted his head above the flood tide, expelled enough water and inhaled enough fresh air to shake off his body's intended lapse into unconsciousness, and to continue surviving—at least for the moment. But his hold was precarious, at best. It soon let go and he was back, once again, in the rage and rush of the creek.

His head ached more like he had been struck a direct blow by a woodsman's axe than by a simple tree limb. The brief respite he had managed with his arm-hold on the second tree limb, however, had enabled him to resume his crouched position and the rhythmic springing away out of the water and into the air for life-sustaining oxygen.

He was doing just that when his upper body was thrust into what he feared might be another punishing excursion through thorns and brush. Hoping to avoid that, he reached out an open hand and succeeded in grabbing a firm hold on a piece of brush. From that, he found another firm hold. Then another. And another. Until, at last, he had contrived to arm-walk his way out of the main current of the flood tide and into an area that, though still deep in water, was relatively tranquil compared to where he had been.

Clinging tightly with both hands, Bill examined with his fingertips the texture of the bush that had saved him. It was yaupon. "As long as I live," he vowed, "I'll never cuss this beautiful stuff again!"

The man's powerful arms had brought him to the main stalk of the obviously large yaupon, yet he was still in water so deep that his feet could feel no ground. While holding fast to the bush with one hand, he reached out in all directions with the other, but could find nothing else to grab onto so that he might arm-walk the rest of the way out of the water; and in the blackness of the night, absolutely nothing was visible. Still, he felt relatively secure in his position, so he had to content himself with continuing to cling tightly to that providential yaupon and wait for dawn.

There are long nights and there are long waits, but the man his young pal had named Bill had never before experienced either a night or a wait as long as that one. For interminable hours, the rain that had spawned the flood continued its inter-

mittent, spurting activity—punctuated by occasionally heavy
downpours that lashed their ice-bullet drops at the unprotected
face of the man in the water. Floating debris kept hitting him
about the head, also—small twigs, large tree branches, forest-
floor flotsam from what must have been miles of land unaccustomed to having creeks flowing across it. Occasionally, he
felt something submerged brush across his lower body—some
unidentifiable, flood-borne something that always made him
jump. Snakes, he knew, are forever a danger in any flooding
situation, and he had no taste for tangling with one of any kind
while dangling from a precarious brush-hold in the middle of a
pitch-black night.

He had no idea how far downstream he had been carried by
the flooded creek, but the velocity had been so great that he
knew it must have been quite a distance. How far—two hundred yards? A mile? Two miles? No way of knowing. He knew
only that it was over—at least he wanted to believe that it was
over. Come dawn, he could work his way out of it and go find
Buddy.

Once again, he was struck with that intense, internal body
blow of anxiety-laden emotion when his thoughts returned to
Buddy; and once they had done so, he could concentrate on
nothing else. His growing affection for the youth, which he had
tried hard to stifle, was now projecting straightaway from the
raw edges of his every nerve ending. The boy he had thought of
as his meal ticket, his grubstake, had grown to mean so painfully much more to him.

God, he admitted to himself, how he enjoyed that kid! What
a great kick he got out of teaching him about the woods! What a
joy it was to see him shoot and react to his own success, or to
delight at the discovery of some insignificant triviality in the
newfound world around him! Nothing in Bill's entire experience could match the satisfaction he felt when, attempting
some esoteric explanation, he could see the light of comprehen-
sion dawn in those expressive blue eyes.

Dangling from the yaupon, neck-deep in water, Bill realized
that the sensation he had been feeling must be truly what it was

like to be a father. Or was it merely that of being a teacher? *But then*, he mused, *being a father is being a teacher, isn't it?*

Whatever it was, it was the most enjoyable, gratifying experience he had ever had. Then self-analysis crept into his thoughts, and he wondered whether all of that enjoyment that he felt was nothing more than ego gratification. Did his experiences with the youth, reflected by the boy's obvious adulation, serve only to massage the man's personal ego? Was it the boost to his own self-esteem that made him feel so good, or was it really genuine affection for the kid?

How could he know? Who can look deeply enough inside a man's soul to determine what his feelings really are? And whose business is it, anyhow? Bill knew, though, that it was his business to determine what he truly felt about the boy . . . and thereby, perhaps, what he truly felt about himself. And it was demonstrably his business to get the boy out of the mess that he had gotten him into.

Aloud, he pleaded in the face of the elements that had overwhelmed him, "Just hang on Buddy, I'll get you out of here. I promise."

There was good reason to believe that Buddy could survive the aqueous onslaught that had swept his kidnapper away, and Bill was sustained by it. There was no way of knowing, of course, how deep the water might have gotten inside the trailer, but he reasoned that there was plenty of stuff inside for the kid to stand on to escape the rising tide. He also knew that the force of the current had been so fierce that it might have swept the tiny trailer along with it, tumbling as it went; and with the boy rattling around loose inside, he could easily have been knocked unconscious. He would then have been completely unable to escape drowning; he would be dead.

It hurt the man terribly to realize that he was responsible for whatever pain the kid might have suffered, or might still be suffering—hurt him worse than the body-covered stinging of his own torn flesh, worse than the aching of his head from the blow of the tree limb, and worse than the icy chill of the creek water in which he must remain immersed the rest of the night. He knew that, had it not been for his own ambition, for his greed, that great kid would never have been there in the first place.

And why, he wondered, hadn't he heeded the hurricane warnings? Why hadn't he hauled-ass out of there as soon as the rain started and been safe? Was he so caught up with his situation, *in loco parentis* there in the woods, and enjoying it so much, that he just couldn't let go? Or was he simply trying to play it safe and not get caught?

Well, he thought, *I played it safe all right. I played it so goddamned safe that I might have gotten us both killed.*

A shiver shook him from head to toe, and he realized that the chill of the creek water was beginning to rob him of body heat. That was dangerous. Trying to stimulate circulation, he began methodically to maneuver his way around the yaupon bush in the same arm-walk that had brought him there, thrashing his legs as he went much as Buddy had done when he plunged into the icy waters for that first bath. At least it was something to do; but he wondered how long he could keep it up, or whether fatigue would overtake him and lull him into sleep.

People go to sleep before they freeze to death, he thought. He knew it was a normal bodily reaction to hypothermia, and he supposed that a person could suffer from hypothermia just as easily by spending the night in a frigid creek as he could trudging through mountain snow. There was a vast temperature differential, of course, but the principle remains the same—a person's body heat gets dissipated, and he's got hypothermia. Then he lapses into sleep and freezes to death; except in Bill's case, if he lapsed into sleep he would drown.

Mustn't let myself go to sleep!

▼ ▼ ▼

As all things must, even purgatory will ultimately come to an end. Bill's did—after he knew not how many hours of arm-walking around the yaupon bush, fighting chill and exhaustion—with the first faint glimmerings of light from a still far-from-rising sun.

The most dense objects, usually the outlines of trees, are always the first things to become discernible in the earliest light of dawn. So it was from the man's water's-eye view; but that was not enough to enable him to negotiate a passage out of the swollen creek. As with the countless times he had sat in a deer-hunting stand in just such a predawn situation, he had to wait . . . and wait . . . eyes straining in effort to hurry the moment when objects finally become defined clearly enough to be identified. Creepingly, the moment came, as it always does.

Bill studied his situation and determined that it could have been a lot better. The yaupon bush to which he had clung throughout the night was a lone island in the creek-sea that surrounded him. There was much, much more water than he had expected. Although he had grossly miscalculated the probabilities of flood before he and the boy went to bed, the source of all that water was clear to him now.

There had not been any great amount of rain there at their creekside campsite, rightly enough; but Bill had failed to consider what a deluge from the hurricane—and that one must have been considerable—might do to the creek's watershed upstream. Obviously, it did plenty, resulting in the tremendous rise there at camp and the uncustomary-for-East-Texas wall of water that had washed him away. How much more, Bill wondered, was he going to miscalculate in his ill-fated attempt at kidnapping?

There was not much to miscalculate now, however; he would simply have to swim his way out to the stretched-away creek bank. Even though apart from the central force of the still-heavy flood tide, there remained ample current at his location to make the swim out a heavy task, though not an impossible one.

Taking a deep breath, he bade thank you and good-bye to the yaupon that had saved his life, and stuck out in a strong crawl stroke. He touched-in amid the prickly embrace of a small holly tree, found his footing, and waded the rest of the way out to sodden, but relatively dry land. At last.

Bone-weary, the man stretched out flat on the ground and lay there for a long few minutes to muster his strength for what he knew would be an arduous and anxious search for the missing

Buddy. Although he had no intentions of doing so, he drifted into a short nap, until he was awakened by the rays of the all-forgiving sunrise shining brightly on his face.

To his surprise, it was a beautiful morning. Anyone who had suffered through what the night had dealt to Bill might have found any kind of morning to be delightful, simply for the sake of visibility; but this one was beautiful even to a purist's specifications. The sun was brilliant and penetratingly warm, accompanied by a few thin lines of clouds across the horizon and only a scattering of puffy, white cumuli to decorate the clear blue heavens above. Who could ever have believed, at such a dawn, that a hurricane had been through the night before?

Having fought off hypothermia for he knew not how long, Bill relished the penetrating heat of the sun. But as he had had only a scant few minutes of sleep, he now began to feel the results of the beating he had taken in every muscle, tendon, bone, and joint of his body.

He knew that he was desperately in need of rest, but there was no time for that now. As he sat up, shaking to clear his head, he discovered for the first time the visible evidence of his flood-borne trip through the briar patch. He examined his head-to-toe lacerations, and the thought occurred that this was one sight he'd rather not even see—but there it was, all over him.

Now a new worry. Some of the scratches and abrasions were obviously serious enough to have caused bleeding, but that had all been stopped by his continued immersion in the frigid water. Many of his helter-skelter body stripes, he noticed, were swollen and puffy beneath their wrinkled covering of water-softened skin.

Looks like a good way to catch typhus . . . or something. And he wondered, *Is it typhus? Is that what you get from open wounds in polluted water? Whatever it is, it looks like I'm ripe for it. But to hell with it, no sense in worrying about that now, there's not a damned thing I can do about it.*

The worry that pre-empted all others, he believed, must be somewhere back upstream. He would have to pull himself together now and go back . . . go back and find Buddy.

Looking around at the terrain, Bill had no earthly idea where he was. His landing spot was not as dense as much of the thicket he had been through, but then it was not the sylvan glade where he and the kid had taken their last swim together, either. As he studied the lay of the land, there was no obviously easy route to take—not for a man with no clothing except a soggy pair of jockey shorts and, worst of all, no shoes.

What the hell? he thought, as he rose to his feet for the first time. *I can't get much more scratched up. And I might as well get a few splinters in my feet to even things up.*

His first, tentative attempt at walking was a shock. The legs moved as ordered, and the feet touched ground more or less as they were directed, but the torso didn't seem to want to follow suit. It tended to sway, to wallow on its underpinnings; and it was when he tried mentally to will his wayward trunk into proper alignment that he noticed his head felt like it was splitting wide open. Remembering the terrific blow he had taken from the tree limb, he reached a hand tentatively up to his temple for a fingertip exploration. To no surprise, he found it swollen and extremely sensitive to the touch. It was only then that the realization struck him that he was lucky, after what he had been through, even to be alive.

Bullshit! his thought countered. *If I was lucky, the whole damned thing wouldn't have happened in the first place.*

Then fortunate, maybe.

Bullshit on that, too. Bullshit on everything.

Especially on aching muscles, and splitting heads, and torsos that tended to teeter.

That's it, fellow, get mad. That'll do it.

And it probably did. Somehow, at least, he did succeed in forcing his body to function as a whole unit instead of a disjunct collection of individual parts; and he started to walk.

Upstream. That was the best he would do—just keep trudging upstream. There was no way of knowing where the boy might be . . . if there was anything left of him.

"Mustn't think like that," he mumbled aloud. Then to himself, *Don't think at all. Just walk. Keep walking. Keep looking. Keep . . . going.*

After a little practice, keeping walking and keeping going became a trifle easier, but looking was a virtual impossibility. There was nothing to look at but Big Thicket woodlands—tall trees and short trees, underbrush and overbrush, Nature at her meanest. Somehow, the Thicket had lost its charm for the moment.

Lacing through it all, with no banks for definition, no markings, no boundaries, was the flooded creek. There was no visibility beyond, nothing but a meandering waterline among the trees and brush. But with nothing else to guide him, Bill had no choice but to continue to follow its outline.

And what the hell, he wondered, was he looking for anyway? Was he expecting to find the lifeless body of his young pal lodged against a tree trunk somewhere? Maybe with his belly bloated? *God no! That's the one thing I don't want to find.* If such were the case, the man thought, he'd rather not find him at all.

"Please God," the devoutly unreligious man murmured aloud, "if that's gonna be it, just let him stay missing. I don't want to have to handle that."

That was cowardly, he realized.

"No," he spoke again, "I'll handle it. Just let me find him, no matter what. I've got to know."

Occasionally, during his desperate walk, Bill would wade out into the flood, heedless of the submerged brambles that kept snagging and grabbing at his flesh, hoping to locate the center of the stream; but each time he did so, he would find himself chest deep in water, with no definable stream location in sight. With the sun to guide him, it occurred to him that he could strike out away from the thicket he was having to traverse and attempt to find the road into camp. The creek meandered roughly northwest to southeast at that point, so such a circumvention would not have been difficult. It was also not the best idea, either, he realized. As painful as it was, he had to keep searching along the water's edge, with occasional forays into the water, for what he fervently hoped not to find.

It was on one such foray that he made a painful, but heartening, discovery. His right leg was sharply pierced in two places—thigh and calf. He took a breath, ducked underwater to examine what had grabbed him, and his exploring fingers identified the unmistakable presence of a barbed-wire fence. Thinking about it for a moment, he realized that there was only one such fence in the area, to his knowledge. He had to drive through it, through a former gate opening, to reach his campsite. If what he figured was correct, that meant that the creek flood, at that point, must be across the road!

To check it out, he struck out north, deeper into the creek, feeling his way along the rusted fenceline as he went. In short order, he emerged out of the brush into a narrow, clear passageway—almost shoulder deep now—and stumbled over the short, wooden approach-railing to a bridge. From somewhere, he grabbed onto a long, stout vine, just in case the current became too strong for him to remain erect. Cautiously, he paid his way out the vine until, ultimately, the rush of the flood water swept him off his feet and he hung there, dangling in the rushing current like a wind-tossed, toy balloon.

Before he lost his footing, though, he felt the wooden slats of the bridge beneath his feet. He was dangling atop the only bridge, across the only road anywhere around there; and the main channel of the creek was directly beneath him. That meant that camp was no more than a quarter to a half-mile away!

Pulling himself hand-over-hand along the vine, back out of the central flood, he relocated the submerged fenceline and retraced it back to where he had entered the water. Then he continued to follow the waterline through the woods once more, and found that it seemed to be receding to the north. Presently, he was in a narrow, clear path again—it was the road, leading directly to camp.

Back into the water now, he waded due north. Somewhere around there, there had to be a trailer, or what was left of one; and a van. There had to be the van!

The first clue he got was a glimpse of something red up ahead, something red shining in the slanting rays of the morning sun. Wading toward it, he was soon able to make unmistakable identification. It was Buddy's skimpy little red bikini underwear!

Trudging closer and ever deeper now, he could see that the boy was lying face down atop something protruding from the water. Then the wheels became evident; and the axle; and part of the tongue. The slender body with the scant red skivvies was stretched out atop the bottom of the upended trailer.

The boy was asleep. Asleep in the morning sun.

Asleep . . . and alive!

Bill's pace quickened. Fatigue disappeared. Muscular aches, painful scratches and abrasions, the pounding headaches—all became unfelt; the man had the strength of a horse. He started running through the water, and when it got too deep to run in, he dove in and began to swim, strongly, against the current that tried to carry him away. When he reached the end of the trailer he climbed aboard, stood up, then halted to study the welcome sight before him. The boy, he reasoned, must be completely exhausted.

He looked so fragile there, so vulnerable lying face down on the trailer bottom with his head cradled atop his right forearm. Trailer bottoms are never pretty; and this one, with its rusting axle and dirty wheels, was downright ugly. But the boy . . . the boy was beautiful. Unclothed, unkempt . . . and beautiful!

Gruffly, to hide his emotions, the man kicked him on the bottom of a foot. "What's the matter kid," he asked, "can't you read the sign? No shirt, no shoes, no service."

The tousled blonde head raised off its rest and a pair of glazed-over blue eyes glanced upward and to the rear.

"BILL!"

Buddy jumped to his feet and threw his arms around the man's waist. "Bill!"

The man clasped the boy to him in a bear hug, and both stood in silent embrace for a long, glorious moment. Neither of them could speak; and neither felt any shame at all about the tears trickling down both of their cheeks.

▼ ▼ ▼ ▼ ▼ ▼ ▼ ▼ ▼ ▼ ▼ ▼ ▼ ▼

14

His face was buried so tightly in the hairy tangle of the man's chest that Buddy had a hard time articulating the words when they did come. It was with a breathless mixture of a deep sigh and a sob that he finally stammered, "I . . . I thought you were dead."

"Who, me?" Bill replied. Strength . . . firmness . . . stolidity seemed the appropriate posture for the moment, although reasoned observation might more correctly have labeled it bravado.

Grasping the boy firmly by both shoulders, he thrust him away from the tight embrace and held him at arm's length, basking in the caress of those now-radiant blue eyes. "I just thought I'd go do a little body-surfing."

"Liar," Buddy observed, half-laughing. The glow of the eyes now covered his entire face as he teased, "You're nothing but a big, fat, hairy, mean, liar!"

"I'm not either fat, you little spoily-ass city brat."

"But you're still a liar!" Buddy half-screamed in near falsetto. His excitement and obvious joy had conspired to constrict his vocal chords and raise his voice almost a full octave. It was only then that he noticed the ravages that had been inflicted on the man's body. Reaching out tentatively, concerned, he touched one of the nastier-looking wounds and asked, "What happened to you?"

Bill looked down at the exploring fingers on his chest, and then back into the blue eyes that he had prayed (in his own way) to see again. That wrinkle of a half-smile, now so familiar to his young friend, appeared in the left corner of his mouth as he replied, "There was a lot of seaweed in the surf." With a light, open-handed slap against the boy's cheek, he asked, "But what about you, did you miss me?"

Buddy joined in the bravado game, "Miss you? Hell, no. It's the first peace and quiet I've had in three days. I was just having a nice nap when you had to come wake me up."

"Can't let you nap on a beautiful morning like this. What say we go for a short swim?"

"How short?" Buddy inquired.

"Like, say, over to the bank over there," Bill replied, motioning to distant south.

"Well, I'm not used to swimming with all my clothes on these days," Buddy said, tugging at his scant skivvies. "But I suppose I could manage just this once."

Bill glanced around the sunken hulk of the trailer beneath them. It had come to rest just outside of the tumultuous mainstream current of the raging creek, which was clearly discernible in front of the trailer's upside-down tongue. The door and windows were all below water level beneath them, inaccessible; their clothing, which they would need to face the world, was buried beneath the swirling torrent.

"I guess we're up shit creek for clothes, aren't we?" he asked.

"I didn't know that was the name of this creek," Buddy replied. "But it sure fits."

"Five will get you ten that the trailer's got ninety feet of sand in it down there, and everything is buried under it even if we could get to it. I guess I could go down and check it out though."

"No!" Buddy quickly responded. "Don't go. We don't have to have clothes."

Enjoying the boy's show of concern, Bill knelt down and dangled his left leg backwards into the rushing water, in apparent preparation for easing himself into it.

"No!" Buddy screamed again, grabbing him by the arm. "I don't want you to. Please!"

It seemed like a cheap trick to force additional show of concern, but Bill perversely enjoyed it, nonetheless. Standing up again, he carefully surveyed the situation now for the first time.

There was little difficulty locating the van. It was only twenty yards upstream from the trailer, with nothing but its left front fender and a couple of feet of bumper protruding above the rushing waters, smack in the center of the strongest part of the current. Bill calculated its position by locating the partially submerged beech trees that had formed the arbor over the once-shallow stream, and he figured that the van must have lodged, tail down, squarely in the middle of the pool where he and his young guest had bathed. Chances were that it, too, would be full of flood-borne silt, and that any attempt at checking it out would result in another rapid ride downstream and a second aquatic bristle-brush treatment. He had no taste for any more of that. Glancing again at Buddy, he could see concern in the boy's eyes; but it was quickly wiped away by a broad smile.

"Right," Bill agreed. "Who the hell needs clothes? Are you a strong-enough swimmer to fight this current and get to that bank?" he asked, pointing.

"Come off it," Buddy replied. "I bet I'll beat you there."

Bill gestured to the swirling waters around the trailer beneath them. "See the way the current is working around here? You'll have to get clear of that in a hurry, or you're going to be in for a wild ride that I promise you, you won't enjoy."

"Piece of cake," the boy announced. "Follow the leader." And he dove in with all the grace of a natural athlete. Bill was close behind.

The boy was a good three yards ahead of the man when they splashed out into wading depth downstream from the spot that was once their serene campsite. "See, you creaky old fart," he said, recalling the memorable epithet from his badminton embarrassment, "I told you I'd beat you."

Both smiling, the two woods buddies locked arms around each other's shoulders and waded the rest of the way out of the water. When they reached a sunny spot, both flopped to the ground to soak up the warmth.

"God damn, kid!" Bill exclaimed, with a broad smile and a sideways nod of his head. "It sure is good to see you."

"Me too," Buddy replied. "I was so scared something had happened to you."

"How did you manage to get out of that mess?" the man asked, gesturing toward the sunken trailer.

"After I looked at it a while ago, I don't see how I did." Shaking his head to emphasize his incredulity, the boy added, "But I did."

"Tell me what happened."

"Well . . . when that big wave hit, the door of the trailer slammed shut and the whole thing just seemed to lift up off of its wheels, and I felt it kinda rockin' back and forth, real hard. I fell down a couple of times trying to get to the door; and then when I got there, the damned thing wouldn't open. I tried and tried to get it to open, but there was just no way. I don't know whether it was broken, or it was just the push of the water outside against it, but the fuckin' thing just wouldn't open.

"I was standing there fighting with the door when the whole trailer just sorta flipped, like one of those big machine-things at a carnival, and I was bouncing around on the ceiling, upside down. I heard a lot of glass breaking when that happened, and pretty soon water was gushing in all over the place. Most of it, I thought, was coming in that big window over there by where the couch and your bed were.

"I couldn't see anything at all. It was totally dark; and I was trying to remember where everything was inside, and trying to figure a way out of that window when the whole thing went end-over-end again . . . twice. That's when I bashed my head against something inside, and my head started pounding real hard."

"Did you black out?" Bill asked.

"No, but I thought I was going to. Water was coming in real fast now, so I fished around with my hands; and the first thing I found was that pole over by the bunk beds—the one you had locked me to with the handcuffs. I figured the best thing I could do was to grab onto that pole and hang on real tight; and that's what I did.

"After a while, the water stopped coming in so fast, and then it stopped altogether. When it did, it left an air pocket—sorta like a big bubble, I guess—up there where my head was, right near the floor of the trailer."

"How big a pocket?" Bill asked.

"Not very damned big. I guess it must have been maybe four or five inches deep. By pushing and stretching with all my might against the pole, I could just barely get my nose and mouth up there out of the water. But there was air there enough for me to breathe, although I didn't know how long it would last."

"So what did you do," the man wondered, "just hang there holding onto the pole with your nose against the floor, or did you try to get out?"

"No, I was afraid to try to get out. I didn't know what I might get myself into if I tried to get out; so I figured that I'd better just hang on there as long as I could—as long as the air held out. I guess I was just too scared to do anything else."

Bill interrupted, "The water got a little chilly during the night, didn't it?"

"Oh shit, did it? I thought I was going to freeze my ass to absolute death. After hanging there a little while, I figured out how I could rest my legs on the bottom of the bottom bunk, the one I slept on. It was kinda weird with the whole thing upside down, but I could just kinda hang there, halfway stretched out, half sitting and half lying down. I couldn't let go of the pole—I was afraid I would float away—but I didn't have to hold on for dear life like I had done before. Every once in a while I would sorta doze off, and my head would sink down in the water. That would wake me up, for sure, and I'd come up sputtering and coughing and grabbing for my pole.

"And then I'd get so cold, so awful cold, and I knew that I had to do something to get some blood going inside me; so every once in a while I would kick my feet and raise my legs up and down as fast as I could. I guess it helped a little bit, I don't know."

"How long did you stay there like that?"

"'Til daylight," the boy replied. "I don't know how long it was—hours and hours. It seemed like forever. Slowly, though, finally, things started getting lighter, until I could just barely see around inside. Mostly the floor of the trailer and that pole were all I could see. It's funny how much I hated that god-damned pole before; but all night last night, I loved the son-of-a-bitch."

"I know how you felt," Bill noted. "I had the same feelings myself for a yaupon bush. But how did you finally get out?"

"After a while, I figured that it was as light in there as it was gonna be, so I had to do something. Probably the only way out, I figured, was through that biggest window by the couch, which obviously was busted. I didn't know how strong the current would be when I got out, but I figured it would be pretty damn strong, so I'd better have something to hold onto. So . . . I dove in and swam around inside a few times and managed to find our blankets. I tied them together, then I tied one end around my pole. Then I held onto that blanket, dove underwater again and went looking for that window. When I found it, I felt around for the broken glass and pulled out a couple of big pieces from it until it felt like the hole was big enough for me to get through."

"Did you cut yourself?"

"Not then, not until I tried to wiggle through it. Then I scratched my stomach a little bit." Buddy traced his right index finger along a four or five-inch, thin-line scratch on his lower abdomen that Bill had not noticed before. "And along my knee," the boy added, displaying a similar tear on his right knee.

Continuing his narrative, Buddy said, "When I figured I could wiggle through the hole in the window, I went back up to the floor—that sounds so funny, I went 'up' to the floor—got myself a deep breath of air, then held tight to my blanket and worked my way out the window."

"I'm surprised you didn't run out of blanket before you got up top," Bill said.

"I did. In fact, I just barely got through the window and started up the side of the trailer toward the surface when I reached the end of my blanket. I could feel the current in the creek pushing really hard against my feet and legs, and it scared the pure-D piss out of me. But I hung on there onto that blanket with my right hand and reached as far up with my left as I could. I caught hold of something on the bottom of the trailer—it was some kind of shelf or something—and I held on real tight. Then I grabbed hold of that with my right hand, too. I raised my head just a little bit and there I was, out of the water and almost on the bottom of the trailer. I stretched out as far as I could stretch and was able to get a good, firm hold on the side of the trailer tongue and pull myself up. It felt so god-damned good being out of the water that I wanted to kiss the bottom of that trailer. The next thing I knew, the sun was shining and I fell asleep. Then the next, next thing I knew, some old fart was kicking me on the feet."

Bill patted him on the leg. "You done good, kid; I'm proud of you."

Buddy smiled, but the smile quickly faded when he remembered his nightlong concern. "I spent a lot of the time during the night worrying about you. I was afraid you had drowned . . . or something."

He then shifted back into bravado and teasing, false nonchalance. "I didn't care, of course; but since I had no earthly idea where in the hell I was, I thought it might be nice to have you around to find the way out of here."

Bill thought about his nightlong anguish over the boy and half-mumbled, "Tears don't show in the water."

"What'd you say?"

"I said it's no fun spending the night in the water. I had to do the same thing myself."

At Buddy's insistence, Bill recounted in full detail his own harrowing experiences in the clutches of the flood, though never once intimating his overriding concern for the safety of the boy. He had shown quite enough weakness and emotion already; it was stiff-upper-lip time again.

In addition to his own inadvertent demonstration of softness, Bill sensed a subtle change in the boy, as well. As Buddy recounted his personal fright-night, Bill could not avoid noticing his suddenly more "colorful" turn of phrase. It could have been due only to excitement, but Bill felt that by sprinkling his language more freely with profanity than he previously had done, the boy seemed to be signaling a desired change in their man-and-boy relationship to one of equal partners. Bill had spoken freely with the youth all along, openheartedly welcoming him into his private world. He now felt as though Buddy appeared to be admitting the man into his, and nothing should any longer be held back.

In Bill's judgment, it was only reasonable for the boy to assume that each of them had been tested with his own trial by water torture, and each had passed the test. Individually and alone, each had taken the worst that nature had to dish out, and had triumphed on his own terms. Now, they were equals.

That meant that there was no room in their relationship for condescension or patronizing (if there ever had been any of that). There was no need to establish or try to maintain dominance or superiority; and the kidnapper-captive arrangement was permanently and completely abolished.

Fine by me, Bill thought. Looking directly at Buddy now, he realized that what he was witnessing in the boy must be a case of instant maturity. And he enjoyed being part of it.

As of the moment they walked out of the flooded creek together, the man believed, they were just a couple of very dear friends, largely interdependent, and faced with the same set of problems. For the time being, at least, neither of them possessed anything more than a skimpy piece of water-soaked underwear to shield his nakedness and vulnerability from the world. That is all either of them had to face a hostile environment, and to fight their way out of a predicament that a cruel twist of fate had dealt—that, and one important thing more: they had each other.

As if to underscore the point, Buddy leaped to his feet, obviously ready to take on whatever came next. "Well, coach, what do we do now?"

Bill looked around at the ruination of his entire playhouse— all of his belongings, all of his plans, and all, perhaps, of his future; then he rose to his feet. "Well hell, Buddy, I guess we punt."

He saw the gesture coming and caught the boy's swinging hand with a resounding, high-five slap. Whatever was to come, they would face it together.

Buddy literally danced away. He picked up a fallen twig and

threw it at the man. Bill caught it and threw it back. "Little punk, I'll get you," and he took off after the boy.

The youngster ducked behind a tree as the middle-aged man futilely grabbed a double handful of air behind him. Buddy then spread his hands widely apart, glanced in every direction and asked, "Which way to . . . wherever?"

"Thataway," Bill replied, motioning downstream. "Thataway."

"What the hell is 'thataway'?"

"It beats the hell out of me. But this much is obvious, it's not going to do us any good to stick around here. We're just going to have to walk this mother out until we get to a highway."

"Then what?"

"I don't know what." He did know, of course; he just wouldn't say it. They would have to separate.

"Won't we look kinda strange walking down a highway in our underwear?"

"Yep. Kinda strange."

"I don't care," the boy declared, his happiness radiating from every pore. "I just don't . . ."

"Don't what?"

"Don't . . . give a shit! But why," he wondered ". . . why don't we just walk out the road we came in on?"

"Because that road is under water," Bill explained. "I came by it on my way back here this morning. We would have to cross the creek to stay on the road, and the current is too swift. We couldn't get across it. Besides, it's fifteen or twenty miles into town if we go by the road. But there's a highway some-where downstream east of here. I figure that if we just follow the creek, we'll hit that highway eventually, somewhere, and then we can hitchhike into town."

"What town?"

"It's called Woodville."

"Then what're we waiting for?"

"Nothing," Bill replied, favoring his friend with a rare, broad smile. "Not a damned thing."

For two guys about to walk their way through what would have to be several miles of prickly thicket, with varying degrees of hardship and bodily punishment undoubtedly in store, light-hearted foolishness seemed the order of the day.

Bill balanced on one foot, swung both arms to the side like a vaudeville performer prefacing his departure offstage, grinned and half-sang, "Weeee're . . ."

Buddy immediately picked up the cue and imitated the gesture, joining in, "Weeee're . . ."

Together they pranced away singing, "Off to see the Wizard, the wonderful Wizard of Oz."

"That's my favorite movie," Buddy hollered in delight. They had a common interest that he was unaware of. "How many times have you seen it?"

"I don't know," Bill replied, "maybe a half a dozen or so."

"Shoot, I've seen it a dozen times at least. I didn't know any grown-ups liked it that much."

"Never underestimate the ability of grown-ups to act like kids," Bill noted. Motioning to his state of undress, he shrugged his shoulders and raised both hands widely apart. "Or hadn't you noticed?"

Buddy smiled broadly. "I noticed." He stared at the unclothed man briefly, then added, "But you're still a creaky old fart!" and he ran tauntingly toward the creek.

A moment of sadness crept into their joyous reunion play when the boy spotted a small blue object at water's edge. Stopping to pick up the Frisbee, he said, "I wonder what happened to Brutus."

Bill didn't want the pleasant feeling to fade. "Don't worry about Brutus," he lied, "he'll be okay. He'll find us sooner or later."

That seemed to satisfy the boy, and he grinned again; then he sailed the Frisbee to Bill. Bill caught it, performed a semi-fancy pirouette, and zipped it back to the retreating youth.

Somehow, curiously, neither of the two celebrants was the slightest bit aware of his own state of near exhaustion. They were too busy with their dance of joy—each with his own personal recognition of having found a warm, live, caring human being to fill that empty spot that had ached within him for so long. They rejoiced in each other, in having each other back from the black, wet, terrifying torture of the night; and they would continue doing so as fully as they could until they reached wherever they were going and they had to do something different. Neither wanted to think about the future beyond that.

They laughed. They frolicked. They tussled and they kidded one another. The "creaky old fart" and the "punk kid," out for a romp through the woods. Once into the woods, the going became a trifle more tedious, but that didn't slow them down appreciably. Buddy, who seemed to want to lead the way, simply waltzed around the thorn bushes and over the shintangle. Bill, on an obvious, almost ridiculous high, followed laughingly along behind.

They were making so much noise, in fact, that neither of them heard the rattle.

As floods do, this one had driven a host of nature's ground creatures from their dens and havens, their nests and habitats. Some could take the inconvenience in stride; others tended to become downright testy about it. The canebrake rattler coiled next to a small cedar tree, right in Buddy's path, belonged in the latter category. It offered its customary warning rattle well in advance of the boy's inexorable dance toward it; but the two kids were making so much noise that they never heard it.

The boy's foot landed less than a yard from the serpent, which was strike-borne even before the toes of the tender-skinned youth touched ground. The fangs caught Buddy in the outside right calf, half-way between the ankle and the knee, and he dropped to the ground in complete surprise, shock, and searing pain.

"NO GOD DAMMIT, NO!" Bill screamed in anguish as he saw the boy hit the ground and the snake begin to slither backwards, returning into a coil.

"You mother-fucking son of a BITCH!" the man yelled, reaching down, completely without thinking what he was doing, to grab the snake by its furiously rattling tail.

He flailed it around at its full length like a heavy chain, until the creature's body slammed against a tree. That seemed like the thing to do, so he executed another sweeping arc, like an

Olympic hammer-swing contestant, and bashed it against the tree again.

By the second bash, the man's eyesight had become constricted into tunnel vision through the intensity of his fury. He could feel his pulse throbbing in the veins of his face and neck as his narrowed vision lit upon the familiar outline of a toothache tree. That gave him an even better idea; so he shifted positions, flailing the rattler at full length all the while, and slammed its head against the cat-claw thorns of that most unusual tree.

Again and again, in his rage, he bashed and thrashed the hated serpent against the thorny trunk, until its head was nothing but shreds. Finally, in a continuing arc, he heaved the now-lifeless creature into the water.

Breathless, he turned his attention to Buddy. The boy's eyes had the same look as they did the night of the cougar scream—wide as pie plates and radiating terror.

Trying vainly to muffle tears, the boy sobbed weakly, pathetically, "Oh shit, Bill. Oh . . . shit!"

The man kneeled beside his buddy, struggling to compose himself. "Where . . ." His voice caught, and he had to swallow hard to muffle a sob. "Where did it get you?"

The boy touched the spot. "Right there."

Bill examined the telltale signal—twin fang marks, an inch or so apart, as plain as day. He looked away in the direction of the hurled-off rattler; it was a huge son-of-a-bitch, all right.

Canebrake rattlers, denizens of wooded areas, mostly, are quite different from the common diamondback rattlers which are much more familiar to Texans and other Westerners. The elongated diamondbacks are not infrequently found to be over six feet long; the canebrake variety tends to grow plump, instead. They are also much more colorful than their longer, more slender cousins. But the specimen that vented its displeasure at displacement on the hapless Buddy was both long and fat. Recalling the size of the slithering assailant through the blinding haze of his anguish, Bill remembered it as being a good four to five inches in diameter—and certainly more than five feet long. It was, indeed, a monster.

And he was scared, scared half out of his wits. His virtually impossible task, now, was not to let Buddy know it. Bill knew that excitement, activity—anything that might increase the pulse rate—are the worst things that can happen to the victim of a poisonous snakebite. Somehow, although so overwrought that he could hear his own heartbeat pounding in his ears, he would have to pretend to Buddy not to be excited.

Stop shaking, you son-of-a-bitch, he silently ordered his hand as he laid it gently on the boy's leg. Then aloud to Buddy—but softly, comfortingly, "Okay, kid. It's going to be all right. Above all else, I want you not to get excited. I am going to take care of you. Now just hold still."

Racing against time, Bill glanced quickly around him—still seeing in tunnel vision, but more sharply and vividly, more quick-discerningly, than he had ever before in his life. Finding what he was looking for, he grabbed hold of a small vine and, with the strength of a mountain, ripped it away from its roots. He cupped his hand and tore away all the leaves and branches from a four-foot length of it, snapped it in two again, and wrapped it half-tightly around the boy's calf, above the wound. Then he broke a small branch off the closest tree and twisted it inside the impromptu tourniquet, as a windlass.

"Hold this tight," he told the boy, "but not too tight. And lie still."

Three hours—that was all the time he had. Bill had read somewhere that a person bitten by a pit viper must get medical attention within three hours, or serious consequences might become irreversible. Paralysis, kidney failure, gangrene, crippling, death—any of that was possible, depending upon the size and strength of the snake, the depth of the bite, whether or not the poison had entered a major artery, etc., etc.

He had also read that medical opinion was divided as to what was the best, least dangerous, and most effective first-aid treatment. Tourniquet, cut, and suck was the accepted method for years and years. Then, along came somebody with the idea that ice on the wound, to slow down the blood flow and decrease the activity of the venom, was the best thing to do. "Why risk infection from a cut in addition to the snakebite?" that line of reasoning argued. "Just put ice on it and get the hell to a hospital."

Sure, put ice on it, Bill thought, sardonically. *There must be a 7-Eleven around here somewhere; I'll just stop in and pick up a nice bag of ice.*

Goddamnit! his thoughts continued, silently railing against the predicament that confronted him and his now-helpless young friend. *I don't even have a fuckin' knife to cut-and-suck with. I don't have a shittin' thing!*

Three hours. His mind raced.

The toothache tree!

He leaped over to that strangely configured tree and reached high, above the spot where he had destroyed the rattler's head, and he gouged off one of the tree's cat-claw barbs with his thumbnail. Then he bounded back to the recumbent victim and knelt down to his stricken leg. Already, Bill noticed, it looked like it was starting to swell.

"Hold still, Buddy; this is going to hurt."

With the tree thorn clenched tightly between his thumb and forefinger, the man stabbed it into the boy's calf and raked the point a half-inch across one of the fang marks. Buddy cried out, but kept himself under control. Bill repeated the procedure ninety degrees across the first cut, to form a quickly bleeding X.

Distantly, almost abstractly, Bill remembered the Indian legend that he had related to Buddy; and he realized that he had, indeed, broken the boy's skin with the barb of a toothache tree. *I'm not after your soul, Buddy,* he thought silently, *but you're welcome to mine if it will help.*

Aloud, involuntarily, he added, "Go ahead, take it!"

As he said that, he inscribed another X in identical manner to the first one across the second fang wound, as Buddy winced and winced again, struggling valiantly to remain calm.

In spite of the boy's courage, it was obvious that the pain in his leg was intense. Bill remembered the magazine article. It stated that in twenty to thirty percent of bites from poisonous snakes, little or no venom gets injected into the victim. Not much chance of that being the case with Buddy—the snake was monstrous big, it had struck full force, and the boy's skin was already starting to turn blue.

Under the skin, Bill knew, tissue destruction had begun immediately after the snake had injected its vile poison. The overwhelming urgency of his crude first-aid procedure was to remove as much of that poison as possible, before the blood stream picked it up and distributed it throughout the body. Fragments of mutilated cell structure, partially digested by the venom, could also have a toxic effect, as they would ultimately be picked up by the body's circulatory system and distributed to the brain, lungs, heart, kidneys and liver.

Buddy loosed an involuntary kick with the injured leg, accompanied by a short, sharp scream that he had not been able to stifle. The action caused the boy to lose his grip on the tourniquet, but he promptly recovered it and tightened down the windlass.

As quickly as he could move, Bill dropped to the ground, picked up the bleeding limb, placed his mouth atop the X marks, and sucked in deeply. Then he reared back, spat out what he had sucked in, and bent back down to repeat the task. Then again. And again.

After about the fourth try at sucking out the poison, he told Buddy, "Relax the tourniquet a little bit now, you've got to let some blood get down into your leg." Buddy complied.

Following the sixth suck treatment, Bill said, "Okay, tighten up on the tourniquet again. But still, not too tight."

As he said that, he caught Buddy's look—directly, head-on. Now starting to cloud over, the once-glowing blue eyes pleaded mutely, *Please, please help me. I'm depending on you.*

"I'll take care of you, Buddy," the man told him. "Have faith in me."

Biting his lip against the pain, the youth blinked an acknowledgement of his faith; and Bill went back to his task. After sucking and spitting for the fifteenth time or so, Bill decided that was as good as he was going to be able to do. It was time to pick up the boy now and get him the hell out of there.

He walked over to the distended creek, picked up a handful of water, swilled it around in his mouth to rinse out the blood and venom, and spat it back toward the floating carcass of the huge rattler. Then back to Buddy.

Three hours.

He glanced upward at the tangle of thicket in front of him. The water's edge—the only thing he had to guide him—was ten feet away curving north, to the left as he faced the morning sun. The thought struck him: Why follow the creek? It will meander around and around in a thousand twists and curves, covering twice, maybe even three times as much territory as a straight-line hike would before reaching the distant highway. He didn't need the creek; he had the sun.

"Buddy of mine," he decided aloud, "we're heading straight east."

Gently, he hoisted the stricken lad off the ground and swung him onto his back for a piggyback carry. "Now you just sit tight, there, Buddy, and everything is going to be all right."

There it was again—almost the exact same sentence as before—and it hit the boy like a thunderbolt. *Now you just sit tight, there, Buddy, and everything is going to be all right.*

The pain in the boy's leg was excruciating, but his mind wouldn't leave the baffling memory. It was the same thing— that familiar *déjà vu* that had troubled him since their first afternoon together. He knew . . . he *knew* . . . that he had heard it somewhere before—some time long ago.

Bill balanced the fragile burden on his back and said, "I just wish the hell we had an airplane. Then I'd get you to a hospital in a hurry."

It was the word "airplane" that triggered it. Buddy was beginning to get dizzy; but suddenly, from deep within the memory bank of his swirling, pain-racked brain, he could see the inside of an airplane. It was full of people, just before takeoff. A man with curly black hair, a man in a uniform, was bending over the small boy, buckling his seat belt. "Now you just sit tight, Buddy Boy," the man said, "and everything is going to be all right."

And Buddy knew. He knew who Bill was! That man who was now about to walk barefoot and naked through hell to try to save his buddy's life . . . that man who had kidnapped him . . . taught him . . . cared about him—the only really tried-and-true friend that he had ever known—was a pilot on his own father's airplane!

They can torture me 'til I die, the boy vowed to himself, *and I'll never tell who he is.*

Bill felt an ever-so-slight change in the boy's hold around his neck. Barely perceptible, it was only a quick squeeze, a hug, and then it relaxed.

He looked at the dense thicket ahead of him, searching for a likely path to head toward the sun, then he closed his eyes and reared back his head to press gently against the forehead of the kid on his back.

Three hours.

▼ ▼ ▼ ▼ ▼ ▼ ▼ ▼ ▼ ▼ ▼ ▼ ▼

15

There was little doing in room B-22 of the Federal Building. Everything was in place, at the ready; and no one dared leave, because it was now critical time. Henry Wilson had spent the night there waiting—waiting for the telephone call that had not yet come. Liddell Peters had put in almost as much time. Four other agents were working in alternate shifts of two, manning television-like screens and the other paraphernalia connected with the highly sophisticated call-tracing equipment that was in place. But still, no call.

Wilson felt certain that it would be today. Saturday. It was the only likely time. The word was well disseminated now of the return of the kidnapped boy's parents to Houston, and it was time, as the radio newscaster had noted, for the other shoe to drop. Any time now.

In the meantime, it was watch and wait. Newspaper crossword puzzles. Gin rummy. Pocket knives cleaning, trimming and re-cleaning fingernails. The lingering smell of hamburgers and onions from yesterday's Jack-In-The-Box lunches tainting the stale air of a room that, until only four days ago, had been long vacant. And a wastebasket full of Styrofoam coffee cups. And boredom.

The black telephone connected directly to the dispatcher at Houston police headquarters still had not rung. Twice, Henry Wilson had ordered an assistant to check it out to make certain that the connection was still workable.

The red phone, though, rang incessantly, jarring the quartet in residence into attention with every jangle; but so far, the calls were only for the Caine parents. Chatty. Conciliatory. Consoling. From friends. But not yet, not one stinking yet, from the kidnapper, from the man who must be calling in very soon now, to press his demands to ransom the youth.

"Otherwise?" Liddell Peters questioned.

"You know damned well what otherwise," Henry Wilson replied wearily. He leaned his head backward and, with both hands, roughly massaged the almost hairless expanse of skin on top. "Otherwise, it might be all over. The kid might be dead."

"I don't want to believe that," Peters said. He was the father of three children, a devoted family man who detested the thought of murdering a child.

"I don't either. But it's a reality we may have to face sometime pretty damned soon, I'm afraid. When someone snatches a kid for ransom, and then is not heard from again for four days, it's the thing you have to start thinking about."

Peters was in his pensive mode again, with a stem of his eyeglasses stuck into the right corner of his mouth. He was as much aware of all of that as Wilson was. He was also aware that fatigue, inactivity, and disappointment can push people into pessimism, and he didn't want to let that happen.

"What do we do then, chief," he asked, "if we don't hear from him?"

"For a while at least," Wilson replied, "we keep on with what we're doing. We stay right here. We man the telephones. And if we haven't heard from him by Monday, we go back to being investigators again."

"Meaning what?"

"I'm not quite sure what," the local FBI boss admitted. "But there have to be lots of people we haven't talked to yet. We still have several hundred prints of the composite photo to stick in people's faces; we just have to use our heads and come up with the right faces to stick them in."

The red telephone erupted jarringly into life, and the tape recorder switched automatically into doing its job.

"Hello," said the voice of Mrs. Hamilton Caine.

"Melanie, this is Betsy."

"Betsy, where are you?"

"We're in Tahiti now. We've been running on the diesels, and we got in some time last night. How are things there?"

"Oh you just can't begin to imagine, Betsy, everything is simply horrible. The police . . . the FBI . . . nobody seems to be able to do a thing but just sit around and wait, and we're all about to go crazy. Why last night . . ."

▼ ▼ ▼

After about a hundred yards or so, the thicket closed in on the man with the woefully wounded boy on his back. Never easy going, the remnants and regrowth of that time long ago, when even the Indians refused to enter, erected a barrier that was brick-wall solid. Nature had hung a sign, NO PASSAGE BEYOND THIS POINT.

Sweat poured down Bill's face, arms, hands and chest—sweat so copious that it lubricated his arm-hold on the boy's bare legs, making him prone to slither backwards out of the man's grip. Bill was forced continually to shift his cargo back into position; and every time he did so, Buddy would grunt in painful compliance and attempt to tighten his hold around the man's neck.

Now faced with a forbidding tangle of underbrush, the man and his boy-burden were forced to turn back, to retrace their tedious steps and find another route around the thorny blockade. Doing so cost them in strength and energy, plus the collection of a few more unwelcome thorns and scratches; but the greatest penalty was the loss of time. There was so little time!

They had to continue east—no other choice now; but with the passage blocked, Bill opted to swing north, to maneuver around the wall of wild shrubbery. It turned out to be a long way north, agonizingly much farther than he was willing to grant, and at ninety degrees to his intended route. But Mother Nature was calling the shots. She held all the cards; and the two weary wayfarers were helpless to do anything other than play them as they were dealt.

The going was at least easier in that direction, and Bill felt akin to the classic story of the nocturnal drunk looking for his dropped keys beneath a street lamp—it wasn't where he'd dropped them, but the light was better there. Similarly, Bill and his piggyback companion were able to make easier progress going north, but east was the direction in which they had to go.

Every time Bill would attempt to swing toward the morning sun, something with sharpened barbs and leg-tangling virtuosity would grab him, thornfully, and deny him passage. Thus, he continued to skirt north.

His legs were bleeding in at least five or six places—not just surface scratches, but deeper, bleeding wounds—when he finally was able to make a cut toward the east. There was a small cedar tree at that point, eight or ten feet tall, with its bark literally ripped to shreds for a length of about three feet, not far off the ground. The clean, white underbark was evidence that the damage had been recently inflicted—solid indication that there was a buck deer resident in the area, scraping the velvet coating from his new crop of antlers. It is a yearly ritual that precedes the estrus period, known to hunters as the "rut"—the whitetail's annual mating season.

Bill glanced briefly at what hunters call a "sign"—in this case, a "rub"—and thought of more pleasant experiences in the Big Thicket; then he trudged on. At least he was now able to make progress toward the east; but there began to be some question as to how much longer he would be able to determine which direction was east.

The nicely decorative sprinkling of morning clouds that had greeted him at sunrise had begun to congeal into a thin overcast. Also, as the sun drew closer to the meridian, the sense of direction became more and more diffuse. Shortly, Bill feared, he would have to be navigating on instinct. Under an overcast in the thicket, forced to tack this way and that, as the brambles allow, instinct is every bit as valuable as . . .

"Tits on a boar hog," Bill mumbled to himself. "That's how much good all my well-trained woods instinct is going to do me."

"Huh?" the boy said, half-moaning and appearing to struggle to retain consciousness. "What did you say?"

"Me say sign look good, Bwana," Bill replied in his best imitation of African pidgin English. "But trail still plenty long. Bwana must save strength."

"Um-gah-wa," Buddy grunted, playing along with Bill's hunters-on-safari game.

It seemed like a good game, something to lift the spirits, so Bill continued. "Many long steps before Great White Hunter get to safety. Much danger. Elephant spoor. Lion spoor. Simba look angry."

The sky was beginning to look angry, also. Bill glanced upward for directions and drew a blank stare in return—the sun was completely obliterated by a sea of gray. He strained to identify some landmark ahead, in the direction that he last thought to be east, but saw nothing but thornbush, yaupon, blackberry entanglements, and ground clutter. The trunks of taller trees were visible only to eye level; their tops were concealed by the brush. Alone, a man has a difficult task picking his way through that kind of terrain. He must dodge and weave—like a halfback threading through a mass of football linemen to get into the secondary—to avoid being tackled by the tangle. But dodging and weaving are restricted by an enormous percentage to a man with a badly hurt boy on his back.

Now, to Bill's body-load of sweat from the stifling September-after-a-hurricane, Big-Thicket heat and humidity, was added the sweat of additional fear—the new fear of losing his way, along with mounting fear for his buddy's life.

The boy slipped in the man's grip again. Bill caught him, shifted him back up, and Buddy grabbed tightly once more to his carrier's neck. That action was followed by another involuntary kick of the wounded leg, and a not-too-effectively-stifled yelp from pain.

"Bwana be still," the man said, trying hard to keep it light. "No can push through bush with Bwana wiggling like sack of greasy worms."

Desperately, now, he tried to sense the right direction. Desperately he sought east, picking and poking—with cat-claws tearing at his every move and nailbeds of ground thorns seeking lodging in his feet with every step. And the sun was gone, completely gone.

Presently, the rough going eased a little. The brush was thinner now. Bill glanced skyward again for directions, but there were none to be had. He looked at the ground, took two tentative steps to the right, and his heart leaped into his throat. There, right in front of them, was the same mutilated cedar tree—the identical buck deer "rub" that they had passed at least a half-hour previous. They had made a complete circle!

During his joyous reunion play with Buddy, Bill had somehow been distracted from the bone-crushing fatigue and the mental exhaustion that had been the result of his nightlong aquatic struggle for survival, and his anguished, frantic journey back to camp in search of the boy. Now it all returned, with knee-buckling intensity. The disappearance of the sun, coupled with the discovery that he had wasted much precious time in the life expectancy of his young pal, walking in a circle, had added depression to the physical and mental burden. For the first time, he began to question whether he could go on. Confidence and hope were all but gone.

Bill sank painfully to his knees and leaned the almost-limp Buddy against the bark-stripped tree. "Gotta rest just a minute," he told the kid.

As he looked down at the sorry sight against the tree beside him, it took all he had to keep from breaking down completely. The once-bright face, with its penetrating, sparkling blue eyes, was now twisted with pain, and there were lacerations across it from encounters with the brush. Bill had tried hard, but it was impossible to shield the fragile countenance behind his head from every scraping twig and bush in their path. The boy's blonde, crowning glory was now atangle with leaves and twigs. His body, always sinewy and taut, radiating adolescent vigor, was dishrag-limp, like a clay statue that had been left too long in an August sun.

But the leg. The boy's right leg was the sorriest sight of all. Bill had thought, before, that it appeared to be turning blue. Now it was solidly so, like an enormous bruise from knee to ankle; and it was swollen almost to the size of his thigh.

"Bill," Buddy said weakly. "I feel sick."

"Nauseous?"

"Yes. I think I'm going to throw up."

"Now's as good a time as any," Bill told him. "See if you can't get it off your system."

The man held the boy by the shoulders as he leaned to the opposite side and vomited. Copiously. Once. Twice. Three times.

"Bill, I'm so scared."

He couldn't say it, but Bill was scared also—scared almost out of his mind. But he covered, "That's all part of it, pal. You have to expect it. But you're going to be all right; didn't I promise you? I'm going to get you to a hospital and you will be all right."

His words may or may not have brought solace to the boy, but they provided the man with a new sense of determination. "Come on, Buddy," he said. "Let's get going." And he hoisted the pathetic youth once more onto his back.

The continuing refrain, once again, asked, "Which direction?" Bill remembered that on his last passage by the scraped-off cedar tree, he had headed off in the direction from which he had just come. East, then, was behind him. When he first encountered the deer sign, he had been wending his way north, following a barely distinguishable line in the brush. He would just have to try going north along that line again.

The sun was gone, no help from that—which left only the meandering waterline of the flooded creek as a directional guide. It had to be to his right, then, intersecting the scant outline of the north-south brushline up there somewhere. It was the only option open, so Bill took it.

The boy felt heavy on his back; he hadn't seemed that way before. Bill reasoned that this was probably because of the short rest. And because Bill had been able to cool off a little during that rest, he could now feel the intense heat radiating from the boy's bare chest, belly and loins that were girdled tightly against his back. The kid was burning up with fever. The thought occurred to Bill that, if they could reach the creek again, it might be a good idea to immerse Buddy in its icy waters and try to reduce that fever. If . . . if they could reach the creek. Right now, the man was taking no bets.

He should have; because he had no sooner thought they might not, when they did. After no more than a few cautious steps past the deer rub, man and boy not only found the water's edge, but they emerged from the tangled thicket into a totally clear pathway. It was covered with water, but there it was—the road out from camp!

Of course, you idiot! Bill thought to himself. *Why in the bloody, goddamned hell didn't you think of this before?*

Now, at last, the quickest, easiest route out was as clear as the mustache on his grizzled face. Painfully, he realized that all that he had had to do, all of that precious, wasted time, was to strike north and hit the road. Even if it was covered with water, it wasn't deep. Bill now remembered that somewhere—not far south of the bridge that he had stumbled over that morning on his struggling way back to camp—there was a vast clear-cut. If he could make it to that, the going would be easier by a hundredfold than his tortuous trek through the thicket. All he had to do now was stay on the road, head for the fence, then turn right when he got there; the clear-cut should be no more than a hundred yards away. At that point, Bill believed, he would have easy walking straight east for at least a mile—maybe two—and that would put them a helluva lot closer to that distant highway, wherever it was.

Bill silently castigated himself. *How many times? How many more stupid miscalculations are you going to make? Are you ever going to stop fucking-up before you kill this kid?*

He shifted his limp-hanging load once more, waded into the roadway and headed out—east, by damn, in spite of the hidden sun. And it gave his spirits a lift.

"The Great White Hunter and his faithful gunbearer, Booga-Booga, emerged from the Mopane shrub and onto the grassy veldt once again," he related, trying to keep both of their spirits going with a crudely mixed parody of Hemingway, Capstick, and Tarzan. "The wait-a-bit thorn had exacted a cruel toll on their tender bodies . . ."

He had no way of knowing whether Buddy could even hear him. He felt so spineless, so limp on the man's back, that he could have passed out for all Bill knew. Occasionally, though,

Bill would stumble or otherwise break stride, and the boy would respond, reflexively, by tightening his grip around his carrier's neck.

Bill continued his make-believe East African narration, "The two intrepid hunting companions knew that the fierce cannibals from the Mothafuka tribe were close behind. Although they were near exhaustion, they dared not stop to rest. Time was of the bloody essence. But the White Hunter knew the territory now. 'We'll be jolly well all right,' he told his faithful gun-bearer, 'as soon as we reach the escarpment.' But then, and he paused—concern was etched across his brow—then we shall have to contend with the river.'"

"What happens at the river?" Buddy mumbled, to Bill's surprise and absolute delight at the boy's display of consciousness.

"Why, we'll have to jump, of course," he replied.

"I still think . . ." With his lips pressed tightly against Bill's neck, the boy was barely intelligible.

"You still think what?" the man wondered.

"I still think you're the world's biggest bullshitter."

"Me think Bwana talk too much," Bill replied. "Shut up and save breath."

"You shut up and save yours," the boy countered. "You're the one . . . doing all the . . . work. I'm just here . . . for the ride."

"Then shut up and enjoy the scenery."

And both did shut up, lapsing from comic relief back into steady, purposeful plodding down the straight, water-covered roadway. Bill's every step was a conscious effort, burdened not only with the weight of the boy, but with the near-blinding internal pressures of physical exhaustion and extreme mental and emotional strain.

He found progress easier to accomplish by setting short-range goals. First, he must reach the fence across the roadway; so he drew a mental picture of that intersection and worked to maintain concentration on it. It was a good thing that there was a gateway there. The Lord only knew, he thought, how he would manage to get the limp body of the boy across a fence without a gate.

When the fenceline goal was achieved, and he was forced with his back-load to penetrate the woods once again, he concentrated his imagination on breaking out of the woods and into the clear-cut.

Thrashing once again through the thicket, Bill mumbled, not at all intending to speak, "It's not fair." Then he went back to silent self-castigation. *The kid deserves better than I gave him. I forced him into this, now . . . now I've got to get him out. Even if it kills me.*

Go on, he silently challenged the fates. *Go on and kill me. But for the love of honesty, spare the boy. Spare my little buddy.*

Inadvertently again, he mumbled aloud, "I must be delirious. Gotta be delirious to talk like that."

His next step carried him out of the brush and into the vast, vacant, jumbled expanse of the clear-cut. "Look here, Buddy," he said to the kid behind him. "Do you know what this is?"

For hundreds of acres in three directions, as they faced the cut, the earth was a disgustingly unsightly litter. The tops of trees—all kinds of trees—lay where they had fallen after they had been felled and their saleable trunks had been chain-sawed off and hauled away. Clearly visible, though, were stacks of seemingly usable tree trunks that had apparently been collected for hauling, but then left behind—wasted—for some unfathomable reason. Here and there, helter-skelter, stood an occasional scraggly, forlorn-looking tree—each a badly scarred, lonely sentinel left standing to overlook the devastation.

The boy raised his head, opened his eyes and surveyed what he promptly recognized as a scab on the face of creation. Struggling to talk, he said, "Whatever . . . it is . . . it's ugly."

"Wrong, Bwana, it's beautiful." Bill set the boy on the ground for another rest. "All that emptiness out there," he continued, with a broad gesture of his left arm, "is going to make it easier for us to get to the highway. By the time we get to the other end of this cut, we'll practically be there; and you'll be as good as into the hospital; and some brilliant doctor will shortly be pumping antivenin into you to kill that snakebite. What do you think of that, kid?"

Buddy's reply was unintentionally rude. He leaned over to his right and vomited again. Twice, this time.

Bill wrapped his arms around the boy's chest from behind, both to steady him in his pathetic activity and to provide as much solace as he could. Almost involuntarily, he rested his forehead against the boy's back and increased the pressure of his embrace ever so slightly. As he did so, he felt a shudder course through the hot, hot body.

Shit! Bill silently cursed himself. *I was going to cool him off in the creek, and I forgot. No time to go back for that now.*

He hated to draw the boy's attention to it, but Bill felt compelled to reach over and touch the hugely swollen right leg. Necrosis, edema and ischemia—medical terms that he had long ceased to remember—were all taking place beneath his touch. Although he couldn't remember the words, their meanings were burning in his consciousness, just as their life-threatening activities were burning inside the boy's venom-racked limb. They meant that tissue destruction was continuing, that there was an excessive accumulation of watery fluid inside the body cells and the muscle structure, producing the waterlogged tissues that caused the awful swelling. In addition, there was an ever-spreading deficiency of blood supply to the bite area, along with deterioration of the blood's ability to clot. At some time down the line, Buddy could be hemorrhaging uncontrollably. In all, it was a hugely dangerous condition.

"Can we go on now?" Bill asked the victim.

The boy didn't reply, he only nodded consent; and Bill eased him gently back into the piggyback carry.

However gentle, the move triggered another involuntary surge of vomitus from the boy's open-sagging mouth, which spilled onto the man's shoulder and cascaded down his right arm.

"I'm sorry, Bill," Buddy said, trying weakly to brush it off.

"All in a day's work, kid; don't worry about it."

As welcome as the clear-cut was, the passage it provided was easy only in comparison to the tangle of the thicket. The ground was as undulant as a washboard, with every pocket a pool of muddy water. The giant machinery that had collected, loaded and hauled out the timber had scraped away the thin layer of sandy topsoil and dredged up the clay-like underlayer known generally in those parts as "gumbo." When wet—and it had been soaked by the hurricane's rains—it becomes a slimy, extremely sticky substance that clings and holds on to any intrusion, like concrete setting around a fence post.

With each step, Bill's legs would sink into the ooze up to his knees. Then, reluctant to part, the nasty material would hold tightly as the man tried to extract his foot for another step, until it finally let go with a vulgar sucking, squishing noise.

The going was particularly bad, in the gumbo respect, in the area adjacent to the timber and brushline, where the bulldozers and articulated log haulers had maneuvered in and about the perimeter of the logging activity. Tire tracks three feet wide, with additional indentations four inches deep from their enormous lug treads, made extremely uncertain footing for the man's bare feet and toes. Frequently, he stumbled.

One stumble was disastrous. Tugging against the clinging mud-hold, his right foot caught on an inch-thick tree branch submerged in one of the many standing-water pools and firmly entrenched in the gumbo. Both man and boy pitched straight forward and landed face down in the ooze.

Sputtering a fluent assortment of expletives, Bill carefully raised the boy's head out of the mud and helped him to sit up. Appearances were not of major concern at the moment; but something had to be done about that face, at least. Tenderly, Bill splashed Buddy's mud-laden countenance with a few handfuls of water from the puddle. Though the wash water was muddy, it was better than a faceful of East Texas gumbo that would soon harden into the consistency of cement.

With the pain-contorted face at least slightly rinsed, Bill struggled to hoist the muddy boy up onto his back once again. The proverbial greased pig would have been just as easy to handle.

And he thought, *Assuming we ever do reach the highway, who in the hell would ever pick us up the way we look now? A grown man and a teenage kid in nothing but their underwear, covered with mud from asshole to elbow . . . we must really be cute.*

Surveying the waterlogged territory in front of them, Bill thought that there had to be a better way. The terrain took a slight rise to his right, toward the south. The ground there was covered with the decapitated treetops that had been left to rot and decay and, coincidentally, to provide firewood for campers who would undoubtedly flood the area in the deer-hunting season—plus cooking and cabin-warming fuel for the scattering of dirt-poor residents of the general vicinity. All that, along with the stacks of perfectly good tree trunks that had been harvested but never made it to the mill, would have to be stepped over or walked around; but the area didn't have as many rain pools, and it appeared not to have been gouged out to the gumbo like the heavily trafficked stretch through which he had been trying to walk. So he headed for the rubble.

Occasionally, a foot would sink in deeper than he expected it might; and he would have to traverse zig zag through the cutover land—stepping over the ground litter with the boy on his back just wouldn't work. Otherwise, Bill did find that the going was definitely easier away from the tire-gouged mud-wallow of his original path.

After about a hundred yards of decent progress, Bill topped a small rise and spotted a familiar sight up ahead, another four hundred yards or so away. Unless he was mistaken, it was a deer hunter's stand; it was certainly in a good location for one.

To occupy his mind as he headed toward the object, Bill thought about how clear-cut areas such as the one he was plodding across—sidewalk conservationists' theories notwithstanding—are quite beneficial to many forms of wildlife, especially whitetail deer. It doesn't take long in the East Texas woods for such a cut-over piece of land to begin sprouting new growth. Wind-borne and bird-carried seeds of the same flora that have been indigenous to those woods for centuries, sprout quickly into living plants, sprinkling the devastated expanse with brightly colored young green things.

Deer love brightly colored young green things, he mused.

Whoever had erected that hunting stand knew what he was doing. When that green stuff starts shooting up, the deer will start coming out of the woods to munch on it, and the hunter in an elevated stand at the right time, in the right place, should not have too difficult a time filling out his deer tags.

Of most importance to Bill, the presence of that deer stand meant the likely presence of a road to it. He knew that with such a prime set-up as that vast clear-cut field and its crop of tender green deer bait, the typical East Texas hunter will usually take the laziest way out. He'll likely locate his stand beside a logging road, so that he can drive his pickup truck right to it an hour or so before light on opening day.

That road to the deer stand will be our route out.

At a distance of ninety or so yards from the stand, the piggyback hikers passed a nicely carpentered feed trough. Wedge-shaped at the bottom, like a primitive cradle, the feeder had a plywood roof to shelter it from the rain. It was filled with seed corn, just in case the new greenery of the field was not sufficient enticement to the antlered, cloven-hoofed residents of the nearby woods. The purpose of the corn was also to attract Bambi and his friends to that particular area of the field, where the intrepid nimrod could be waiting a sighted-in distance away, in his sheltered enclosure, to ambush some unsuspecting white-tail.

That wasn't Bill's way of hunting, but he couldn't fault it; it was just the way it's done in those parts. It was man-the-predator's way of engineering an edge against the much keener senses of the prey. Bill preferred to take his chances at taking game inside the woods, where man is at such a noisy disadvantage.

But Bill was not hunting animals now. He was hunting the path of the hunter; and his reasoning as he had approached the tall stand had been exactly correct. From ten yards adjacent to the stand, there was an easily discernable, if muddy and water-pooled, two-track road leading away in a curving path toward the forest in front of him, now less than a hundred yards distant. It was a clear, easy-going, almost certain route out.

Breathing a deep sigh of relief, he kneeled to the ground and rested his slack-limbed cargo against a leg of the hunter's stand.

"Buddy," he announced with more confidence than he had felt in hours, "the end is in sight. We're going to make it."

Dizzy, with milky eyes, Buddy stared at the structure above him. It was a four-by-four square box, standing on wooden legs twelve feet tall and supported on each side by a long guy wire to a heavy iron stake in the ground. Access was gained by a ladder, straight up from the ground to a trap door in the center. Each of the structure's four sides contained a rectangular observation and shooting port that was sealed off with a sliding panel. The slanted, plywood roof was covered with composition shingles.

"What is that thing?" Buddy asked.

"It's a deer stand."

"What's so dear about it?" The boy would obviously remain smart-mouthed to the end.

"A deer-*hunting* stand, wise-ass. And the dearest thing of all about it is that it is sitting right next to a road. And that road is going to get you and me out of here."

Buddy smiled. It was weak, and it was wan; but it was fresh mountain air, nectar and ambrosia to Bill.

The man pondered silently, *How long has it been? How much of the kid's precious three hours have I used up? No way to tell. Can't do anything about it anyhow. Just gotta keep going.*

"How fah . . ." Buddy's voice caught, then he gagged, coughed, and leaned over to vomit. Nothing was forthcoming, though, so he cleared his throat of everything he could assemble and spat it onto the ground. Then he continued, "How far is the . . . highway?"

Bill reached over to the boy and tenderly brushed away from his eyes a mud-filthy shock of hair that lay across his forehead. "I don't know," he replied, "I just don't know. But we're going to find out—you and I—just as soon as these tired, dirty old legs can get us there."

At that moment, there was a distant sound from off to the east. It began as a barely perceptible whine, then crescendoed to a sort of thumping roar, only to diminish to a whine once again. Then it disappeared. Unmistakable.

"Did you hear that?" Bill's face was beaming. "Do you know what that was?"

"A car, a truck maybe?" the boy replied.

"That's an eighteen-wheeler, baby. It's on that lovely high-way over there. And from the sound of it, it's not too damned far off. Come on, let's get at it!"

Gamely, the remnants of the proud youth stretched out his arms for the man to lift him. He nodded his head, smiled the best he could, and agreed. "Right on."

▼ ▼ ▼

There was no sign of civilization in sight when the two grimy, bedraggled, weary citizens emerged from the woods—only the narrow strip of asphalt running straight as a chalk line from northwest to southeast. Woodville, Bill calculated, couldn't be more than five or six miles away, to the left.

He crossed the roadway and deposited Buddy on the gravel shoulder, where the limp boy slumped into a heap. The spiritual boost had worked wonders at the hunter's stand, but the effect was transitory, and he was all but comatose once again. Withal, he wrapped his arms around Bill's legs and held them tightly together.

"Hang on now, kid," Bill told him. "You've got to hang on. We'll get there in a little while."

It was obviously not the busiest highway in East Texas; but somebody, something, had to be coming along sooner or later. Sooner became later, but she did come.

Minerva Goodsen was the quintessential old maid. Now in her mid-seventies, she lived alone with two mongrel dogs and an uncountable number of cats in a down-at-the-heels clap-board house on Pine Mill Road, just off State Highway 1097. Her house was exactly five-point-nine miles by the odometer of her ancient Chevrolet from the Tyler County Courthouse, in Woodville.

She remained active enough in the local First Baptist Church to get into most people's hair, and met regularly with a group of biddies who gathered every other week to exchange gossip and stitch on a group-made quilt. She eked out a living on Social Security and the scant proceeds from her inherited forty acres of farmland that were tended by a family of sharecroppers.

The spinster lady's jaw dropped so hard it almost shattered when she and the old Chevrolet drove by on their way home from their weekly trip to the grocery store in town. She couldn't believe the scandalous sight—a man and a boy ensconced on the other side of the road, practically naked, and filthy as hogs in a wallow.

She was on the telephone to the County Sheriff's office as quickly as she could reach the house. "Hello, Betty Sue, this is Minerva Goodsen. I have to talk with Sheriff Cantrell right away. Hurry."

After a long wait, the sheriff's voice came on the phone in its most unctuous, placating tones. "Hello Miss Minerva, nice to hear from you. And how in the world have you been?"

"Well, just fine, Joe Walter." Everybody in Tyler County knew the sheriff by his initials, J.W.; but Minerva Goodsen had known him since he was a baby, and she still called him Joe Walter. "Just fine, except for that ol' back of mine. You know how it gets to hurtin' every time we get a change in the weather? Why, when that hurricane blowed in, 'twas the other day, I swan, I thought my pore ol' back would break plum in two. But I knew it was comin' . . . knew it for two days. How is everything at your house?"

"Just fine, Minerva, just fine."

"Tillie and the children all right? Let's see, that oldest of yours is just about in high school now, isn't he?"

"He graduates next June," the sheriff replied, wondering if she had called in such a hurry merely to inquire about his family. "Now, I'm kinda busy right now, Minerva. Uh . . . what'd you call about?"

"Oh yes, I almost forgot," she admitted. "Joe Walter, there's a couple of them mud-rasslers standin' over on the highway just about naked. It's a man and a boy, looked like, wearin' hardly nothin' at all, and covered up with mud. They can't be up to no good, seems to me. I think you better go out and arrest them."

"Well, I'll sure look into it, Minerva. I'll send a deputy out to check them out right away." Never forgetting that the office of the County Sheriff is an elected position, he added, "And thank you for calling. It's always a pleasure hearing from you."

"Well thank you, Joe Walter. And tell that deputy he'd better be careful, you hear? Well, bye now."

The sheriff had no need to ask the lady the location. He knew where she lived; and he knew that she never went anywhere but that short stretch of highway between her farm house and town. It was curious, though. Mud rasslers?

▼ ▼ ▼

The siren of Deputy Alvin Ralph's county vehicle gurgled a short, low growl as he wheeled around in the highway and pulled alongside the bedraggled pair. An insignia on the front door featured a large, silver star and the words TYLER COUNTY SHERIFF'S DEPARTMENT. Bill grabbed the back door handle, flung the door open wide, then picked up the slumping boy and lifted him onto the seat.

"Just a minute there, you," Deputy Ralph warned, as he shifted a quid of tobacco to the left side of his mouth. His face was aghast.

"The boy's snake-bit." Bill's voice was urgent, pleading. "Canebrake rattler. Now please, get us to the hospital immediately, before it's too late."

Deputy Ralph struggled to collect his wits—both of them. Looking into his vacant eyes, Bill had the impression that he could see all the way to the back of the man's head.

"Please," Bill pleaded. "Hurry!" And he thought, *This guy would have to stay up late nights for two weeks, studying hard, to pass a stupidity test.*

"Yes sir. You bet," the deputy finally agreed. Then he turned on his red light and siren, slammed the car into gear, and sprayed gravel for thirty yards in hasty departure.

Just as they were leaving, Bill heard a dog bark; but he thought nothing of it. The woods are full of dogs, and they are always barking.

This one—a large, yellowish beast of indeterminate ancestry—emitted a short, plaintive whine as it emerged from the woods across the road, then began to lope after the car with the silver star as it sped away. Gone.

▼ ▼ ▼ ▼ ▼ ▼ ▼ ▼ ▼ ▼ ▼ ▼ ▼

16

The deputy picked up a deeply stained coffee can from the floor of his county patrol vehicle and spat into it a copious, brown stream of excess tobacco juice. He wiped his mouth on a handkerchief held in his lap, then asked, "You folks from around here?"

"Beaumont," Bill lied.

"Whatcha doin' gettin' yourselves snakebit around Woodville? And how come you ain't got no clothes on?"

"We were camped in a little cabin over east of here," Bill replied. "The storm blew it over last night right onto our pickup. I think it must have been a twister. Everything we had blew away, and we had to walk out. My boy got bit on the way out."

Deputy Ralph spat another wad of tobacco juice into the can, then turned around to study the black-and-white contrast of the mud-encrusted, worn-out-looking man and boy. Incredulous, he asked, "That your boy?"

"Yeah," Bill replied.

The deputy shook his head. "You shore must have a awful blonde wife."

"You got that right, friend," Bill said. "She's blonde . . . and she's awful."

A fine spray of tobacco juice splattered the windshield of the car as the deputy erupted into laughter. His wad of chewing tobacco caught in his throat and he started to choke—so badly that he had to pull the car off the road and spit out the quid entirely to bring himself under control. Then he laughed out loud, wheezing as he did so.

"I heard that!" he exclaimed, pulling the vehicle back onto the pavement and resuming his emergency hospital run. "I shore 'nuff heard that!"

Wheeze. Giggle. Wheeze.

"Shhh-oot! I did hear that! I reckon she shore as hell is. She's blonde . . . and she's awful. (Giggle) Shoot yes she is."

Picking up his radio microphone, he called, still chuckling, "This is three to base."

"This is base, come in," the radio answered back.

"Betty Sue, I got these two subjects from the highway with me. The boy's snakebit, and I'm takin' 'em to the hospital," Ralph reported, followed by another chuckle.

"Ten-four, Alvin," the sheriff's radio dispatcher replied. "What's so funny about that?"

"His wife's blonde . . . and she's awful."

"Come back on that?" the radio asked.

With Buddy's upper torso and head resting on his lap, Bill could feel the boy's rib cage vibrating with suppressed laughter.

"Shhh!" Bill admonished.

In spite of his pain, there was a large grin spread across the youth's face, and he looked as though he wanted to speak. Bill leaned over and put his ear to Buddy's mouth.

Weakly, the boy whispered, "Absolute world's biggest bull-shitter."

"Shut up," Bill whispered back.

His one, quick quip had completely disarmed the inquisitive deputy, and he felt that if he could just keep the dimwit laughing, he could avoid any penetrating questions that might lead to detection. With a little more inane giggling, Bill hoped, they just might make it; the outskirts of town were already passing by the car windows.

"Alvin," the radio intoned, "your wife wants you to call her."

"Oh Lord, I forgot," the deputy replied. "I was supposed to take her to get her hair fixed."

Betty Sue Blankenship, the comedienne of the East Texas

airways, replied, "That's too bad, Alvin; I didn't know it was broke."

"Ain't broke," her radio foil replied, "just wored-out." And he giggled again, with the mike still open. "Don't you know, Betty Sue, she's awful brown-headed." Then he shut off the mike, held it at arm's length and chortled, "She's brown-headed . . . and she's awful! Whoo-oo!" And he exploded once again into a gale of laughter at his own sparkling wit.

"Shoot yes she is," he said into the microphone again. "Betty Sue, call her and tell her that I'll be out to pick her up just as soon as I get these fellers t' the hospital."

"Ten-four," the dispatcher replied. "But you'd better hurry in after that, J.W. will want a report before you go to the house this ev'nin.'"

"That's a ten-four. Unit three out."

Deputy Ralph was still chuckling when he roared the car into the emergency room driveway behind the East Texas Medical Center. "Shoo-oot yes, she is," he repeated just one more time, as the car braked to a screeching halt.

Nurse Vivian Allen, standing in the doorway, saw the county car pull up and, instinctively, started wheeling a gurney out the door. Bill had the car door open and the boy in his arms before the dust settled.

As the man tenderly placed the rag-limp youth onto the stretcher, the nurse took a long look at the spectacle of the mud-encrusted pair and observed, "My Lord, maybe there is a wrath of God."

"You're a darling, and you're all heart," Bill replied. "Now please get my boy in there. He's been bitten by a rattlesnake."

All business now, the nurse responded, "I can see it. Right calf." As the emergency room door opened again, she called to another nurse who was standing there, "Get Dr. Conrad, the boy's been snakebit. Here," she said to Bill, indicating the handles of the gurney, "help me with this."

Bill took control of the wheeled stretcher and broke it into a gallop as Nurse Allen held the door open.

"How long ago?" she asked, as they hurried down a back hall;

then she motioned for him to stop and indicated a doorway on the left. "In here."

"I don't know," Bill replied. "Some time this morning; maybe about nine o'clock." Both glanced at the large clock on the emergency room wall. It was 12:24.

A youngish-looking doctor materialized in the room, fitting his stethoscope to his ears. Dr. Alan Conrad wore his sandy hair cropped short, a pair of 1890-looking eyeglasses, and a look of concern.

"It's critical, Doctor," the nurse announced. "Rattlesnake. Maybe three hours or more ago." Bill saw that she was spraying some kind of cleansing solution onto Buddy's hugely swollen leg. Then she wiped it away gently, with a towel. Buddy winced, and the leg made an involuntary jerk.

"Canebrake or diamond back?" the doctor asked peering over his tiny, round spectacles to look Bill directly in the eyes. He, too, was all business.

"Canebrake," Bill replied. "A big one. Over five feet."

The doctor listened to the boy's heart, then placed the stethoscope's probe to his rib cage. Leaning down to speak into Buddy's ear, he asked, "Are you conscious?"

"Um-huh," Buddy managed to reply.

"Then breathe deeply a few times."

Buddy complied the best he could. After the doctor had heard the lungs, he put his hand to the boy's mud-encrusted forehead. "He's burning up," he announced, to no one in particular. "How did he get so filthy? Both of you?"

"We fell in a mud puddle," Bill replied.

"All these lacerations on his face and head," the doctor observed, "where did they come from?"

"Tree branches and thorns. I had to carry him out through the thicket; and I couldn't always duck enough."

"Out from where?"

"From where we camped, out southeast. It all blew away in the storm."

"I see." Giving the man a worried look, the doctor asked, "Have you given him any kind of first aid?"

"Best I could, Doctor," Bill answered. "I broke off a tree

thorn to cut the fang marks, and sucked out as much of the venom as I could."

"Good," the doctor said, as Nurse Allen entered the room with an I.V. bottle and rigging paraphernalia.

"Okay," the docter said to Bill. "We'll take over now." Glancing obviously at Bill's own heavily lacerated torso, he asked, "All those tree thorns . . . is that how you got so cut-up?"

"I'm okay, Doctor," Bill replied. "Just take care of the boy."

"I am taking care of the boy. He's in good hands, don't worry about him. During my residency, I studied with Dr. Ruben Villafranca, in San Antonio, who is one of the foremost authorities on pit-viper bites in America. We'll give your boy a good dose of antivenin and all that other good stuff. We may have to do a debridement, I don't know. I'll have to make an exploratory incision to find out."

"What's a debridement?"

"Tissue removal. Snake venom destroys tissue, and it's often best to remove some of it, if you can. I won't do it unless it looks like it's necessary. But if it is necessary, it is absolutely so. You his father?"

"Yeah," Bill lied.

Just as the deputy had done, the doctor looked at Bill with studied incredulity.

"His mother's awful blonde," Bill explained, with a nod.

"Well, you'll have to sign some consent papers."

As he said that, the doctor saw Bill's eyes close briefly, and he saw him sway, almost imperceptibly.

"You may think you're all right," he told him, "but you obviously need a good dose of hospitalization yourself." Turning to the nurse, he asked, "Do we have any beds, Vivian?"

"Yes, sir," she replied. "Plenty of beds."

"Find someone to put him into a room and get him out of those filthy shorts, into a shower and a clean smock. We'll take care of his lacerations as soon as we get the boy stabilized. Who are you?" he asked Bill, without looking up. He was intent upon fingertip examination of the boy's neck.

"Name's Hamilton. William Hamilton."

Hamilton—Buddy's given name; it was the first thing that came to Bill's mind. He figured the boy would probably refer to him as "Bill," so he added the "William."

"And the boy?"

"His name's Buddy."

"That his name, or his nickname?" the doctor asked.

"It's his name."

"Okay, Mr. Hamilton. We'll take care of Buddy. Now go get a shower and get into bed. I'll be with you in about three quarters of an hour, but the nurse will be there before that."

Bill could see intensity and urgency in the doctor's eyes, behind the funny glasses, as they now looked the lying kidnapper directly into his.

"And remember," Dr. Conrad warned, "there is no equivocation. If we are to save your boy's life, you must sign those consent forms." Then he turned to the second nurse, now standing beside Bill. "Now get him out of here, nurse. We've got important work to do."

Bill liked him. No holds barred. No extraneous bullshit. Right down to business. He felt confident, and relieved, that his woefully hurt Buddy was, indeed, in good hands.

As for Bill, he wasn't quite certain what kind of hands he was in. They could have been those of a female Marine Drill Instructor.

"In there," Nurse Thompson ordered (identified by her name tag) pointing to the bathroom in the two-bed, semi-private room into which she had ushered him. Happily, both beds were vacant.

"Get out of that filthy mess and into the shower. When you finish, put this on," and she handed him one of the characteristically flimsy, tie-in-the-back hospital gowns. "You needn't go to too much trouble tying the string, though, 'cause it'll have to come off so Doctor can look at those nasty-looking cuts of yours. I don't know what you and that boy got into, but you sure musta screwed up."

"Love your bedside manner, pet," Bill chided. "You want to come in and scrub my back?"

"Sure," she replied. "Just as soon as I go get me a nice, stiff brush."

"Never mind, love, on second thought. I'm afraid you might like it too much."

"Well?" she demanded, glaring at him with hands on hips. "Are you getting into the shower, or aren't you?"

"Are you going to stand there and watch me when I do?"

"You want me to?"

"No."

"Then do it. I'll be back," she said. Then she walked out the door and pulled it shut behind her.

"A threat if I ever heard one," said Bill.

Weariness, near-exhaustion, finally caught up with the man in the relaxing steam of the shower, and he almost fell asleep standing up. Once dressed in his dainty little smock and propped up in a bed, he struggled in vain to stay awake and wait for the old battleaxe Thompson to return. When she did, he was sound asleep.

"Wake up, mister," she intoned, harshly. "You've got to sign these forms. What'd you say your name was?"

The cobwebs in his brain were thick as putty.

What the hell did I say my name was? Oh yes, the kid.

"Caine," he said aloud.

"How do you spell that? C-A-N-E?"

"No, P-A-I-N," Bill replied, suddenly realizing his mistake. He rubbed his still-swollen left temple and added, "I said I've got a pain right here."

"We'll give you something for that in a minute. Now what's your name?"

"Ham . . . Hamilton," he finally remembered. "William Hamilton."

"And the boy?"

"Buddy. Yes, Buddy's his name, not a nickname."

"Sign this form right now," the Marquis de Sade's answer to Florence Nightingale demanded, "and fill in your home address. The doctor's ready to operate." She shoved her paper-stuffed clipboard virtually into his face.

Bill scribbled his latest *nom de plume* in the several spots where she had made X-marks and asked, "Will you bring Buddy in here with me after the doctor's through with him?"

"No way, mister. He goes into ICU."

"Into what?"

"Intensive Care. He could be there for as much as a couple of days. Snake bites are nothing to laugh at." And she marched out of the room.

"Neither are you, you old bat!" Bill exclaimed, tossing the world-famous, one-finger salute at the closing door.

He was in deep sleep, once again, when Nurse Allen placed a gentle hand on his shoulder. "I hate to bother you with this, good-lookin', but you've got to have this shot."

Trying to surface through his mental fog once again, Bill asked, "What kind of shot?"

"Antibiotic. You've got a good chance at infection there, and we've got to put it down. Are you allergic to any medication?"

Bill shook his head.

"Then roll over and turn the other cheek."

"Is everyone in this hospital a comedian?" he asked, exposing his bare posterior.

"You have to learn to live with a lot of suffering in a place like this," she explained, jabbing the syringe into the man's left buttock. "Sometimes you can't help letting off a little steam with the patients you think can take it."

After she extracted the needle, Bill rolled onto his back again and asked, "What happened to King Kong?"

The nurse smiled; she was truly a sweet lady. "You mean Nurse Thompson?"

"Yeah, her."

"She got off at three. We're short-staffed, so I'm staying a little late today."

Bill abruptly sat up. "At *three*? What time is it now?"

Glancing at her wrist watch, the nurse replied, "Quarter to four."

"My God! Where's the doctor? Where's Buddy?"

"Your boy is all right, under the circumstances. He's in ICU and probably still sedated. The doctor came in to take a look at you, and you were so deeply asleep that he figured you needed the rest, right now, more than you needed bandages. But the important thing is to get that antibiotic to work."

"Can I see Buddy? I want to see him."

"Sure," she smiled, softly. "Come on, I'll take you over there."

Bill stood shakily out of bed, and the untied smock flared revealingly in front of him. Hastening to tie the strings across his bare behind, he asked, "Isn't there some way that I can make this thing a little more secure?"

"Hold on just a minute." And the nurse left the room.

She returned, presently, with another smock and said, "Here, put this one on backwards. Then you can tie it in front and nobody will be able to see your hind-end."

"You're a sweetheart. What say you and I run off and get married?"

"That might be fun," she replied without a hint of a blush, "but I've got to cook supper for a lumberjack husband and three kids tonight." Affixing a bow knot in the front of the smock for him, she added, "Come on."

Buddy was the only patient in the Intensive Care Unit. The room was small, but apparently equipped well enough to do the job. There were racks of esoteric-looking equipment scattered about—assorted monitors, life-sustaining machines and the like—with a lone nurse on duty, seated at a desk.

The boy lay on a bed with siderails raised; and there was an intravenous feeding bottle affixed to a pole at the end of the bed next to his head, providing a steady drip-drip of some kind of fluid into a vein in his left arm.

He lay there in drug-induced sleep looking pale, drawn, and more fragile than Bill might ever have imagined. A shock of mud-flecked, but still golden hair lay across his forehead, almost dangling into one of those once-radiant, now sadly closed eyes. Bill wondered whether he might ever see their sparkle again.

As he reached down to push the unruly shock of hair back onto the boy's forehead, Nurse Allen explained, "We cleaned him up only as much as necessary. We'll get him spick-and-span after he wakes up."

From Buddy's forehead, Bill ran his open hand along an uncharacteristically sallow, sunken-looking cheek. Plainly visible, over the left side of his upper lip, was a small scab marking the spot where the youth had cut himself shaving the night before. *Was it only last night?* Bill wondered.

Staring at what his own money lust had caused, the kidnapper could no longer avoid the obvious. As much as he had tried to suppress the truth, he finally had to admit it: he loved that kid.

Without comment, Bill turned quickly away and walked out of the room.

The name tag on the door of the room adjacent to his identified the patient inside as a Mrs. Emily something-or-other. That wouldn't do. Across the hall, there were two patients, with the door ajar, and Bill could hear voices inside. That wouldn't do, either. Next door to that, a single name tag listed the room's occupant as Fred Zoller.

Let's see what Mr. Fred Zoller looks like, Bill told himself, as he softly opened the door and stepped inside.

With his left arm in a cast suspended by a cord from the ceiling, Fred was obviously asleep. And alone. Bill quietly opened the closet door and found the man's pants, shirt, shoes and socks. Sizing them up, quickly, he decided that they would do; then he gathered them up and quietly closed the closet door.

"Thanks a lot, Fred," Bill whispered, as he closed the outer door and tiptoed back to his own room.

They weren't all that bad a fit, considering the circumstances—blue jeans, a plaid, short-sleeved shirt that exuded evidence that it's owner's deodorant had long since given out on him, and a pair of steel-toed work shoes that provided Bill with plenty of toe-wiggling room. He concluded that Fred was obviously not a bank president.

Bill found a pencil and a scratch pad in the table drawer beside his bed and wrote:

This is the Caine boy who was kidnapped from Houston last Tuesday. Please take good care of him.

Bill folded the note, stuck it into the pocket of Mr. Zoller's borrowed shirt, paused, then pulled it out again. He unfolded the note, picked up the pencil and added:

He's a hell of a good kid!

There was a safety pin in the table drawer, so he took that with him, also.

The nurse at the desk in the Intensive Care Unit gave him a hard look when he entered the door, but she recognized him as having been there with Nurse Allen, and allowed him to enter.

"Don't you need to go change somebody's bed pan or something?" Bill asked her.

"ICU nurses don't change bed pans," she replied, icily.

"I'm sorry, I didn't mean any offense. But shouldn't you be assisting in open-heart surgery or something? I'd just like a few minutes with my boy. Please?"

"Your boy is under heavy sedation. You won't be able to communicate with him."

"Lady, I can communicate. He'll get the message. But sweetheart, there are some things a man needs to tell his boy at a time like this that feel better being said without someone listening in. Please?"

She tried her best to be stern, but the soft, brown eyes and curly, black hair were too much for her. "All right," she replied, "but not for long. I'll be back in five minutes—no longer."

"You're a doll. Thank you."

Now that he was alone with the unconscious boy, Bill really didn't know what to say. The kid looked the same as before— pathetically, tragically sad. Bill thought that even if Buddy was unable to hear him, he might could get the message by touch, so the failed kidnapper pulled back the sheet that covered his former captive and picked up his limp right hand.

"Buddy . . . pal . . ." Bill began, hesitantly. "I've got to go. I'd rather leave my right leg on the table over there than to leave you here like this. But you know as well as I do that if I stick around here, they'll catch me; and then I wouldn't be worth a damn to you in jail, for sure. We got by that stupid deputy, but I'm not so sure we fooled the doctor.

"I think you're in good hands. I really do. I have faith in the treatment this doctor here is giving to you. And I know . . . I just know that you're going to be all right.

"Remember what I told you last night? I promised that some day, some way, I'd get back with you again. Well, I'm renewing that promise right now. Come hell or high water, buddy-of-mine, we'll be together again."

Bill put his buddy's arm back to his side and replaced the cover sheet. As he pinned the note to the boy's pillow, he added, "Just one more thing before I go. You've got to know, pal, that if I had been able to write the specifications personally, I could never have dreamed-up a son I'd rather have more than you. Get well, kid."

From their position behind the plate glass window, at the opposite end of the room, Dr. Conrad and Nurse Allen were all but invisible to Bill's bedside testimonial; but they could see every move that he made.

"What do you intend to do, Doctor?" the nurse asked.

"Nothing. He's doing it himself."

"But shouldn't you call the sheriff?"

"There'll be plenty of time for that. Tomorrow, maybe. We'll find his note tomorrow. After all, he did save the boy's life; and then he brought him here. That took dedication. Dedication and guts. I'm all for saving lives. And dedication. And guts, too. Whatever he did wrong, he did this right."

Recalling what the curly headed, mustached man in the skimpy hospital smock had said to her, the nurse sighed, half-wistfully, "Maybe I should have."

"Should have what?" Dr. Conrad wondered.

"Run off with him and got married."

The youngish-looking physician removed his studiedly small, round eyeglasses and smiled benignly; then the doctor and the nurse watched as the man in the stolen clothes walked quietly out the door.

▼ ▼ ▼ ▼ ▼ ▼ ▼ ▼ ▼ ▼ ▼ ▼ ▼

17

In a small, Texas country town, especially if it's the county seat, Saturday afternoons are always the busiest of the week—when farmers and laborers are in town from miles around to stock up on their week's supply of groceries and other necessities.

But that was no longer true in Greater Metropolitan Downtown Woodville. A shopping center—not a big, air-conditioned, covered mall, just a strip shopping center with a major discount store—had opened south of town and virtually killed all of the town-square commerce that had been the lifeblood of the community for decades.

As a consequence, the town looked almost deserted that late Saturday afternoon when Bill escaped out the emergency entrance of the hospital and went looking for some place to hide—searching for some inspiration as to how to get his soon-to-be-sought-after personage out of town . . . in a hurry.

The perfect answer presented itself as he approached the back parking lot of the town's only hardware store. It was a pickup truck, with an emblem emblazoned on the side identifying it as the property of the Alabama and Coushatta Indian Reservation. Adding to its apparent effectiveness as a means of escape, there was a large quantity of assorted stuff and junk in the truck's bed, including the most desirable commodity of all—a large tarpaulin.

The Indian reservation was some sixteen miles west of town, halfway between Woodville and Livingston, and deep in the Big

Thicket woods. Bill hoped that if he could sneak a ride to the reservation, he could be much more than miles ahead of his pursuers when they inevitably took out on his trail. Who would think to look on the Indian reservation? And besides, he would be in the the woods—not out on a highway somewhere.

Carefully, he climbed into the back of the pickup truck, shuffled around its load of debris, lay down and covered himself with the tarpaulin.

Not long afterward, he heard some kind of unidentifiable shuffling and bumping-around outside. Suddenly, the pickup was rocked, as though something heavy had been dumped into the truck bed beside him.

Then he heard the panting. And he felt the poking. Ultimately, he sensed the corner of the tarp nearest his face being pushed aside; and some searching, sniffing something moved toward his face. When it located its target, a long, wet tongue began frantically to lick him all over the face.

"Brutus, you old son of a bitch! How in the world did you find me?" he exclaimed, as quietly as he could.

Immediately, the back end of the pickup truck was an uproar. Brutus pawed and clawed away at the tarpaulin, trying to uncover Bill, who, just as frantically, was trying to remain covered. Brute strength, determination, and the upper hand won out, finally; and Bill gave in. He hugged the loving beast, tousled his ears, and accepted another face-bath of long-tongued, wet kisses.

When the reunion finally subsided, he struggled to get big-old, loving Brutus to lie down beside him; then he covered them both with the tarp, to await the arrival of whoever it was that had brought the Indian pickup truck to Woodville.

He didn't have to wait long. Soon there were voices, and Bill felt the impact and vibration of something being dropped into the bed of the truck. Brutus lurched. And then . . . ominous silence.

Slowly . . . cautiously . . . the tarpaulin moved away; and Bill found himself looking right into the stern and reproving eyes of two rather stout-looking Indians.

"How," he said meekly, raising his right hand.

"How is right, mister," one of them replied. He was the one with the long ponytail. "How in the hell did you get into our truck? And how in the hell long did you think you were going to stay there?"

"Oh, just maybe as far as the reservation? Maybe?" Bill replied, tentatively, affecting his most ingratiating smile.

The other Indian, with full-cut hair but no ponytail, said, "Looks to me like Keemosabe here is trying to get out of town."

"Yeah," said the other Indian, "and he's even trying to take his damn dog with him, too. How come, Lone Ranger?"

Just what I need, Bill's inner voice whispered, *a couple of hip, smart-ass Indians.*

"Okay, you got me pegged," he responded. "I'm in a little bit of trouble, and I need to get out of town in somewhat of a hurry."

"What kind of trouble?" ponytail asked.

"Big trouble," Bill replied. With only the slightest hesitation he added, "With . . . with Mr. Hendricks."

"Boss Hendricks?" It was ponytail again.

"Yeah," Bill acknowledged. "Do you know him?"

"Know of him," said Indian Number Two. "Everybody in these parts knows about Boss Hendricks. He owns half the world around here. What's he after you for?"

"A slight indiscretion," Bill stated, with his mind racing in creative fabrication. "I work for Mr. Hendricks . . . or, at least I did . . . in his headquarters office. But I'm afraid I got caught dipping into the wrong well."

"You mean dipping into the company cash box?" asked non-pony tail.

"No, not that well. Mr. Hendricks' daughter. They caught us at the Dogwood Motel together."

Indian Number One (with the pony tail) glanced knowingly at Indian Number Two. "What kind of work did you do for Boss Hendricks?"

"I worked in the office. Accountant."

The two red men exchanged knowing glances again, and Number Two asked, "You a CPA?"

"Yes," Bill lied.

After yet another exchange of knowing glances, Number Two said to Number One, "We could sure use a CPA to help straighten out our books. That oil drilling has put a strain on the operation, and we have no way of knowing if they're screwing us."

Number One nodded in agreement. "Okay, Keemosabe," he said, pulling the tarpaulin back over the white man and his yellow dog. "Any enemy of Boss Hendricks is a friend of ours. You're going with us."

▼ ▼ ▼

Although it was only a short ride to the reservation, Bill had plenty of time to reflect. This American-aboriginal Tweedle Dum and Tweedle Dee were a godsend. He had never heard Indians talk like they did—obviously a studied affectation; but then, he had never heard Indians of any kind talking much of anything, other than trying to peddle rubber-stamp Navajo rugs and deadly dull turquoise-and-silver jewelry around the square in Santa Fe.

He did know, however, that in spite of the nationwide downturn in the petroleum industry, oil had been discovered on the Alabama and Coushatta reservation, and there was at least a minor-league drilling program under way there. If his guess was right, whichever oil companies were involved were probably putting the screws to the Indians. After all, white men had been doing that for several centuries.

But as far as helping them with their bookkeeping? Forget that! Bill had a hard enough time keeping his own meager bank account straight. His lie would be discovered soon enough; but he decided that he would meet that train when it pulled into the station. At least he was getting the hell out of Woodville—and with the best possible cover.

The Indian reservation was just about what he might have expected it to be, at least in the main headquarters area—a collection of National Park-looking buildings housing a restaurant, curio shop, museum—that sort of thing. It had been a long, long time since those Indians or their forebears had shot an arrow into the hide of a buffalo. Or trapped a beaver. Or skinned a bear. Bill quickly formed the opinion that, for many years, the only thing that got skinned around that particular reservation was tourists.

From their highway billboards, newspaper and magazine articles, and their advertising, this combination of two long-ago tribes might well be dubbed the "show-biz" Indians. For years, the modern-day remnants of those two tribes that had sought refuge in Texas in the 1780s, after the French-Indian War, had eked out an existence by operating their reservation as a full-fledged tourist trap.

It wasn't that way in the beginning, when the Alabamas and the Coushattas were said to have controlled an estimated nine million acres of the Big Thicket. That vast quantity dwindled drastically under the onslaught of the white man's logging axe until, in the mid-1850s, the federal government created the 4,600-acre reservation. That was still a lot of land; and at the time, there was still plenty of game to hunt and trap. The Indians managed to get along quite well with little interference or influence from the white man's world outside.

But things change; and change is not always for the better— particularly, as history seems time and again to repeat, for the Indians. So, their tribal existence degenerated into a carnival side show. They gave twice-daily performances of the sort of tom-tom-and-tomahawk tribal dances that American tourists have been conditioned by years of Western movies to expect— for the delight and edification of tourists, along with elementary and junior high school children who were bussed-in each year from Houston and other school districts within a two- or three-hour drive. They sold the pottery, handcrafted jewelry and other gimcrackery expected of a tourist trap; and they lived in semi-poverty in modest brick homes subsidized by the federal government.

The discovery of oil on the reservation held promise of alleviating some of that poverty, but nobody in the know was taking any bets. And one thing was certain: a non-accountant, brought to the reservation with his big, yellow dog in the back of a pickup truck, was not going to be of much benefit to them. Still, he had to play it out.

Bill learned that the improbable-talking duo who had aided his escape—both apparently in their late twenties—were named Emerson Langley and Jason Furst . . . not exactly the "Howling Coyote" or "Running Bear" monikers expected of the plains Indians of the movies. But then, the Texas Big Thicket was a long way from the Western Great Plains—by a couple of thousand miles and about one and a half centuries.

Langley was the one with the ponytail. He was not very much short of six feet tall, with broad shoulders and the characteristically high cheekbones of the American Indian—with round, puffy cheeks beneath them and dark, virtually impenetrable eyes. His hair was jet-black, pulled tightly across his temples and tied at the base of his neck with a rubber band or some such, then left to dangle, loose-stranded, for more than a foot down his back. He wore the venerable, sleeveless cotton undershirt that had become dignified on West Coast beaches and elsewhere with the name of "tank top," and some sort of three-quarter-length trousers that fit semi-tightly just below the knees, almost like knickers—but they weren't billowy above the knees like knickers. To complete his costume, he wore long, mid-calf-length socks inside high-top, black tennis shoes. Bill doubted that he would make the pages of *Gentleman's Quarterly*.

Neither would his companion. Jason Furst was slightly shorter and more stockily built. His hair was trimmed to shoulder length all the way around—a "page boy" do, on the order of Prince Valiant. He wore blue shorts and a white polo shirt, with low-top sneakers and gym socks.

Their skin was uniformly dark—darker than the average Latin American of Bill's acquaintance, though not as dark as the many darker-hued black residents of Houston. And it was a mystery to Bill how they ever got the nickname "redskins." The skin of those fellows was brown—nothing akin to red. But then, he realized, there is nothing white-skinned about the white man, either.

Bill was even further bemused by the curious twist of logic that had persisted in calling the native American inhabitants

Indians at all—ever since Christopher Columbus's original act of mistaken identity.

But there he was, with a couple of non-red, red men—Indians who had nothing to do with India—about to have to admit to them that there was considerable about himself that was also false.

Langley and Furst stared at Bill as he, in turn, stared blankly at the record books they had placed before him in the tribal headquarters building.

"You don't know a damned thing about accounting, do you?" It was ponytail Langley who made the observation.

With his head tilted down, the white interloper raised his eyes at the inquisitor—the sort of look an accountant would make peering over his reading glasses . . . if he had been an accountant, and if he had worn reading glasses.

"No," was his simple reply, accompanied by a slight shake of the head.

Furst added the observation, "No, you ain't no accountant; but I'll give you one thing—you are something else as a bullshitter."

Sounds just like Buddy, Bill thought. Then aloud, trying to remain cool under fire, "Why do you say that?"

"Boss Hendricks doesn't have a daughter."

"Oops," was the best the imposter could reply. He knew that he was had.

Then curiously, a broad grin began to spread across the previously stern countenance of Indian Number One. It was picked up by Indian Number Two, and soon both of them were laughing good-humoredly. Langley reached out with his right hand and slapped Bill lightly on the shoulder.

"But there's no law against not being a CPA," he said. "And if Boss Hendricks did have a daughter, you're probably just the kind of guy she'd get caught in bed with."

"So what the hell do you do?" the other Indian asked.

Bill smiled, relieved. "I lie a lot."

"I hear where you're comin' from, friend," said Furst. "Do you need a place to hide out? Is that it?"

"Yeah," Bill admitted, with a slight twist of his head, "that sure as hell is it."

"Well," said Number Two, "any man running from white man's law is okay with us . . . as long as you didn't kill nobody. You didn't kill nobody, did you?"

"No," Bill shook his head. "I didn't kill anybody. I just almost got killed myself."

"I don't know of any law against that," Furst said to Langley, "do you?"

Ponytail shook his head in reply. "No way, Keemosabe," he said, shifting back into the phony dialect. "We fix you up with job and place to hide. Okay?"

"Right at the moment, I can't think of anything better than that," Bill answered, barely managing not to add, "Tonto." At their beckoning, he followed the pair out the door.

▼ ▼ ▼

From his untethered position in the back, Brutus barked happily at nothing in particular as the pickup truck rumbled down the oyster-shell road—crushed oyster shells were frequently trucked-in from the Gulf Coast to serve as all-weather road beds, cheaper than gravel. Sitting on the bench seat up front with his two benefactors, Bill could see the crown of the drilling rig on the left, ahead, protruding above the tops of the surrounding pine forest.

On their way there, the Indians explained that the two of them were what they called "go-betweens," a more or less official liaison between the tribal rulers of the Alabama-Coushattas and the oil company that was drilling the wells on the Indian land.

"They might have some work for you over at the well," Langley said. "We can't order them around, you know, but they pretty much have to do it when we ask them real hard to do something."

The road, newly constructed solely for the well-drilling operation, took a turn to the left. After another hundred yards or so, it terminated in a five-acre clearing. From that spot, a road constructed of heavy wooden planks led up to the towering drilling rig. A sign at the start of the board road read: AUTHORIZED PERSONNEL ONLY. PROPERTY OF DEEP EAST TEXAS DRILLING COMPANY. RIG NO. 6. HARD HAT AREA.

Unless it is placed in the middle of downtown Manhattan, a well-drilling operation will dominate any landscape. This one was no exception. The rig, itself, was of the relatively portable variety, with a derrick structure, more accurately referred to as a "mast," that was first pieced together horizontally on the ground, then jackknifed under its own power into vertical position. And its position was commanding.

Painted white with dark-blue trim, the derrick sat atop a fifteen-foot-high substructure that contained the blowout prevention equipment beneath the operating floor of the rig. Looking like a collection of super heavy-duty plumbing devices, the "preventers" were designed to control and shut off, if necessary, any sudden surge of high-pressure liquid or gas from the well. The classic "gusher" was a thing of the past; and any such occurrence with modern drilling activity was an embarrassing and extremely costly accident.

A cluster of small buildings and trailers was arrayed on one side of the derrick structure like a flotilla of escort vehicles hovering around a giant aircraft carrier. One trailer belonged to the oil company that was paying for the drilling of the well, the "company man's" trailer, and another, parked adjacent, was headquarters for the drilling contractor's operations. Yet a third trailer, parked remotely, housed the mud-logging unit, where material brought to the surface in the drilling mud was periodically analyzed for mineral content.

There were other buildings that housed the giant diesel engines which powered the rig, storage facilities for drilling mud, and assorted other things . . . plus a cluster of small, steel buildings that were unfamiliar to Bill. He had never encountered their like.

The ground area atop which all of that assorted equipment and buildings were located was entirely paved with heavy wooden planks, in the same manner as the final one hundred yards of the road that led to it—common practice on Gulf

Coast drilling locations, in particular, where heavy rains could turn the scraped-off drilling site into an impassable swamp.

The planks of the board road clickety-clacked beneath the wheels of the Indian reservation pickup truck like a shaky road-bed beneath a passing train.

"Ever been to an oil well?" asked one of the Indians.

"Yeah, lots of times," Bill replied, but he volunteered no further information.

The rig company's drilling superintendent—a job known in the oil patch as "tool pusher"—was as delighted to see the two Indians as a crippled elk is to see a pack of hungry wolves.

"What the fuck do you want now?" he asked, as a greeting.

"You got any jobs around this chickenshit place?"

"You must mean this fellow here," the tool pusher replied, motioning to Bill. "I know you two ain't interested in working."

"Yeah, me," Bill interrupted the cordiality.

The tool pusher, a leather-skinned, hard-bitten-looking sort named Mack Ferguson, sized-up the newcomer. The truth was that, not only did he have a job opening, he was desperate for a man to do the toughest—perhaps the most dangerous and demanding—job on the rig.

Glancing sideways at the man heretofore known as Bill, he asked, "Can you run pipe?"

Not really comprehending what he meant by that, Bill replied, "Sure I can."

"Well, you're probably lying," Ferguson noted, "but my derrickman on the morning tower just drug-up, and I've got to have somebody to take his place. We're going to be taking a trip tomorrow afternoon sometime, and I've got nobody to run pipe. None of the rest of those sonsabitches out there has got the balls to tackle it."

As a pilot flying tools and personnel into the southern Louisiana swamps, Bill had visited drilling rigs many times, often having to stand around and wait for protracted periods before making his return flight. Thus, he had often watched the goings-on aboard the rigs. When he realized the job to which the man was referring, he had to suppress what might otherwise have been an audible gulp. Then he glanced out the window of the tool pusher's trailer to the top of the rig—easily one hundred and fifty feet off the ground.

"You mean up there?" he asked, pointing.

"I mean up there."

Desperate as he was, Bill had no other options. "You just show me how to do it," he said, "and I'll do it."

"Well, I've never seen nobody yet could make a derrickman right off, without fuckin' somethin' up," Ferguson said. "But right now I've got no choice. I'll give you a shot at it; and if you can handle it, you've got yourself a job. And if you can't, you don't. And if you get yourself killed tryin' . . . I never heard of you."

"Go check with the cook over there," he added, pointing to the group of portable metal buildings that Bill had found unfamiliar, "and tell him to find you a place to sleep. If you last, you'll work seven on and seven off, and you'll get your bed and meals right here on the location. What's your name?"

"Harrison," Bill replied. "William Harrison." If he had thought quickly enough, he would have come up with some other given name; but he seemed to be stuck with "Bill," and it came out virtually all by itself.

"Okay, Harrison. Now get the hell out of here. Most of the crew's already had supper, I expect; and you'd better get your ass over there before it's all gone."

"I appreciate it," Bill replied, offering his hand for a handshake.

"Okay, Keemosabe," the Indian Furst said, offering his handshake also. "We'll see you later."

As Furst and Langley drove away, Bill looked around the drilling site. For his situation, the setup could not have been more perfect. Not only was it a job—and he now had absolutely nothing except the stolen clothes he was wearing—but it was also a place to live. And with free food, to boot.

Brutus seemed to like it also, as he went barking after another mutt. There was never any shortage of dogs around an oil rig.

Bill tilted his head up until he almost leaned over backward, and he stared at the lonely, tiny-looking platform a third of the way down from the top of the towering rig structure.

But oh, shit! It's going to be interesting.

He turned and strolled into the building that he guessed would be the dining room.

It was at the right end of the long, low, cluster of portable buildings—windowless, square, modular, put-together structures that were the crew's living quarters. Bill had never visited such a setup. All of the live-on-it drilling rigs he had ever been on were self-contained barges, which were towed into place by tug boats through freshly dredged channels in the swamplands that lined the coast of southern Louisiana. He had visited a few land rigs, for some obscure reason that he could not recall, but none of them that he had ever been on were what were known as "camp" locations. On the ones he'd seen, all the rig workers commuted back and forth to wherever they lived by car.

But this one was absolutely perfect. It was close enough to where he had last been seen, in Woodville, so that if any dragnet were to be formed, it would likely pass by in a hurry. It was located deep in the woods of the Indian reservation, where no one would likely come looking for a workman—they'd be searching for a fugitive on foot, one who would most likely be sticking close to the main highways in an effort to put as much distance as possible between him and the slow-paced little town in the East Texas forest.

The more Bill thought about the drilling site as a refuge, the better it appeared to be. Attempting to second-guess police— and the FBI, most likely—he reasoned that they might believe a sought-after fugitive such as he would try to beat it to another state, where the heat might possibly not be on as heavily as it was in Texas. Louisiana, a strong possibility, was little more than fifty miles away—east; but the Indian reservation and the deep-woods drilling location were *west* of the hospital where he had left his gravely stricken Buddy.

Besides, he reasoned further, continued flight would require some money; and he had none. But there, on Deep East Texas Drilling Company's rig number six, fate had provided him with a job, and the opportunity to save every penny he earned—at least after he bought some better-fitting clothes. His feet would just have to find a way to exist on the tiny platform way the hell up on that derrick. Bill determined, then and there, that he would find a way to hack it.

"You can sleep here," said the bulge-bellied cook in the holey T-shirt, as he motioned to the top bunk in a small cubicle across the hallway from the shower room in the crew quarters.

In addition to the two bunk beds, the spartan accommodations contained a small table and a one-piece unit that was a combination clothes closet and chest of drawers. The walls of the room were decorated with cut-out photographs of female genitalia from "adult" magazines—pictures that would have appeared equally at home in a gynecologic journal.

"Now come on into the kitchen and get yourself some food," the cook told him.

At a table in the small room that served as lounge area and dining room, Bill ate heartily for a while. It had been a long time since his last meal, and that had been a skimpy one, at that—their last supper in his creekside trailer, when he and his young pal Buddy had both been too melancholy about parting to be much concerned with food. So long ago, now . . . so painfully long ago. Last night.

At the recollection of it all—the play in the woods, the admiration and trust in the boy's blue eyes, the hurricane floodtide and, most of all, the horrible snakebite—Bill's stomach tightened up with a kink that felt like a knot on one of those huge ropes that are used to secure large ships to their moorings; and there was no more desire for food.

After he had scraped his plate into the garbage can, dropped it into the sinkful of sudsy dish water and sauntered to his room, Bill crawled into his bunk and quietly sank out of sight. Exhausted.

The next thing he knew, there was a hand shaking his shoulder.

"Hey," a voice was insisting. "You the new guy?"

Bill struggled to surface from his slumbering position deep within the bowels of the earth.

"Huh?"

"Come on. It's time to get up. We're fixin' to make a connection; and Bulldog says to take you up top and show you how to do it."

"Who's Bulldog?" Bill asked.

"Ferguson, the tool pusher."

"It fits."

Before he was fully awake, Bill found himself being fitted into a leather harness around the waist, which was secured to a cable strung to somewhere up there toward the top of the derrick. As the dull knife of consciousness hacked through the peanut-butter fog of weariness that still clouded his brain, he finally realized what it was that he was being required to do. Looking straight up, he asked, "Up there?"

"You better believe up there, friend," the still-unidentified voice replied.

What the man was saying, Bill realized, was that he was now going to be required to climb what appeared to be something just slightly short of ten thousand steps up to that minuscule platform near the top of the rig.

"This is a safety line, right?" he asked, holding the small cable in his hand.

"Right," the other man, whoever he was, replied. "You can't get hurt. Fall off the ladder and you'll just hang there."

"Wonderful," Bill noted. "Sounds like a gang of fun."

"Sure it is. Better'n a carnival ride. The only thing that can hurt is all that hard stuff you bang into while you're dangling there and they lower you back down."

"Thanks," Bill said. "You're a pillar of confidence." And he started to climb.

Every sinew in his back, arms, and legs—particularly the hamstrings—was beginning to ache by the time he was halfway up. Bill found little comfort in the knowledge that he had made it that far; because he still had that much farther remaining to go. To add to the degree of apprehension, it was now night. There was plenty of light for the crew to see what it was doing on the rig floor below, but not much of it spilled onto the narrow ladder that he was trying to climb.

"When you get up there," the man who had launched his

journey called from below, "unhook the cable and let it swing loose. I'll pick it up down here."

"Right," Bill replied, with a meant-to-seem casual wave of his left hand.

Finally, he did get there; and he crawled tentatively from the ladder to the derrickman's platform high above the works and workmen below. It was way, way up there; but the view was terrific—a bunch of floodlit machinery below, most of it obviously capable of causing instant maiming or death at the slightest miscue, lighted by large, mercury-vapor floodlights that managed to glare blindingly into his sleep-starved eyes, while scantly illuminating his perch. All of this goodness was surrounded by a sea of jet-black, absolute darkness. Somehow, he thought, this job was going to be hard to love.

It didn't start to look easier, only more intimidating, when the man who had launched him skyward suddenly came catapulting up the ladder that Bill had climbed so laboriously, and with such great pain. He only touched a foot to it now and then on his rocket ride up. Ultimately, Bill realized that the man was not climbing at all, but riding the safety harness, which must have been being pulled by some quick-turning winch motor somewhere.

"Beats the hell out of walking," the man said as he alighted on the platform beside Bill, like a circus aerialist joining his partner for the next stunt.

Bill only stared at him.

"You get used to it up here after a while," the man said, then he introduced himself. His name was Jim Bob Carter, and he was the derrickman on the evening "tower"—a peculiarity of oil-rig pronunciation, the term is actually "tour," as in tour of duty—just as Bill would be on the morning "tower." If he survived.

Presently, the steady grinding and groaning of the drilling rig halted; and the rotation of the huge swivel, beneath the equally huge pulley that hung suspended from the top of the rig, came to a halt. In due time, there was a flurry of activity on the rig floor down below, and Bill watched as a piece of drill pipe that was lying on a steel rest that slanted away from the bottom of the rig, was affixed to a hook and steel cable and half-dragged, half-hoisted aboard the rig.

Jim Bob fastened a safety line that was attached to a railing at their stratospheric work station to the safety belt around his waist, and gave a second one to Bill, to attach likewise.

In good time, the top of the thirty-foot-long pipe that Bill had seen picked up below was hoisted up the center of the rig, and Jim Bob leaned out against his harness and stretched his arms to grab onto the pipe and pull it over to him. Then he steadied and helped guide it into position down below.

To Bill's fatigue-numbed brain, the rest was a blur. But somehow, in whatever order, there was a flurry of activity on the rig floor below, in which a pair of giant tongs was employed to help unscrew the drill pipe in the hole from the solid-steel shaft that drove it from above—activities that were accompanied by a lot of mechanical grunting and groaning, with the rig's big diesel engines being revved-up and retarded again. That brought a cloud of diesel smoke that wafted straight into the faces of the two men high up on the platform. At some point, Jim Bob repeated his aerial act, helping guide the long steel pipe into position down below; and presto-chango, a new section of drilling pipe was affixed firmly in place, and the methodical thump-thump and occasional squeaking of routine drilling activity had begun again. Bill was certain that he could remember exactly what he had to do . . . for a full thirty seconds.

"Is that all there is to it?" Bill asked his instructor.

"Yeah, that's more or less all," Jim Bob replied. "Until we have to make a trip."

"Where are we going?"

The man stared at Bill for a moment. "You really don't know from shit, do you?"

Bill quickly thought of at least a couple of spiffy rejoinders, but trading insults with the man would avail him nothing. "No, not a helluva lot," he replied. "But I can learn. All I need is a little teaching. I'll make it."

"A trip," Jim Bob explained, is when we have to pull out all the pipe that's in the hole and break it loose, three joints at a time, so that they can put on a new drill bit. When we do that, we have to stack the stands in the rack over there—you or me— until all the pipe is back on the rig."

"How many is that?"

"Depends upon how deep we are at the time. Right now, we're only about five thousand feet deep; so you can figure it out for yourself . . . three joints to a stand, each joint is thirty feet, divided into five thousand feet. When it really gets to be fun is when we get about thirteen thousand, fourteen thousand feet or so deep. I think this well is permitted for something a little over fifteen thousand."

"Divided by ninety, times three?" Bill asked.

"You've about got it figured. And then," he added, almost as an afterthought, "we've got to push all that pipe back to them to go back into the hole."

After a pause, Bill asked, "And what do you do for recreation?"

"Drop wrenches and hammers and things on the roughnecks down below. It keeps 'em on their toes."

Bill winced at the thought.

"You want to ride the cable back down?" Jim Bob asked, as he fastened the previous winch cable to the leather harness still around his waist.

"No thanks," Bill replied, realizing that the man meant descending in the same manner as he had previously zoomed up to the platform. "I think I'll wait 'til daylight to try that little number."

"Whatever you say," the other man replied. Then he climbed out onto the skimpy-looking ladder, waved his left hand to somebody down below, and down he flew, like some crazy rock climber rappelling off a cliff.

Watching the descent, Bill mumbled, "Thanks, but no thanks. I believe I'll walk this time."

▼ ▼ ▼ ▼ ▼ ▼ ▼ ▼ ▼ ▼ ▼ ▼ ▼ ▼

18

In time, Bill became used to it. He found the way to fake it, a couple of times, through "making a connection"—hanging on one piece of drill pipe, as Jim Bob had done—before being tested with the gruelling and unfamiliar routine of "making a trip." Doing that was tough. But he managed to acquit himself without embarrassment or, as Bulldog Ferguson put it, having to be "run off."

In time, he settled into the routine of living at the drilling location, and he contrived—through simple hard work and doing what he was told, without talking back—to pick up a second job at the rig during his normal off-time.

The regular work schedule for all the roughnecks and roustabouts was one week on duty, working twelve hours a day and living at the rig, and one week off. Since Bill had nowhere else to go—no home, no family, no car in which to go anywhere—he talked the rig superintendent into letting him do odd jobs around the rig, on a semi-regular but not rigidly routine basis, during his week-off periods. The advantages were three-fold: he earned extra money, he kept away from the eyes of the law, and he kept his mind busy and somewhat eased from the mental burden that he carried so heavily.

Withal, it didn't stop his reading the newspapers and watching television news shows—almost every evening at both six and ten o'clock—for news about Buddy.

The first word came on Bill's second morning on the job,

when he picked up a Houston newspaper that a drilling mud salesman had left lying on the couch in the small sitting area of the mess hall/living quarters. The headline read: CAINE YOUTH FOUND IN EAST TEXAS HOSPITAL—SNAKEBIT BUT ALIVE

The story detailed how the kidnapped boy had been picked up by a medical evacuation helicopter and flown to John Sealy Hospital, in Galveston, for treatment at that institution's famed Poison Control Center. Details were sketchy, the story related, because the boy was heavily sedated and could not give much testimony. The article hinted that, despite the hospital's refusal to comment, the boy was barely clinging to life.

Bill groaned aloud when he read that, in addition to the near-fatal snakebite wound, the boy was also heavily lacerated about the face and head, apparently from vicious beatings at the hands of the kidnapper.

According to the newspaper story, there were contradictory statements from medical personnel at the hospital where the Caine boy had been found, in the small East Texas town of Woodville, and sheriff's department officials in the same community. As best the story could be pieced together, according to the newspaper, the kidnapper had apparently forced his captive to walk nearly naked from a cabin where he had been held, to a State highway outside of Woodville. The boy, already beaten and emaciated, had been bitten by a rattlesnake during the forced walk out.

The story went on that after the snakebite—according to the Tyler County Sheriff's Department—the kidnapper must have carried the captive youngster on his back to the highway, still in hope of trading off the stricken youth for ransom money. Tyler County Sheriff J.W. Cantrell was quoted as saying that the kidnapper apparently decided to give up the ransom attempt, and fled from the East Texas Medical Center wearing clothing stolen from another patient. Ironically, the story noted, the stricken Houston youth and his kidnapper had been picked up on the highway, five miles outside of Woodville, and taken to the hospital for treatment by a deputy from the same Sheriff's Department.

As the days and weeks went by, the story did not become a

great deal more clear—nor more accurate, either. Buddy recovered and was released from the hospital, and he returned to Houston to a virtual hero's welcome. He became an instant celebrity.

News stories related that the youth was apparently healthy and on the mend, although he was forced temporarily to walk with a cane while his leg continued to heal following the surgical removal of a small quantity of poison-destroyed muscle tissue. There were hints, though, that there was other damage to the River Oaks scion in addition to the injured leg. The secondary damage, the stories hinted, was emotional—if not mental. At times, they said, his recollections of his whereabouts and activities while being kept prisoner for four days were hazy. At other times, they were conflicting.

As best the authorities could establish from the boy's testimony, the kidnapper had secreted the youth in a small, unpainted wooden cabin somewhere southeast of Woodville—east of State Highway 1097; but the cabin had been destroyed by the winds of Hurricane Elizabeth, which had been reported to reach eighty-four miles per hour when the eye of the still-potent storm passed east of that small, East Texas town.

The papers reported that an extensive search of the area was underway, in hope of finding some clue to the identity of the kidnapper; but that so far, no such cabin as the boy described had been located. Although hazy in some details, according to authorities, the boy appeared to be quite certain about the relative location of the cabin hideout.

"I remember when we were walking out," the Caine boy was quoted as saying, "the morning sun was to our backs . . . always to our backs."

"That little son-of-a-gun!" Bill exclaimed when he read that. "He's lying . . . to protect me."

If Bill needed further proof of that, he had to look no farther than the composite picture that the Caine youth pieced together of his kidnapper, both printed in newspapers and shown on television. It looked more like the giggling, dimwit deputy sheriff than it did Bill.

As time wore on, according to the news accounts, authorities began to think less and less of the boy's story. The FBI was particularly doubtful. The case became even more muddled when the variety of witnesses to the man's appearance—the kidnapped boy himself, the deputy in Woodville, the doctor and the nurse in the Woodville hospital—all came up with composite pictures of the kidnapper that were widely different. The two that bore the closest resemblance to each other were those assembled by the deputy and the one put together on the day of the kidnapping by the Caine family chauffeur.

"The boy spent four days in his hands," argued Houston Police Chief Arnold Campbell. "He ought to know. Those people in Woodville didn't have the time to study the man that the boy had. We'll have to believe in the boy's picture."

"Not so," argued the FBI's Henry Wilson. "He just might be confused; or maybe his memory was affected."

That was what he said for publication. Privately, though Bill had no way of knowing this, Wilson was adamant.

"The little son of a bitch is lying," he told Liddell Peters and his other cohorts. "I don't know why, but if I could just have my hands on him alone for a few hours—with no judges, no attorneys, or no parents looking on—I'd damned sure find out."

Bill read that Wilson was pushing to have the Caine boy psychoanalyzed—perhaps even hypnotized—because of various conflicting elements of his story. But his family refused to allow it; and no judge was about to issue such an order in the face of the political clout no doubt available to the boy's father, Hamilton Caine, Sr.

A leading Houston psychologist, meanwhile, was quoted as saying that the lapses and contradictions in the boy's testimony were easily explainable and quite normal, under the circumstances. He was traumatized, the doctor explained, from what must have been horrible experiences at the hands of the kidnapper—although the boy protested otherwise—and his brush with death from the snakebite. What the boy was undergoing, the doctor explained, was what is known in psychological circles as "post-traumatic stress syndrome."

"Not only has that muddled his recollections," the doctor stated, "but it also has manifested a continuing fear of retribution—of punishment—from the kidnapper. You might say that, although the boy is now safely at home, he is still subconsciously scared to death of the man."

Bill enjoyed that. The kid who had begged to get to see him again is "still scared to death" of him. *That's rich.*

He truly did enjoy knowing that Buddy was recovering, but he was saddened to learn that he was forced to walk with a cane, even if it was only temporary. And he was delighted at the knowledge that the kid seemed to be dancing rings around the truth in order to protect the man he had named "Bill."

The sun was always at his back, Bill quoted to himself. *I love it. Before it disappeared entirely, the sun was directly in our faces, and Buddy knows it. And that bit about the wooden cabin—he obviously got that from the yarn I spun for that tobacco-spitting deputy sheriff. And bless his heart, he's sticking to his story. Those sonsobitches can search themselves blue in the face for a torn-down cabin east of that State highway. They might find one, but it won't be where we stayed; our camp was way the hell west of the highway.*

Bill was not totally caught up in a stultifying routine of all work and no play. Occasionally, on paydays, he would catch a ride into the town of Livingston (avoiding Woodville) to cash his paycheck. It would have been nice to have a few beers with the boys while shooting a game of pool or something, but that was impossible. The entire county was dry—no beer, no booze, no anything. The same held true for Tyler County, of which Woodville was the county seat. Those East Texas counties were part of what has come to be known over the years as the Baptist Bible Belt—among the last bastions of true, dedicated hypocrisy in the State of Texas. In order for Bill or any of his working cohorts to purchase alcoholic beverages of any kind, they had to journey halfway to Beaumont, in Hardin County, where, in true Texas fashion, a cluster of liquor stores dotted the county line. And the highway to and from was lined with empty beer cans.

Bill learned that, to compound the hypocrisy, he could check into a motel in either county and receive a free membership to that establishment's "private club." There, it was "belly up to the bar, boys," with beer, mixed drinks, or whatever a man's thirst might desire. Bill wasn't interested in paying for a motel room, though, just to be able to buy drinks across the bar; saving money was his goal. Besides, it wasn't necessary—there were Langley and Furst.

As is always the case in any liquorless area, bootleggers fulfilled the desire; and for the men of Deep East Texas Drilling Company's Rig Number Six, this meant the Tweedle Dum and Tweedle Dee of the Alabama and Coushatta tribes, Emerson Langley and Jason Furst. One or two evenings each week, they would appear with their pickup truck loaded with booze—hidden under the providential tarpaulin that had covered Bill in his escape—to sell to the crew members at outrageous prices. Bulldog Ferguson protested loudly, and he threatened vehemently to expose the bootleggers; but to no avail. The men wanted it; they were going to get it no matter how they had to do it; and the rig boss couldn't risk the enmity of Langley and Furst. It was an unusual ball game for him, because he was drilling on the Indian's land; and they had the upper hand. Thus, it was all Ferguson could do to keep not the booze, but the drinking of it, away from the rig. Consequently, there were many drunken parties in the nearby woods.

Bill found that not only did his two Indian benefactors enjoy selling the stuff for profit, they also had a strong affinity for consuming it, as well. And they liked to play games, along with it.

One day-after-payday, the pair appeared at the rig and invited Bill to go off into the woods with them for a little alcoholic conviviality. That sounded all right with Bill; and he learned that, just like in the movies, Indians and firewater definitely do not mix. In fact, they all three got bombed.

And then they pulled a gun on him.

"Relax, Keemosabe," ponytail Langley advised, while irresponsibly waving around a monster-big .44 magnum revolver. "I just want to take a little target practice." With that, he leveled the pistol and blammed off a shot that hit a beer can a scant five yards away.

With slurred speech, he asked Bill, "Can you do that?"

Bill stared at him, saying to himself, *The day will never come when I'm so drunk that I can't outshoot either of you two bastards.*

He took the gun and leveled down on the same can, only it had been bounced a full ten yards further away by the impact of Langley's bullet. With Bill's shot, it bounced even farther.

"Pretty good for a paleface," Langley said, good-naturedly. "Bet you can't do it again."

"What's your bet?" asked Bill.

"Five bucks. I bet you five bucks you can't hit that can right over there," the Indian challenged, pointing to an empty beer container some fifteen yards away.

Jason Furst joined in the challenge. "I've got another five bucks says you can't either."

"You're both on," Bill accepted.

He considered, momentarily, that he might bend over and shoot the target from between his legs, just for fun. The can was only about fifteen yards away; and he knew that a .44 magnum, in the right hands, is accurate to at least one hundred yards. Supremely confident (booze has a way of inspiring confidence) Bill knew that his were the right hands. But he decided against the trick shot. After all, it was possible that, through his booze-clouded eyes, he could miss and lose ten bucks. Besides—in a position like that, the report of the always-loud .44 magnum would make his ears ring for a week.

They rang anyway. And so did the can. Bill collected his winnings.

"Now you wanna bet that I can't do it?" asked Langley.

"Right," Bill replied, in the true spirit of competition; and he waved a five-dollar bill in the air.

Langley pulled the trigger, and the big handgun blasted. It blasted the air, it blasted the ears, and it blasted a huge hole in the dirt—a good one and one-half feet to the right of the target beer can.

"Pay up," Bill demanded. The Indian grudgingly dug into his pocket for a roll of bills, pulled off a five, and handed it over.

"Let me see the gun," Furst demanded. "I'll bet you ten that I can hit that damn can."

"Yeah," Langley joined in. "I bet he can too."

Again in the spirit of competition, and heady with his winnings, Bill called both bets.

The Indian with the page boy hairdo cradled the big gun in both hands, took careful aim, squeezed the trigger and sent the beer can flying.

Bill nodded his head. "Good shot." And he paid off both bets.

"Let's try it again from a little further out," Furst proclaimed. His speech was slurry, but not quite as much so as Langley's had been.

"Tell you what," he continued. "We'll set up a bunch of cans and we'll both shoot, for twenty-five bucks a shot. You hit one and you collect. I hit one and I collect. If we both hit, it's no win. Fair enough?"

"Suits me," Bill agreed.

At the rig crew's deep-woods drinking spot, there was no difficulty rounding up a half-dozen empty beer cans; and the two Indians gleefully set them up in a row, about twenty-five yards from their pickup truck.

Furst took a long drink from the bourbon bottle the trio had been nursing on, and fired. He missed. Then he handed the bottle to Bill, indicating that he, too, should take a swig. Bill put the bottle to his mouth, slugged down a quick drink, casually cradled the pistol in both hands, and fired. A can went flying. Langley didn't shoot; he held the bet money.

On the second round, both shooters drank again, and both connected; so there was no win or loss. Both drank and hit their targets again on the third round, and Furst suggested that they double the bet and back off another ten yards or so from the aluminum can shooting gallery. Bill agreed to that, and they did so; whereupon Bill's bullet hit its can, and Furst's missed. Time for another drink apiece.

Bill knew that he was being hustled almost from the minute the pistol had been passed from Langley to Furst. It was an old, old game—set up the mark with an easy loser, then raise the bets and hand off the gun to a better shooter. The Indians failed at their attempt for either, or both, of two reasons—Furst was not really all that good, or he couldn't handle his booze.

Bill allowed the drinking-and-shooting game to continue long enough to win three hundred and seventy-five dollars, and to anger his opponent severely. Also, by that time, Jason Furst was practically falling-down drunk.

"Time to quit," Bill announced. "Too much firewater."

"Fuckin' paleface," Furst declared. "C'mon man, let's shoot some more."

"No way, Tonto." Bill was adamant. "You know what they say in the movies. Redskins and booze don't mix. Redskins and booze and shooting—bad medicine. Now come on, put the gun away and let's get back to the rig. It's almost supper time."

"Next time, Keemosabe," Furst declared. "Next time I hang your scalp on my tepee."

"Next time," Bill warned, "before you try that old hustle, better not drink so much."

▼ ▼ ▼

In Houston, Buddy was feeling fine once again, although he still had to walk with a cane; and he had begun to enjoy his celebrity. He was interviewed countless times for local television news programs, and all three major TV networks carried his story with pictures from the boy's hospital bed in Galveston. Long articles with photographs of him beside his Adoring Mother appeared in both Houston daily newspapers, and the gossip columns were abuzz almost daily with the latest tasty tidbits about this or that activity of the Caine youth and/or his long-suffering, but devoted parents.

There was only one persistent rock in the road of young Ham Caine's recovery and, most significantly, his peace of mind: Henry Wilson. The agent who headed the Houston office of the FBI just would not give up.

He questioned the boy interminably, dedicated to breaking

what he felt certain was the kid's pack of lies concerning practically everything having to do with the kidnapping. He questioned Buddy at home, and he grilled him at the bureau's
downtown office. So obsessed was the agent, in fact, that he
even had the youth shadowed on his daily trips to and from
school. If called down about it, he intended to proclaim that it
was only for the boy's own safety; but in truth, he was looking
for some kind of rendezvous. Wilson's latest theory was a nag-
ging suspicion that somehow the boy was in league with the
kidnapper, and had been all along; and that the snakebite was
an accident that put a halt to their mysterious, but doubtlessly
nefarious plans.

Whatever the truth might have been, Wilson was determined
that he was going to cut through the fog of that boy's lying
testimony, and then capture and prosecute that kidnapper—or
accomplice, as the case may be.

He was still convinced that the perpetrator was someone
known to the family, and he frequently bore down on Buddy in
questions to that effect. Did he know the man? Had he ever
seen him before? How much contact did he have with people
who worked for his father's company? And, most significantly:
had he ever flown with his family—or without, for that matter—in any of the Texas Consolidated airplanes?

It all began to wear heavily on the boy; and the more he was
questioned, the more confused his story became.

Although he actually had lost interest in the goings-on,
Hamilton Caine, Sr., was the one who ultimately put a stop to
it all; and brief though it was, he enjoyed doing it immensely.

The senior Caine had never forgotten the brittle meeting between the FBI agent and himself that afternoon in the company
airplane hangar when he and his wife returned from their sailing cruise. Wilson had bested him; and Caine swore to get
even.

With just a little prompting from his wife, the rationale was
simple. The boy had had enough. He was back home; he was
safe; no ransom had been paid; and there was no use in putting
him through any more anxiety from continual, probing questioning. As Caine knew it would, one telephone call to his

friend in the White House was all it took; and the case was officially closed.

As could be expected, Henry Wilson was furious.

"Just what in the god-damned hell did they expect of me?" he asked Liddell Peters, who was acting as his sounding board.

"Am I supposed to let some son-of-a-bitch come in here, haul off a rich bastard's kid and hold him for ransom, let the kid get snakebit and almost die, and then simply drift away like a fart in the wind?

"He could do it again," Wilson continued to rage. "He got away with this one, so he could do it again."

"He didn't get away with any money," Peters reminded.

"But he still got away with the crime!"

"A lot of people in this town might argue that he saved the boy's life."

"Bullshit! He *endangered* the boy's life. He's the one responsible for that kid's getting bit by the rattler. He put him there. And he's the one that . . ."

"He carried him out on his back," Peters interrupted. "The man you seem to think you're after would have just left him to lie there and die; and no one would ever have known."

"So you're buying it too?" Wilson began to feel that his number one assistant was going over to the enemy camp.

"Henry, I'm not buying anything. What I'm really trying to do is just to get you to accept it. The case is closed; orders from headquarters. Old man Caine said he was going to do it to you, and he did it. Give up. Go home. Take a few days off. Get a rest."

"And let that lying little shit get away with it, huh? You know he's protecting that bastard, don't you?"

"Probably so," Peters agreed. "But what you've got to do is forget it. It really is not important any more."

"Like shit it isn't!"

Important or not, the Special Agent in Charge finally did cease openly investigating, because those were his orders; but he never closed the file.

▼ ▼ ▼

During it all, Buddy's popularity grew. He was recognized and the center of attention everywhere he went. So great was his celebrity, in fact, that it almost enabled him to achieve a long-sought ambition.

The occasion was a Thanksgiving holiday party given by Marsha Horton, a classmate at Wingate School, at her parents' beautiful home in the forested "Memorial" section of Houston. There was nothing particularly special about the party, just another of many such holiday affairs—except that the youth who had been so much in the news, after having been kidnapped and having nearly died from a poisonous snakebite, Hamilton Caine, Jr., was the guest of honor.

The weather that afternoon was unsettled—gray and overcast. The heat of summer was gone, but the refreshing briskness of autumn was nothing more than spasmodic, at best—an air-cleaning, fresh-breathing cool front once in a while, then back to the leaden-sky, heavy-air doldrums.

But such is the stuff of which Houston weather is made. Natives and longtime residents are used to it; so it should do nothing to put the damper on a festive, holiday, teenage party. And it didn't.

A live rock band who called themselves The Organisms was playing at multi-mega decibels in the Horton's spacious, back-of-the-house family room, while a gang of clean-cut, well-dressed, obviously well-provided-for teenagers writhed about in what they chose to call dancing—pretty young girls in expensive, frivolous party dresses, and handsome youths in sport coats and ties. And all of them wealthy.

Sadly, though, the guest of honor could not participate in the dancing. It had been scarcely two months since that kind, youngish doctor in the small hospital in that quiet, slow-paced East Texas town had sliced away on the muscle tissue in the boy's right calf. The operation had been absolutely necessary, and the leg was mending nicely; but it still hurt a bit, occasionally. And dancing was out.

The kid didn't hurt for attention, though. In fact, it followed him around like a swarm of bees around a portable hive. Everyone wanted to know details. What had it been like? What was the kidnapper like? How was he treated? What kind of snake was it? How big? All good, kind, show-of-interest concern and admiration, requiring Buddy to stay constantly on his toes in order to keep his lies straight. But it all became wearying after a while.

Still, it provided extraordinary opportunities the youth had never known before.

One of them, in fact, seemed furtively to be looking at him, during the party, every time he glanced in her direction; but she would quickly avert her gaze each time he caught her at it. He had never met the girl—she didn't go to his school—but he knew who she was, nonetheless. The daughter of an automobile dealer—Stinson Chrysler/Plymouth/Jeep—she could be seen almost any night, late, on Houston television. Her fat, crass, father had been using her in his loud, tasteless, hard-sell commercials ever since she was two months old; and though she was seventeen now, he still referred to her, on the air, as "Baby."

She was blonde—every bit as much so as Buddy—and stunningly good-looking. But as he watched her milling about the party crowd, it seemed to him as though there was a certain fragility about her that belied what one might expect from her commercial TV persona. And so, bolder than he had ever been, he decided to find out.

Buddy wasn't sure exactly how he did it, but he actually managed to make his bumping into her appear to be quite casual and accidental.

After the requisite apologies, she said, "Hello, I'm Bonita Stinson. It's nice to see you getting along so well after all that happened to you."

Buddy quickly observed that she was even prettier up close than she had been from across the room—and far more so than on television. Her eyes were the color of the crest of an ocean wave, backlit into sparkling radiance by the transilluminating rays of an early morning sun. Her skin was soft and caressively smooth, all the way from her barely made-up cheeks into the tantalizing depths of her low-cut party dress.

"Was it just awful, what happened to you?" she asked, almost the same as most of the others had done.

Buddy twisted his head, a trifle shyly, and said, "Oh, it wasn't so bad."

He appeared to be agitated; and her response could not have been more welcome.

"Would you like to get out of this mob scene for a little bit and go outside for a breath of fresh air?" she asked. "Maybe we could talk out there."

Half-eagerly, the boy nodded and replied, "Yeah. I'd like that."

Outside, the vast expanse of the Horton's back lawn and garden was lovely. It was dusk, and shadows were deepening among the mimosa trees, the oleander hedges, the poinsettias and other ornamentals that had been carefully cultivated among the natural-growth, East Texas pine forest that pervaded the general area. The lot sloped gradually toward the back, where it was bordered by a meandering, dry creekbed, adjacent to which a largish, white gazebo had been constructed.

Although the air was leaden, Buddy felt the presence of an unusual spark.

"What do your friends call you?" the splendidly put-together darling of late-night automobile commercials asked as they strolled into the garden away from the noise and the crowd. "Hamilton seems so stuffy, so formal."

"Some of them call me Ham," he replied. "But I most like being called Buddy." It was the first time that he had ever mentioned that name.

"Buddy's nice. It kinda goes with my nickname, too."

"I know what that is," he told her. "It's Baby, isn't it?"

"Yes," she replied, almost with an air of resignation. "But how did you know?"

"Aw, come on," Buddy replied. "Everyone who's ever stayed up watching a late movie knows who you are."

He couldn't get over how fragile, how absolutely innocent she looked. It just didn't fit.

"And everybody in the whole world who's looked at a newspaper or watched television in the last two months knows who you are, too," she said.

With a shy grin, Buddy observed, "So we're both famous, then. But I guess you're used to it by now."

Almost wistfully, the girl replied, "Yeah. And sometimes I get awfully sick of it."

"What do you mean?"

"Well, you probably know. People seem to think that just because they see you on TV all the time, that they can paw all over you—I mean, all kinds of creeps."

Buddy made no reply. The thoughts that were crossing his mind might label him a creep.

"That's why it's so nice getting out here for a while, in the peace and quiet," she added.

"Yeah," Buddy agreed. "It was getting awfully stuffy in there, anyhow. I wish kids wouldn't smoke—not cigarettes, not pot, not anything. It louses up the air."

"I think so too."

Not nearly as tentatively as he might have thought he would, had he thought about it in advance, Buddy reached for her hand; and they walked in silence for a few steps. His other hand held the cane.

Then she asked, "Does it get tiring for you to walk too much, or stand around? I mean, does your leg hurt you?"

"Yeah, once in a while," Buddy admitted.

Considerately, she suggested, "Why don't we go sit down and rest in the gazebo out there?"

"That would be awesome."

The young couple had barely been seated on the small bench when the leaden skies fulfilled their threat and slow, gentle rain began to fall, bringing a slight chill to the air.

"Br-r-r-r," the girl complained. "I should have brought a sweater or something."

That sounded like a cue if he had ever heard one; so Buddy took off his jacket and wrapped it around her shoulders, leaving his right arm where it naturally came to rest. Sometimes, even a neophyte can be guided by sheer instinct.

She responded by snuggling tightly against him. Two years' difference in age, between fifteen and seventeen, makes an absolute world of difference in experience of that sort.

"That better?" he asked.

"Uh-huh," she replied, pressing ever tighter in his one-arm embrace.

Buddy felt strangely protective, as her sense of fragility, of vulnerability, seemed all the more apparent now. But even as protector, he could not avoid staring deeply into the fascinating, deliciously rounded depths within the sharply plunging neckline of her frilly, blue, off-the-shoulder party dress.

Presently, he was aware of an unaccustomed—not unwelcome, just unaccustomed—stirring within his loins; and he wondered just what in the hell he was going to do next. He hated for her to think that he was "pawing at her," but he would certainly have liked to give it a try. He decided for the moment, though, just to savor it all as it was.

And it was well worth savoring.

The two beautiful, blonde, young people were snug and warm now against the elements—and the more snug they became, the warmer they got. The gently falling rain caressed every leaf and flower in the November garden, unleashing a heady aroma that washed tantalizingly across the two of them— stronger than the Persian Market with all its perfumes uncapped, and sweeter than honey squeezed fresh from the hive and ladled atop young love.

Amidst all this, there they sat in splendid isolation—protected from the party goers inside by the rain, and shielded from the shower by the sheltering embrace of the gazebo.

Gently, the rain continued to fall. And gently, too, she placed her right hand on the knee of his injured leg.

"Does it hurt you much?"

"Not when you touch it." It hurt all right—but not on his leg.

Oh my God! Buddy barely managed to keep his exclamation to himself as her hand slipped slowly, haltingly, but steadily upward from his knee onto the inside of his thigh.

"I kinda wanted to touch it," she said.

"So . . ." his voice caught. "So did I." Throwing all caution to the winds, he reached out with his left hand to find a natural repository high on her rib cage, just below the voluptuous curve of her right breast. He ached to inch it the rest of the way up.

All of a sudden, Buddy felt as though they were no longer under the gazebo in the back-yard garden. They were in a cave in the Congo, beneath a waterfall, where the gentle creatures of the forest had brought them to play out their primordial ritual.

They were alone in the pristine, unsullied world after Creation. He was Adam and she was Eve; and each was thrilled by every inquisitive, discovering, tender touch of the other. They had not yet found the apple—nor the fig leaves.

They were Anthony and Cleopatra, cruising in exquisite luxury on a barge down the Nile. She was peeling and feeding him grapes—one delicious, succulent bite at a time; and he was basking in her concentrated attentions—alone in the world, and they owned it all.

But Anthony and Cleopatra were passionate lovers. With just a little luck, that might be the case here, also—in the gazebo . . . under the waterfall . . . floating down the Nile . . . in Eden. Step aside Mark and Cleo, Adam and Eve, Tristan and what's-her-name; it was time for Buddy and Baby to carry on the tradition.

Her face raised slowly to his—only a whisper away—and her eyes mutely posed the question. In response, hoping not to embarrass himself, he crossed that whisper-distance to place his lips on hers. But nobody had ever told him that he would have to turn his head before doing anything like that. Clumsily, his nose bumped into hers; and they both jumped. He felt the red rush into his cheeks.

"It's okay," she whispered consolingly. "Just hold still." And she took it from there.

As he felt her lips press onto his, his mouth parted automatically, unconsciously, and her tongue slipped quickly, probingly inside. At the same time, he felt her right hand slide the rest of the way up and come to caressing repose between his legs.

An atomic bomb went off inside his head, followed by a simultaneous series of lightning bolts that coursed through every tissue, blood vessel, and nerve fiber within him. It was the end of the world, and the beginning of a new one . . . the dawn of creation and the cataclysmic explosion of a star. There was nothing else in the universe—only her tender, pliant young body held vibratingly next to his.

He shook all over, pulsating beneath her ever-tightening caress—because he knew. He knew for certain that the moment he had yearned for . . . wondered about . . . couldn't wait to happen . . . was now upon him. If he could just figure what the next step should be and not mess it all up, this was *it*. The big act. Event number one. And he felt sure, now, that nothing could stop it.

And he was wrong.

"Hey, what's going on out there?" was the loud call from the direction of the house. Suddenly the walls of the cave collapsed; the forest of Eden came crashing to the ground; and the barge sank into the Nile.

"Fear no more," somebody called, as a delegation from the house ran up the gazebo stairs with two oversized golf umbrellas. "Your rescue party has arrived."

Adam and Eve jolted erect and tried their best to brush off Eden and get their fig leaves straight.

"Looks like we're just in the nick of time," the pretty young hostess, Marsha Horton, announced from beneath her umbrella.

The boy with the other umbrella noted, "Or maybe we should have waited a little while longer."

"Yeah," Marsha observed with a wicked smile. "Maybe a lot longer."

"Better luck next time," grinned the boy who had accompanied her.

The music . . . and the dancing . . . and the holiday socializing lasted for another hour or so; but for Hamilton Robert Caine, Jr., guest of honor, the party was over with the arrival of the golf umbrellas. Exactly as she had appeared, beautiful, blonde, Baby Stinson seemed simply to melt back into the crowd. They had come so close; but she was gone.

And the boy with the cane—just a couple of hours older and only a tantalizing bit wiser—knew that she had been like a match that flames brightly, and then is gone forever. Somehow, he felt certain that except on the late, late show, he would never see Baby again.

▼ ▼ ▼ ▼ ▼ ▼ ▼ ▼ ▼ ▼ ▼ ▼ ▼

19

"If I was you, I wouldn't mess around so much with them damned Indians," said Bulldog Ferguson, giving Bill the benefit of his years of experience growing-up and living here and there in East Texas.

Bill was sitting with the tool pusher at the rig on one of his days off, waiting for the Indians, Langley and Furst, to come by and pick him up. They were going on a run to buy booze to bootleg in to the rig workers, but Bill had told his boss nothing about that—only that they were going to go out. After all, he had no car—Ferguson knew that; consequently, the only opportunity he had to go anywhere was when someone invited him. And the Indians had invited him to go "shopping" with them.

Ferguson didn't like it. "You keep messin' around with them mother-fuckers and they'll end up knifing you in the back, just as sure as shit stinks. They're no god-damned good, the whole mother-fuckin' lot of them."

"That's what I like about you, Bulldog," Bill told him. "Not an ounce of prejudice in your body."

Ferguson had taken a liking to the mysterious stranger who just happened to appear that day in September looking for a job. There were a lot of questions about him that were unanswerable; but as far as Ferguson was concerned, he was diligent, honest, and a hard worker. He kept his nose clean and didn't cause trouble; and that was good enough for the tool pusher on a drilling rig deep in the Big Thicket woods of East Texas. Ferguson had worked in the oil patch for over twenty years, literally all over the world; and he felt as though he had seen just about every variety of scoundrel and ne'er-do-well imaginable when it came to trying to hold together a crew of men who would give him an honest day's work in exchange for an honest day's pay. But he had never encountered anyone quite like this man who called himself Bill Harrison.

Bill seemed to have a lot more class than the average rig hand. Oh, he got filthy and cussed and spat with the rest of them, but Bulldog could see through that. Much of it, he could tell, was just an act—a concentrated effort at trying to meet the rest of the workers at their own level. And it seemed to have worked; everybody got along well with him.

That was, in large measure, the reason that the rig boss gave Bill the extra work that he sought. Ferguson could see that the man was obviously stony, on-his-ass broke when those two Indians had brought him to the rig looking for work. When he asked for more work, during his days-off period, Ferguson had first hesitated at allowing it; but Bill had done the work, and he'd done it well. And now, he had been given additional opportunities and responsibilities.

Number one among them was keeping what the rig boss insisted on referring to as "them mother-fuckin' Indians" off his back. Bill seemed to be able to handle them better than anyone else could; and that alone made him worth a lot as far as Bulldog Ferguson was concerned. But still, he meant every word in his warning to Bill about staying away from the two all-too-ubiquitous red men in his personal life. Chalk that up as another of life's little ironies, because it was his "messin' around" with the Indians that made Bill so valuable to his boss.

One of his most notable contributions to Ferguson's serenity occurred when the well where Bill had originally signed-on was completed, and it came time to move the rig off of that location and onto another.

Five wells were planned in the development drilling program on the reservation, with the one where Bill first went to work being well number two. That well was completed in December. By that time, the two delegates from the reservation had come to believe that they knew so much about location-building and well-drilling that they made complete nuisances of themselves trying to tell Ferguson all about how to go about doing it. That was where Bill came in.

"Get them shit-heads out of here," the always refined Mr. Ferguson told him. "I don't care what you do, just keep them the hell away while I'm tryin' to get this fuckin' well started."

Bill complied by inventing various fool's errands to go on— needless alarms and excursions in which he would take one of the drilling company's cars or pickup trucks, haul Tweedle Dum and Tweedle Dee off with him, and be gone all day. It worked so well that Ferguson gave him a raise.

As the year wore on, and drilling continued well after well, hardly a day went by that Bill didn't think about the kid with the tousled, shining blonde hair and the probing, inquiring, laughing, penetrating, blue eyes. He wondered, after all that time and all the boy's noted celebrity, whether the kid ever thought of him. Some days he imagined that, yes, Buddy might have missed him as much as he missed the boy. Other days, and those were downers, he felt that the kid probably had erased from his consciousness the good times between them there on the creek, and that he was having too much fun in his increasingly glorious teen years to give another thought to the man he had named Bill. The man found some consolation, though, in his certain knowledge, gleaned from news reports way back there in September, that the kid had lied through his truly loyal teeth to protect the kidnapper that had become his friend. That was a good feeling; but it was also months ago.

If you think he's forgotten you, fellow, Bill asked himself, *then why are you saving every nickel you earn just like the second Great Depression is going to begin tomorrow? Why, if not in the hope that when you get financially healed, you can go find him again?*

His reply to himself was, *Oh, shut up!*

▼ ▼ ▼

By late spring, when drilling was under way on development well number four, Bill's unofficial function as liaison with the

Indians had made him virtually indispensable to his boss. He was still nothing more than a derrickman on the morning tower, as far as company payroll was concerned, but he had become *de facto* right-hand man to the man they called Bulldog. After a couple of raises, plus a lot of extra work and virtually no living expenses, he had been able to save a considerable sum of money.

The Indians knew this. They didn't know just how much he had, nor where he kept it, but they knew that he must have saved a bundle. But then, they weren't doing too badly for themselves, either, what with the occasional under-the-table payoffs that Ferguson was obliged to ladle out to them, along with their thriving bootleg whiskey operation.

They talked to Bill about cutting him in on the action. It was their idea that a man on the inside could likely peddle a lot more booze to the rig hands, on an always-available basis, than they could on their occasional, nocturnal forays to the drill-site in their pickup truck. Knowing that, by now, Bill had considerable money stashed away, they also felt that with that extra cash available, they could purchase the stuff in larger quantities and get a better price break: thus, more profit—all good, sound, American free enterprise.

"No way, guys," Bill told them when they broached the idea. "Bulldog Ferguson would fry my hide for lunch and feed the leftovers to the coyotes. He puts up with your bootleg goings-on because he knows he can't really stop it. But if he thought he could, he'd shut you down in a minute, and have the Texas Liquor Control people haul you off so fast your heads would swim."

"Okay, Keemosabe," Furst replied. "We just thought you might like to make a little extra white man's wampum."

Bill considered it of somewhat more than passing interest that, during that discussion, his two Indian friends seemed awfully curious about just how much money he had put away. They tried a number of ploys to get him to tell them just how much, but they were entirely unsuccessful.

So, he had no interest in their business; but as soon as they arrived he was going to accompany them on a booze-buying expedition to Beaumont—just to get away from the rig for a while. The day before had been payday; and doubtless, the boondocks entrepreneurs would be back to the rig later that evening, peddling their illicit wares once again.

"Maybe in the meantime," Langley had told him, "you and us can go out and play a little modern Indian stick ball. So bring plenty of money."

Just what that might mean, the man known as Bill Harrison had no idea. But the thirteen hundred dollars or so that he had in his pocket while waiting for the Indians to arrive was, at least to him, not only "plenty of money," it was a bundle.

What it amounted to was two weeks' pay from his two rig jobs combined. His original job as derrickman paid fairly well, with his odd-jobs pay for his off-days being little more than half as much; but the two, combined, amounted to a substantial wage for a man in his circumstance.

As was his regular routine, he had cashed his bimonthly check at a bank in Livingston. Because there had been no time for it that day, he would later deposit virtually all of it in an interest-bearing account at a savings and loan. After a full seven months of work, Bill's accumulated savings, in which Langley and Furst had been so interested, now amounted to something approaching twenty thousand dollars. Therefore, the game which Langley had called "modern Indian stick ball" probably meant a couple of Indians trying to get their hands on as much as possible of their white friend's money.

And so it was.

The "stick" to which they referred bore no resemblance to the pre-Abner Doubleday equivalent of a baseball bat—it was the same Ruger Super Blackhawk .44 magnum revolver to which Bill had already been introduced. And the ball, or balls, would be the 240-grain, soft-point, jacketed ammunition that it shot.

"Time for a rematch, Lone Ranger," Langley announced as he pulled the pistol from its sheepskin-lined, leather sheath. Both Indians seemed never to tire of their pseudo-Lone Ranger, "B"-movie, language affectation.

They were in the latest edition of the rig worker's beering and boozing spot—a recently cut-over area of some ten to fifteen acres not far from the current drilling site. A freshly opened bottle of cheap bourbon had just been passed around for a good swig by all.

Furst, who had proved to be the better shot of the two in their previous shooting competition, kicked an empty beer can a few feet away and said, "Here, see if you can still hit one of these things." He handed the pistol to their paleface pal.

The man called Bill looked him straight in the eyes. The Indian obviously knew better than that; the can was not even ten yards away. Bill realized that wagering was undoubtedly going to be the order of business—that was what this "modern Indian stick ball" was going to be all about. He also knew that he could probably handle the big, potent, single-action revolver well enough for whatever the Indians had in mind—and probably better than most. Although he had never owned one just like it, he had fired a couple of them; and he had owned, and shot extensively, both .22 caliber and .357 magnum versions by the same manufacturer. It was the .22, in fact, which he had carried with his now sorely missed young friend Buddy on many of their excursions into the woods along the creek so long, long ago—the one the boy had filched in his show of determination to be taught to shoot. The big .44 handled and balanced much the same, it was simply bigger and heavier—one helluva lot bigger and heavier!

He also divined, at the outset, that his Indian friends were undoubtedly going to try to work some kind of scam on him. Another hustle. He would just have to remain alert, wait it out, and see what their plan was to accomplish it.

Believing that he might as well call their hand right off, Bill asked, "How much?"

"You name it," challenged Furst, as he pulled out a large roll of bills from his pocket, with many one hundred dollar notes evident. He obviously was intent on some serious betting.

Tactic number one in working a hustle—and Bill knew it—is quickly to get your intended victim greedy; thus the large roll of bills.

"Okay," Bill agreed. "Ten bucks a shot. And I call the shot."

"You're on."

Bill took the pistol in hand with his back to the beer-can target. "Ready?"

"Whenever you feel like it," said Furst.

"You in on this too?" Bill asked Langley.

"Right," he replied. "I've got ten bucks on Jason."

Bill nodded agreement and looked each of his gaming adversaries in the eye. Then without warning, he whirled, cocking the hammer as he did so, and shot the can from the hip—no aim at all. The can jumped high.

"Your turn. And remember, you start with your back to the target; no aim."

The challenge might have been more than the Indians bargained for. On the other hand, losing early-on is a standard gambit in the operation of any good hustle. Bill collected twenty dollars.

"Now I call it," Furst declared; and he kicked the same can a good twenty yards away. "One handed."

"Wait a minute," Bill declared, and he opened the door and rummaged around inside the Indian pickup truck. He emerged shortly with a piece of Kleenex, which he tore into quarters. Then he squeezed two of them into wads as small as he could and stuffed them into his ears. "No use going deaf while you fellows are taking my money. You still in?" he asked Langley.

The Indian nodded.

The man who was in charge of keeping the Indians out of his boss's hair then took the big revolver in his right hand, stuffed his left hand into his hip pocket, and leveled down on the beer can. At the loud report, the can went flying.

Both Indians merely nodded. Then Langley-of-the-pony-tail dashed over to place a second beer can in the approximate location of the one Bill had blasted, and returned back to the shooting location. Furst's shot connected solidly; no winner. Next, Langley passed around the whiskey bottle for each to have a drink. It was obviously going to be drink-em and shoot-em time again.

As he took a swig from the bottle, Bill thought that either those guys had very short memories, or they had something else up their sleeves. Furst had gotten loaded on their last shooting competition, and lost badly because of it; surely he wouldn't be so stupid as to try the same thing again.

Bill found out what that something else up the sleeve was when Furst took his drink. He watched as his Indian competition's Adam's apple jiggled in a manner that was supposed to look like copious guzzling; but there was no lower throat movement to follow. He was only pretending to drink the booze. If that was the scam, Bill figured, he would have to adjust his own drinking accordingly.

"Okay, Tonto," he said, joining in the phony Lone Ranger talk. "You call the bet, and I'll call the shot."

"Fifty dollars."

Without being asked, Langley added, "The same goes for me," as he walked over to place a second can alongside the target already in place. They were still approximately twenty yards away.

Bill looked hard at each of them and then nodded agreement. His back was to the target. "Do you know who Pocahontas's parents were?" he asked.

Without waiting for an answer, he bent over and aimed at the target—upside down and backwards, between his legs. "Two fuckin' Indians!" he said, answering the riddle as he pulled the trigger.

In his far-from-steady position, Bill was nearly knocked over by the recoil of the big gun. He managed to stay on his feet, but the can didn't.

Straightening up, he handed the pistol to the other shooter and said, "Don't forget the punch line."

Furst glared at Langley, assumed the position and said, "Two fuckin' white-eyes!" With the report of the big magnum, he, too, nearly toppled over; but he didn't. Neither did the beer can; and Bill was one hundred dollars richer.

Time for another drink.

"Try swallowing some of it this time," Bill said as Jason put the bottle to his lips. "It goes down so much better that way."

The Indian wiggled his Adam's apple a lot, again, and swallowed but a little. Then Bill, too, took a small drink; and the shooting game continued.

As the contest progressed, the shooting distances increased. So did the betting; and Bill continued to outshoot his Indian opponent. He hadn't kept count, feeling that, as in a poker game, it would be bad luck to count his winnings. But by the time the Indian started challenging double or nothing, Bill figured that he must have taken at least fifteen hundred dollars from the red men's large roll of bills. The previous shot had been for five hundred.

"Have you got a thousand left in that wad of yours?" Bill asked.

"We've got it," Jason Furst declared, as he reloaded the weapon.

"And that's your bet?" asked Bill.

"You got it."

"Okay," Bill agreed. "Money on the ground." He peeled off an even one thousand dollars from his winnings and dropped it on the ground.

Langley, who was now acting as their banking agent, dropped another thousand to the ground and declared, "Now it's my turn to call the shot." Furst handed the gun to Bill.

The curly headed rig worker waited gun-in-hand for the call, as Langley went back to the pickup truck and returned with a box of vanilla wafers. He opened the package, extracted one of the small, round cookies and declared, "In the air."

"Oh shit," Bill said. "Looks like poker just went up."

"And so will this cookie," Langley replied. "You ready?"

"Ready as I'm gonna be."

The taller of the two Indians tossed the wafer twelve feet into the air. As he raised the gun, Bill cocked the hammer, tried his best to track the flight of the vanilla projectile, aimed and fired.

Miss.

Next, it was the Indian's turn. When his constant companion tossed a second cookie, Jason Furst raised the gun and fired. All that was left in the air was a cloud of vanilla dust.

"Double or nothing again?" he asked Bill. And he handed the gun to the white man.

As Bill took the gun, he glanced quickly and unobtrusively at the end of the bullet cylinder; and the contents were clearly

visible. Every other bullet in the gun had a blue tip on it . . .
snake shot!

So that was their scam! When it was Bill's turn to shoot, he
had a bullet forty-four one-hundredths of an inch in diameter
with which to hit a two-inch flying cookie. But the next shot—
the Indian's turn—would bring up one of the shot-filled projectiles, which, at the range they were shooting, would fire maybe
a couple of hundred tiny pellets in a pattern two or more feet
wide—a virtual cinch.

He remembered that Buddy had called him a cheat when he
shot the tin can the boy tossed into the air with a much smaller
shot load from his .22 magnum pistol. Vividly, Bill recalled
explaining, "When it's you against the world, you utilize every
advantage you can get hold of."

And Buddy had responded, "Especially if you want to show
off and impress somebody, right?"

The Indians were not trying to impress. They were intent
upon swindling their friend out of his hard-earned money.
Smiling inwardly, he told himself, *You can't hustle an old hustler.*

Then he reached into his pocket and counted out two thousand dollars; it was almost all he had. "The bet is two thousand,
I believe. Right?" He bent over and lay it on the ground.

As he straightened up, he faced away from the Indians,
shielding the gun with his body. Quickly and quietly, he rotated
the cylinder of the .44 mag one notch, which meant that the
remaining shot loads would now come up on his turn to shoot.

"Go ahead, Geronimo," he said to Langley. "Toss your cookies."

The small, round target that sailed off the Indian's fingertips
exploded into powder before it had flown ten feet.

Bill handed the gun to a slack-jawed Jason Furst, waited for
the Indian bet of two thousand dollars to be placed, then said,
"Okay, friend; see if you can do it twice in a row."

He couldn't.

Bill took the pistol back in hand and said, "That's my four
thousand on the ground. You gonna match it?"

Two centuries of pent-up Indian bitterness at the perceived

injustices of the white man blazed in the eyes of Emerson Langley as he counted four thousand dollars from their now-dwindling stake and dropped it to the ground.

"Ready?" he called.

Bill nodded in reply; and a cookie went flying—sideways.

"No shot!" Bill called, without even raising the gun. Then to Langley, he said, "Try it again, friend; but spin it broadside this time."

Bill recalled what his tool-pusher boss had told him would happen if he kept "messin' around" with Langley and Furst. "They'll knife you in the back." Bill was determined that he would not allow that to happen.

Once again a cookie flew; and once again Bill's shot exploded it like a tan, miniature clay pigeon at a championship shoot. There remained only one bullet left in the pistol; and Bill knew that it would be out of sequence, because he had rotated the cylinder to bring one of the blue-tipped shot shells in line for his turn—two shots ago. That meant that if the Indian adversary, Jason Furst, attempted another shot, no bullet would fire; and Bill's counter-ruse would be discovered. It was time to lay down his cards.

Quickly locating the live bullet in the cylinder, he raised the barrel of the big magnum skyward, cocked the hammer and pulled the trigger. There was a loud click.

"Must have a bad bullet in here," he said. Then he repeated the action, with the same result.

"Looks like we seem to have lost a shot," Bill said, to the wide-eyed stares of the Indian would-be scam artists. "Now suppose you let me reload it this time; just hand me the bullet box. And while you're at it, you might as well get that little package of bullets with the cute little blue plastic tips on them, too. You know, the ones with the bird shot in them that make it so easy to hit the flying cookies."

Langley asked, "What you trying to pull, man?"

"Nothing," Bill replied. "Nothing at all—except that I'm not only trying, but I *am* pulling out of this phony hustle you guys are trying to pull on me. That money on the ground is mine; now you get me those bullets like I told you—both kinds—then get your crooked asses into your goddamned pickup and clear the hell out of here." With that he cocked the hammer of the pistol, bringing the remaining live round in line with the barrel.

"Remember," he warned, "there's still one good .44 magnum pill left in here; and I don't think either of you wants to be the one that gets it."

"You won't get away with this," Furst threatened.

"Wrong, Geronimo," Bill replied. "*You* are the ones who *already* didn't get away with it. You tried to cheat me; but you just weren't smart enough."

Bill picked up two hundred and fifty dollars off the ground and handed it to Furst. "This gun's worth a good two hundred on the used market. Keep the change—but don't forget the bullets."

Grumbling loudly, the outsmarted Indian adversaries climbed into the cab of the truck; and Langley, on the side nearest the white man, threw both boxes of bullets onto the ground. Then with angrily spinning wheels, the vehicle from the Alabama and Coushatta Indian reservation roared away in a cloud of East Texas dust.

"Give my regards to Pocahontas," Bill called after them. "And to both of her parents, too."

▼ ▼ ▼ ▼ ▼ ▼ ▼ ▼ ▼ ▼ ▼ ▼ ▼

20

Following the Christmas holidays, Buddy's celebrity began to wane; and that suited him just fine. It had long since become a drag, as far as he was concerned.

When classes began again in January, he was not the same Ham Caine that the faculty and students of Wingate School had known and enjoyed the previous semester. Somehow, the sparkle had gone out of him. He was becoming increasingly able to hobble along on his healing right leg without the cane; but sometimes, on bad days, he was forced to resort to using it again, so he kept it around.

But his leg was obviously not the problem. Children and youths have gutted through the mending of broken arms and legs since time immemorial; and his affliction was no worse. The big problem appeared to be emotional.

Buddy seemed to have retreated within himself. He became moody, melancholy, and often dispirited for no apparent reason whatsoever. To make matters worse, he was frequently short-tempered and argumentative—most decidedly a troubled young man.

His friends never actually deserted him; but they ceased to take any great delight at being around him. Most people, though—both faculty and friends—were solicitous of him; because they all knew what was bothering him. Almost everyone realized that after all the excitement of his homecoming, following his close brush with death, he had truly succumbed to the so-called "post-traumatic stress" referred to by the psychologist who had been quoted in the news media. Everything had been all right for a while; but as the school year wore on, the psychological wounds he had undergone were apparently more lasting, in the long run, than the terrible trauma to his injured right leg.

That is what everyone thought; and Buddy was just as happy to have them think it. At least it made them tolerate him, more or less, when he occasionally sank into a deep, brown funk.

After all, how could he tell anyone what was really troubling him? How could he begin to explain how much he longed to be back in that little clearing beside the creek somewhere up in that long-ago Big Thicket woods? There was no one to whom he could explain his longing to hear again the night sounds, as the forest sank vibrantly into evening—alive with the stirrings of the woodland creatures and pulsating with the vitality of life in the sure-enough raw.

And the daytimes—hot, sweltering, with a body-load of good, honest sweat budding up on his skin and trickling along his arms, his legs, and down his face. He recalled with pleasure even his own body stench from all that sweat, and the sense of delight at being totally, completely filthy—like never before in his sheltered, sanitary young life.

They were exciting days, filled with activities that were completely new to him and totally enjoyable. They were filled, also, with the most meaningful personal relationship he had ever known—a friendship warmer than he might previously have even imagined.

He missed the stars at night, and the glorious rays of sunlight threading through the woodlands at dawn. He thought at times that he could almost feel again the exaltation he had experienced when he waded softly into the ice cold creek that dark and early morning before his squirrel hunt—alone in the universe, and at one with all of nature.

He longed to feel again the chill of the creek tunnel where he and the man who had taken him into that completely different world had discovered the paw prints from that big cat.

He wished, even stronger than before, that he could hear that creature scream again—just once, up close—and feel the hair stand up on the back of his neck . . . wished that he could hear again the yodeling yelps of the pack of coyotes and feel, through them, his own kinship with the wild and free.

He missed that freedom. He missed the forest, and the ice-cold creek. He missed the fun. But most of all . . . he missed Bill.

And he couldn't even talk about it.

As the school year wore on, he continued to sink ever more deeply into his own, private thoughts. Every once in a while, during class, he would fish out and reread the wrinkled newspaper article that he always carried in his pocket. It was one of the earlier stories, written while he was still in the hospital; and he carried it, not for reference to what the article said about him, but for the single passage that he had underlined in red ink:

A curious aspect of the character and purpose of the kidnapper has come to light with a note that Houston investigators uncovered, written by the kidnapper. Pinned to the pillow of the stricken youth as he lay recovering from a life-saving operation in the small Woodville hospital, the note read: "This is the Caine boy who was kidnapped from Houston last Tuesday. Please take care of him. He's a hell of a good kid!"

By mid-March, Buddy's studies had fallen off so badly that his school counselor asked to arrange a meeting with his mother—privately, without the boy. Something had to be done.

The obvious answer was counseling. The boy needed a psychiatrist to help him adjust—to cope with the psychological scars that had been inflicted upon him, and to straighten up and prepare for a life with advantages and possibilities that few youngsters his age will ever have the opportunity to enjoy. So they agreed to send the kid to a shrink.

Dr. Loren E. Newton was just the man. Handsome, somewhere in the mid-forties and graying at the temples, he exuded an air of competence. Of knowledgeability. And of patience.

After all, for one hundred and fifty dollars an hour, he was delighted to have all the patience in the world.

His practice was well-peopled with the economically advantaged who, often as not, just needed someone to talk to. And that was all well and good; they usually benefitted from it.

Hamilton Robert Caine, Jr., also needed someone to talk to. Desperately. But he wasn't talking—not to any "goddamned society shrink," as he liked to refer to the good doctor. Still, he had to go through the motions.

"How long have you had this feeling of insecurity?" the doctor asked the youth during an early session.

Buddy stalled—glancing around the expensive-looking office, with its walls richly panelled in some sort of silk brocade and sprinkled with decorator-hung European landscapes. He was actually lying supine on a leather couch—he couldn't believe it!

"I don't know," he finally answered. "I don't keep a diary."

"Have you always been this belligerent?"

"Ask somebody else. I don't feel belligerent; that's your idea."

"You're not helping me," the doctor complained.

"My folks aren't paying you so that I can help you. You're supposed to help me, remember?"

"I can't help you one bit. You have to help yourself. My job is simply to help you find the answer inside you."

"Find the answer, huh?" was Buddy's quick response. "What was the question?"

The doctor wished that he could say, "The question is why are you such a little smart-ass?" But he thought better of it.

In time, Dr. Newton was able to worm himself into his young patient's inner self to some degree; and what he found surprised him. He wrote in his journal, in fact, that he was chagrined at allowing himself to be taken in by the boy's apparent dissembling. That fifteen-year-old kid, he ultimately discovered, had been laying a con on him. And he had swallowed it—hook, line and little stinker.

"I've got to admit that you had me fooled there for a while," he ultimately told his young patient. "I really bought it."

"Bought what?" Buddy asked.

"Post-traumatic stress syndrome. I know you know all about

that, because that's what you have been trying so hard to make me believe. That you are all shook up . . . all mixed up in your head over the horrible things that happened to you . . . and that your generally antisocial behavior is because of it. What was it that psychologist said in the papers? I have the clippings, you know, in your file. He said something to the effect that even though you were home safe and sound, you were still scared to death of your kidnapper—or something like that. You remember?"

"Yeah," Buddy recalled, "something like that."

"Do you know what that is, young man?" the doctor asked.

Buddy shook his head.

"It's bullshit, that's what it is!"

Buddy's jaw landed on the floor. Society shrinks were not supposed to talk to delicate young patients like that.

"I've finally got you pegged, Mr. Hamilton Caine, Junior," the doctor continued. "The question now is what are we going to do about it?"

"I don't know what you mean."

"Have you ever heard of Patty Hearst?"

"No," Buddy answered. "Who's that?"

"She was an heiress to an outrageously large fortune, mostly from a publishing empire. Lived in San Francisco. Sometime back in the seventies, she was kidnapped by some far-out group of would-be revolutionaries who called themselves the Symbionese Liberation Army. You ever heard of them?"

Buddy shook his head.

"She was kidnapped for ransom, just as you were; only those people wanted more than just money. They wanted notoriety . . . publicity for their cause, whatever that might have been. They wanted to make a big splash.

"Well, they got it all right. And in the bargain, they even got Patty, too. By a strange psychological quirk—which I might as well call the Patty Hearst syndrome, to keep it simple—she fell in with their cause. That bunch of crazies robbed a bank; and she was photographed by one of the bank security cameras, participating in the holdup. She was actually holding a gun.

"It was nothing new in psychological circles, this thing that I called the 'Patty Hearst syndrome'; but it was new to the general public. It is a sort of psychosis that grows out of a person who has been kidnapped being totally dependent upon his kidnapper—or kidnappers—for his very survival . . . for life itself. They literally hold their captive's life in their hands; and ultimately, the victim becomes grateful to his or her kidnapper for his continued existence. The kidnappers have then become, in effect, substitute parents; and the victim, to continue the analogy, is the dependent child. And because of this, in many cases, the captive actually forms an affection for the kidnapper.

"And that, young man, is what has happened to you. All of this time since you got out of the hospital, you have not been 'scared to death,' like that learned psychologist said. You have been protecting your kidnapper!

"This current melancholy of yours is a manifestation of a sort of perverse desire to return to the clutches of that man who kidnapped and then brutalized you. In my opinion, this may indicate an incipient psychosis—perhaps not unlike masochism."

Buddy raised up from the leather couch, upon which he had struggled so valiantly to keep the truth from coming out, and he looked the psychiatrist straight into the eyes for a long, silent moment. Then he stood.

"Doctor," the patient announced. "I didn't understand half of what you said. But whatever it was, you can take it and . . . stick it in your ear!" And he walked out the door.

End of analysis.

▼ ▼ ▼

The twenty-seventh of May was a lazy afternoon—the last day of school. Teachers of any competency know, of course, that they can expect little in the way of attention or accomplishment from their students on that final day. The exams are over, the grades are passed out, and everything else is only a formality. Attendance is more or less mandatory, but that is about all that can be expected.

Hamilton Caine, Jr., though, was a special case. He had been doing nothing but showing up for months. His last-period class that day was English literature; and his knowledgeable and exceedingly kind teacher was a Mrs. Stephany Knapp—a lady who cared not only about the subject she was teaching, but she also cared about the subjects whom she taught. And she was quite concerned about young Master Caine.

Ham Junior—Buddy—was all but totally unaware of anything going on around him that last hour of school. He was staring out the window, but seeing nothing of the beauty of the late spring day in the forest of western Houston. He also heard nothing of the excited, last-hour-of-the-last-day chatter around him.

What he saw was a glowing campfire, and the dimly visible meanderings of a tree-arbored, sandy-banked creek flowing gently, quietly along a few yards beyond. And what he heard was a funny call from a bird that sounded like a horse, and the rattle-chatter of squirrels, invisible in the trees around him. And the coyotes; he also heard the coyotes.

And Bill was telling him, "That band of yodel-pups out there is probably a mixture of everything canine imaginable. They are coyotes, yes; but there are also wild dogs mixed in among them—wolves, too; and they all run together. And they inter-breed, so that their true bloodline has become all mixed up, indistinct. That's what happened to the red wolf; it screwed around with the coyotes and wild dogs so much that it lost its identity. Now, they say that it is totally extinct in the wild."

Bill the naturalist. Bill the woods guide. Bill the teacher. Bill . . . the friend.

Bill the badminton player. And then Buddy was no longer sitting at the campfire; he was bounding around their makeshift badminton court, returning some shots and missing others—cussing and fussing and laughing a lot. And then he and his kidnapper were skinny-dipping, reveling in the ice-chill of the deep-woods creek and discoursing on tea-brown creek water and soap that floats.

And then the bell rang.

"Hamilton," said Mrs. Knapp. "If you would, please stay just a few minutes. For the rest of you, have a glorious summer; and I look forward to seeing all of you next fall. Class dismissed."

When the last students had gone out the door and the noise of everyone going home had subsided behind them, the teacher told Buddy, "Hamilton, I know that it has been a difficult year for you. Everyone has seen that; and we have all been concerned—extremely concerned.

"You are a very likable young man, but I'm afraid that you are going to be wasting a perfectly wonderful potential unless you do something to get yourself out of the hole into which you seem to have sunk. Are you aware of what I'm saying?"

Buddy only nodded. He had heard so much of that! So much probing and prying—all well-intentioned meddling into his preferred-to-be private self. And he was up to the ears with it.

His teacher continued, "Didn't you play tennis last summer? It seems as though your leg has healed well enough now for you to get back into that. It would be good for you. You need to get out and have fun and recreation with other young people again. You seem to have crawled deep within your . . ."

"Mrs. Knapp," the boy interrupted. "Have you ever gone skinny-dipping in an ice-cold creek? I mean buck-ass naked?"

The eyes of the kindly, earnestly concerned teacher almost popped out of their sockets. She could not begin to utter a reply.

"Your balls completely disappear!" Buddy said. And he walked out the door.

▼ ▼ ▼

Outside, the new chauffeur waited. In just one more month, Buddy would be sixteen; and he would have his own car. It was the last . . . absolute last . . . ultimate last . . . never again last time that he would have to suffer through the indignity of having a damned chauffeur pick him up after school.

This one, at least, wasn't as creepy as the last one. After the famous kidnapping incident, the Hamilton Caines had fired Jimmy Jamison. They couldn't stand the sight of the man who had allowed their son to be kidnapped. In fact, so deep was their revulsion at the memory that they even got rid of the Cadillac limousine and purchased an even longer, stretched Mercedes. The new chauffeur was named Friedrich. He was of staunch

Germanic descent—older, but much more sturdily built than his perverted predecessor. Thus, the Caines reasoned, he would be more capable of fending off another kidnapping attempt if such should ever happen again.

Buddy didn't mind him so much, even though he did display an ancestral Teutonic inclination to enjoy a trifle too much of the schnapps now and then. That resulted in an occasional aroma of beer breath inside the limo when the soon-to-be-sixteen-year-old climbed into it to be delivered home from school.

The last day of school was no exception, and the eau-de-beer-parlor was strong, all the way to the back seat. But Buddy didn't care; in fact, he almost liked it. Not the aroma, that was raunchy; but it was the statement that it made—a declaration of personal independence and forthright, go-to-hell manliness that Buddy had never felt displayed until that episode in the Big Thicket woods way back last September.

This time, though, Friedrich's inadvertent, boozy pronouncement only helped to strengthen the youth's resolve. He had been toying with the idea for several weeks—planning and scheming, along with a lot of wishful thinking—and he was determined to go through with it, even if he ended up in jail.

His father probably would put him in jail, too, Buddy decided; but he would have to catch him first.

Thus, on the very next morning, he managed to con Friedrich out of the keys to the Jeep Grand Wagoneer station wagon so he could "take it for a ride around the block." The vehicle got very little use at all, and Buddy was able to convince the chauffeur (he knew that Friedrich was actually a kind sort, deep down) that it would be all right for the kid to get a little driving practice. He had finished driver's education training; and next month, when he turned sixteen, he could get a license. A little solo practice, therefore, seemed in order. Friedrich understood the need, as he had once had a young son himself; but that boy was long since grown up and about to start his own family.

Cautiously then, but good-naturedly, the chauffeur handed over the keys to his employer's only progeny, paying no notice at all to the satchel the youth carried with a shoulder strap.

Buddy often used it to tote books and other gear to and from school, so Friedrich was quite accustomed to seeing it.

Only this time it was not school books and gear in the satchel . . . it was maps. There was a Texas map, which would be needed at first; and then, most important, a minutely detailed sectional map (the kind used for aerial navigation) of the area abutting and southeast of Woodville, Texas. There are just some things, Buddy had told himself, that a man's got to do.

Of course, if a man has never done anything like them before, things can tend to get a little dicey.

Driver's training notwithstanding, he was really not prepared for the first time he hit a Houston freeway, solo. No one ever is.

Almost right off, the blast of an air horn nearly sent him into celestial navigation, as the pilot of a huge Peterbilt invoked the truck drivers' perceived right of eminent domain over any stretch of concrete, asphalt, or macadam anywhere in the continental United States (Hawaii had yet to be tested). Buddy ducked, instinctively, until he realized that such an action would do nothing to forestall annihilation. The only thing left to do was to stomp on the gas pedal. That he did, sending the simulated wood-sided family four-by-four lurching ahead of the bellowing behemoth.

That turned out to be fun, as the youthful vehicle operator learned the joys of acceleration in and out of freeway traffic—of sudden, heavy breaking, and of forcing and filling a gap between fellow travelers where none actually existed. He even once had the opportunity to employ the universal freeway salute, shooting the finger with aplomb at a bespectacled, Oriental-looking fellow in a dirty-white Toyota, who took horn-honking umbrage at just such a maneuver. It was all very juvenile, all extremely immature and potentially dangerous behavior—exactly as it is done minute-by-minute, hour-by-hour, every day of the year on the Houston freeways . . . where manliness is a large V-8 engine, and courtesy is *not* helping a little old lady across the street. Somebody might get hurt that way.

The God of Fools was smiling on young Hamilton Caine, Jr., as he managed to thread the Wagoneer all the way out of Houston without a single fender-bender. The remainder of his journey northeast, on U.S. 59, was uneventful, without even so much as the presence of a single black-and-white cruiser from the Texas Department of Public Safety to reinforce the youth's stomach jitters about being intercepted on his first-day-after-school escapade.

The route he had red-pencilled on his map called for him to turn right, at Livingston, onto highway 190; and thence, on to Woodville—another thirty-two or so miles over heavily forested, rolling hills. Halfway there, he passed the large, billboarded entrance to the Alabama and Coushatta Indian Reservation.

I'll be damned, he declared to himself. *Bill wasn't bullshitting. There really are Indians here.*

Unbeknownst to the boy, it was the area in which the man whom he sought had been living and working for almost the entire duration of Buddy's school year.

The man he sought, indeed. The hopeful youth realized that there wasn't the chance of a snowcone atop a barbecue grill that he would be able to find Bill, who might or might not be hiding-out somewhere in those East Texas woods. Also, there was another fear that nagged at him. What if—he could not avoid thinking this—what if Bill was not interested in seeing him again? It was only reasonable to assume that the man knew exactly where to find the boy, yet he apparently had not attempted to do so for the painfully long period since they were last together. But for the man's one-time buddy, attempting to locate his former kidnapper was nothing less than like trying to find a grain of salt in a sack of sugar. The kid reasoned that most likely, if Bill had been able to pull it off, he would have been long since gone to East Bejesus or somewhere by now—or B.F.E., as Buddy's contemporaries liked to say: "Beyond Fucking Egypt."

So why was the River Oaks teenager making such a pilgrimage? He couldn't answer, even to himself; but a long highway trip allows plenty of time for introspection and deep study of just what a young man's needs and goals in life amount to. And all of that, Buddy felt, was so much bullshit. He was just going, that's all. He was not actually running away from home per se; in all likelihood he would be back in his River Oaks bed that night. It was only that, as he had told himself before, there are just some things that a man's got to do. By extension, the same thing applies to a boy.

And what was that? Go find the camp. Go find that twisty little creek with its dense, arboreal overhead shelter. And walk in the creek and let the icy chill on his feet and legs permeate his body and cleanse his soul once again, as it had done before. And maybe strip off and go skinny-dip in that little pool, and feel his testicles run for cover as far as they could get into his warm body cavity, away from the chill-bath.

And maybe, just maybe that green van and trailer might still be there—upended, as he and his middle-aged friend had left them—in the middle of the creek. If they were, then perhaps he could nose around and find license plates, or serial numbers, or something to identify the derelicts and lead him to the identity and whereabouts of the man he called Bill. It was worth a try.

Small Texas towns tend to look their sleepiest at midday, which was about the time Buddy arrived in Woodville. The lulling effect of that sleepy look was dispelled with pulse-pounding intensity when, negotiating his way around the county courthouse, he discovered what appeared to be the world's supply of police cars parked outside. There were at least a half-dozen, with door-side emblems identifying them to be of both county and state registry. To compound the fright, two Smokey-The-Bear-hatted highway patrolmen were climbing into one of them at the moment the boy drove by. The urge to pee in his pants was strong, but he managed to resist it.

He was hungry, but any thought of grabbing lunch somewhere was out of the question—not in the town where he had been found hospitalized and recovering from snakebite, and where he was thereby, most likely, even more famous than he was in Houston; and not in any town that seemed to be as chock-full of the constabulary as that one was.

Suck it up, Buddy, he told himself.

▼ ▼ ▼

Finding his way along U.S. highways for the first time on his own was one thing. Finding jeep trails and timid little winding creeks, as indicated on a sectional chart, was another. According to the chart, they were everywhere; but according to all the meandering youth could locate as he drove along dusty country roads and unlikely fencelines, they were nowhere. Still, he believed that without the sectional chart, his mission would have no chance at all for success.

Buddy had learned of the existence of such charts during his prolonged grilling by Houston police and the FBI, as they tried in vain to cut through his lie about the location of the kidnapper's camp. He contrived to get one of his own, near the end of the semester, by having the accommodating Friedrich drive him to a small private airport on the western edge of Houston, on the pretext that he was getting some material from there that he needed for a school project.

He had spent hours at home poring over the sectional chart, using the highway to which Bill had carried him on his back as an initial point of reference. That road, State Highway 1097, was clearly identified; and Buddy reasoned that his kidnapper's creekside campsite had to be somewhere west of there. But from the way Bill had talked, the road to the camp did not intersect that highway; so it had to come from somewhere else. As Buddy read the map, the most likely looking prospect was a country byway known as Trenton Road.

From that, he attempted to thread the big four-wheel-drive station wagon down the first, then the second of the two most likely looking side roads—as best he could translate from the printed theory on the large map beside him, into the reality of the Big Thicket all around. Each time, the winding little dirt roads—alternately powder-fine or surfaced like a washboard—terminated into dead ends. On a third attempt, he ventured into an area that had recently been logged, and got lost for half an hour wandering around a labyrinth of extremely rough, cut-through roads that headed off in every direction. On each attempt, he ended up either in another dead end, or back where he started. His quest was beginning to look impossible.

Buddy brought the vehicle to a halt and studied the chart once again; and it was then that he discovered his mistake. He had been driving back and forth, up and down, on a road that just might be parallel to the one he was looking for. He plotted an escape route back almost to where he started, off Trenton Road, and retraced his path. He almost missed it again; but as he drove along the sandy road, he just barely noticed a gap in a barbed-wire fenceline, heavily overhung with trees of all varieties. A crude gate constructed of three strands of barbed wire held together by a trio of spindly cedar posts was stretched across the opening. Although barely discernible, there was an apparent road—just two track indentations in the knee-high weeds— headed away from the sandy main road he was on.

A city boy who has never encountered such a gate is likely to get severely frustrated, and painfully pierced by barb wire, before he can figure out how to get one of those contraptions open and drive a car through. Buddy was no exception. He cursed and sucked blood from a quickly bleeding puncture wound on his right thumb, then he mustered every ounce of determination he had left and pushed as hard as he could against the end pole that was held by a barbed-wire loop above. That time it worked, sending the gate flopping to the ground and tearing a gouge in his designer blue jeans. But never mind that. Without even bothering to drag the limp gate out of the way, he simply drove the big Jeep station wagon across, mindless of the possibility that barbed wire can puncture tires as well as fingers and blue jeans.

Not versed in the proper etiquette with regard to country fences, which declares that gates, once opened, must be promptly closed, he simply continued driving.

Once through the gate, the youth felt in his heart-of-hearts that the almost invisible road he was now traveling was the one to the creekside campsite of his fondest memory; but appearances told him otherwise. Nothing looked even vaguely familiar—not until he had proceeded at a virtual crawl for a mile and a half, perhaps two miles, and he drove bumpily over a small wooden bridge. It spanned a narrow creek; and just past the bridge, the road took a turn to the right, through a gateless gap in an ancient-looking barbed-wire fence.

Finally, something felt familiar. Without knowing why, Buddy could sense that beyond that turn lay the giant clear-cut field through which he had been carried, raging with fever and the unbelievable pain of a hugely swollen, snakebit leg. It had all been at least partially under water, but he was almost certain that that was the spot. If he was right, the campsite should not be far away; he was almost there.

In short order, he was there. And to his great shock, someone else was there as well. As the runaway boy in the stolen vehicle drove to the road's end, where an umbrella of beech trees arched across a gently flowing creek (*That one over there is a beech*, he remembered. *This smaller one here is a son-of-a-beech*) he drove right into an empty camp. A tent was pitched in just about the same spot where Bill's trailer had been, and a tall, black, tough-looking, four-wheel-drive Chevrolet Blazer with stout, oversized tires was parked nearby. But there was no one in sight.

He then did just what he should not have done. One just doesn't get out and walk uninvited into someone else's camp, but Buddy did exactly that. He stopped the car, got out and started to look around.

There was no trace of the trailer; no van to be seen anywhere. The creek was flowing just as tea-brownly as it had been the previous September, only perhaps a little higher in its banks.

A deep, aching hole began to develop in the pit of the boy's stomach. That was the place, without doubt; but his hopes of finding a clue to help locate his dearest friend ever were dashed. And he realized that if he didn't get the hell out of there in a hurry, he might find himself up to his eyeballs in trouble with whoever it was that had pitched that camp.

Run—that was what he should do if he had any sense. But then, if the youth had any sense, he would not have filched his parents' automobile and gone wandering off a hundred and fifty or so miles into the woods in the first place. What he did, instead, was take off his shoes, drop them onto the floorboard of the Wagoneer, and saunter barefoot down to the creek.

The water's temperature was no disappointment, as his feet became instant blocks of ice the moment he stepped in. But the cold didn't stop him. He continued to wade in, with total disregard to the soaking being inflicted on the legs of his trousers, until he was knee-deep in the center, like he had been that dark and early morning before the squirrel hunt way back then. Remembering the sensation, he raised his arms skyward and stretched until he could feel the muscles tighten in his back—exactly as he had done before.

"Where are you Bill?" he asked softly of the trees above. "Why won't you let me find you?"

An announcement from God of the imminent arrival of doomsday could not have had a more shattering effect on the boy than the voice that yelled out from somewhere within the thicket beside him.

"WHAT THE HELL YOU DOIN' HERE, BO?"

If it were truly possible for a human being to jump out of his skin, Buddy would have done so. Failing that, he merely dropped his arms and froze reverently still. The first person to emerge from the brush was not a person at all. It was a lumbering, yellowish, very large dog; and it lunged right at the kid in the creek—right at his face, with a long, eager tongue.

"BRUTUS!" Buddy yelled. "Is that really you?"

The dog responded with a deep, bass bark and another wet lick across the boy's face. As soon as Buddy could recover, he looked up; and there the man stood in cut-off jeans, open shirt and sneakers, on the edge of the creek.

Tears welled instantly in the young blue eyes, obscuring vision to the point that they were unable to ascertain for sure whether or not the same thing might have happened to the mature brown ones that were now studying him so intently a few yards away. Neither man nor boy spoke or moved; they simply stood here, each silently drinking-in the sight of the other; and each aching, within himself, to run and throw his arms around his too-long missing pal. But that was not the manly thing to do; so they just stood still. Staring. Aching.

It was Bill who broke the silence.

"How long are you going to stand there freezing your feet?"

"I guess I've done it long enough for now, anyway."

Buddy splashed out onto the bank and sat down. He had been instantly, emotionally drained. Bill sat down beside him;

and with the most his masculine reticence would allow, he popped the kid on a knee with the palm of his hand.

"Good to see you, kid."

Buddy bit his lip to try to control himself, shook his head and replied, "Oh shit, Bill, it's so good to see you, too."

They were almost like children at their first party—each studying the other and not knowing what to say or do next.

"I see your language hasn't cleaned up a helluva lot," Bill noted.

"Nope," Buddy agreed. "Probably won't, either. I guess you're a bad influence."

"*I* am?"

Buddy nodded affirmation. "But what are you doing here?" he asked.

"Oh, I don't know, just a sentimental journey, I guess."

Buddy smiled, a trifle wanly. "Yeah, me too, I guess. But what happened to the trailer? And the van?"

"I hauled them out," Bill replied. "I was afraid that some day, somebody might find them and start putting two and two together."

"Yeah, so was I."

After another few moments of awkward silence, Bill asked, "You got any plans for the summer?"

"No," Buddy answered, picking up a stick and tossing it into the creek. "I thought about trying to get back into tennis again . . . but, I don't know. I was just kinda hoping . . ."

"Hoping what?"

"Oh, I don't know. You doin' anything?"

"Well," Bill replied, "I'll tell you what I've been thinking about doing."

"What's that?"

"In Colorado," Bill said, "there's still snow on the mountain tops. The creeks are running clean and cold, and they're swarming alive with tender, young trout. I happen to know a spot that would be a helluva place to go hide out and spend the summer. Of course, it wouldn't be any good alone. But if I had a friend—someone about sixteen years old, say, who could handle my little Blazer over there and help with the driving—we could leave Houston in the afternoon, drive straight through and be there the next morning. That is, assuming I could get some help breaking camp here."

Buddy leaped to his feet and almost yelled, "*Could* we? Do you really mean it?"

"I don't know what's to stop us; not if we decide that's what we're going to do."

"That would be awesome. Absolutely, totally *awesome!* But what about my parents?"

"They probably wouldn't want to go, so let's don't even ask them."

"You mean just . . . go?"

"That's it," Bill said. "Just up and go."

"But when?"

"Would tomorrow be too soon?"

"Are you kidding? Hot damn!"

Buddy was walking aimlessly around in circles, talking to the trees. Talking to the air. Talking to a smiling providence. "Hot damn!"

Struck with a sudden, urgent motivation, he said, "But there's one thing I want to do before we go."

With that, the boy shucked his shirt and tossed it deliberately onto the ground. Then he unbuckled his belt, pulled off his jeans and piled them atop the shirt. His underwear was quick to follow; and he dashed nakedly to the creek.

"You've got to come in with me," he shouted back at Bill.

"I think I'll pass this time," Bill declared, knowing more about the temperature of that creek in May than Buddy did.

Mimicking his mentor, the boy yelled from the water's edge, "The thing you've got to do is dive in head first and get wet all at once. It's the only way." And he proceeded to do just that.

"Holy shit!" he hollered after surfacing. "It's colder than it ever was. Come on, Bill. If you don't come in with me, then I'll know for sure it's true."

"What's true?"

"That you're nothing but a chickenshit, fat-ass, creaky old fart!"

"That did it!" the man replied.

He ran straight into the water, clothes and all, and grabbed onto the teasing youth—locking his arms tightly around Buddy's shoulders. They tumbled together into the creek with a resounding splash—so invitingly that Brutus felt compelled to romp in and join in the fun.

Bill struggled onto his feet and into shallower water, still holding tightly to the deliriously happy kid with both strong, muscular arms. He raised him up, plopped him back into the water, then hoisted him high again—like an old-West cowboy rinsing off a dirty saddle in a badlands creek. Through it all, the boy's shoulders remained tightly clamped in the man's vice-like grip, while his head stayed pressed as closely as he could press it to the wet, hairy chest of the man he had named Bill.

And they laughed. Loudly. Uproariously.

They laughed.

And they laughed.

And they laughed.